More praise for the novels of
Virginia Kantra

"Virginia Kantra's books are on my keeper shelf."
—Suzanne Brockmann

"An involving, three-dimensional story that is scary, intriguing, and sexy."
—*All About Romance*

"Kantra creates powerfully memorable characters."
—*Midwest Book Review*

"Spectacularly suspenseful and sexy. Don't miss it!"
—*Romantic Times*

"An intriguing story that glued my eyes to the pages."
—*The Best Reviews*

"Smart, sexy, and sophisticated—another winner from Virginia Kantra."
—Lori Foster

"Packs a wallop!"
—Elizabeth Bevarly

"Kantra once again proves her remarkable ability to pen strong romance with a twist."
—*Wordweaving.com*

CLOSE-UP

VIRGINIA KANTRA

BERKLEY SENSATION, NEW YORK

THE BERKLEY PUBLISHING GROUP
Published by the Penguin Group
Penguin Group (USA) Inc.
375 Hudson Street, New York, New York 10014, USA
Penguin Group (Canada), 90 Eglinton Avenue East, Suite 700, Toronto, Ontario M4P 2Y3, Canada
(a division of Pearson Penguin Canada Inc.)
Penguin Books Ltd., 80 Strand, London WC2R 0RL, England
Penguin Group Ireland, 25 St. Stephen's Green, Dublin 2, Ireland (a division of Penguin Books Ltd.)
Penguin Group (Australia), 250 Camberwell Road, Camberwell, Victoria 3124, Australia
(a division of Pearson Australia Group Pty. Ltd.)
Penguin Books India Pvt. Ltd., 11 Community Centre, Panchsheel Park, New Delhi—110 017, India
Penguin Group (NZ), Cnr. Airborne and Rosedale Roads, Albany, Auckland 1310, New Zealand
(a division of Pearson New Zealand Ltd.)
Penguin Books (South Africa) (Pty.) Ltd., 24 Sturdee Avenue, Rosebank, Johannesburg 2196, South
Africa

Penguin Books Ltd., Registered Offices: 80 Strand, London WC2R 0RL, England

This is a work of fiction. Names, characters, places, and incidents either are the product of the author's
imagination or are used fictitiously, and any resemblance to actual persons, living or dead, business es-
tablishments, events, or locales is entirely coincidental. The publisher does not have any control over
and does not assume any responsibility for author or third-party websites or their content.

CLOSE-UP

A Berkley Sensation Book / published by arrangement with the author

PRINTING HISTORY
Berkley Sensation edition / July 2005

Copyright © 2005 by Virginia Kantra.
Excerpt from *Home Before Midnight* copyright © 2005 by Virginia Kantra.
Cover design by George Long.
Interior text design by Kristin del Rosario.

ISBN: 0-425-20679-3

BERKLEY® SENSATION
Berkley Sensation Books are published by The Berkley Publishing Group,
a division of Penguin Group (USA) Inc.,
375 Hudson Street, New York, New York 10014.
BERKLEY SENSATION and the "B" design are trademarks belonging to Penguin Group (USA) Inc.

PRINTED IN THE UNITED STATES OF AMERICA

10 9 8 7 6 5 4 3 2 1

ACKNOWLEDGMENTS

Special thanks to Pamela Baustian and Melissa McClone; to my sister-in-law, retired corrections officer Virginia Grisez; to account manager Kimberly Smith; and to everyone in every sheriff's department across North Carolina who took the time to answer my questions with patience and good humor. I owe each of you a lot more than a copy of this book. If I've taken liberties or made mistakes, it's not your fault.

To my husband, Michael, and to Jean, Drew, and Mark . . . I owe you everything. Thank you for believing in me.

CLOSE-UP

ONE

THE woman scrambling over the stockade wall had a really nice ass. So it was a damn good thing she wasn't his sister.

At least, Jack Miller hoped she wasn't his sister. Because that would make things really complicated, and he had more than enough complications in his life already.

Concealed in the shadow of trees outside the militia's compound, he watched as the woman's head followed the rest of her over a ten-foot wall of rough-cut pine. The sunlight fired her short blond curls.

Nope. Definitely not his sister. His sister Sally wore her hair in a long dark braid. Or she had the last time he saw her, what was it now, seven years ago? Eight?

Ignoring the familiar twinge of guilt, Jack narrowed his gaze on the blonde. Okay, so the hair was wrong. But the getup was right—the long skirt and sandals, sort of Haight-Ashbury goes Amish. She must be one of them. The Holy Rollers. The Disciples of Freedom or whatever the hell they called themselves.

But if Blondie there was a member of God's little army,

why was she tearing up her clothes and her hands going over the wall?

So far, none of the compound's sentries had noticed her break for freedom. Lax of them, Jack thought. But then, what did they have to worry about out here? Bears? Timber snakes? They were in the middle of the Nantahala National Forest, eight and a half miles of rough backcountry from the nearest access point and a long day's hike from the nearest town. The deep gorges and steep hills all around probably made even paranoid militia men feel safe from intrusion.

At least, that's what Jack was counting on.

But the blonde wasn't taking advantage of the guards' inattention to make a run for it. Scared? Jack wondered. He was too far away to see her face or her knuckles, but she sure seemed reluctant to let go of that wall. His muscles tensed. *Come on, sweetheart,* he urged silently. *It's not that far. Three feet. Four, tops.*

Her sandal dropped. And then Blondie did, too, crumpling as her feet hit the hard-packed ground. There were no bushes to break her fall. The Disciples had cleared the area around the compound of brush, which explained why Jack had set up his stakeout thirty yards away, outside the perimeter of trees.

He watched as the woman lurched to her feet. Was she hurt, or just jarred? Jarred, he decided, as she stooped for her sandal. At least she had the sense not to stop to put it on.

She hopped toward the tree line, her shoe clutched in her hand, angling for the thick laurels on Jack's right. Good. She wouldn't lead her pursuers straight to him. Assuming she attracted pursuit. As long as Jack didn't do anything stupid to call attention to himself, like offer her shelter or help . . .

But he wouldn't.

He couldn't.

He had to think of Sally.

His blood pumped. Adrenaline flooded his body. He had no ties to the mystery blonde, no stake in her escape. But he caught himself rooting for her as she stumbled for cover, ungainly as a mother partridge distracting a fox from her nest. He sure hoped she had some goal, some thought, some plan beyond making it to the bushes.

She didn't carry a bundle. No sleeping bag or supplies. What was she going to do tonight when the sun went down and the temperature dropped thirty degrees? Spring was beautiful in these North Carolina mountains, but fickle. And cold. Kind of like his ex-wife, actually.

Yep, the blonde definitely needed a plan to survive.

A shout sounded from inside the compound.

Jack stiffened. Shit.

The blonde's head jerked up like a startled deer's. At this distance, Jack could see she was young. Cute, too. Under her loose pink top, her breasts were nice and round. No wonder somebody didn't want to let her go.

After that one frozen second, the woman dropped her chin and ran like hell over the rocky ground. Her skirt snagged behind her as she plunged into the bushes, a flag to watching eyes, and then it, too, disappeared.

Jack released his breath. Time for him to do the same, before Locke sent his thugs out after the pretty fugitive.

He withdrew silently through the trees, grateful for his drab jacket and camouflage pants. Poor Blondie. Her pink shirt and full, flowered skirt would show up against the browns and greens of the forest like tracer bullets in the night sky. He heard her crashing through the woods on his right and scowled. She'd be better off lying low until her pursuers had passed. Plenty of hiding places in this wilderness.

Like that oak over there . . .

Jack's gaze narrowed. The forest giant had toppled many seasons ago. Its leaves were gone; its branches broken; its roots raised in a broad wedge of crumbled clay and rock. The gaping hole left behind was an obvious hiding spot; the depression under the trunk, sheltered by a tangle of brush and leaves, made a much better one.

Jack was no Daniel Boone. He'd gone camping with his old man exactly once, and the trip, like most of their attempts at father-son bonding, had been a disaster. But he'd picked up some basic survival skills at Uncle Sam's insistence and taxpayer expense.

Squatting, he poked under the log with a stick. The hollow appeared dry and snake-free. He'd need to squeeze his shoulders through the narrow opening, but beyond that the ground fell away. He wasn't crazy about being stuck in a hole in the ground, but this one had plenty of room to move and breathe.

Jack tossed the stick away. Shrugging out of his pack, he shoved it out of sight, under the trunk, and crawled in after it.

LEXIE ran, blind with pain and panic.

Her ankle jarred with every step. Her breath grunted and whistled. Branches lashed her arms; tree roots tripped her feet.

She snatched at a sapling, keeping herself upright through sheer luck and force of will. Her heart hammered. She had to get away. She couldn't let herself be captured, wouldn't let herself be used again . . .

The ground heaved, and a man rose up practically under her feet.

Oh, God. She was caught.

He was as massive as the mountain, dusted in dirt and leaves and dressed like a nightmare out of *Soldier of Fortune* magazine.

Whirling, she bolted.

He grabbed her from behind, yanked her against his large, hard body, and covered her mouth with his hand.

She bit him.

"Shit." His breath hissed against the side of her face as she kicked and clawed his arm. "Hold still, will you? They'll hear us."

His voice penetrated her panic. He didn't sound angry. Exasperated, maybe, but Lexie exasperated lots of people. Typical male reaction, really.

And that *us . . . They'll hear us . . .* Wasn't he one of them, then?

She stopped struggling.

"You okay?" he growled close to her ear.

She was not okay. She was scared out of her wits. Her side ached, her ankle throbbed, and she had Locke the Lunatic and his band of baddies hot on her trail.

But she nodded. At least, she tried. It was hard to signal agreement with that big hand clamping her jaw.

The hand relaxed slightly. "You won't scream?" His breath was hot against her cheek.

Why would she scream? Nobody would hear. No one who would help, anyway.

She nodded again. And then, fearing he'd misunderstand her response, she shook her head.

"Right."

Those fingers eased their grip. Slowly, as if her captor was as suspicious, as reluctant, as she, he released her.

Lexie twisted in his arms and took a step back. Pain shot to her knee. She staggered.

Oh, dear Lord.

Lexie had seen enough militia-style getups in the past few days to recognize trouble. And this man, with his slouch hat pulled over burning eyes and his stubbled jaw, would look dangerous with or without the uniform. Dangerous, disreputable, and—despite his intimidating attitude and the three days' growth of beard—very, very hot.

Lexie licked her dry lips. She didn't *do* intimidating men, she reminded herself. Growing up with an overprotective, ultracontrolling father had put her off tall, dark, and dangerous for life. And if her upbringing hadn't already convinced her to steer clear of macho males, the past couple days surely would have.

She never should have trusted Ray.

Just because this guy wasn't one of the crazies inside the compound didn't mean she could trust him, either. As much as she'd railed and rebelled against her father's paranoid view of the world, she had to admit now there were some seriously bad people out there. Man Mountain could be anyone. Anything. A hunter. A hillbilly. An escaped convict.

She shivered. "Who are you? What are you doing here?"

He looked at her as if she was the crazy one. "At the moment, I'm saving your ass. Get in."

Lexie blinked. The drugs they'd forced on her were out of her system, but she still felt woozy. Get in what? Get in where?

The woods crackled behind her.

The big man swore. Grabbing her elbow, he dragged her toward a fallen log and shoved her to the ground. Lexie caught herself with her hands. A hole gaped in the earth, dark and spidery and uninviting.

Her stomach quailed. In *there?*

But she had no choice. Anyway, the man behind her wasn't offering her one. He nudged her into the crack, crawling and sliding in after her. Lexie fought a burst of panic. How could they fit? There was no room, no air . . .

And then he levered his body somehow, bracing himself on his hands and his toes, and stretched out on top of her.

That was better. And worse. His thighs trapped hers. His chest flattened hers. His arms were heavy with muscle. She could feel the tension in them as he splayed above her.

He weighed a ton.

"They're coming." His voice was a vibration at the back of her neck. "Don't talk."

Talk? Lexie wasn't sure she could breathe.

She turned her cheek against the cool, decaying leaves and inhaled carefully through her mouth. Her ankle throbbed in time with her pulse.

The man on top of her moved his lips to her ear, his jaw rough against the side of her face. "Dogs?"

· Lexie's heart lurched to her throat. Oh, God. If her pursuers were hunting with dogs, their hiding place was worse than useless. They'd be caught. Trapped.

She swallowed her panic. She hadn't seen any dogs within the compound. Of course, drugged, tied, and confined, there was a lot she hadn't seen. And some of the things she had . . . She shivered.

Don't think about that now, she ordered herself. *There's nothing you can do about that now.*

"No dogs," she said.

He grunted, apparently satisfied. The sound, low and intimate in her ear, made something inside her clench and then soften. She lay still, her senses straining. No shouts. No gunfire. Only the pounding of her heart and the slow, steady breathing of the stranger above her and—

There. He must have heard it, too, because he stiffened. A stealthy disturbance of the forest floor, too loud to be a bird and too deliberate to be a squirrel, moving away to their right. Footsteps? Someone was after them. After her.

Lexie squeezed her eyes shut and held her breath. She was acutely aware of the man pinning her to the soft, damp ground. His size. His strength. His . . .

Oh, my goodness. Her eyes popped open. He was aroused. That wasn't his belt buckle pressed hard against her bottom. It was too long, too hot, too thick, to be mistaken for anything but, well, what it was.

Lexie exhaled. Now what?

Under normal circumstances, she would have made a joke and moved away.

But things had slid from normal to nightmare three days ago.

And nothing in her past experience, none of her father's dire warnings or her mother's frank instructions, offered a clue on what to do when you were being hunted through the woods by armed religious zealots and a significant portion of your rescuer's anatomy was poking your backside.

Lexie's hands fisted against the cool, soft earth.

Well, fine. If he could endure it, if he could ignore it, then so could she.

Lexie bit her lip. Anyway, she could try.

JACK gritted his teeth and tried hard not to react to the fluffy little blonde under him.

No such luck.

In the darkness he could barely see her, but he could smell her. Even sweaty, she smelled good. Female. Sweet. God, he hoped she was right about the dogs. It wouldn't take a K-9 dog to pick her perfume out of the regular scents of the forest.

At least she hadn't screamed. Or squirmed. Not that her lack of response seemed to make a damn bit of difference to his happy dick, but maybe she was too scared to notice.

Yeah, right. And maybe she was too smart to care. She probably had bigger things on her mind than the horny ass-hole who had pulled her to safety.

Of course, she might worry more if she knew his last involvement in a domestic dispute had ended with the woman dead.

Jack scowled, trying to distract himself from Mr. Happy's reaction to the feel of her under him, all smooth and soft and sweaty. Would she be better off if he made a break for it? Drew her pursuit away? Locke's men might dress like soldiers, but Jack bet they had no more training than your average pickup full of rednecks in town for a Saturday night. He could lose them in these woods and circle back for her.

On the other hand, the army of God's very lack of professionalism meant things could get ugly fast. Every cop knew that drunks and fanatics were illogical. Unpredictable. Dangerous. And these particular fanatics were better armed than he was and on their home turf.

Leaves crunched not ten yards away.

Jack sighed. Well, that settled that. He couldn't leave

her now. By the time he untangled himself and crawled from their hiding place, Locke's men could be right on top of them.

Crunch, crunch, crackle.

Christ, they were close. One man? Two? They must have fanned out to search, which meant they had only a general idea which direction their quarry had taken. They'd be moving fast, trying to catch her before she reached the road or one of the hiking trails. Not much hope for her either way. The only road—if you could call it that—was a track connecting the Disciples' camp to an old logging road. The nearest public trail was miles away. He'd studied the maps, waiting for Sally.

Beneath him, the blonde was wound so tight she was vibrating. Trembling, Jack thought and tried to broadcast some kind of mental reassurance. *It's all right. You're going to be all right. I won't let anything happen to you.*

Yeah, like she'd believe that, with his hard-on lodged against her tush.

A shadow crossed the chink of light. One man.

Jack's pulse drummed. He could take him. The weight of the Glock tugged on his hip, a reassurance and a temptation.

Bad idea. He had no backup. He had no jurisdiction. He couldn't even be sure he had accurately identified the situation. No cop worth his badge operated without understanding the circumstances and consequences of his actions. A cop had to be in control of himself and his situation.

Which explained why, technically speaking, Jack wasn't a cop anymore.

Crunch, snap.

Damn, he wished he could see. He had to assume whoever was out there was armed and dangerous. But he'd sure like a better look at the guy and whatever weapon he carried.

Jack concentrated on not making any sound, which he was actually pretty good at, considering he'd been regular infantry and not special forces or anything. The guy outside apparently didn't care if he made noise or not. He tromped off through the underbrush, headed downhill.

That was good, because he left without spotting them. And bad, because as the perimeter of the search expanded, it would be harder to predict and evade.

The blonde released a quick breath.

Jack moved his mouth to her ear. "Five minutes," he said, real low.

Sooner or later, Locke's men would realize they'd missed her and backtrack for a more thorough search. Jack had to get her clear before then.

He heard her swallow before she nodded.

He was glad she hadn't freaked out. That was the danger of working with civilians. Women civilians. Women civilians in a domestic dispute were the worst. You couldn't help them if they refused to help themselves. And if you tried . . .

He set his jaw. Don't go there. Do *not* go there.

A minute crawled by. Jack focused on the sounds of the forest, listening for a sign the guys with guns had wised up and doubled back.

They didn't.

Two minutes. Three. Being buried alive was bad enough. Being buried alive with a beautiful blonde added a whole new level of discomfort. It got tougher and tougher to ignore how great she felt under him. And impossible to disguise his reaction. Maybe it would be easier if he'd had sex sometime in the past four months.

Jack tried lifting his weight off her, but moving didn't make things any better. In fact, it made things—it made his thing—worse.

He went back to listening and breathing, trying not to notice that sexy little catch in her throat or the way her hair smelled against his face. Jesus. She must think he was some kind of pervert, sniffing her hair.

Four and a half minutes. Long enough.

He shifted and felt her shudder in response.

"I'm going to take a look around," he explained so she didn't get the wrong idea. "Stay down."

He couldn't see her face, but she did as she was told, lying still as he crawled over her and out. Well, if she'd thrown her lot in with the Disciples of Freedom, she was probably all about that obedience and submission crap.

Except she'd run away. Which was more than Sally had managed on her own.

Cautiously, Jack straightened, scanning their surroundings: bare brown slopes, naked gray trunks, bright green buds hazing the branches. No flash of binoculars. No glint of guns. No wannabe Rambos playing soldier in the woods.

"Okay. You can come out now."

She wriggled from under the fallen log. Leaves flecked her hair. Dirt smudged her cheek and the front of her pink top. She scrambled to her feet, not quite meeting his gaze.

She probably didn't know what to say to him. *Hi, my name is Bambi. Was that your Mr. Friendly poking my ass?*

Shrugging out of his fatigue shirt, Jack handed it to her. "Put this on."

She looked up at him then. Her eyes were blue. With those blond curls and big eyes, she looked like one of his sister's baby dolls. She might as well have the word *victim* tattooed on her forehead.

"I can't take your jacket," she protested.

It couldn't smell *that* bad. "Take it. It'll help hide your clothes."

"Oh." Her face turned pink to match her top. "I didn't think of that. Thank you."

Very polite. More like a runaway from some pricey private girls' school than a defector fleeing a survivalist compound. What was she doing with them? And what was he going to do with her?

He watched her slide her arms into the sleeves. The cuffs fell over her hands. He could still see the hem of the blue flowered skirt and her pale legs, but she was covered. Mostly.

"Okay, let's make tracks," he said.

She narrowed her eyes at him. They weren't that blue, he saw. More like gray. "Where?"

He hadn't figured that out yet. "What the hell does it matter? Away."

"No." She shook her head. "I'm sorry, but I can't."

"Why not?"

"I don't know you."

He gave her points for caution, even if it was costing them valuable time. Reaching into his back pocket, he flipped her his ID. "Jack Miller."

She caught his wallet one-handed and studied the driver's license inside, really studied it, like a bouncer or a cop. "This says you're from Pennsylvania."

"That's right."

"You're a camper?"

When Jack left Clarksburg two days ago, he hadn't told anybody where he was going or what he was planning to do. He sure as hell wasn't explaining his reasons to a woman from the Disciples' compound. "I'm doing some camping, yeah. You?"

"I . . ." She handed his wallet back. "I'm Lexie. Lexie S—Smith."

Yeah, right. And he was Gandhi.

"Nice to meet you, Lexie Smith. Can we get going now?"

"I can't."

Exasperation stabbed him. "Why not?

"Well . . ." She smiled weakly. "I don't think I can walk."

Jack looked down. She was telling the truth about one thing at least. Her ankle had swollen to the size of a grapefruit.

Shit. They couldn't stand around waiting for Locke's goon squad to return. Which left him no choice.

"Then I'll carry you," he said.

TWO

LEXIE twisted her hands together in an agony of indecision. Things were moving too fast for her. *He* was moving too fast.

But not moving could get them both killed.

He unbuckled his belt, and her heart ricocheted into her throat.

"What are you doing?" she asked sharply.

Jack Miller shot her a God-save-me-from-hysterical-females look. "Making a splint. For your ankle."

A little of the tension leached from her muscles.

"So I can walk?" she asked hopefully.

"No. So you don't bounce while I carry you."

Squatting, he dragged his pack from under the tree that had sheltered them.

Lexie watched as he rooted inside. Her head hurt. Her ankle throbbed. She'd already exhausted her limited reserve of strength and her tiny stock of courage escaping the compound. So it should have been easy to let this large, competent man take charge. To go along, quite literally, for the ride.

But some small spark of initiative, once lit, refused to die. She swallowed. "Is that really necessary?"

He pulled out a map. "It is if it's fractured."

"No, I meant . . ." The burning in her ankle rose like smoke to her brain, fogging her thinking. She had no idea where they were. The mountains, obviously. But which mountains? How far was she from home? From help? "Do you have a car?"

He re-folded the map into a stiff square. "We're not going to my car. Sit down and stick out your foot."

Lexie subsided onto the trunk of the fallen tree, squinting at the folded map. Growing up with two ambitious and intensely driven parents had taught her to let go, to go with the flow, to get with the program. Maybe she should just ask him what state they were in.

And when he asked her why she didn't know? What would she say then?

He dropped to one knee in front of her, like a football player on the sidelines. Lexie fought a shiver. Even kneeling, he dwarfed her. If she had to run from him . . .

But she wouldn't have to run. He was going to carry her, he said. He was trying to help.

Yeah, like she could tell a stand-up Samaritan type from a lying rat bastard. Lexie pushed the thought away. She *needed* his help.

He leaned forward to shape the map to the back of her heel. She focused on his hands. Big, square hands, hard and warm. He smelled like earth and leaves and sweat, musky and not unpleasant.

"There's a road," she said. She knew that much. She'd seen it from the compound.

"A road your people use. A road they're watching."

They weren't *her* people, Lexie wanted to object. But she didn't. She'd noticed people very rarely paid attention to her objections anyway. Maybe it was because she was small and blond and female.

And maybe it was because she was a wuss.

"How did you get here?" she asked.

"Parked at the trail access off Highway 143." He adjusted the angle of her foot. The pain took her breath away. "Came across country."

Bringing the sides of the map around her ankle on either side, he began to wrap the makeshift splint with his belt.

Lexie inhaled carefully. "Couldn't we do that?"

"Not today. It's eight and a half miles of strenuous hiking. Even if you were in any condition to try it, we couldn't make it before dark. And I won't even attempt it with me carrying you." He buckled his belt on the outside of her ankle and scowled at his handiwork. "Is that too tight?"

The top of the map cut into her calf. Her blood pulsed against the bindings in rhythm with her heart.

"It's fine," she lied. She offered him her most conciliatory to-the-client smile. "You must have been a Boy Scout."

"Infantryman."

She attempted to ease the awkwardness with a joke. "Then I guess you've had a lot of practice marching with one hundred and twenty pounds of deadweight on your back."

He didn't smile. "Yeah." Pivoting on one knee, he presented her with his broad, muscled back. "Let's roll."

His T-shirt stretched from shoulder to shoulder. But it wasn't his linebacker's body that riveted her attention.

She stared at his waistband. "You have a gun."

Her father's training flashed through her mind. Should she make a grab for it?

No, no, *no*.

And anyway, the chance was lost. In one smooth motion, Miller withdrew the gun from the holster on his belt and cradled it casually between his thighs.

"Yeah. Hop on."

She peered over his shoulder. "That's not . . . standard camping issue, is it?"

"It's good for bears."

"You hunt bears with a handgun?"

"No, I use it to scare them away. They don't like the noise," he added blandly.

Let it go, Lexie. She should let it go. She would let it go, except she'd recently developed a vast distrust of men with guns who told her what to do.

"Do you have a permit to carry a concealed weapon?" she asked.

Miller gave her a narrow look over his shoulder. "Is this really an issue for you?"

"No." *Yes.* "What if you need your hands free?"

"Then I'll drop you." She couldn't tell from his voice if he was kidding or not. "Now unless you want to still be here jawing about it when your friends come back, you put your arms around my neck and your legs around my waist and we get the hell out of Dodge."

Unless you want to be here when your friends come back . . .

Lexie shuddered. Despite the experience of the past few days, she didn't really believe Locke's men would kill her. They needed her to put pressure on her father.

But they might kill the man who tried to help her.

She put her arms around his neck. She put her legs around his waist. He shifted his holster and then lurched to his feet, grabbing her under her thighs to boost her up. He scooped up his pack.

"I could carry that," she volunteered.

"I've got it," he said dismissively.

She tightened her clasp on his neck. "Where are we going?"

He didn't bother to answer. Maybe he was saving his breath. Or maybe he didn't want to be heard. He set off in a direction perpendicular to the one her pursuer had taken.

The forest was shadowy and quiet as a church. The trees formed columns, arches, vaults overhead. Gnats danced in a shaft of sunlight. A squirrel chattered a warning and fell silent.

Lexie strained to expand the circle of her senses, alert to

every flicker in the trees, every rustle of the leaves, every pop of a twig underfoot. Despite her weight and the uneven ground, Miller strode steadily through the light under-brush, setting his feet with precision among the rocks and leaves.

A bird swooped from the branches ahead of them. She clutched him convulsively.

"Jesus," he said. "Relax."

"Sorry. I thought it might be—"

Locke's men.

She stopped, struck by a new dilemma. Did he even know the identity of the men chasing them?

Miller shook his head. "Honey, unless they sent an army after you, they're nowhere near us by now."

Guilt stirred. She stared at the back of his head. Beneath his hat, his hair was short. Shorter than she liked, really. A faint line of sunburn showed above the collar of his T-shirt.

Poor man. He really had no idea just what he'd gotten into.

"How do you know that?" she asked.

His shoulders rose in a shrug, making her shift her grip. "My guess is they'll concentrate their search in the obvious places. People who are lost tend to follow anything that looks like a way out. Creeks. Drainage ditches. Ridge lines. If we steer clear of the road and the most likely routes, we should be able to avoid them."

Well, that explained why he seemed to be picking his way at random across country.

"What if they don't stick to the obvious routes?" she asked finally. "What if we run into them?"

Miller stepped over a fallen sapling. "That depends."

Her heart beat faster. "On what?"

"On what you did to piss them off and how bad they want you back."

It was a not-so-subtle dig for information. The thin edge of the memory card tucked inside her bra chafed her breast and her conscience.

She owed him . . . something. More than thanks. An explanation.

But she didn't know him well enough to guess how he would react to the news of who she was and why Locke's men were after her. Sure, he was helping her now. But where did his he-man protective impulses end and his instinct for self-preservation kick in?

Lexie cleared her throat. "In that case, it might be better if we could avoid them."

"No shit," Miller said.

HE ought to have his head examined.

Jack scowled. Oh, wait, he had, and it hadn't done him a damn bit of good with the review board. His lawyer could argue self-defense till he was blue in the face, but Jack knew and the department quack guessed that he'd quite simply lost control.

For a cop, whose job and whose buddies depended on him staying in and being in control, that loss was devastating.

Jack trudged up a thirty-degree incline, the woman on his back a deadweight. She kept stiffening, as if trying to keep the maximum distance between their two bodies.

Like all that squirming kept his mind off sex. Just having her thighs clamped around his waist was enough to remind him how she'd felt, how she'd smelled, under him.

What, he didn't have enough problems, his *sister* didn't have enough problems, he had to jeopardize her safety and screw up his timetable by getting the hots for some baby-doll blonde? And not any blonde, either, but one who could blow his chances of getting Sally safely away. What was he thinking?

He wasn't thinking, Jack admitted as he topped the ridge and started down the other side. His boots fought for purchase on the slippery pine needles. At least not with his head. He'd reacted on instinct, driven by his damn sense of responsibility and urged on by Mr. Friendly.

He hadn't learned a thing from the last time. And that was too damn bad. For him. For Sally. And for Blondie.

Because the last woman he'd tried to help was dead.

"You never said where we were going."

The remark jolted Jack from his funk. Like it or not, until a better option presented itself, he was responsible for this woman's safety. He needed a plan.

And he had one, sort of, but she was going to hate it.

"I'm camped about a mile and a half east of here," he said, glad he didn't have to watch her face. "We can make it there by dark."

"To your campsite," she repeated.

"Yeah." He rolled his shoulders to ease the strain. He prided himself on being in good shape for a thirty-five-year-old guy. He worked out. Ran. Hell, since his suspension he hadn't had anything better to do with his days. But despite his boast, he hadn't done a forced march with a full pack since right after the first Gulf War. "You got a problem with that?"

"Nope. Better the devil I don't know," she said lightly.

He couldn't believe her. A woman fleeing—whatever it was she was fleeing—well, she ought to act more scared.

"Pretty trusting, aren't you?" he asked grimly.

She flinched. "Under the circumstances, I don't have a choice," she said. He supposed he should be grateful she wasn't having hysterics. "And I can't imagine tonight could be any worse than last night."

Shit. Had she been raped?

But he didn't want to know. He didn't want to be any more involved in whatever mess she was in than was absolutely necessary. She was not his problem.

"Is there anybody you can call?" he asked. "Somebody who's, like, waiting for you?"

Unaccountably, she stiffened. "Why do you ask?"

Jack set his jaw. He was going to regret this. He knew it. But like she said, he didn't have a hell of a lot of choice under the circumstances. "Tomorrow—if your ankle's not busted—I could take you as far as the trailhead where my car is parked. You could get a ride from there."

She was silent a moment. "Couldn't you drive me into town?"

No, he couldn't.

But what came out of his mouth was, "Which town? Bedford?"

"Bedford." She seized on the name as if it was a lifeline. "Yes."

Sally had mailed her last letter from Bedford. Apparently women from the compound were allowed into town once a month to buy supplies. Maybe Blondie had met someone or knew someone there.

"They have a police department, don't they?" she continued.

Well, shit. They probably did. Except Jack wasn't ready to turn control of the situation over to whatever passed for law enforcement around here. The last thing he wanted was some redneck cop with a gun rack mounted on his pickup truck storming the compound to stir things up.

Yeah, like Blondie going over the wall hadn't stirred things up already.

"There's probably a sheriff," he said cautiously. "You thinking of pressing charges?"

She went still. He could have told her it was a dead give-away, but he didn't want to waste his breath.

"I haven't decided," she said finally.

Yeah, Sally hadn't wanted to go to the cops, either. Which explained why Jack was busting his hump hauling Blondie—who for all her baby-doll looks was no feather-weight—over a freaking mountain.

Of course, Baby Doll might not be escaping a battering husband or boyfriend. He looked down at her hands, clasped around her wrists in front of him. No rings.

But she was obviously in some kind of trouble. Maybe she'd transgressed some weird cult rule.

Or maybe she'd gotten fed up with conditions inside the

compound and decided to split. Locke might not take kindly to losing pretty young female disciples.

But leaving any kind of abusive relationship—and despite what Sally had told him over the years, Jack figured relationships inside the compound bordered on abuse—was the most dangerous time. By leaving when she did, Blondie had put herself in danger and Sally at risk.

Hell.

Jack hit the bottom of the slope, jumped the ditch, and began to climb.

"It would help if you leaned your weight forward," he said through his teeth.

"Sorry." Obediently, she adjusted her weight, shifting her grip to her elbows. The movement pushed back the cuffs of his fatigue shirt. "Is that better?"

Jack's gut clenched. It was worse. Because now he could see what her hands and his jacket had hidden.

Her wrists were rubbed raw, and not from her holding on to them, either. A string of corrugated abrasions, purplish brown, circled each wrist like a bracelet. Like a rope.

Somebody had tied her up.

The observation stuck in his throat like undercooked meat. He was still chewing on it when a rifle shot cracked from the hills behind them.

THREE

FIGHT or flight. The body's inborn, primitive response to attack. Adrenaline demanded he choose.

Jack dropped to a crouch, the woman bouncing on his back. His mind raced, clear and sharp, even as everything around him slowed to a viscous crawl.

No way could he fight. At least, he couldn't fight and win. He was outgunned. Outmanned, too, if the sound of shots brought the hunt down on them.

Running was out as long as he was burdened with Baby Doll.

He needed other choices. *Flight, fight . . . or take cover?*

Jack glanced up at the white scar on the dark bark of a pine trunk four feet overhead and then around at the tumble of scrub. Something—someone—crashed through the woods far behind and to the left. *Take cover.*

He dumped Blondie on her round little butt and pivoted on his heels. She gaped at him, face pale, mouth opening silently like a fish. At least she didn't scream. He clapped his hat over her betrayingly bright hair and dragged up the low branches of a giant rhododendron. She ducked and wriggled under cover without any fuss or hesitation at all.

Jack rolled after her, praying his decision hadn't just landed them both in poison ivy.

Or worse.

THEY *had* to stop meeting like this, Lexie thought, an entirely inappropriate bubble of hysteria rising in her throat. She swallowed hard, forcing the laughter down with the fear and bile already churning her stomach.

Miller wasn't laughing. They squashed together, intersecting at sharp and awkward angles. He'd turned his head toward the slit of daylight filtering through the dark leaves. She could see the prickle of beard along his jaw, the sweat in the crease of his neck. In profile, his expression was as hard and flat as if he faced down armed gunmen every day of his life.

She fought a shiver. Maybe he did.

Lexie squeezed her eyes shut. What you didn't see couldn't hurt you. Growing up in her parents' narrow brownstone house in Georgetown, she'd learned to tune out the sound of raised voices downstairs, to turn a blind eye to her father's displeasure, to overlook her mother's disappointment.

She'd always been a visual person. That, as much as anything, explained why she'd drifted into photography. But in this case, closing her eyes only made things worse. With her normal conduit to the world blocked, all her other senses were heightened. Sharpened. She was uncomfortably aware of something knobby sticking into her hip. The heat and tang of Miller's body. The rasp of his breath. The whine of a mosquito.

And voices.

Male voices. Two of them. Coming closer.

Miller heard them, too. The muscles in his arms and legs went rigid. Lexie resisted the urge to bury her face against his chest.

". . . right around here, I tell you," the first voice insisted, sounding aggrieved.

"Not a thing." The second voice was deeper and disgusted. "Lucky for you. Blaine'd have your ass if you'd shot some hiker."

"It weren't no hiker. We're miles from any trail."

"So he'd have your ass if you shot the woman."

The woman. Lexie's heart clutched. They were talking about her.

"Stop her, he said."

"Yeah, stop her. Not kill her. She's no use to anybody dead."

She was dying already. Any second now they could say something that would tell Miller who she was. Any minute now they would find her.

Panicked, she opened her eyes. Miller's gaze bored into hers, dark with warning.

"I don't see that she's doing us any good anyway," groused thug number one. "If nobody knows she's here—"

"You questioning Blaine's orders?" the second speaker asked softly, but his tone affected Lexie like the snap of a twig in the stillness of the forest.

Miller didn't move. Didn't blink. She wasn't even sure he was breathing.

"No. Hey, no. I was just thinking—"

"We don't think. We follow. We're soldiers in a holy war, just like Blaine says."

"I'm following, aren't I?"

"Are you? Because I wasn't the one firing into the bushes and leaving my search area."

The first man fell sullenly silent. Leaves rustled. Footsteps crunched. Lexie swallowed, unable to look away from Miller's hard, hooded eyes.

"Blaine said to follow the ridge line as far as the creek and then beat the ground on the way back to the compound." More rustling. Lexie tensed. They were searching.

Moving. Moving . . . away? "If none of the patrols have picked her up, we'll go out again at first light."

"What if she gets away during the night?"

The other man's voice drifted back as they moved on. "She won't get far. Not by herself. Anyway, after a night alone in these mountains, she'll be begging us for rescue."

Lexie was afraid he was right. She wasn't brave. She'd never been brave.

But she wasn't alone now, either.

Miller's gaze locked on hers. His eyes were dark. Her heart pounded. The moment crackled between them, charged. Significant.

She licked her lips. *Who are you?* she wanted to ask.

But she wasn't going to be the one to speak and give their position away. So she lay counting her heartbeats, ceding responsibility to him.

Miller apparently didn't feel the need to speak at all. He rolled from their hiding place. Lexie eased up on one elbow to follow him, but he raised his palm in an unmistakable signal. *Stay put.*

Like she was going to be any safer huddled under the bushes if he got his head blown off.

The image made her shudder. She subsided against the pulpy, prickly ground. One one thousand, two one thousand . . . Her ankle throbbed. Bug bites bloomed and itched on the back of her legs.

After long moments, Miller's shadow returned. He gestured for her to come out.

Taking a deep breath, Lexie crawled shakily from the safety of the bush. Wordlessly, Miller turned, presenting her with his broad back. She eyed it with a combination of gratitude and misgiving. Their little rest under the rhododendrons had been just long enough for her to stiffen up.

The first thug's voice came back to her, sneeringly confident. *She won't get far. Not by herself.*

She sighed. Linking her arms around Miller's neck, she climbed on. He lurched to his feet.

Lexie winced as little-used muscles in her thighs gripped and adjusted. Her skirt bunched around her thighs. His hands clasped her butt. This was moving beyond awkward and into uncomfortable. Not to mention she could get the top of her head blown off at any moment.

"I feel like I've got a big old target tattooed on the base of my skull," she whispered at last.

Miller grunted. "Good thing you're wearing the hat, then."

She started. Was he joking? Could her surly rescuer actually possess a sense of humor?

"Besides, you're no use to anybody dead," he added.

So he'd heard that. "That's comforting," she said.

Oops. Sarcasm.

"It should be," Miller said. "Nobody ever minded taking a shot at me."

Oh, dear. Guilt tweaked her as she studied the line of sunburn above his collar. She should never have gotten him into this.

A frown formed between her eyebrows. If she *had* gotten him into this. What had he been doing outside the compound in the first place? She was pretty sure he'd lied about the bear gun. She didn't hold it against him. Men lied to her all the time. Ray lied to her. It was like one look at her—Betty Boop goes blonde—convinced them she would believe anything. *I'll call you. Of course I care about you as a person. You can trust me.*

No, she could forgive Miller his lie. After all, she wasn't being completely honest here herself. But she had issues with men who made a practice of getting shot at. *Thanks, Dad.*

"Really?" she asked in her chipper, wedding photographer voice. "Does it happen a lot?"

A muscle bunched in his cheek. "Lower your voice. We don't want to give away our location."

He didn't want to give away anything, Lexie thought as he trudged on. But that was all right. She could live with that.

At least, she hoped she could.

She grimaced at the back of Miller's military-style haircut. The problem was she was completely dependent on him. On a stranger. On scruffy, suspicious, is-that-a-gun-in-your-pocket-or-are-you-just-happy-to-see-me Jack Miller.

He plugged on, steady as a donkey, sure-footed as a mountain goat. Strong. She didn't date clones of her father. No congressional mall rats with gym-toned muscles. No law enforcement types, Secret Service lean, SWAT team buff. She preferred lanky artists, earnest students, average Joes with reassuring padding around their middles. Youth ministers.

Lexie pulled another face. And what a disaster that had turned out to be.

Under the circumstances, she should appreciate Miller's sheer male power. The heat of his body soaked through his T-shirt and was absorbed by her chest. She wiggled, trying to find a less intimate position, and his hands tightened on her butt.

"Relax," he ordered.

She apologized automatically. "Sorry. I've never been in this position before."

Now there was an understatement. All she'd ever wanted was a quiet life as far as possible from her parents' high-stress jobs and higher expectations. She'd certainly never planned on being drugged or kidnapped or forced to flee armed men through the mountains. She'd never dreamed . . . Never imagined . . . In her mind, she heard again the thunk of stones, the electronic shutter of her digital camera. She saw the woman fall, her open hand curled against the rocks of the yard like a starfish.

"Didn't your dad carry you piggyback when you were a kid?"

Lexie blinked the nightmare visions away. "No." The

harshness in her voice startled her. She sounded abrupt. Angry. She took a careful breath. "He wasn't that kind of father."

Miller shifted her weight to tackle another hill. "A pony ride, then. Ever ride a pony?"

"Oh, yes." Her mother had insisted on riding lessons. "But that's different from riding a man."

Miller made a choking sound.

Lexie loosened her hold on his neck and then realized what she'd just said. Her face burned.

"I mean, I wouldn't do it the same way," she clarified.

"Don't like to be on top, huh?"

He sounded more amused than nasty, but Lexie was tempted to strangle him anyway. She wasn't normally a violent person, but being kidnapped by the Disciples could have turned Mother Teresa into one of the mujahedeen.

"I haven't thought about it. Getting away is a bigger priority for me than getting laid," she said and had the satisfaction of seeing Miller's jaw clench.

JACK gritted his teeth. He'd just gotten his chops busted by Goldilocks. And served him right.

What kind of fuckhead made suggestive comments to a battered woman on the run?

His kind of fuckhead, he thought, disgusted. The kind of guy who conducted relationships with his dick instead of his brain. The kind of cop who let his rage overwhelm his training, his instincts overcome the law. Obviously, neither his divorce nor the recent wreck of his career had taught him a damn thing.

He plodded on, one foot ahead of the other. Kind of the way he'd made it through his days since he'd lunged for Tony Boyle in a haze of blood and fury. Four cops, they'd told him later. Four buddies to pull him off, and Rooney was still pissed at him for busting his nose.

One task at a time. One day at a time. *Make the coffee. Read the paper. Leave a message for the lawyer. Go to the gym.*

Jack stared up at the sky, fading blue between black branches, and down at the compass hanging from his neck like his old dog tags. He'd have been happier following a city grid or even a trail of breadcrumbs than this maze of deer trails through miles of unchanging scrub pine. It didn't help his concentration any that the woman on his back vibrated with tension like one of those massage chairs at the mall. Although she'd been pretty quiet for the past quarter mile. Drowsy, maybe. Or offended.

The gurgle of a snowmelt stream trickled into his consciousness. Jack cut to his left, following the sound of water, looking for landmarks: a tree doubled over like an arthritic old man, a rock jutting up like a headstone. He passed the stand of bushes where he'd dug a shallow latrine and saw, two hundred feet farther on, his blue bear bag hanging from a tree. Home sweet home.

He cleared his throat. "Hey." The blonde didn't speak. Didn't stir. He jogged her, not too gently. "Can you stand?"

She slithered from his back. His hands slid from her thighs to her butt. Just for a second, she staggered and clutched at him. He was almost sorry when she let go.

"I think so."

She didn't sound too sure, so Jack turned to check her out. She stood off-balance, her eyes dazed and dark, like a woman who'd had too much to drink or not enough sleep or a couple hours of slow, satisfying, do-it-to-me-one-more-time sex.

His body constricted in sudden, undeniable lust. Fuck.

Or not.

Probably not.

Her hand crept to her cheek, pink and creased from his shoulder. "What's wrong?"

He couldn't tell her that her breasts squashed against

him, her heat riding the small of his back, had made him hard. So he turned the question back on her. A cop's trick, even if he wasn't a cop any longer.

"What makes you think something's wrong?"

"I don't know." She attempted a smile, and he thought again how pretty she was. How nervous. "Maybe because you're looking at me like I have drool on my face?" Her eyes rounded with comic distress. "I didn't drool on you, did I?"

Jack scowled at the images that conjured up. "Nope. No drool."

"Well, that's a relief." She pulled off his hat and fluffed her short blond curls. "I can't believe I dozed off."

"Stress. It takes some people that way." He watched her stagger and ordered, "Sit. I want to take another look at that ankle."

Her smile faded at his abrupt tone, but she looked around obediently for a perch. She was either remarkably good-humored, unnaturally submissive . . . or scared to death of him.

The thought made him scowl even more fiercely. "I'm not going to hurt you."

"I know," she said quickly. Too quickly? She waited until he'd returned from the tent with the first-aid kit before adding, "And I appreciate everything you've done for—*Ow.*"

"Sorry." He gentled his touch as he eased the jerry-rigged splint from her leg.

She peered down at him. "Is it broken?"

"Hard to say without an X ray." The joint was still swollen, her skin hot to the touch. Except for her toes. Her toes were like ice. "Can you wiggle your foot?"

"I think so." Her brows pulled together in pain or concentration. Gingerly, she flexed her toes and rotated her ankle. "How's that?"

"How does it feel?" he countered.

"Sore," she admitted. "But not as bad as it did before."

That was the first encouraging news he'd heard all day. "Any numbness? Tingling?"

She shook her head.

He stood, satisfied. "We'll wrap it in some cold cloths for now. You can rest it while I get our dinner."

"Can I help?"

He didn't bother to answer. *One step at a time,* he thought as he walked to the stream to re-fill the canteen and soak the towel that was all he had in place of ice. She swallowed the painkillers he gave her, making a slight face at the taste of the purification tablets in the water. Huddled in his drab jacket, she watched as he lowered his rations from the tree. *Light the lantern. Kindle the fire. Fill the kettle.*

She roused when he pulled his cup from his pack. "I can help."

"It's okay." As long as he was busy, he didn't have to think about what he was going to do with her. About what her escape might mean for Sally.

But the blonde was determined to be perky. It beat whiny, but not by much. "I've never cooked over a campfire, but I can boil water."

"We're not cooking over the fire," he said, aware he was acting like a bastard and irritated enough not to care.

"Oh." She shrank within his fatigue shirt, watching the flames. "What's for dinner?"

He did a quick survey of the pack's contents. "Beef enchiladas, chicken tetrazzini, or turkey with mashed potatoes and gravy?"

She laughed. "Oh, turkey, of course."

Opening the foil package, he activated the flameless heating unit inside.

Her eyes widened. "You weren't kidding."

"Nope." He handed her the warmed MRE.

"Thank you." She studied the military label on the side before digging in with the plastic spoon packaged with the meal.

"You said you were in the Army?"

"I was. Six years ago." He might have re-upped for a third tour, but Patty hadn't wanted to stay married to a soldier. Turned out she didn't want to stay married to a cop, either, but he didn't blame her for that.

"Rangers?" Lexie asked.

Maybe she was hoping he was here to do the Rambo thing and blow the compound up. Not happening, babe. He couldn't even claim to be a cop anymore.

"Infantry. I got the grub from an online camping supply," he said to forestall further questions.

"It's good," she said politely.

It wasn't good, but it was filling and easy to carry. He wanted to tell her he usually ate better than this, but in fact, since his divorce, he didn't pay much attention to food at all.

The kettle hissed and sputtered. Jack wrapped his hand in his handkerchief and reached to take it from the fire.

Lexie stirred. "Let me."

The last thing he needed was for her to burn her hand or fall into the fire. "I've got it."

She settled back. "I'm not completely helpless."

"Yeah, you are," he said grimly.

Her chin stuck out. "I got over that wall by myself."

True enough. He wouldn't have guessed she'd have the guts. Or the opportunity.

He dumped crystals into two mugs and handed her one. The scent of coffee mingled with wood smoke and pine. "How did you manage that?"

"I convinced . . . the person watching me that I was sick."

"You lied?" He was surprised. Not that she lied. As a cop, he was used to criminals who lied, informants who lied, witnesses who lied. But Lexie S-Smith was not a convincing liar.

"I threw up." A note of pride crept into her voice. "Repeatedly."

A corner of his mouth kicked up. "Good for you."

Maybe she was more resourceful than she looked. Which was a good thing, because he couldn't help her. "So what will you do now?"

She stared at the mug cradled in her hands. "I've been thinking about that. Am I allowed one phone call?"

She wasn't his prisoner, for Christ's sake. "You can have my cell. But it won't do you any good."

"Why not?"

"Mountains, babe. No signal."

"Oh." Her voice was small with disappointment.

Not his responsibility, he reminded himself. Not his problem.

"There's a public phone in the parking lot by the trail-head," he offered. "Who were you planning to call?"

She hesitated. "My—my mother."

Relief flickered through him. So she did have somebody outside the compound to turn to. Unless her "mother" was actually a boyfriend, a lover, some lowlife loser she was boinking on the side. Not that it made any difference to Jack.

Considering what she was running from, it might not make any difference to Blondie, either.

"Is she expecting to hear from you?" he asked.

Another hesitation. She really was a lousy liar. "I think it's likely if I don't check in with my parents in the next few days, they might call the cops."

Jack scowled and shoved a spoon in his own MRE. Someone ought to explain to her that "might call the cops" wasn't going to deter anybody from abusing her body and dumping it down a ravine. But it wasn't his job to educate her. He'd helped her enough already. Now it was payback time.

"They know where you are, though, right? Or where you've been?"

He could almost feel her debating with herself what to tell him. "Not the details," she said at last. "I didn't want to worry them. My father tends to overreact to things."

Maybe that was true. It sounded true. And maybe it was time he gave her a piece of the truth in return, a foundation of information he could build on. Establish a rapport. Create trust. Sometimes one confession elicited another.

"Finding out your daughter's mixed up with a survivalist cult would upset most parents," he said. "It makes me nuts, and Sally's only my sister."

Lexie put down her half-eaten MRE. "You know who they are?"

They, he noted. Not we. "The Disciples of Freedom. I checked them out on the Internet." Bible-spouting, gun-toting, government-hating believers in Daniel Locke and Second Amendment rights.

"And your sister . . ." she breathed.

Jack nodded. "Is married to one of them."

"Sally?"

"Yeah." Dark-eyed, adoring little sister Sally. *Jack, can I play? Jack, you have to talk to Dad. Jack, when are you coming home?* He broke out in guilt like a sweat. Forced himself to ask the question that burned in his gut. "Do you know her?"

FOUR

❧

LEXIE met Jack's hard, dark eyes and felt a chill that had
very little to do with sex.

Well, at least now she knew why he'd been hanging
around outside the compound. His sister was one of them.
A Disciple.

"Know her?" she croaked. "I don't know—" Panic tightened her throat.

Anybody.

She'd spent the past thirty-two hours drugged and
bound in the back of a van or locked in a room the size of a
closet with the window nailed shut.

Not a great way to make new friends.

No one had responded to her cries for help, her pleas for
information, or her tears. Certainly not the women who
slipped like ghosts in and out of her room. They wouldn't
speak to her. They barely looked at her. They dressed
the same—in blouses, skirts, and kerchiefs—like the Stepford nuns or something. Lexie had a hard time telling them
apart. Jack's sister could have been the woman who

brought Lexie her tray or took away her clothes or escorted her to the bathroom.

She could have been the woman stoned in the yard outside her window.

Lexie shuddered. Or one of the ones throwing rocks.

There was simply no way to know. And no way to confess her doubts to Jack Miller.

She stole another glance at Jack, trying to trace some resemblance between his strong, hard-featured face and the smooth, self-effacing women of the compound. Nothing.

She cleared her throat. "I'm not sure . . ."

"You probably know her as Sarah." Jack picked up a charred and glowing stick to poke the fire. "Sarah Blaine. Ray Blaine is her husband."

Shock opened a hole in Lexie's chest. Jack might as well have jabbed her with that stick he was holding.

Ray was *married*?

Of all the lies Ray Blaine had told her, this one was the most personal. Pain and fear and rage ran from the edges of the hole like blood.

That bastard. He'd come into the camera shop several weeks ago when Renae was on break, dark, compact, and intense, exhibiting the white teeth and sleek assurance of a Doberman. Lexie had been both attracted and repelled. She didn't do intense any more than she went for intimidating. The last thing she needed in her life was another decisive, dominant male. But she'd been flattered when he'd sought her out, reassured by his expressed lack of interest in politics, impressed when he didn't grope or grab her on their first date. It wasn't like the singles scene in Lovingston, Virginia, offered a wide range of dating options. Ray was clean, straight, and employed—a visiting youth minister, he'd told her. He'd seemed genuinely interested in her, asking about the details of her work and her schedule, encouraging her to talk about her family. Ha.

She'd convinced herself the slight anxiety she felt around him was part of the getting-to-know-you stage in any relationship. She'd been afraid of hurting his feelings, afraid of doing the wrong thing. And so she'd let him persuade her to go on one more Sunday picnic in the country . . .

God, she was dumb. Dumb and spineless. An easy target.

Ray had never been attracted, never been interested in her at all, only in her relationship with her father. No wonder he hadn't had trouble keeping his hands off her. *Thank God,* she thought now, with another shudder.

He'd *used* her.

He was married.

To Jack's sister.

Her mind grappled with the implications of that while the hollow in her chest oozed some more. Jack, the man who had rescued her, the one guy who could help her, was related by marriage to Daniel Locke's second-in-command.

She didn't just have bad judgment. She had lousy luck.

Lexie licked her lips, staring across the fire at the most recent man to challenge her faith in the basic fairness of the universe.

"So you're here on . . . what? Some kind of family visit?" she asked.

Jack tipped his head to watch her, his expression noncommittal, his body indolent. So why did she get the impression he was coiled, ready to pounce?

"Is that why you're here?" he asked.

He sounded like a cop, Lexie thought, her heart banging against her ribs. Cops did that, answered one question with another question.

"I asked you first," she countered.

A corner of his mouth quirked, and she thought for a second that once you got past the macho, master-of-the-universe routine and the fact that he carried a gun, he was really quite attractive. Not that she could afford to be attracted, but still . . .

"I was hoping to see her, yeah," Jack admitted. "Since I was in the area."

"Camping," Lexie said, not quite making it a question.

"That's right," he agreed blandly.

Liar, she thought.

"When was the last time you saw her?"

He sipped his coffee, watching her over the rim of his cup. "Are you always this nosy?"

He was doing the question thing again.

"No," she said honestly. "I'm trying to turn over a new leaf."

His eyes narrowed. "Under the circumstances, maybe you're being too pushy."

Doubt shook her. Maybe she was. Jack Miller had hidden her, helped her, carried her, and fed her. Did she really want to alienate him now?

She took a deep breath to steady herself and said, "It's not pushy to want to know if I can trust you."

Silence rose like smoke between them, broken only by the hiss and pop of the fire. "You can trust me to take you as far as the trailhead tomorrow," he said at last. "You can trust me to share my tent and not roll on top of you in the middle of the night. And that's all you can trust me for. Is that good enough for you?"

Lexie swallowed hard, refusing to let him see how much he intimidated her. "It will have to be, won't it?" she said.

HE'D scared her, Jack thought, watching the muscles move in her throat. Her eyes were wide as a rabbit's. Good. Maybe if she was scared, she'd stop asking questions. Keep her distance. Be more careful.

Yeah, and maybe she'd panic and make a mistake that would kill them both.

Disgusted with her, with himself, he stood, trying not to notice when she froze like a startled fawn. Shit. Unzipping the tent flap, he hauled the bag with his clothes out by the fire.

Under the trees, it was already dark, the temperature

steadily dropping. He pulled a sweatshirt and two pairs of
socks from the bag.

Lexie watched him, arms crossed against her chest. You
didn't have to be a cop to read that kind of body language.

He yanked the sweatshirt over his head. "How's the
ankle?"

Silently, she stuck out her foot for his inspection. Still
swollen. He was impressed she hadn't complained.

"I'll wrap it now. And you can put these on." He tossed
her the socks.

She caught them. "Thank you," she said, unshakably
polite.

Maybe they taught etiquette inside the compound. Jack
squatted and cradled her calf in his hands, frowning at the
bruises against her pale skin. Or maybe she'd had the shit
kicked out of her for talking back.

"Don't thank me until we see if you can walk on it." Her
knees raised, making a tent of her long skirt. If he leaned
just a little bit forward, he could bury his head in her lap.

Dickhead, he thought, disgusted.

He wrapped the bandage over and around her foot, careful not to look up her skirt as he secured the end with a pin.
"Right. On your feet."

He helped her up, her hand warm and soft in his. Obviously, her duties inside the compound hadn't included
scrubbing floors or splitting firewood. He caught himself
rubbing his thumb over her knuckles and made himself
drop her hand.

He watched critically as she hobbled a few cautious
steps.

"Latrine's behind those bushes," he said. "Do you need
help?"

She smiled, the wry humor in her eyes sliding under his
guard like the sharpened end of a prison spoon. "I've been
going to the bathroom by myself since I was three years
old. I think I can manage."

"Fine." He handed her the flashlight and his roll of toilet

paper. He could use leaves, but he didn't trust her not to grab a handful of poison ivy in the dark. He waited until she was almost beyond the ring of firelight before he called softly, "Watch out for snakes."

She cast one startled look over her shoulder before she disappeared into the shadows.

Jack grinned and then shook his head. He shouldn't tease her. He couldn't afford to like her. He needed to get rid of her so he could concentrate on the job at hand and find Sally.

The bushes rustled and Lexie was back, lifting the kettle from the fire. "There aren't really any snakes, are there?"

She sounded nervous. He was tempted to reassure her, but she'd be safer if she watched her feet.

"Copperheads and timber rattlers," he said. "Somebody should have warned you. In case you left the compound."

She splashed water over the towel and pressed it to her face and throat. Her skin was damp and pink. Her eyes closed in pleasure.

Jack sucked in his breath. He didn't miss Patty anymore. But he missed lying in bed at the end of the day, watching his ex-wife perform those small female rituals—brushing her hair, creaming her face, unhooking her bra.

It was a conditioned response, he told himself. Like Pavlov's dogs.

Water ran down Lexie's neck and blotched the front of her shirt. ". . . don't think anyone expected me to leave the compound," she was saying.

Jack dragged his gaze from her breasts, struggling for his place in the conversation. "Ever?"

She hesitated. Preparing to lie again.

Disappointment stabbed him. And then he was irritated with himself for being disappointed. "Look, don't bother, okay?"

She widened her eyes. "Excuse me?"

He wasn't falling victim to that big-eyed look.

"I don't need to know about your personal life. I don't

care about your personal life." He'd lost everything—his job, his friends, his self-respect—because he'd let a case get personal. Because he'd cared about Dora Boyle and her daughter too much. "Just don't lie to me. If you can't be honest, don't talk at all."

He stalked off to rinse their cups in the stream, leaving the little blonde staring after him like Bambi after the hunters shot Mama Bambi. Way to be a jerk, Miller.

But it worked. She didn't try to fob him off with a bunch of stories. In fact, she didn't say another word. Not even when she stooped inside the tent and saw the single sleeping bag.

"We can spread it out," Jack offered gruffly. "So we both have something to sleep on. I have an army blanket we can cover up with."

Pressing her lips together, Lexie sat to take off her sandals.

"What?" he asked, goaded by her silence.

She looked at him. "Wouldn't it be warmer if we lay on the blanket and pulled the sleeping bag over us?"

He met her gaze in surprised approval. "Yeah. We could do that."

She nodded and unzipped the bag. Practical. Willing. She rolled to her hands and knees to spread out the blanket, and even swaddled in his jacket and that stupid skirt, he could see the swing of her breasts and the sweet curve of her ass.

He kicked himself. Okay, there was a really bad thought to be having before they went to bed. Securing the tent flap, he dragged his clothes to the head of the tent to use as a pillow. He shucked off his holster and put his gun where he could reach it in the night. They arranged the sleeping bag on top of themselves, careful not to tangle legs or bump shoulders. And then he blew out the lamp.

God, it was dark. No house lights, no street lights, no cars. Even the stars were blocked by the nylon walls of the tent.

In the darkness, he could hear her breathe, a ragged sound too quiet for tears, too uneven for sleep.

Jack willed himself not to move. Not to respond. So what if she was awake? He was awake, too. Pretty soon they'd give in to exhaustion and then they would both be asleep. He lay with his eyes open and his arms behind his head, staring up at the black roof of the tent.

But the sound of her breathing snuck up on him in the dark, like the warmth of her body or the scent of her hair. In this tight, confined space, it was too easy to remember how good she'd felt under him, soft and sweaty, her warm, round butt pressed against him.

He was hard as a tent pole. Maybe he should walk the perimeter. Maybe he could try counting sheep. The one thing he couldn't do was handle the problem himself. Not with her lying next to him, listening.

Correction. That was the *other* thing he couldn't do.

She shifted, and her foot brushed his calf. She jerked it back, like she was scared even to touch him.

Jack exhaled through his teeth. "Sorry if I was"—*hard, don't say hard*—"rough on you earlier."

He heard her swallow. "That's all right."

She was being understanding. Shit.

"Don't be nice about it, or I'll feel like an even bigger dirtball."

"It's all right," she repeated.

"You mean, I'm forgiven?" Jack asked.

A pause. "No, I meant it's all right with me if you feel like dirt."

He almost grinned.

The night settled around them. Gradually, the small tent filled with her, the whisper of her breath, the shampoo-and-wood-smoke smell of her hair, the tickling awareness of her body just out of reach . . .

A rock stuck into the small of his back. Jack stretched cautiously, trying to dislodge it.

"I'm sorry about the sleeping bag," Lexie volunteered out of the darkness. "Are you very uncomfortable?"

He strangled on a laugh, caught between a rock and a hard place—one that was getting harder every minute.

"Don't worry about it," he said in a voice that should have warned her to shut up.

But she was braver than he gave her credit for. Or more foolish.

"Is there anything I can do?"

Oh, baby. "Do you want to do anything?" His voice was flat. Challenging.

This time she was silent.

"That's what I thought."

"It's not that I don't appreciate your protection," she said stiffly out of the darkness. "You saved my life today. I'm grateful."

Grateful was good. Naked and horizontal would have been better.

Jack knew cops who claimed sex as one of the perks of the job, a kickback like free doughnuts or coffee. There were guys who figured it was a waste not to take what was offered, who regarded a blowjob as a reasonable trade-off for turning a blind eye.

But he didn't kid himself. If he took advantage of her and her gratitude, he wouldn't be one of the good guys anymore. Not even in his own mind.

"Is this where you offer me your body as a reward?" he drawled. "Sorry, babe, but the virgin sacrifice thing doesn't do it for me."

She sucked in her breath, and Jack wondered for a moment if he'd gone too far.

"I'd find that really reassuring," she snapped. "If I was a virgin."

Whoa. Not tearful. Hostile. "Look, I—"

"But I'm not into sacrifice, either." She cut him off. "So I guess sex is still out."

"You know," Jack said, recovering. "You're not what I expected."

"You were hoping for naked and grateful?"

He winced. Direct hit. "I was thinking more along the lines of scared and submissive."

Another of those pauses while she figured out what to say.

"I don't know about submissive," she said at last. "But I'm plenty scared."

Jack frowned. They were clearly headed for a discussion about feelings, which was almost always a bad idea. But it was better than having sex. Or better than lying here next to her thinking about how they weren't going to have sex.

Resigned, he asked, "What are you scared of?"

SARAH Blaine wavered in the door of the storage room, twisting her hands in her apron. Should she strip the bed? Or leave it? Nobody was sleeping in here tonight. The last of the search parties had returned more than an hour ago. And Tuesdays were laundry days. If she stripped the sheets now, she'd have a start on her chores for tomorrow.

The acrid odor of onions competed with the pine cleaner Sarah had used to ready the room for their "important guest." She'd known better than to ask why any guest of importance was sleeping in the pantry with the window nailed shut. No wonder the poor woman had gotten sick. The smell of vomit lingered in the air, richer than sweat, sharper than fear.

Strip the bed, Sarah decided, but her feet wouldn't move from the doorway.

A thirty-two-year-old woman ought to be able to make a simple housekeeping decision. But she was frozen with fear, paralyzed by her earlier mistake.

"Sarah," said her husband.

For a second she thought she'd imagined his deep preacher's voice. She lived with that voice in her head, chiding, remonstrating, reproaching her. His sure, sincere, persuasive voice.

Christ, Sally, Jack had snapped after his one meeting with Ray. That disastrous meeting at the diner when Ray suggested it was better if Jack and Sarah didn't see each other again. *The guy sounds like a fucking cemetery plot salesman. He'll bury you.*

She'd picked up her purse and followed her new husband without another word. Ray was waiting for her in the car, the engine already running.

Once she'd loved that, Sarah remembered. How sure he was of everything. Of himself. Of her.

She'd believed in his sincerity when he swore he wouldn't do it again, that it hurt him as much as it hurt her, that it was only for her own good, that she made him do it with her sinfulness and her pride.

When she was seventeen, she would sneak downstairs at night, her heart pounding with love and excitement, and stand by the locked front door of her father's house, listening for Ray's voice on the sidewalk outside. He could persuade her to do anything then.

She still listened for his voice. It still made her heart beat faster. But not with eagerness anymore.

"What are you doing here?" he asked.

She turned, tension knotting her stomach.

Her husband watched her, his eyes bright narrow slits in his controlled face. He was still so handsome, trim, and well muscled, his body as disciplined as his soul.

Or his wife.

"I thought I might strip the bed," she offered.

"Why?"

"I . . . Well, because I . . . Because she's gone." Wrong answer, she realized instantly, watching his eyes.

"It's laundry day tomorrow," she said, as if that would matter to him.

"And whose fault is it that she's gone?" Ray asked.

Sarah wet her lips. *Holy Mary, Mother of God . . .* Father Daniel didn't approve of such prayers, she knew, but Sarah had been raised a Catholic.

"Mine," she whispered.

Her husband shook his head. Heavily. Sorrowfully. "That's your pride talking again, Sarah," he said, and the slippery tension in her gut tightened. Sometimes the knot got so bad she was tempted to provoke him, just to get what happened next over with.

But of course she never did. Not intentionally. It was always something she hadn't intended that set him off, a careless word, an immodest look, an involuntary slight.

"I'm sorry," she stammered. "I didn't mean—"

He cut her off. " 'The head of the woman is the man,' says Paul. Your failure is my failure. The responsibility is mine."

"I could go to Father Daniel," she offered desperately, knowing it was already too late. "If I explain to him I was the one who took her to the bathroom—"

"Sarah, Sarah." Her husband's voice was soft. Sad. His eyes were very bright. "It's not your place to speak with Father Daniel."

"Ray, please . . ."

"You must be taught your place," he told her, and the quiet finality in his voice made her shiver. "Get the rod, Sarah."

WHAT are you scared of?

Lexie flushed.

Everything, she thought. You. Me. Making a mistake.

Her father didn't make mistakes. At least, he never admitted to them. Kind of like a politician seeking reelection. Her mother, a prominent surgeon, made life-and-death decisions every day.

But Lexie dreaded knowing that one misstep, one missed call, and people could *die*. Because of her.

None of which she could confide to tough guy Jack Miller.

What are you scared of?

The musty room, the bloody rope, Ray's quiet, lecturing voice, and the sound of screams outside her window . . .

"Getting caught," she said. "Going back."

"How'd a woman like you get mixed up with the Disciples in the first place?"

Her heart beat faster. She could lie. Despite—or perhaps because of—his sister's ties to the Disciples, Jack obviously wasn't sympathetic to their cause. And lying was working, she told herself. He'd already promised to take her as far as the trailhead tomorrow. What good would telling the truth do?

Besides making her feel like less of a sleaze.

She shrugged, forgetting he couldn't see her in the dark. "How does anyone? Met the wrong people. Made the wrong friends."

"Meaning a man," Jack guessed.

She was silent. He was right. If she'd never met Ray Blaine, if she'd never agreed to go out with him, she wouldn't be in the middle of nowhere, dependent on some macho commando.

"Shit." Jack sounded disgusted. "I'll never understand how a bright, good-looking woman can stay with a guy who believes he has the God-given right to smack her around."

"I didn't have a choice," Lexie protested, which was true, though not perhaps in the way he'd take it.

"Baby, there's always a choice," Jack said.

She felt a sudden burst of fury for that nameless woman, sprawled and bleeding on the stones of the yard. "How would you know?"

"It takes a victim of domestic violence an average of seven contacts—seven—to leave the guy who's knocking her around. Social workers, doctors, cops—all trying to help. And they don't listen. They don't learn. These guys don't change. These women should accept that."

"Oh, that's great," Lexie said. "Blame the victim."

"That's not what I—"

"They do listen. They do learn. They listen to men who tell them they're worthless, helpless, incompetent. That they deserve what's coming to them. That they're overreacting. And after a while, they believe it."

"Is that what happened to you?" Jack asked quietly, his voice an invitation in the dark.

Her heart pounded. Of course not. They were talking about battered women. Not the pampered and protected daughter of Washington's elite.

Lexie had never had her judgment questioned, her abilities downplayed, her faith in herself eroded.

She stared dry-eyed at the tent over her head.

We're only doing this for your own good.

Honestly, Alexandra, we expected better of you.

If you'd just apply yourself . . .

Lexie blinked the memories away. "It happens to a lot of women."

"Like my sister."

His sister. Oh, God. How could she even consider telling him the truth now, when her very presence put his sister at risk?

"I guess her, uh, marriage isn't going too well?" *Or her husband wouldn't be trolling for victims in the Virginia suburbs.* A bubble of hysteria rose in Lexie's throat.

"You could say that," Jack said grimly.

She could say a lot more than that, if she dared. Lexie swallowed. "How long have they been . . . ?"

"Fourteen years. She ran off with him when I was in the Gulf. I didn't even meet him until I came home on leave."

"What about your parents?"

"Our mom died when Sally was nine."

Lexie noticed he didn't mention how old he'd been. As if his age, his loss, hadn't mattered. Tough guy. But a reluctant compassion stirred in her heart. "Your father?" she asked.

"Was as glad to get Sally out of the house as she was to go."

Oh, dear. Lexie had been relieved when her own parents divorced and she could live with her preoccupied surgeon mother. But she'd never doubted that her father took a real and continued interest in her life. Whether she wanted him to or not.

"You don't have any other family?" Lexie asked. Surely there were overprotective grandparents. An interfering aunt. Somebody to share the burden of responsibility.

"Sally has a little boy, Isaac. He's almost seven now."

Not the answer Lexie was hoping for.

The darkness pressed down on her, flattening her spirit, making it hard to breathe. Her dash for freedom had taken all her strength and more courage than she thought she had.

She wanted rescue.

She wanted out.

She wanted her life back, damn it, and her quiet apartment with her automatic coffeemaker and her plants in the window and her framed photographs on the wall.

She wanted all this to be over. And instead it was getting more and more complicated. Jack's only family, his sister and his nephew, were inside that compound. Which meant he had a real conflict of interest if he tried to help her.

No, that wasn't right. If Lexie didn't count Jack's very obvious reaction when he'd been lying on top of her, he didn't have any interest in her at all. If there was a way out, if there was a way back from this nightmare, she would have to find it herself.

FIVE

❧

"YOU'RE awfully quiet all of a sudden," Jack said.

Lexie squirmed, prodded by conscience and a root under her shoulder blades. "You told me not to talk."

If you can't be honest, don't talk at all.

"I told you not to lie."

She didn't want to talk. She definitely didn't want to talk about lying.

"What do you care?" she asked defensively. "Guys never listen to what I say, anyway. Unless it's 'Come up for coffee.' Or 'Your pictures will be ready on Friday.'"

"What pictures?"

She jolted. What . . .

"What?" The memory card burned a hole through the lining of her bra.

"You said, 'Your pictures will be ready on Friday,'" Jack repeated patiently. "You work in a camera store or something?"

Oops.

"Sometimes," she admitted cautiously. "To make ends meet."

"And the rest of the time?"

She could tell him. What harm could it do? "I'm—I used to be a contract photographer."

"Yeah? What kind of pictures did you take?"

Her heart raced. *Gee, before the Stepford Disciples took my camera and my clothes away, I got some really nice shots of a bunch of women stoning another woman to death. Maybe when we get back to civilization you'd like to look at them and tell me if you recognize your sister.*

"Portraits, mostly," she answered. "Weddings, events, kids." *Stonings.* "Even passport photos."

"Were you any good?"

She raised her chin in challenge, forgetting he couldn't see her in the dark. "Good enough."

"I'm not questioning your ability, babe. Just your job prospects after you get out of here."

She was instantly embarrassed. He was being *nice*. He was concerned for her welfare.

"I'm sorry. I guess I'm a little . . ." Shaken. Scared. Confused. "Out of sorts," she said finally. "It's been a long day."

"Tomorrow's going to be another one."

She didn't want to think about it. Her ankle throbbed. Her back and shoulders ached from strain and contact with the hard ground. She was at the end of her resources, at the end of her rope, and tomorrow she had to hike five and a half miles through the wilderness only to be abandoned in a parking lot.

She wanted to go home. She needed to call her father.

No, not my father, Lexie thought, tucking her hands into her armpits for warmth. At least, she couldn't call her father with Jack around. Because if Jack overheard her, he would know that his sister and everyone else inside the compound were toast. Waco burgers. Lexie was only fifteen when the Bureau joined the siege of the Branch Davidians, but she'd watched the footage from the Texas compound. She'd read about Ruby Ridge.

She bet Jack had, too.

Guilt seeped into her like cold through the groundsheet at her back. She hated lying. But how could she possibly tell him the truth? *Hi, my name is Alexandra Scott, and my father is Trent Scott, the director of the FBI.*

Jack would never believe her.

And if he did . . . Well, he wasn't stupid. He would know her abduction meant the full force of the U.S. government was about to move on the compound with his sister inside.

She could try to persuade him that she was no threat to his sister. That Trent Scott would move with care and discretion against the armed survivalists who had held his daughter. After Waco, the crisis-intervention teams had been reformed and reorganized. But her father, a political appointee eager to establish himself as tough on terrorism, might not be guided by his own experts. Lexie might convince her father that there were innocents inside the compound who should be spared. But she wasn't confident he would listen to her.

He never had before.

Trent Scott still saw the world in sharp, uncompromising shades of black and white like a high-contrast photograph. Good guys vs. bad guys. Evil-doers vs. innocents. Law enforcement vs. civilians. Us vs. Them. Lexie thought he was paranoid. He thought she was foolishly naive. She'd been mortified when, as a lower-level bureau chief, he'd investigated her friends in high school, miserable when he'd busted her college boyfriend for drug possession.

I was right, wasn't I? Trent had demanded when Lexie protested. *The kid's a junkie. You're a lousy judge of character.*

Wouldn't he be pleased to be proven right again.

Because—Lexie winced—she *was* a lousy judge of character. If she hadn't trusted Ray Blaine, she wouldn't be in this mess right now.

Dizzy on drugs and speechless with shock, she had

listened as Ray patiently explained it all to her this morning. The Disciples of Freedom believed the only true safety rested with vigilant, armed, free men protecting their families and their faith from the corruptions of the outside world. Their leader, Daniel Locke, preached that the United States was powerless to protect its citizens, even the daughter of the man charged with its highest security.

And Ray had kidnapped her to prove it.

"You're quiet again," Jack observed.

"I don't feel like talking," she mumbled.

"Then go to sleep."

Sleep? She was exhausted. But her mind was spinning. Her heart raced.

"I'm too wired to sleep."

"You want to have sex?"

The question thumped low in her stomach. Did she?

Oh, God, adrenaline and lack of sleep were clearly affecting her brain. *"No."*

The sleeping bag slithered as Jack shrugged. "You're running out of options, babe."

And wasn't that the truth.

Lexie sniffed and curled into the fetal position. If she'd had a pillow, she would have pulled it over her head. The wind fretted and poked at the fastenings of the tent. A night bird screamed and fell silent. Inside, the air was close and still.

"I suppose things might look better in the morning," she offered at last, tentatively.

"Maybe," Jack said in the kind of voice that meant *Or maybe pigs will fly.*

She flopped back over on her back. "Or maybe I'll wake up and discover the past thirty-six hours have all been some horrible dream."

"Like that season of *Dallas,* huh?"

"Like what?"

"Never mind. You're too young."

"I'm twenty-seven. How old are you?" she asked.

He muttered something that sounded like, "Old enough to know better." "Thirty-five," he said out loud.

She wriggled to find a more comfortable position. Her knee bumped his thigh.

"Will you hold still?" he said through his teeth.

She sighed and subsided. "Sorry."

She curled on her side and listened to his breathing, deep and slow. *He* wasn't wired, she thought.

You want to have sex?

She flushed with heat in the darkness. What a question. Offhand. Almost indifferent. As if he would deal with that need as casually and competently as he'd dealt with everything else. He could have been offering to buy her a cup of coffee or bring her a glass of warm milk before bed. *Can't sleep? Would you like some sex?*

She tried to summon some indignation and found herself grinning instead.

Smiling, she drifted at last into sleep.

WARM. She felt warm and safer than she had in a long time.

Lexie burrowed closer to the source of heat and woke up straddling a man's hard thigh, with her nose pressed to his neck and her head pillowed on his shoulder. His arm was close around her waist. His jaw scraped her forehead.

Not just any man. Jack Miller.

Oh. Dear. Lord.

She swallowed, barely daring to breathe. Was he awake?

His hand splayed lightly against her back, under her T-shirt. His breath was hot and even.

Asleep, she decided.

Very cautiously, she raised her head to study his face in the gray dawn light. His hair stuck up all over his head like a little boy's. But even unconscious, he didn't look relaxed. Or innocent. He looked hard and faintly dangerous, his

face constructed of shadows and angles. Tension lurked between his brows and secrets in the corners of his mouth.
His lips were full and slightly parted. She wanted to take
his picture, to capture the contrast between that hard face
and those soft lips, between his dark, thick lashes and his
stubbled jaw.

She wanted to touch him. She wanted to trust him.

But that was her hormones talking.

Lexie sighed. Hormones, or the desire to shift the burden
of responsibility onto someone else. Anyone else. She was a
wedding photographer, for God's sake, not some kick-ass
female operative. She didn't do karate. She looked terrible
in leather. She felt like the perky host on *Trading Spaces*
thrown into Jennifer Garner's role on *Alias*.

Unfortunately, her awareness that she was woefully
miscast was no excuse for turning over her part to Jack
Miller. How well did she know him, after all? Just because
the man had an interesting face didn't mean she could trust
him to—

His hand, warm and callused, slid up her back. His
thigh shifted, settling her more solidly against his body.
Lexie sucked in her breath. Wow. His hot, hard, male, thoroughly aroused body.

Her heart jumped into her throat, in fear and . . . Fear,
she decided. Anything else was just too embarrassing to
contemplate. She wasn't the type of woman who got turned
on by dangerous strangers. Certainly not by an unconscious one.

She should move. Quickly, before he woke up. Slowly,
so she didn't jar him awake.

Swallowing, she flattened her palm against his chest.
Sometime during the night, his shirt and sweatshirt had
ridden up his ribs so his flat, bare belly rubbed hers. She
was acutely conscious of hot skin, rough hair, smooth muscle, and the bulge of camouflage below. She eased her knee
down, feeling the drag of his pants material all along the
inside of her thigh.

His other hand came up and cupped her breast. Her heart stopped.

"Nice," he murmured. His thumb rubbed a lazy circle around her nipple. It sprang to attention.

Okay, she really should move.

She would move.

Any second now.

She was not kinky. She did not engage in risky behavior. She was not lying here, panting and dry-mouthed, while some weekend warrior in army surplus fondled her.

Lexie stared, transfixed, at the dark hand against her pink shirt, gently squeezing her breast.

Except she was.

His long, blunt fingers traced the outline of her nipple. "Patty," he said.

Lexie froze. *Patty?*

Oh, dear Lord. He had a wife. A girlfriend. She really *didn't* know him at all.

She scooted back to her side of the tent, her heart pounding. And she didn't trust him, either.

"WHO'S Patty?"

Jack squinted over his shoulder at Lexie, hobbling down the trail behind him. She couldn't have said what he thought she'd just said. Hell, she'd been giving him the silent treatment all morning.

She hobbled to catch up with him, leaning on the walking stick he'd trimmed for her. It was rough going. He'd avoided the trails today, and the ground was slick with pine needles and treacherous with fallen branches. But she had never complained. She was a trooper. He'd give her that much.

"What?" he asked.

Lexie stopped for breath, her cheeks as pink as her shirt, her gray eyes narrowed. "Who is Patty?"

Shit. He was operating on low fuel and less sleep, chafing with worry and edgy with sexual frustration. The only thing he needed to make his day abso-freaking-lutely perfect was a discussion of his ex-wife.

"How do you know about Patty?"

Lexie's round chin tilted up. "I don't know anything. If I did, I wouldn't have to ask."

Jack gave her his don't-mess-with-me scowl, the one he used to break up bar fights and scare teenagers into confessing. It hadn't done a damn thing to stop Tony Boyle from killing his wife, but it worked great on pint-size blondes.

Her gaze skittered away. "You mentioned her in your sleep last night. Is she your wife?"

"I'm not married."

"Girlfriend?"

She really wasn't letting it go, Jack realized with reluctant admiration. "My ex."

"I'm sorry." She actually sounded sincere.

He wondered if he could use her sympathy to develop a rapport, draw her out, and then dismissed the idea. She wasn't his case. He wasn't her friend. He wasn't getting involved. Once they reached the trailhead over the next rise, his responsibility to her was over. "Don't be. I'm not."

"Then why did you get married?" she asked, more tartly than he expected.

"Why does anybody?" She looked flushed. Hot. He handed her his canteen. "I wanted a home, I guess. A family."

Lexie drank thirstily. He watched the movement of her throat, the pulse that beat under her jaw.

She passed the canteen back to him. "Do you have children?"

"Nope. Patty didn't want any." *Now why the hell did I tell her that?* he thought, annoyed.

"Is that why you divorced her?"

Jack screwed the cap back on the canteen. "What is this, my online dating personality profile?"

Lexie's Kewpie-doll mouth compressed, and her face turned even deeper pink. Shit. He'd hurt her feelings.

"Or maybe she divorced you because of your lack of conversational skills," she said.

Jack smiled wryly. "That was part of it," he admitted.

"And the rest?"

Her color was better, and her breathing had evened out. They should get moving. She had a better chance of catching a ride into town before dinner, and he still had to hike back to his campsite tonight.

He sorted through the reasons for the failure of his marriage and offered her the simplest. "She didn't like my job."

"What is it you do?"

"I'm—I was a cop."

Her hand flexed on her walking stick. "You *were*?"

Jack set his jaw. "Yeah."

"But you're not anymore."

Where was she going with this? "Nope."

"So maybe the two of you will work things out," Lexie suggested.

He shook his head. "I'd rather go back to the job than my wife."

Lexie sniffed and limped ahead. "Well, that explains why she wasn't crazy about your job."

"Hey." He was amused. Offended. "Some women find the gun and badge thing a turn-on."

"Not me."

He hitched his pack against his shoulders and started after her. "So, no handcuffs on the first date, huh?"

"Now who's filling out the online dating personality profile?"

Jack laughed. Waited. He'd been good at that once, leaving a question dangling in silence, angling for a response.

But she didn't bite. Wary little fish.

He threw out another line. "Is it cops in general you can't stand, or do you just hate me?"

She glanced back at him, her eyes rounded. "I don't hate you."

Hooked, he thought in satisfaction.

"Cops in general, then," he said.

"One in particular."

Jack scrambled up the ridge line where a bare outcropping of rock gave him a view of the trail ahead. Trees blocked the distant parking lot, but he could just make out the distant hum of the rural highway. Almost there. Almost safe. Almost done with the danger and with her. The thought didn't sit as comfortably as he expected.

He slid back down. "And what did this one cop in particular do to piss you off?"

Lexie tilted her head. His hat covered her short, sunny hair, but it couldn't dim her smile. "Well, for starters, he married my mother."

Jack almost smiled back before the sense of her words sank in. Ah, Jesus. "Abusive stepfather?"

But she shook her head. "Father. And he wasn't abusive."

Jack didn't want to know about it. He couldn't afford to care. But he asked anyway, driven by male interest and a cop's curiosity. "So what was the problem?"

"The problem was he was already married."

Whoa. "To another woman?"

"To his career."

He met her gaze. Her face was flushed, but her eyes were perfectly steady. The echo of his own words jangled between them. *I'd rather go back to the job than my wife.*

Well, hell. He'd known it was a mistake to ask.

LEXIE tightened her grip on her walking stick, wincing with every step. It wasn't just her ankle that was screwed up. Clearly the past several days—lack of sleep or surfeit of drugs, the fall, or the fear—had affected her brain. And her mouth. Her big mouth.

She dug the tip of her stick savagely into the ground. Dumb, dumb girl.

Of course, maybe it didn't matter if she'd offended him. It wasn't likely that Jack cared about her opinion anyway. In half an hour, he was washing his hands of her and she'd never see him again.

And wasn't that a cheering thought.

At the top of the rise, the canopy thinned. The afternoon sun slanted through the branches, creating texture and depth under the trees. But she didn't have time to think about the play of light or the scenery. Jack changed direction, plunging into a wave of greenery. The branches bent and sprang back around him. Lexie waded after him, grateful for the socks that protected her from ticks and poison ivy.

"Watch your step," he ordered.

She pressed her lips together. What did he think she was doing?

"Here." He stuck out his hand, a big, strong hand with a ridge of callus along the top of the wide palm. Just because she was unaccountably mad at him was no reason not to take it. She gripped tight as he supported her down the slope, through the brush, and onto a trail.

An actual trail. Rooted and rocky, it wound through the foliage like the wake of a boat. She could even see a trunk ahead spray painted with a colored dot.

Jack dropped her hand as if she had cooties. "Almost there."

Her chest hollowed. "Wonderful," she said.

Now she had a whole new set of problems to deal with. And all by herself, too.

The track broadened like a stream spilling into a lake of gravel. Weeds shot up on either side. A brown and white trail sign marked the primitive steps leading down to the parking lot.

Jack stopped. "You should be able to get a ride into town from here. Summer traffic hasn't picked up yet, but there are plenty of day hikers."

Lexie's heart banged against her ribs. He was leaving her. Here? Before they even reached the parking lot?

"Great," she said.

He scowled at her, thrusting his thumbs through his belt loops. "If you get stuck, there's a pay phone at the far end of the lot."

"Okay."

He stood there, looking broad and competent and cross.

A lump rose in her throat. She was not going to ask him for a ride. He couldn't wait to get rid of her.

"So." She swallowed the lump and her pride. "Is your car parked down there?"

He nodded. "The white Civic."

Come on, she thought. *You can do better than that. Ask me.*

She could do better than this. She could ask him. She drew a deep breath.

"I can't drive you," he said abruptly. "It could be sunset before I got back."

"Right." She exhaled, deflated. "You can't find your way to your campsite in the dark."

"Yeah."

Wordlessly, she slipped out of his fatigue shirt and handed it to him.

He took it. "I guess you'll be all right now?"

"Absolutely," she lied.

He still didn't move.

"You want your socks back, too?" she asked, only a hint of bitterness in her tone.

He looked startled. "No. You keep 'em."

"Well." This was awkward. "Thank you. For everything."

"No problem."

It was like some horrible end-of-date experience. No good-night kiss, only tension and frustrated expectations.

Lexie stuck out her hand firmly. *Don't leave me, you selfish son of a bitch.* "Good-bye."

His hand engulfed hers one more time. "Take care of yourself," he said seriously.

Like she had a choice.

She watched him walk away, ignoring the flutter of panic in her stomach. She didn't need him. She needed a phone and food and medical attention. She needed to turn over the memory card in her bra to whatever passed for local law enforcement around here and get a message to her father.

Lexie sighed, imagining Trent Scott's probable reaction to the news that his daughter had been kidnapped by a survivalist cult in . . . in . . . Oh, God, she didn't even know what state she was in. Maybe she *would* call her mother first.

Yeah, because her mother would love to be the one to tell her ex-husband, the president's appointee, that Daniel Locke was right. He really couldn't keep this country or their daughter safe.

Lexie winced. Phone first, she reminded herself. Then food. She'd deal with her parents' politics later.

She limped down the log steps, trying to shake off the feeling that unwashed men with guns were going to leap out at her from the bushes. She and Jack hadn't encountered any signs of search or pursuit all day. Everything was going to be fine. Nothing was going to happen to her. Nothing ever happened to her.

Of course, she'd told herself the same thing two days ago when Ray had pulled his car to the side of the road . . .

Her heart was pounding as she hobbled into the open. But the lot, a strip of grass and gravel ringed by woods and edged with rocks, was nearly empty.

Okay. That was good. A state trooper would have been better, but she was prepared to deal.

She spotted a white Honda Civic—Jack's car—with Tennessee plates and also a battered pickup from Virginia. A late-model Ford parked under the pines. The sound of voices made her nervous, but it was only a middle-age couple on folding camp chairs picnicking from the open trunk of their car. The woman was eating from a bag of chips. The man wore a ball cap, a fanny pack, and white socks halfway to his knees. No danger there, unless they intended to assault her with their cooler or a folding chair.

The woman looked over curiously and nudged her husband.

Lexie tugged on the ends of her hair. She probably looked like shit. Not to mention she was dressed totally inappropriately for these mountains in a long skirt and sandals.

She flashed the picnickers an embarrassed smile, resisting the urge to ask if they had an extra sandwich packed in that cooler, and sidled past them to the phone.

It stood on a pole in a dimpled metal box, weeds tufting around the base, its severed cord dangling. It took Lexie a moment to realize it had been vandalized. Disbelieving, she stared at the empty cradle where the receiver should be.

She could handle this, she thought desperately. She had to.

Hot tears sprang to her eyes.

"Do you need some help, dear?"

Lexie blinked and sniffed.

It was Chip Woman, in a flowered blouse, yellow pants, and a pink lipstick that looked too youthful for her pleasant, middle-age face. "Are you all alone?"

"Yes. I . . ." She needed something plausible. Unthreatening. Unextraordinary. "I got separated from the person I was traveling with."

Because the rat bastard wouldn't give up one night in the wilderness to drive me into town.

"You trying to call somebody?"

"Yes. Do you . . ." Lexie sent a breathless prayer to the gods that her luck was about to change. "Do you have a phone I could borrow?"

The woman's round face creased. "Oh, gosh, we sure don't."

No. Of course not.

"Clyde doesn't believe in those cell phones," the nice woman in the flowered blouse confided. "They're unsafe, you know. People driving with their hands full and their mouths flapping. And I heard if you was using one and pumping gas, why, your tank would explode."

Lexie blinked. "Really." Somewhere the gods of luck and fate were laughing their asses off.

"But we could give you a ride," the woman continued. "To the next rest area. Phone there might be working."

"Really?" Lexie repeated. Her voice squeaked. "You would do that?"

"Sure," the woman said kindly. "It's worth a shot. And Clyde and me, we're about done with our lunch. Time to be heading back anyway. Hey, Clyde." She raised her voice. "Young lady here needs a ride."

Her husband looked up from stowing the cooler in the trunk. "Where to?"

"Where are you headed?" Lexie asked.

"Home. That's Benson," the woman explained.

"Benson." Lexie committed the name to memory. "That's the nearest town?"

Clyde slammed the trunk shut. "Nearest one of any size."

"Clyde's the pharmacist," his wife said with pride.

"Could I . . . Would it be possible for you to give me a ride that far?"

Clyde hitched his belt and regarded her from under the brim of his ball cap. "Guess so."

"Thank you. I really appreciate this," she said.

She did, too. The way she looked—and smelled—right now, she wouldn't have offered herself a ride.

The nice woman beamed at her. "We know what it's like to be lost."

The car interior was worn and clean, the tang of cigarettes overlaid by the pine air freshener dangling from the rearview mirror. Lexie sagged against the broad backseat with a sigh of gratitude. She was sitting down. At last. She didn't even have to drive. She didn't have to do anything.

The engine grumbled to life. The door locks clicked shut. The car reversed slowly, its tires crunching on the gravel. As it nosed up the ramp to the road, the sun shot through the windshield. The nice woman flipped down her visor. She had some kind of holy card, a saint's image edged in gold, stuck up there with her insurance and registration. Not St. Christopher.

Lexie squinted. Her Catholic mother only took her to church because it annoyed her father. She'd stopped after the divorce. But Lexie was pretty sure she'd seen that smooth, ascetic face before, those pale blue eyes fixed on higher things.

Her breath stopped.

She had.

Recently.

The smiling, saintly image over the visor was Daniel Locke.

SIX

~~

"WE must pray," Daniel Locke said, leaning back in his executive leather desk chair to regard Ray with vague blue eyes. "And God will provide a solution."

Ray Blaine schooled his face not to betray impatience. He wouldn't need divine intervention if Alexandra had accepted her place in his plan. If Sarah had done her duty. If the men assigned to the search had done their jobs. How could he be expected to succeed when he was surrounded by unfaithful servants? Weaker vessels.

And really, Ray thought with a pinch of irritation, when it came to implementing their vision of a new society, Daniel wasn't much better. They were at war with a government that usurped their parental rights. Their God-given liberties. Believers everywhere were only waiting for a voice crying in the wilderness to lead them from the ways of promiscuity and homosexuality, from race-mixing and baby-killing.

Daniel fancied himself that voice now. Ten years ago, he'd been kicked out of his Mississippi congregation. With his few adherents, he had wandered to his family's dirt-scratch farm in Nantahala. Gradually, as his following grew, the work of the settlement shifted from raising goats and tobacco to raising an army for the Lord. Daniel's short-wave radio broadcast reached hundreds every week. His website received thousands of hits each month.

But it was Ray's plan, Ray's efforts, that would bring the Disciples glory, that would rally the faithful and win the nation to their cause.

As long as he wasn't frustrated by incompetents.

"I'm not sure we can wait for a reply from the Lord this time."

Daniel drew himself up behind his desk. "Do not overstep yourself, brother. 'Cursed is the one who trusts in man, who depends on flesh for his strength and whose heart turns away from the Lord.' "

Ray lowered his gaze. He needed to step carefully here. Daniel was already unhappy with him for meting out justice to Martin's whorish wife. Ray couldn't risk usurping Daniel's authority or losing his support. Not until Ray had solidified his own position.

"Of course, Daniel. What I meant was, you are more effective at prayer than I am. You have chosen the better part."

"Like Mary at the feet of our Lord."

Ray breathed again. "Exactly."

"While you worry and obsess over details, like Martha."

Important details, Ray thought resentfully, but he didn't make the mistake of speaking his thoughts again.

He was grateful, now, that he'd delayed announcing their victory until the false trail was laid. He still had time to recover Alexandra before the Beast descended on these hills.

He'd ordered patrols on every hiking trail and stationed watchers at every access point for a radius of ten miles. He'd even enlisted their members living outside the compound, whose dedication was less fervent or whose jobs or connections in the community were too valuable to sacrifice.

"Only to serve you, Daniel," he said stiffly.

Daniel nodded, accepting his submission. "See that you

do." His pale eyes met Ray's, suddenly not vague at all. "Or I'll find someone who will."

LEXIE'S heart drummed in her ears. Her mouth went dry.

She had to get out. Get away.

Her gaze flicked to the car window, where grass and gravel gave way to asphalt. And she had about five seconds to do it, before the car pulled onto the highway and picked up speed.

The nice woman in the front seat turned around and smiled. "Don't forget to fasten your seatbelt."

Oh God, oh God, she didn't want to do this . . .

Lexie lurched forward and grabbed at the passenger-side door lock.

"Hey!" the woman cried, startled.

Lexie jammed the heel of her palm down on the handle and threw her shoulder against the door. It fell open. She tumbled out.

The ground jumped up and hit her. Bit her. Wrist, elbow, hip. Gravel tore her skin and clothes. The woman screamed as Lexie rolled.

She lurched to her feet—*ow, ow, ow*—and stumbled down the ramp toward the parking lot.

"Turn around! She's getting away!"

The engine gunned. Tires spun. Panicked, Lexie looked over her shoulder. But there was no room in the narrow turnoff for the Ford to maneuver. The driver would have to pull onto the highway to turn around.

She ran.

Her sandals slapped and slid on gravel, every step a beat of pain. *Ow. Ow. Ow.* Her breath sobbed in her lungs.

She ran.

Back to the parking lot? There was nobody there. She would have to take her chances on the trail.

No. They would find her. Catch her. She would never get away again.

Her heart pounded. Her vision swam. *Think, dummy, think.*

She burst into the parking lot. There was the pickup, empty. The white Honda, abandoned. Behind her, she could hear the rumble of an engine and stones spitting from the road. She was in such big trouble now. Would they stone her?

Wildly, she looked around. No phone. No help. No hope. No Jack.

She picked up one of the rocks that ringed the parking lot and smashed it through his windshield, setting off his car alarm.

SHE was fine.

Jack stomped down the trail, no longer concerned about making noise.

Wonderful, she'd said. *Great,* she'd said. *Absolutely all right.* All she had to do was hang around the parking lot doing the helpless blonde chick thing, and eventually somebody would come along. AAA, maybe, or the highway patrol. A couple campers or some hikers or a bunch of gang-bangers in a pickup truck . . .

Shit.

He stopped to stuff his jacket into his pack. He was too warm to want it now, but he'd be grateful for it tonight. And his sleeping bag. And some quiet.

You want your socks back, too?

He grinned and then shook his head. See, that was the problem with taking on a female. They got inside your head and messed with your priorities. He couldn't be wondering or worrying about Lexie S-Smith when his own sister was depending on him.

He straightened slowly, slinging the pack on his shoulders. Although, you know, it wouldn't hurt Sally if he stuck around here a little longer. The hike back to his campsite would be a lot faster without Lexie slowing him down. He might walk to the parking lot and make sure she was okay.

He didn't have to stay. Just until she got a ride. That wasn't the same as getting involved.

He was already turning when the car alarm went off.

Shit. He started running.

LEXIE'S heart rose in her throat as Clyde hauled himself from behind the steering wheel and lumbered toward her.

The car alarm still split the air. Where the hell was Jack? Where the hell was anybody?

"I don't want to hurt you," Clyde said.

Lexie skittered to the other side of Jack's car. "Good. Go away."

Clyde frowned and walked closer, arms outstretched as if he were shooing geese. "I can't do that. Please, get back in the car."

"You must be kidding," Lexie said.

From the corner of her eye, she saw his wife open her door and bounce from the car.

"Now, don't make a fuss," the older woman scolded. "You're ruining everything."

Lexie's mouth dropped open at the injustice of it. She'd been kidnapped, drugged, stripped, threatened, chased through the woods, and abandoned by the man she'd spent the night with, and *she* was ruining everything?

Clyde lurched for her. She dodged and ran behind the pickup. Puffing, he came after her.

"You be careful!" his wife called.

Great. Maybe he'd have a heart attack.

Okay, not a productive thought. Lexie hobbled around the hood of the truck. Could she beat him to the highway and flag down help? Or would she only attract more trouble?

But even as Lexie eyed the road and gauged her chances, Mrs. Clyde climbed behind the wheel of the Ford and gunned the engine. Lexie's heart sank. No way could she outrun the car. Not to mention the last thing she wanted was to wind up the victim of a hit and run.

Almost the last thing. She wasn't crazy about winding up back at the compound, either.

Clyde lunged.

Lexie hopped away, still keeping the truck between them. The car alarm blared. Her ankle screamed. She couldn't take much more of this. Neither could Clyde, apparently. Beneath his cap, his face was red and shiny.

Hope welled inside her. If she couldn't outrun him, maybe she could outlast him?

He fumbled below his paunch for his fanny pack and pulled out a gun. A big gun. A .38 Browning, just like the one her daddy taught her to shoot during their awkward and infrequent visitation weekends.

Lexie's brain blanked. Her mouth dried.

Clyde pointed the gun over the hood of the pickup. "I don't want to hurt you," he repeated breathlessly. "Get in the car."

Lexie stared appalled at the wavering muzzle, feeling as though Casper Milquetoast had suddenly and unfairly morphed into Dirty Harry. She knew, because her father had drilled it into her since she was six years old, that you never got into a car at gunpoint. Your chances of survival were always reduced once your abductor was mobile.

But what she knew and how she felt faced with the business end of a .38 were entirely different things. She swallowed, hard. Coward.

"Drop your weapon," commanded a cold, hard voice from the trees.

Jack.

Lexie sagged in relief.

Clyde whirled to face the trailhead and squeezed off two quick shots.

Lexie squeaked and ran for cover, expecting a bullet in her back at any moment. Or her shoulder. Or her knee. *I don't want to hurt you.*

She heard a pop and an answering blast behind her. Oh, God. She crashed through bushes. Oh, Jack.

She stumbled on, pausing once to glance over her shoulder. Through the trees, she glimpsed Jack's Honda, its front tires shot out, its windshield shattered, its car alarm still shrieking. The Ford's door was open. Clyde's wife cowered behind the dashboard, her hands pressed to her ears. Lexie faltered. Where was Clyde? Where was Jack?

Her steps lagged. Should she go back? Could she go back? What good would it do?

"What the hell are you waiting for?" Jack growled beside her. "Move it."

"We can't stop now," Lexie said.

Jack punched 9-1-1 on his cell phone. Was it too much to ask for one decent relay tower in this godforsaken state?

Apparently, it was. He flipped shut the phone in frustration.

"They'll come after us," Lexie insisted. "We have to keep moving."

She was limping and out of breath, and she wanted to run?

Jack raised his eyebrows. "You really see the old guy chugging through the woods?"

"No," she admitted. "But they could have called somebody. Other Disciples."

"You said they didn't have a cell phone."

"I don't *think* they had a cell phone. But they could have been lying about that, too. And they could drive to a gas station or someplace to call for help. Reinforcements."

"Relax." He enjoyed her indignation for a moment before he added, "They're not going anywhere soon. I took their keys."

Her mouth dropped open. "You took . . ."

"Their car keys. The old lady wasn't in any position to argue."

"But the gun . . ."

"I took that, too."

He slid it from the belt at the small of his back and showed her, like a kid trying to impress his friends at show-and-tell.

She shuddered and looked away.

Jesus, what did he think, she was going to go all gooey-eyed and say, *Good job, Jack?* He stowed the gun safely in his pack. At least she wasn't crying or clinging to him or screaming how this was all his fault, the way almost any other woman would do. That was one thing to be thankful for.

His gaze dropped from her face, pink with exertion, to her damp shirt.

Not that clinging was always a bad thing.

He dug blindly in the pack, trying hard not to remember how she'd felt under him yesterday, all smooth and soft and sweaty, her round ass cradling his dick.

Oh, yeah, he absolutely shouldn't remember that. She probably didn't need the sex, and he definitely didn't need the distraction.

He unfolded and refolded the map, glad to have something to occupy his hands and his brain.

"Okay, here's what we're going to do," he said gruffly. "There's a mountain shelter less than a mile from here. We can make it before nightfall, easy. It's early in the season, but there will still be hikers and rangers on the trail. I'll stay with you until somebody comes."

"No," she said.

One word. Just like that. Like she had a choice.

"What do you mean, 'no'?"

Her round chin set. "I'm not going with anyone else. I don't trust anyone else. I'm staying with you."

He struggled to keep his tone even. Reasonable. "You can't stay with me."

"Why not?"

Jack took a deep breath. Could he tell her? He couldn't before. Nine times out of ten, an abused woman ended up going back to her abuser. He didn't want to risk telling her his plans if she was going to spill them to Blaine or Locke to buy herself out of a beating.

But Lexie had proven she was no Dora Boyle. She wasn't going back. Not willingly, at least.

He looked at her serious eyes, her soft mouth.

If he could make her understand . . .

And she didn't rat him out . . .

"I told you my sister is married to Blaine," he said abruptly.

Lexie nodded.

"Well, she wants to leave him. Finally."

"That's good," Lexie said. She frowned, watching his face. "Isn't it?"

"It's great. I never liked the son of a bitch. But . . ." He stopped. How much could he trust her?

I'm not going with anyone else. I don't trust anyone else. I'm staying with you.

"But . . . ?" she prompted gently.

"But she can't do it on her own. Not with the kid and all. She needs help."

"And that's why you're here."

"She wrote to me." Jack looked away, unwilling for Lexie to see how much the damn letter had meant to him. "She doesn't have anybody else."

"That's very . . ." Lexie hesitated.

Jack set his jaw. "Stupid?"

"Nice," Lexie said. "Very nice of you."

He could hear another "but" in her voice. "Yeah, so?"

"I was just thinking. Wondering," she corrected carefully, as if the wrong word would set him off. "Couldn't you wait until—"

Guilt lashed him. "No, I can't. I'm supposed to meet her tomorrow. It's not like I can call her and tell her there's been a change of plans."

Lexie fell silent, digesting that. She had to see he was right. She had to agree. The best, the *only* thing he could do was get her to a shelter as quickly as possible.

"How long do you think it would take us to reach that town?" she asked. "Benson?"

Christ. Didn't she ever give up?

"Too long," Jack said.

"If we drove?"

"Drove what?" he demanded. "My car's a total loss. And that's before your buddy back there rounds up his friends and takes it apart."

"I'm sorry."

Even though he knew better than to fall for it, her big-eyed routine made him feel like he tortured puppies or pulled the wings off flies. "It's not your fault. Anyway, it's a rental."

"But won't it be harder now for you to get your sister away?"

Fuck.

"We'll manage," he said tightly.

"How?"

Talking to Lexie was like playing whomp the gopher at the midway, he thought, exasperated. Every time he thought he'd swatted her down, she popped up with something else.

"There are other cars. I'll borrow one."

Her gaze turned speculative. "You can do that?"

In the Army, Jack had learned to hot-wire damn near anything. "Yeah."

"Then why can't you do it now?"

"I could, if I wanted to go back to the parking lot and get jumped by your friends. Or arrested by the locals for auto theft."

"I'm sure if we explain—"

Jack's knowledge of southern law enforcement was based on the *Dukes of Hazzard*. He couldn't afford to get locked up by some self-important local sheriff who took a week to write a traffic ticket.

"I don't have time for explanations."

Lexie frowned. "You're right. I wasn't thinking."

Jack felt a flash of relief.

And then she spoiled it by adding, "I'll just come with you and wait somewhere."

"Where? You're not safe in these woods."

"I'm not safe anywhere." She met his gaze. The trust shining in her eyes made him nervous. "Except with you."

She had to be kidding. The last woman who had trusted him with her life was dead. "You don't know anything about me," he said harshly.

"I know you came back for me."

Big mistake, he thought. But just for a moment, looking in those smoky blue eyes, he believed in second chances. He believed in himself.

And that was an even bigger mistake.

SEVEN

LEXIE watched as Jack hunkered down to inspect the gear piled at the back of the wilderness shelter and told herself the revulsion she felt was completely unreasonable.

So she had privacy issues. It was her father's fault. Trent Scott's attempts to keep tabs on his teenage daughter had made her feel isolated and somehow ashamed. She'd given up keeping a diary. She'd dreaded the soft click of the second line when she was on the phone with her friends. And she'd hated knowing her father knew the contents of her underwear drawer as well as she did.

But this was different. This was life or death. Jack wasn't pawing through some unsuspecting hiker's personal possessions out of curiosity.

He held up a pair of jeans as if measuring the waistline of the woman who fit inside, and the twelve-year-old girl inside Lexie cringed.

"Is this really necessary?" she said.

He shot an impatient look over his shoulder. His shirt pulled tight across his back, exposing the shape of the gun on his hip and his tight, muscular butt. "What are you, nuts?" He tossed the jeans at her. "Put these on."

She gaped at him.

"Hurry up," he ordered, and bent back to his business. "These clowns will probably file a police report," he said over his shoulder. "If it makes you feel any better, you can track them down when all this is over and pay them for what we take."

Mollified, she sat and began pulling the jeans on under her skirt. "Wouldn't it be simpler to just go back to your campsite?"

Oh, God, now she was whining. She hated whining.

But Jack didn't seem to notice. Or maybe—she winced—he didn't expect any better of her.

"You can't walk that far. Not twice in one day. And not on that ankle."

Secretly, she acknowledged he could be right. But pride demanded she protest. She stood and wriggled the jeans over her hips. "I'm tough."

"You were lucky." He sounded distracted.

She glanced over and found him watching her. "What?"

He shook his head and pulled a small pot from the pack in front of him. "We'll find someplace closer tonight. Someplace Blaine's men won't be looking."

Yeah, and maybe since they were so *lucky,* they wouldn't freeze to death without a tent or sleeping bag.

No whining, Lexie reminded herself. At least, thanks to Jack, she wasn't on her way to the compound with Mr. and Mrs. Clyde.

She fastened the top button on the jeans—they were a tight fit, but she could do it—and stepped out of her skirt. "Can I help?"

He nodded toward the other pack. "We need food. Dinner tonight and at least two meals tomorrow."

Life or death, she reminded herself. She knotted the skirt to make a sling. "What about the people the food belongs to? Don't they need it, too?"

"The people it belongs to aren't getting shot at. They can hike out to Burger King."

Lexie pressed her lips together, determined not to quarrel.

Jack exhaled. "Fine. Take half. Anything they have duplicates of. But hurry. And no cans."

"We could, um, borrow a can opener."

"We don't want the weight."

"Right." She rummaged. Trail mix, crackers, a jar of instant coffee, foil packages of tuna . . .

She dug deeper. There at the bottom, wasn't that . . . Oh, joy. *Yes.* Bright yellow disposable cameras, sealed and ready at the bottom of the bag, familiar as peanut butter and more comforting than cocoa. A way to put her world in perspective. To hold it at a distance.

"Come on." Jack dropped to his knees beside her and started shoveling her selections into his already-bulging pack.

"I've got it," she said.

Anything they have duplicates of . . .

Her hand hovered over the cameras.

Jack grinned. "Thinking of taking pictures for the yearbook?"

Her face flamed. She drew back her hand as if he'd slapped it. "No. No, of course not."

Jack stayed on his haunches, regarding her with too-seeing, too-mocking eyes.

She offered him an embarrassed smile. "I guess it's kind of like you and your gun. I feel naked without a camera in my hand."

"You naked is good," Jack said. "But take a damn camera if you want one."

She shook her head. "I don't need one."

Jack muttered a curse and dug in his back pocket. Surprised, Lexie watched him peel off a couple twenties and tuck them into the bag. Grabbing a camera, he tossed it into her lap.

"Let's go."

Lexie watched him stride silently out of the shelter and off the trail.

Speechless, she shouldered her makeshift sling and limped after him.

DEPUTY Sheriff Bobby Greene stuck his head in the door of Will's office.

"Got a minute, Chief?" he asked and then flushed.

Will Tucker kept his face impassive, pretending not to notice Bobby's slip. When he was one of them, all the deputies had called him "Chief," a semi-teasing reference to his Cherokee blood. But since the old sheriff was laid low with a stroke and Will stepped in to fill his post, they all called him "Tucker" or "Sheriff." Or tried to. Old habits died hard in the mountains.

Old prejudices did, too.

To most in Dorset County, Will would always be the big, silent, black-eyed kid from Scrub Hollow, Jenny Tucker's half-breed bastard. He'd joined the Army fresh out of high school, seen the world—well, Germany— served in the Gulf, gone through college on the G.I. Bill, and never planned on coming home again.

But even though Will had never known his father's people, had never been accepted by his mother's, his blood was in these mountains and the mountains were in his blood. He'd joined the sheriff's department seven years ago and worked his way up to chief deputy. And now, at least until the next election, he was the sheriff.

"Sure," he said, pushing back from his desk. "You got anything on that gunshot report by the highway?"

Bobby shook his head. "Might have been hunters."

"Nothing's in season. Except wild turkey."

Bobby helped himself to a handful of the M&Ms Will kept on his desk since he'd quit smoking. "That never stopped some kid with a gun from going after squirrel."

"They shouldn't be that close to the road or the trail, though." Will frowned. "Isn't the Disciples compound out that way?"

Unlike the national parks, national forest lands could only be purchased from willing homeowners. Even deep in the designated wilderness areas, there were still pockets of privately held homesteads and farms handed down through generations. The Disciples had moved onto the old Locke homestead while Will was in the Army.

"About three miles in."

"That's a long way to hike for shooting practice," Will observed.

"Oh, they wouldn't be involved in something like this," Bobby said.

Will raised his brows. In an area where most folks attended one of three churches in town and hunting was a cherished tradition, the Disciples' God-and-guns attitudes went down easy with their neighbors. What had the government ever done for the people of these hills but move them off their land and threaten their way of life? The Cherokee, yes, but white settlers, too, forced out by mining companies, logging companies, railroad companies, and park programs. The Disciples' distrust of outsiders and suspicion of big government found plenty of sympathizers.

But there was still something hinky about them.

Maybe Locke's weekly shortwave radio broadcasts preaching the evils of government didn't sit too well with this government employee.

And maybe, Will admitted, he didn't like them because they didn't like him. The Disciples of Freedom was definitely a whites-only club.

"You think?" he asked. "You friendly enough with them to know?"

"I know most of them don't need target practice," Bobby said. "And Locke doesn't want any trouble. They keep themselves to themselves. You know that."

He did. They did. The Disciples homeschooled their

children. Even their women only came into town once a month, in carefully shepherded groups.

A memory teased Will: a sweet-faced woman with a long dark braid, licking an ice cream on the bench outside. He pushed it away.

"So, what's up? You didn't come into my office because of some boys shooting squirrels."

"No. The thing is, that wasn't all they were shooting at. There was a car in the same lot with its front tires shot out."

"Deliberately?" Will asked.

"Hard to see how it could be an accident. The windshield was broken, too. By a rock."

Will scowled. "But nobody was hurt?"

"Nobody was there." Bobby took another handful of candy. "Probably just vandalism. The phone was out, too."

"Probably," Will agreed. "You run it through PIN?"

The sheriff's office had recently added a Police Information Network terminal. That was one good thing to come out of homeland security.

Bobby looked down at his notes. "Car—white Honda Civic—registered to an Ames Rental in Knoxville."

Right over the Tennessee border.

"Stolen?" Will asked.

"Nope. Rented to a John Miller from Clarksburg, Pennsylvania, last Saturday. His vehicle's still on their lot."

Will leaned back in his chair. It was probably nothing. Vandalism, like Bobby said. But . . .

"Notify the phone company about the repair. We'll increase patrols in the area for the next day or so. I'll call the ranger station, tell them to keep an eye out for your Mr. Miller. He's not going to be happy when he comes off the trail."

LEXIE trudged, concentrating on putting one foot in front of the other, again and again. Her ankle throbbed, and her conscience pinched. Her left sandal was rubbing blisters through her sock. But she'd never get anywhere thinking about the things that made her uncomfortable. She had to focus on where she was going. She'd worry about what she was doing later.

At least Jack hadn't dumped her ass back at the shelter. He'd even "bought" her a camera.

He strode ahead of her, looking broad-shouldered and competent in a T-shirt that clung to his biceps and hugged his waist. Lexie fought an unexpected shiver of guilt and lust.

She was using him.

Lying to him.

The way Ray had used and lied to her. And she felt just terrible about it.

The shadows collected under the trees. Despite the thickening chill, a line of sweat ran down Lexie's spine. What would Jack do when he found out?

She trusted him. She did. To a point. It seemed stupid to trust the guy with her life and not trust him with the truth. And he had come back for her. But would he have rescued her if he knew she was carrying evidence around in her bra that could implicate his sister in a murder?

She eyed the back of his head. Maybe he would understand. He was a cop. Ex-cop.

An ex-cop who had dropped everything to come to his sister's help. *She doesn't have anybody else.*

Lexie sighed. Nope, she definitely couldn't tell Jack the truth.

Because right now she didn't have anybody else, either.

Not a cheering thought.

Jack turned to steady her down a slippery bank.

"I'm okay," she said stiffly. "I don't need your help."

Which was another big, fat lie. She didn't sound strong and independent. She sounded ungrateful. And sulky. She sounded like a big, fat, ungrateful, sulky liar.

He gave her an annoyed look. "Don't be stupid. You're slowing us down."

"Sorry," she muttered, and took his hand.

His palm was warm and square. Hard. Strong. A jolt of awareness contracted her insides. Oh, no. The situation was complicated enough. She was not going to complicate it further with sex.

But maybe Jack didn't see sex as a complication. Maybe he took things more casually. His question from the night before thumped in her stomach. *Would you like to have sex?*

Hastily, she let go. "Thanks. I'm good now."

At least, she was trying to be.

His mouth quirked. In his hard face, his mouth appeared unexpectedly soft. He had a long upper lip and a full lower one. "Not cut out for wilderness hiking?"

"Not cut out for any of this," she confessed without thinking.

Oh, dear. Now he would think she was a real loser and regret even more his decision to bring her.

"I'm a good photographer," she added defensively.

He started down the slope ahead of her. "Great."

"And I get along well with people. Most people," she said to his back.

His shoulders shook. "That'll be a big help next time the shooting starts."

He was laughing at her. The bastard.

"You think I should forget the people skills and channel my inner bitch instead?" she asked sweetly.

Jack turned, his eyes narrowed. In annoyance? Or amusement? "I think you should quit worrying about it. You got away, didn't you? Twice. That took guts, and it took smarts."

She gaped at him.

"Now haul ass," he said.

Uphill and down, over jutting rocks and tangled roots. *You can't walk that far. Not twice in one day. And not on that ankle.*

Ha. Like this was so much better.

The shadows lengthened and deepened, making the footing even more treacherous. Lexie slithered, grabbing a sapling for balance. Her flat-bottomed sandals weren't any more suited for dashing and hiking than she was.

But Jack thought she was gutsy? He'd said she was smart.

She gritted her teeth against the pain pulsing in her ankle and let go of the tree. One more step. Another. She lost her balance, stumbled forward, and bumped into Jack.

"Watch it." His hands came up automatically to steady her. He was holding the map.

He smelled like sweat and earth, musky and male. She took a step back. "Why did we stop?"

"I'm looking for landmarks." His tone was abstracted.

She pushed her hair out of her eyes. "We're surrounded by landmarks. What are you looking for? A hill or a tree?"

His mouth twitched. "An adit."

"A what?"

"Old mine entrance. These hills are riddled with old copper mines. They went bust because they were too far from the railroads." For Jack, this was positively chatty. He scanned the hillside in front of them. "There."

She looked where he pointed at a cut, a crack in the side of the hill. A spill of shale served as a threshold. Overgrown grass sprang up on one side. Overgrown bushes curtained the other. She couldn't see inside the tunnel at all.

As tourist attractions went, it was a complete bust. "Okay, we've seen it. Let's go."

Jack's jaw set in a way she was beginning to recognize. "We're not going anywhere. We're spending the night here."

"Why?"

"It's shelter."

"It's a hole."

"It's protected."

She took another look. Maybe. "It's creepy."

A faint, pungent odor from inside made her suspect they

weren't the first or only animals to take refuge here. She picked her way after him across the rutted stones. "What if there are . . . I don't know . . . like, bears or something?"

He grinned sharply. "That would certainly discourage anybody from sneaking up on us in the dark."

"The *bears* could sneak up on us in the dark," she muttered.

He ignored her. Pushing back the foliage, he leaned in. Her heart beat faster. Close up, she could see the rough opening was supported by stacked rock and black timbers. The floor, a drift of leaves over hard-packed earth and stone, was more or less flat. Cold breathed from the blackness of the tunnel. Lexie shivered. Jack ventured a few yards deeper into the mine, feeling his way with hands and feet.

She twisted her own hands together so she wouldn't grab him and jerk him back from the edge of . . . the edge of . . . "Be careful."

"It's a horizontal tunnel." His voice came out of the darkness. "The shaft must be farther in."

"I don't suppose this is going to be like in the movies where there's a hidden elevator to your super-secret, high-tech lab with a fully supplied kitchen and hot showers?"

She would kill for a shower. A hot meal would be nice, too. And a big, round bed with satin sheets . . . She blushed, grateful he couldn't see her face or read her thoughts.

Jack re-emerged from the dark. "You want James Bond, babe. I'm just a cop. *Was* a cop," he corrected himself.

"You keep saying that like it's something deeply significant I'm totally not getting. What are you now? Chopped liver?"

He scowled at her. "Did anybody ever tell you you talk too much?"

"All my life," she assured him. "Why aren't you a cop anymore?"

If they were talking, maybe she could stop thinking

about spending the night in that creepy dark hole. Spending the night with him. Alone. Pressed together to share body heat, waking together, her hand on his naked stomach, his hand on her breast.

"I'm suspended," he answered shortly.

That got her attention.

"Why?" she asked, startled. A cop could be relieved of duty for a number of reasons. None of them good.

"I beat somebody up."

"Oh." Lexie chewed her lip. Violence of any kind made her uneasy, and police brutality made her cringe. But she could be fair. She wanted to be fair, for both their sakes. "I understand sometimes you have to use force to apprehend—"

"I wasn't apprehending anybody. The guy was already under arrest. Restrained." Jack met her gaze, his eyes flat and challenging. She got that uh-oh feeling in her stomach. "I beat up a suspect in custody."

MUSCLES braced as if for a blow, Jack waited for Lexie to condemn him.

Except Lexie wouldn't tell him off. She was too polite. Too kind. Or maybe too scared. She'd just look at him with those big, serious eyes and think . . . And say . . .

"Why would you hit someone who was already in custody?"

He wasn't expecting her to say that. He scowled. "It doesn't matter why."

Her chin tilted. "It does to me."

"Well, it shouldn't," he said, relieved she hadn't sentenced him without a hearing and angry he was relieved. "You're a cop's daughter."

"You know, I'm getting pretty tired of people holding my father's job against me."

Jack was momentarily diverted from his self-disgust. "What?"

Lexie sighed. "Never mind. Just tell me why I should judge you because my father is in law enforcement."

"Because you should know the job is all about control," Jack said tightly. "Being in control. Staying in control of yourself and the situation. And I lost it. I lost control."

She eyed him warily, like she was afraid he was going to lose it again. "You still haven't told me why."

A picture of Dora Boyle and her daughter ripped red across his memory. So much blood. But it wasn't the blood that sickened him. It was the waste. The waste and the stink of his own failure.

Lexie's gaze sought his. He didn't need this. He didn't need another abused woman looking to him for answers. For reassurance. For hope.

"Don't worry," he said harshly. "I've never hit a woman."

"I didn't think— I'd never say— Where are you going?" she asked, her voice rising with alarm.

"We need water." He needed to get out of there before he said something else they'd both regret. "I'll be right back. You're safe enough. For now."

Slinging the canteen over his shoulder, he stalked into the gathering dusk.

LEXIE watched him go. *Safe enough?*

Safe from what? she wanted to yell at his departing back. The Disciples? Him? Herself? *Bears?*

But of course she didn't yell any such thing. She was too repressed. Too uncertain. Too afraid of hurting his feelings.

Much too big a wuss.

She hugged her elbows tight. His confession definitely made her uneasy. She should have demanded answers. Details. But she wasn't nearly as upset by what Jack had said as by the things he wouldn't say. Reasonable or not, she was hurt by his refusal to share something that so obviously bothered him. She was not some total incompetent who had to be protected from the truth.

Okay, maybe she was, but she could handle more than he gave her credit for.

Than her parents gave her credit for.

Than she gave herself credit for.

Jack's voice sounded in her head. *You got away, didn't you? Twice. That took guts, and it took smarts.*

Lexie straightened her shoulders. Right. So maybe it was time she quit dithering and did something productive.

HIS voice came out of the dark. "Good job, Girl Scout."

Lexie jumped. She fed another branch into the fire, hoping to hide her hands' trembling. "I wasn't in the Girl Scouts."

Jack stepped into the circle of firelight and took her breath away. When he was away from her, she could make him over in her mind into a man like the men she was used to. A man she could handle.

But when he came up on her unexpectedly, like now, the shock of him hit her all over again. His size. His strength. His hard, beard-stubbled face and potential for violence.

A corner of his mouth lifted, and the pounding of her heart settled into a purely feminine flutter. "So how did you learn to make a fire?"

She tipped her head back to smile at him. "I watch a lot of *Survivor*."

He crouched by the fire, knees spread, supporting himself easily on his strong thighs. "You go for that?"

She looked away from his crotch, aware of a heat in her cheeks that had nothing to do with the fire. "Go for . . . ?"

"Those reality shows. You ever want to take a trip to a tropical island for adventure and a chance at a million dollars?"

She couldn't believe they were discussing her taste in television programming. What was next, the weather?

But at least they were talking. He was trying, she thought, to make up for his earlier surliness. To put her at ease. It was sweet of him.

I've never hit a woman.

She shivered and held her hands out to the flames. "I'm not a big fan of adventure. Heck, there are times I'm not a big fan of reality, either."

"Is that why you left the Disciples?"

The softly spoken question jolted through her. Put her at *ease?* Ha. He was interviewing her. Establishing rapport. Softening her up with a show of interest before the wham-bam interrogation.

Lexie recognized the technique. Her father had used it often enough.

"I left the Disciples," she said precisely, "because I don't like being used."

Jack met her gaze, held it. "Neither do I."

She dropped her eyes, her indignation stained by embarrassment. She *was* using him. Lying to him. And he was smart enough to know it and to turn it against her.

"How was Locke using you?" he continued, his voice deep and inexorable.

She was silent.

"I thought at first you were bailing out on a bad marriage," he said, poking the fire. "But you're not wearing a ring, and somehow I don't see Blaine calling out all the troops for one runaway wife."

Lexie swallowed. "Why not? Isn't that why you're here? To help your sister when he comes after her?"

"You're not my sister," Jack said. "Which is another reason I've got to know—Are you married?"

Her heart thumped. She was deceiving him on so many levels. Surely she could tell the truth about this one thing? "No. No, I'm not married."

"So why are they so damn anxious to get you back?"

The fire hissed. The silence crackled. Her blood drummed in her ears.

They don't want me, Lexie wanted to protest. *This isn't about me. I'm just a tool they can use against my father.*

"Do you know something?" Jack asked at last. "Did you see something?"

I saw a woman stoned to death. What I don't know is whether or not your sister helped murder her.

"I don't want to talk about it," Lexie muttered.

He didn't move, but she felt his withdrawal. His eyes were shadowed. Expressionless.

"Your choice," he said.

She felt chilled despite the heat of the fire. "It's nothing personal," she offered.

He met her gaze then, and the heat banked in those dark, dark eyes licked a warning along her nerves. "It sure felt personal this morning when I woke with you draped over me like a blanket."

She drew a shuddering breath. "Okay, I really don't want to talk about that."

His eyebrows raised. His mouth turned up very slightly. "It happened."

"Yeah, well, it's not going to happen again."

He didn't answer, and she remembered, too late, they didn't even have a sleeping bag tonight. After spending most of her adult life struggling to be self-reliant and self-supporting, she was completely dependent on Jack for food, for protection, even for body heat.

His words mocked her.

Your choice.

EIGHT

IF he smirked, she would kill him.

Lexie looked from the makeshift bed at the mouth of the mine to Jack's carefully expressionless face. Okay, actually killing him was probably out. Even if she could overcome her long-standing aversion to violence, there was no way she could overwhelm a fully grown man who was almost a foot taller and at least sixty pounds heavier than she was. And no way Jack would simply lie there and let her . . . let her . . .

Her mind skittered back to this morning, to the brush of his hard, muscled belly and the bulge below. Her pulse picked up.

No way.

After their meal—crackers and tuna washed down with weak instant coffee—Jack had cut branches to form a kind of mattress, topping the pile with the green wool Army blanket they had used the night before. From his pack, he produced a thin, crinkly foil he identified as a thermal emergency blanket. Stolen, he told her, before she could ask. It was the most he'd said to her all evening.

So she was spending the night huddled under a space-age tarp on a pile of buggy branches in a bear-infested cave beside a taciturn man who brought every red blood cell in her body to agonized attention. Maybe she should have let Clyde shoot her this afternoon and put her out of her misery.

Whining, she reminded herself. No whining.

Jack watched her with dark, impenetrable eyes, his hard face sculpted by the red glow of the fire. The muscles in her thighs went lax.

He lay down on the lumpy blanket.

She pressed her knees together.

And then, very deliberately, he turned his back.

Well. Lexie inhaled. Okay. Stiffening her wobbly legs, she hobbled over to their bed. Gingerly, she lowered her body onto the makeshift mattress. The branches crackled and yielded beneath her. Leaves pricked through the rough wool of the blanket. She curled in a ball on her side, her arm pillowing her head, warmed by the flames in front of her and Jack's solid weight at her back.

The night rustled and settled around them.

She could hear Jack's controlled breathing, sense each slight movement in the slide and crinkle of their shared blanket, in the scratch and shift of their shared bed.

Lexie squeezed her eyes shut and willed herself to sleep. It did no good. No good at all.

Awareness of him seeped into her senses and pooled low in her body. The air around them thickened with the things they had said and could not say.

Want to have sex?

Oh, God, yes.

She bit her lip. Oh, no.

She wasn't normally a sex fiend. Take it or leave it was her attitude. And lately, mostly, she'd left it. She liked comfort more than risk. She preferred a night with the TV more than a casual hookup in a bar and her own routines more than the demands of a live-in lover.

She lay on the cold ground, listening to Jack's even, indifferent breathing, and burned. Beneath her bra, her nipples were tight. Her insides were loose and achy.

It was so unfair. Why now? Why him?

Maybe she was simply feeling the effects of danger. She could be confusing adrenaline with some other hormone.

Maybe it was the forced break in her routine. She'd been snatched from her usual patterns, stripped of her usual defenses, deprived of her usual conveniences. It wasn't her fault if she yearned for a lover's unfamiliar comfort.

Jack shifted, crushing their bed of leaves and branches, making her rock toward him. He didn't touch her, and yet her body reacted as if he had, as if he'd rolled over and on top of her, pressing her down on the rough blanket, pushing his way between her thighs. Her mouth dried in desire and despair.

Maybe it was him. Jack.

Her senses were raw. Open. Straining. Something fluttered overhead. She felt the movement of the air like a caress on her cheek, like a finger drawn down her spine.

"What was that?"

"Nothing." But Jack's voice was tight. Maybe he wasn't as indifferent as he pretended.

Or else he'd heard it, too.

There it was again, a vibration, a disturbance in the air, like a sigh from the cave behind her. Her heart jolted. Her eyes popped open.

Bears?

A brush. A rush. A shadow. A flap of wings, swooping, soaring, falling faster than leaves blown in the wind.

Not bears. *Bats.*

Lexie screamed.

"Jesus Christ." Jack bolted upright beside her. "What's the matter?"

"Bats!" she shrieked, throwing her arms over her face.

Rats with wings. Flying Willards. Overhead, everywhere,

pouring out of the mine shaft into the night. Horrible, horrible. She screamed again, grabbing the foil blanket, trying frantically to pull its thin protection over her head.

"Okay. Jesus. Okay. Shh." Jack rolled on top of her, covering her with his body.

She burrowed into him, shuddering, shaking, clinging to him for comfort and dear life. *Bats.* Yuck.

"It's okay," he said again, over and over, stroking her hair, murmuring into her ear.

His weight crushed her into the blanket. He weighed a ton. Lexie clutched him, grateful for his broad shoulders and hard torso, for the solid barrier of his body between her and fear. She would have climbed inside him if she could.

She heard a squeak, a flutter overhead, and cringed, turning her face into Jack's neck. He was trembling, too. He must be scared, too. And yet he held her, covered her, comforted her.

She eased her grip and raised her head to thank him. Her eyes narrowed. He was laughing.

He was shaking with laughter.

The *bastard.*

She made a fist and punched him in the shoulder as hard as she could. "You *jerk!*"

His face was alight with amusement. "Ow, honey, hey—"

"It's not *funny.*" She slugged him again, punctuating her words with her hands. "I was *terrified.*"

"Yeah, I could tell. You—"

But she wouldn't let him finish. All the feelings she'd pushed down and denied for days now bubbled up and surged out of control. The trickle became a torrent, the torrent a flood, and all the fear and horror and rage she'd dammed inside came pouring out.

"I hate this," she sobbed, pounding her fist into his chest. "I *hate* being scared all the time."

Jack caught her wrists, the laughter fading from his face, and held them so she couldn't hit him anymore. He pinned her against the rough blanket, using his weight to control her. She fought against his greater strength, her grief and fury spilling from her in wave after wave of tears.

She cried as she hadn't allowed herself to cry since she'd been kidnapped, cried in shock and betrayal, cried in fear and anger, cried in terrible pity for the woman stoned outside her window. She gasped. She sobbed. She wept until her throat was raw and her eyes were nearly swollen shut.

And instead of trying to dam her outburst, Jack held her, simply held her through it all, absorbing her struggles and her tears.

At last she lay still. Drained. Empty. Exhausted.

"Feel better?" Jack asked dryly.

"No." She sniffed. Her chest felt hollow. "My nose is stuffy."

She'd also totally humiliated herself, but it was too late to do anything about that.

Jack levered himself off her slightly to dig in his back pocket. "Here."

None of the men she'd ever dated carried handkerchiefs. She eyed it with a mixture of gratitude and suspicion. "Is it clean?"

His mouth compressed. Was he disgusted with her? Or controlling a smile? "Not very trusting, are you?"

"I used to be," she said.

His brows raised. "Bitter?"

Yes.

"No," she said, recalled to her manners. She took the handkerchief, rubbed her eyes, and blew her nose before offering the crumpled ball back to him. "Thank you."

"Keep it." He caught a strand of her hair between two fingers and stroked it back from her forehead. Her face felt hot and puffy. "So, you're fine with being tied up, hurt, chased, and shot at, but you've got a problem with bats, huh?"

"I am not fine with being shot at. And I'm not afraid of bats." She shuddered. "Are they gone?"

Jack glanced toward the mouth of the shaft, where smoke shimmered against the shadow of trees and the brilliant sky. "Yeah."

He still lay on top of her, his chest squashing her breasts, his belly pressing her belly, his hips cradled by her thighs. Why didn't he move?

"I'm sorry I made a fuss," she mumbled.

"'S okay. Everybody's afraid of something."

"You're not," she said, half resentfully. He'd laughed—*laughed*—at her.

"Sure I am."

"Name one thing you're afraid of."

He was silent.

She snorted. "See?"

"All right." He glared at her. "Being buried."

Oh, Jack. Involuntarily, she flattened her palms on his back, holding him closer. "Well, that's natural. You were a soldier and a police officer. Both dangerous professions. An awareness of death is—"

"I'm not scared of dying," he interrupted roughly. "I'm afraid of being buried. Alive. A buddy of mine—" He stopped, his mouth a grim line.

A huge dark chasm opened at Lexie's feet. She quivered on the edge of discovery, on the brink of a question.

She should let it go.

Every time Jack lowered his barriers, every time she stepped beyond hers, it became harder and harder to keep her secrets. She couldn't afford to connect with him. She couldn't afford to confide in him. Their growing intimacy was as seductive as sex—and even more dangerous.

Step back from the edge, she ordered herself.

She opened her mouth and jumped in with both feet. "An Army buddy?"

Dumb, dumb girl.

Jack shook his head. "This was after I got out. I'd only

been on the job a couple months. Patty was still happy. Things were looking up."

He didn't sound very cheerful about it.

"And then . . . ?" Lexie prompted. *Shut up, shut up, shut up.*

"And then this guy on my shift—Denny O'Brian, nice guy, big joker—walks into a 7-Eleven robbery when he's off duty and, bam, he's dead."

Lexie's breath escaped in a soft exhalation of sympathy. "Oh, Jack . . ."

He continued as if he hadn't heard. "I can't believe it, you know? I figured my war was over when I left the Gulf. So I'm at Denny's funeral in my new dress blues, watching them lower his coffin into this hole, and I keep expecting him to bang on the coffin and yell, 'Hey, guys, only kidding. Let me out.' Like that was going to happen with his head blown half away."

Lexie's heart clutched. She did know. She'd grown up knowing the toll the job could take on law enforcement officers and their families. Alcoholism, heart disease, depression, divorce. Even her own parents . . .

Okay, on her Top Ten Mental List of Things She Didn't Want to Think About, her parents' divorce hovered at number three, right after number one, *Fanatic militia men are trying to kill me,* and two, *I'm a murder witness.*

She yanked her attention back to the present. The present, and Jack. "Did you ever talk to anyone about it?" she asked.

He slanted a derisive look at her. Not hard to do, considering he was still on top of her. "You mean, like a shrink?"

He sounded like her father. The woo-woo boys, Scott called the Bureau's Behavioral Science Unit. His attitude hadn't done a lot to endear him to the agents under his command.

A week ago, Lexie would have backed off, warned by Jack's tone and influenced by a lifetime of making nice.

Screw nice. She was right. Years of therapy couldn't be wrong.

"You need some way to deal with job-related stress," she insisted.

His lips twitched. "Besides drinking?"

"Or swearing a lot and punching things. Yes."

His face tightened. Too late, she remembered he had punched someone. A suspect in custody.

He rolled off her and onto his back.

She should have been relieved. He weighed a ton. She didn't need his iron strength above her, his planes and angles fitted so perfectly to her hollows and curves it was hard to tell where he left off and she began. She didn't want this intimacy, low voices sharing in the dark, supporting, confiding.

But in the emptiness created by his absence, the lines between what she needed and what she wanted shifted and blurred. Her body mourned the loss of his.

"What's the matter?" she asked.

Which made her feel like an even bigger fraud. Because she knew.

"This guy you're running from," Jack said, staring into the shadows of the tunnel roof. "The one you're not married to. The one who marked your wrists. Did he hit you?"

Surprise and tenderness clogged her throat. She didn't want to think about Ray. *Jack's brother-in-law.*

But while she was wondering and worrying about Jack's suspension, he was thinking about *her.* Observing her, with an attention to detail that suggested a cop's eye and a real concern. Worrying about her and what his history of violence might mean to her.

"No," she said. Betrayed her, drugged her, tied her up . . . But he hadn't hit her.

Even in the dim light, she could see the muscle bunch in Jack's jaw. "Because I don't want you thinking I—"

"I don't," she assured him honestly. Whatever demons drove him, Jack wouldn't hurt her. "I trust you, remember?"

More than was wise.

"More than you should," Jack muttered.

She swallowed hard. What if he was right? "So, what do you do to blow off steam?" she asked lightly.

Their eyes locked.

"I run," he said. "Lift weights."

Her heart pounded. "Does that work for you?"

"Not really."

She watched his mouth, distracted by the disciplined cut of his upper lip, the dizzying sweep of the lower. Tension thickened the air, sharp and sticky as pine sap.

She should say something. Anything.

"Maybe you should try yoga," she blurted.

"Yoga," Jack repeated without expression.

She flushed. Or maybe not. He wasn't exactly an inner peace and tranquillity kind of guy.

"It's not as bad as aromatherapy," she said defensively.

"And not as good as sex."

"I wouldn't know."

"You should try it sometime."

The words thumped low in her midsection, another matter-of-fact invitation to disregard the risks and damn the consequences in favor of . . . in favor of . . .

"What are you offering, exactly?"

That mouth, that wicked, distracting mouth, quirked. "What did you call it? Stress relief? A chance to blow off steam?"

Casual sex. Her pulse raced.

Or maybe not so casual. His big, solid body was rigid as a rock. His eyes were dark and intent.

Lexie moistened her lips. "With you," she said, so there could be no misunderstanding.

"If you want."

She barely restrained a pout. He was leaving the choice, the decision, to her. It was reassuring. Flattering.

Frustrating.

"Oh, like it's all up to me," she scoffed.

"Shouldn't it be? Unless you have rape fantasies."

She shivered, remembering the cot and the rope. "Not . . . No."

"No," he agreed quietly.

His hands were linked behind his head. His broad chest rose and fell with his breath. In the firelight, with three days' growth of beard on his jaw, he looked like an outlaw. Or a pirate.

Rape fantasies, her ass.

"Sorry. I'm not good at this," she said.

He smiled slowly. "Babe, I'm not going to score your performance. If you're willing, that's good enough for me."

Her face flamed. "I wasn't apologizing for my lack of . . . experience. I meant, I'm not used to making decisions."

Jack didn't apologize. He didn't even have the grace to look embarrassed. He said, matter-of-factly, "That figures. Locke doesn't exactly preach self-determination and equal rights for women."

Oh, dear. Their conversation was like one of those scary fun-house mazes she'd hated as a kid. Every time it took a turn, she was confronted with another unflattering image of herself, bumped into another lie.

She struggled to find some truth, one piece of her real self she could share.

"It's not Locke," she said. "I wasn't in the compound long enough to . . . I wasn't there long." *One day.* "It's me."

She snuck another look at Jack. He hadn't moved. He didn't speak. He just waited, patient as a priest hearing confession. She wanted to crawl on top of him.

Lexie bit her lip. Not a priest. If she had thoughts like that about a priest, Ray was right and she was going to hell for sure.

"I grew up with two, um, very strong-minded people. My parents were always telling me to take initiative. To stick up for myself. But they didn't really like it when I did. They fought," she said, using very short sentences, as if that would help him understand how it had been. "With me. With each other. *Somebody* had to keep the peace. To go with the flow. So that's what I did."

"News flash for you, babe. You've been grown up for a while. You don't need to please your parents anymore."

She flushed. "And I don't. But that doesn't mean I go around imposing my vision and my opinions on other people. To get a good portrait, you have to put yourself, your ego, in the service of someone else. You are not the subject. The other person is the subject. So you have to understand them. You have to empathize. You have to know what they want. And then you have to deliver."

Jack grinned. "So, if I tell you what I want, you'll give it to me?" He shook his head. "Oh, babe."

"I was talking about my work," she protested, with as much dignity as she could muster. "I'm perfectly capable of saying 'no' in my private life."

Although she hadn't with Ray. She'd let his expectations and her dread of scenes, her dislike of hurting his feelings, pressure her into their last date.

And look how that had turned out.

Jack's eyes gleamed beneath half-closed lids. "So is that what you're saying? No?"

Her breathing was fast and too shallow. Her mind raced. "No" was smart. "No" was safe. Another big, safe lie. Jack was just waiting for her to say "no" and then he'd turn his back and they could both go to sleep.

The intensity of her disappointment shocked her.

But if she said yes . . .

A quiver ran through her, two parts desire and one part fear. If she said "yes," she wouldn't be able to claim afterward that she'd been swept up in the moment. She couldn't pretend, even to herself, she didn't know what she was doing. "Yes" was raw and real and honest.

She couldn't possibly say "yes."

"I'm saying I can't make a decision."

"Bullshit," Jack said.

Lexie blinked. "Excuse me?"

"You've been making decisions since I met you. For both of us. *I'm not going with anyone else,*" he quoted. *"I don't trust anyone else. I'm staying with you."*

Guilt made her squirm. "I didn't have much choice."

He gave her a flat, bland cop stare. "You mean you don't want to take responsibility."

She didn't say anything, and the stare sharpened, deepened, became another kind of look entirely, the kind of look that went to her head like smoke. She was lightheaded. The fire at the tunnel entrance was drawing away their oxygen. Burning up all the air.

She opened her mouth to breathe and felt her throat go dry with possibilities.

"Is that it?" Jack asked softly, still watching her. "You waiting for me to make my move, Lexie? No 'yes,' no 'no.'" He turned on the blanket so he faced her, his weight supported on one elbow. "Only this."

His big hand cupped the back of her neck and pulled her close. His lips brushed the corner of her mouth. His kiss was teasingly soft, temptingly warm.

"And this," he growled, and his hand fisted in her hair and his mouth covered hers.

Lexie's head exploded. He rolled on top of her, his solid weight welcome. Reassuring. Erotic. She opened her legs. She tilted her hips, and he made a sound low in his throat and kissed her roughly, thoroughly, deeply, his hand in her hair and his tongue in her mouth.

Dazed, she clung to him, dizzy from lack of air and drunk on the taste of coffee and some darker, richer flavor she could only identify as Jack.

No "yes," no "no." Only him. Only this.

No fear, only this humming urgency he evoked in her flesh and her bone, this danger as sharp as delight, this risk worth taking.

No responsibility. Only the heat of the moment and his body hard against hers.

He kissed her again, and she gave herself up to it,

opened herself up to him, embracing the dark and the heat and the buzz in her blood. He was slow and thorough, using his teeth and tongue, as capable at kissing as he was at everything else. Lexie writhed beneath him, wanting more. Wanting it all. She was desperate for him to touch her.

His free hand slid to her breast, finding the nipple with devastating accuracy through her clothes. He palmed it, rubbed it, kneaded it, until both breasts drew to tight points and her inner muscles contracted. She arched into him with a moan of pleasure.

Tugging her shirt free of her waistband, he pushed it up under her armpits and yanked on her bra. Lexie held her breath in anticipation of his touch.

Nothing.

She opened her eyes.

Jack poised above her like the angel of death, his face a granite mask.

Misgiving squeezed her heart. "What is it?" she asked.

"Funny," he said in a voice completely empty of humor. "I was going to ask you the same thing."

Bewildered, she said, "I don't—"

His fingers brushed her ribs. Her nipple beaded at his touch. Ignoring her reaction, he held up a thin black square between his thumb and middle finger.

Lexie's heart stopped. The picture card from her camera. It must have worked out of the slit she'd made in the lining of her bra.

She met his eyes and shivered.

"So, what is it?" Jack asked.

NINE

JACK was aroused, frustrated, and furious. He'd been looking to get laid. Instead he'd been had, by a baby-doll blonde with trust-me eyes and a fuck-me mouth. Her deception was worse than humiliating. It hurt.

"So, what is it?" he asked, doing his damnedest to sound like a mean son of a bitch instead of some horny teenage stud who'd failed to get his rocks off in the backseat of his daddy's car.

And apparently he succeeded, because Lexie went from willing and bewildered to scared and confused in under three seconds.

Way to ruin a sure thing, ace.

"It's a picture card," she said with only a hint of a wobble in her voice.

Nice touch, he thought.

"I can see that." It was printed clearly on the side: *Fuji film 16MD xD-Picture card*. "What are you doing with it?"

"I'm not doing anything." She struggled to sit, jerking up on her bra and down on her shirt at the same time.

He glimpsed the round fullness of her breast, the pale curve of her belly, and his eager dick reminded him he wasn't finished with her yet. They'd barely gotten started.

"You've been holding out on me, Blondie," he said grimly.

She stopped tucking her shirt into the narrow waistband of her jeans long enough to glare at him. "Obviously, I wasn't holding out enough."

He almost grinned at her flash of spirit. He wanted to tell her the hell with it, they could get naked now and talk later. But he was pretty sure, looking at her face, that the moment was gone. He wasn't going to have sex with her anytime soon. Probably not in this lifetime.

The thought didn't soften his mood any. Or, unfortunately, his dick.

"You're the one who's big on talking to get over your problems," he said. "So talk."

The chin went up. "I don't know what you want me to say."

The echo of their earlier conversation cut to the bone.

You have to empathize. You have to know what they want. And then you have to deliver.

So, if I tell you what I want, you'll give it to me? Oh, babe.

Could she be as guileless as she seemed? Or was she just that good an actress?

He held up the camera card. "Let's start with what you're doing with this."

"I told you, it's a picture card. I'm a photographer. I take pictures."

"In the middle of the woods," he said with heavy skepticism.

"Nature shots," she said.

It was so ridiculous he wanted to laugh. Except there was nothing remotely funny about the situation. "That's crap," he said. "Where's your camera?"

"I had to leave it behind."

"Right. You left your camera. You ran away without food, without water, without decent shoes—" Just thinking of her in danger made him angry.

"I was in a hurry," she said.

"In fact, the only thing you manage to bring with you is a picture card, concealed in your bra, and you want me to believe it's full of photographs of squirrels and trees."

Lexie nibbled her lip, her big eyes fixed on his face. Was she searching for a way to apologize? Or debating with herself what new lies to tell him?

Shit. He'd thought he could trust her. He'd thought she trusted him. He wasn't sure which loss hurt more.

Her hands twisted in her lap. "You've probably guessed . . . You can probably tell I wasn't exactly in the compound of my own free will."

Relief fissured his chest. Had she decided to come clean after all? But he carefully kept all trace of emotion from his face and voice. A good interviewer was impartial. Neutral. Open-minded. "What does that mean? Exactly?"

"If you must know, I was kidnapped."

He buried his outrage. "Why?"

"Because of who I know."

That made sense. That was consistent with what she'd said before. Jack waited. She was still holding out, holding back. Lying? Fearful? Embarrassed?

"Somebody in the Disciples?" he prompted.

She hesitated. "Yes."

Lying, he decided, with regret. "So, about the pictures?"

"They're for my family."

Another wait. Don't ask leading questions. Don't rush a response.

She stumbled on. "He . . . The Disciples took my clothes. And my camera. I had a nice, lightweight Fuji F420 zoom that just fit in my jeans pocket."

He let her go on about the camera, let her develop an

increasing comfort with her subject, before bringing her gently back to the part that interested him. "The pictures for your family . . . What kind of pictures were they?"

"Identifying pictures." Her chin went up another notch. "I told you my father was in law enforcement. I wanted my parents to have a place to start searching if my body turned up in a couple months."

Admiration swamped Jack. Her courage and resourcefulness nearly left him speechless.

"That was smart," he managed. "Real smart."

She blushed like a little girl with pleasure. "Thank you."

But the itch at the back of his neck—the itch that told him there was something else, something more, something wrong—refused to go away.

"You're not a reporter on a story?" he asked.

"Nope," Lexie said, so cheerfully he believed her.

"Or an undercover fed investigating cults?"

She laughed a little wildly, her gaze sliding from his. "Goodness, no. Nothing like that."

Maybe, he thought. She sure didn't act like a fed. Or react like a fed. No "Out of my way, I'm making the world safe for democracy" about Lexie. But why wouldn't she meet his eyes? "What are you, then?"

"I told you. I'm just a photographer who got mixed up with the wrong guy."

"And your parents?"

"My parents may not even know I'm missing yet. At least, that's what I hope."

"This guy . . ." This bastard who took you, hurt you, *had* you . . . Jack unclenched his jaw. "He wasn't after money, was he?"

Lexie looked uncomprehending.

"Ransom," he explained. "Would he have contacted your folks for money?"

"He can't," she said triumphantly. "He can't ask for anything now. He doesn't have me anymore."

Guilt knotted Jack's stomach. "Don't look so happy," he growled. "You're not out of the woods yet."

"Well, obviously," Lexie said, rolling her eyes toward the dark trees outside the circle of firelight.

"I'm talking about tomorrow," he said through his teeth. "When I go to meet my sister. I'll be taking you straight back into danger."

"Not really. Not unless you're meeting her at the compound. You're not, are you?"

"Hell, no. There's a waterfall off one of the trails. Sally said she could bring the kid that far. But if Blaine comes after her, he could find you."

"He won't be looking for me. At least, he won't be looking for me with you."

"Don't kid yourself, babe. By now, your friends back at the parking lot have told Blaine you hooked up with a guy on the trail. By tomorrow, the Disciples will be looking for both of us."

He wanted to scare her into confiding in him. But Lexie, he was discovering, didn't scare easy.

"We'll have to be careful, then," she said.

Jack scowled. "It would help if you told me why the hell they want you back so bad."

She smiled self-deprecatingly. "You don't think it's because I'm warm and sexy and fun to be with?"

She was all those things.

It wasn't hard to see why a man, any man, would want her back.

And too damn easy to imagine what this bastard would do to her if he got his hands on her again.

"You're a pain in the ass," Jack said.

Her smile slipped for a second before she hauled it back and fixed it into place. "Gee, thanks," she said lightly. "Why don't you tell me how you really feel?"

Shit. "I didn't mean—"

"It's all right," she said, her tone bright and determined.

"I don't need you to like me. I just need you to get me as far as Benson tomorrow."

And that was that, Jack realized. He wasn't getting any more out of her tonight. No more answers.

And definitely, definitely no sex.

"JOHN Miller," Ray Blaine repeated softly, turning away from his view of the yard. Daniel sat outside in a circle of children, teaching the day's lesson.

Inside, Tod Hawley waited respectfully for further instructions, pimples raw from a recent shave. One of the younger recruits to the cause, he understood that preaching and teaching were no longer enough to save America from the erosion of its moral values.

The war for the country's soul required soldiers, Ray reflected.

And casualties.

"In a rental car, you said?"

Hawley stood at even straighter attention. "According to the sheriff's office, Miller rented the car in Knoxville and drove it here. Ranger Long said he's probably a hiker."

"So you think the presence of his car in the parking lot where Brother Clyde failed to accomplish his mission was a coincidence?" Ray said.

Frankly, Ray didn't give a damn for Hawley's opinion. But it might give him a clue to how Daniel was likely to regard the incident.

Hawley looked confused. "Well, yeah. But the sheriff's department asked Ranger Long to keep an eye open for the car's driver on the trail, and you told me to inform you of any developments that came through the ranger's office, so—"

"Yes," Ray interrupted him. "Thank you."

He turned back to the window. He could see his son Isaac's smooth, dark head rising above the rest of the children in the circle. The boy would be tall. As tall as his uncle, one day.

Jack Miller. What was he doing here?

"Is it important, sir?" Hawley asked from behind him, his voice almost cracking with eagerness.

No one inside the compound knew of Sarah's connection to Jack Miller, that agent of corrupt government. It didn't matter. It couldn't be allowed to matter. She was his now. She belonged to him and to God.

Isaac hunched as Daniel addressed something to him— a question or a rebuke, perhaps—and Ray frowned. Sarah babied the boy. It was past time their son was admitted to the Men's House. But he had promised Sarah, in a moment of weakness years ago, when he still believed there would be other children, to wait until Isaac's seventh birthday. One more week before the rod of correction could drive the foolishness from his child's heart and make the boy more perfect. His seed. His son.

"No," he said slowly. "No, it's not important."

His family must be perfect. Above reproach. Or his leadership could be questioned.

Clyde had reported a man with Alexandra, Ray remembered. Was it possible Miller had been sent by the government to help her? But no. That really would be a coincidence. The Beast, when it came, would come with many men, guns, and helicopters. It would be the start of a holy war, the establishment of a new order.

But then why would Jack Miller be here, now?

Unless God had chosen the search for one woman to reveal the duplicity of another. Ray's lips drew back from his teeth. Unless Sarah had sent for her brother.

The suspicion spoiled what should have been perfect, like a worm in an apple, like the snake in the Garden of Eden. Rage uncurled in Ray's heart.

Hawley was still at attention, waiting for his instruction.

Ray met his eyes calmly. "Find my wife," he said. "Tell her to come to me."

THE blue tones of morning had been swallowed by the flat colors of midday. Now the warm, slanted light of afternoon cast interesting shadows under the trees and played on the surface of the water.

Lexie shaded the lens with her free hand and framed her shot of the waterfall.

"What are you doing?" Jack asked behind her.

She almost dropped the camera in the water. Lowering it, she glared at him. A navy ball cap covered his dark hair. He'd exchanged his drab khaki T-shirt for an equally forgettable gray one and his Army fatigue pants for old jeans. The small changes might divert a Disciple spy armed with a description, but they didn't do a darn thing to disguise his broad, powerful chest or his massive shoulders or the danger in his eyes . . .

She clutched her camera tighter. In self-defense? "I'm taking pictures."

The smile leaped to Jack's eyes, making him even more alarmingly attractive. "Yeah, I can see that. Why?"

Heat washed her face. She'd always been a camera geek. A photographer for the yearbook. An observer on the sidelines of life. Even now, as the hours crept by and Jack's sister still didn't come, the familiar actions, the absorbing considerations of scale and contrast, comforted and distracted her.

Like she could say any of that to Mr. Imperturbable Stakeout Guy. He didn't need a distraction. And he didn't want her comfort. *You're a pain in the ass.*

She stuck out her chin. "You know, we're surrounded by some of the most beautiful scenery in the world."

"Yeah. It would be nice to stay alive to appreciate it."

"The camera is part of my tourist disguise."

"Nice," he approved.

A warm glow settled on her midsection.

His mouth quirked. "Of course, you might want to save your film until somebody's actually watching."

The waterfall was far enough from the main trails to discourage casual hikers. Foot traffic had been light: one father and son pair, a weathered married couple looking like a page from an L.L. Bean catalog, and a chattering church youth group portaging their canoes around the falls.

Lexie had stiffened when the kids tromped into view like a many-legged monster at a Chinese New Year's parade. Ray had claimed to be a youth minister. But these teens all wore bright yellow T-shirts proclaiming Grace Baptist Church, and the round-faced man shepherding them never looked in her direction as they unloaded their boats and tromped off for a picnic.

Every time voices approached, Jack tensed. Anxious about meeting his sister again? Lexie wondered. Or assessing a threat?

But he didn't say anything, and his face gave nothing away.

"Sorry," she mumbled, and slipped the camera in her pocket.

His pocket, actually. She'd done her best to alter her appearance, too. She wore Jack's slouch hat and fatigue shirt over her "borrowed" jeans and the ruins of her pink T-shirt. Her hair was filthy. She would have killed for a toothbrush. But she figured they looked like any other couple who'd been sleeping out and living rough on the trail for a couple days.

Jack picked his way down the moss-covered rocks. She'd chosen to shoot the falls from below to emphasize the height of the tumbling white water. Spray filmed her jacket. The toes of her socks were damp.

"Nervous?" he asked. "Or just bored?"

She blinked, surprised by his observation. "Maybe a little of both," she admitted.

He nodded, his dark gaze scanning the tree line above.

If she was nervous about his sister's nonappearance, he must be worried sick.

"I like to keep busy," she offered, to relieve the waiting. It wasn't that different from making conversation with the bride at the back of the church. "If I was home, I'd bake cookies or clean my closets or rearrange my bookshelves."

He slanted a look down at her. "So you're one of those."

"One of what?"

"A nester. One of those make-a-house-a-home types."

She was insulted. "It's not nesting to want a comfortable and organized living environment."

"Hey, I meant it as a compliment. You should see my house."

"I don't have to. I can guess. Dust over everything and the living room decorated in newspapers and pizza boxes." Her parents, ambitious professionals with a disdain for housework and schedules, had lived the same way. She used to hate coming home after school to the neglect and disorder of her mother's crammed condo or her father's empty townhouse.

Jack shook his head. "Babe, I learned how to clean in the Army. It's the other stuff I'm no good at."

"What stuff?" she asked suspiciously.

"The curtains, pillows, candles stuff." He grinned, and her insides suddenly melted. "Girl stuff."

"Didn't your wife . . . ?" Lexie asked before she thought better of it.

"Patty?" Jack shrugged. "Not really. I'm not saying our marriage was all newspapers and pizza boxes, but I remember a lot of magazines and Chinese takeout."

He didn't sound disgruntled or condemning, Lexie thought, studying his hard-featured face. More . . . *wistful?*

A remnant of their earlier conversation drifted in her memory, insubstantial as the mist at the foot of the falls.

Then why did you get married?

Why does anybody? I wanted a home, I guess. A family.

Jack's gaze locked with hers. Her throat tightened.

Something shimmered and hung in the air between them like a rainbow.

"Hey, folks."

Jolted, Lexie looked up. A heavyset man in a khaki uniform with a red Christmas tree sort of patch on the sleeve stood at the top of the bank. A ranger.

Lexie sagged with relief and anticlimax. Another day, another minute, and she'd be offering to make sacrifices and light candles like some sort of domestic goddess. Instead, she had a line to the authorities and a ride into town.

"I'm looking for a John Miller," the forest ranger said. "You wouldn't happen to be him, would you?"

Lexie frowned. How did the ranger know Jack's name? Unless his sister had found this way to get a message to him.

Beside her, Jack shifted his weight. "What's up?" he asked easily.

The ranger's smile never faltered. "May I see some ID, sir?"

"Sure," Jack said, reaching slowly for his wallet. "Can you tell me what this is about?"

"A car rented to a John Miller was found vandalized in a lot near here. Sheriff needs you to come in and fill out some paperwork."

That sounded reasonable. But . . .

"We're in the middle of our vacation here," Jack said. "Can it wait a couple days?"

The ranger—Long, his badge read—shook his head regretfully. "'Fraid not. Sheriff thinks he caught the boys who did it. He needs a statement from you to press charges."

Lexie looked at Jack, an uncomfortable feeling in her stomach. *Boys?* There were no boys. Only Clyde and Mrs. Clyde.

Jack's face was calm. Set. "Right. We'll hike out, then."

"Be a lot easier if I took you in my truck," Ranger Long offered, staring hard at Lexie. "It's parked on the service road a little ways from here. Might be tight with three across, but we can do it. If you folks don't mind."

Lexie shrank into her jacket. She minded. She minded a lot. She wasn't going anywhere with this guy.

"No problem," Jack said. "Let me just get a few things out of the canoe."

Canoe?

"Need a hand?" the ranger said.

"We've got it," Jack said firmly. He turned Lexie toward the bright-colored canoes beached and abandoned by the youth group. "Come on, honey. Let's grab your pack."

She ducked her head and picked her way to the nearest canoe, her steps slow and her heart racing, listening for Jack's footsteps on the rocks behind her. Her sandals splashed in the water. God, it was cold. She was shaking, her knees rubber.

"Uh, folks . . ." the ranger said.

"Now," Jack ordered, low. "Get in."

She scrambled over the high, ribbed side and lurched for a seat, banging her shins, tripping over a paddle. Rocks scraped. The canoe slid, pitching her into the prow. The ranger yelled something, lost in a splash. Water sloshed. Jack surged forward, pushing the boat into the current. Lexie made a grab for the side and missed.

"Paddle!" Jack roared.

She dug between her knees for the paddle. The canoe tipped wildly as Jack hauled himself in. The bottom of the boat filled with water. The ranger plunged down the bank and slogged after them into the stream.

"Go, go!"

Lexie dug her paddle into the water, making the canoe dip. The ranger lunged forward, reaching for the side of the boat. Jack snatched an oar and smacked his knuckles. A scream swelled in Lexie's throat. Struggling for balance, she plied the water on both sides of the boat as the ranger thrashed and Jack shoved and the canoe bobbed up and down. Sweat broke out on her face and under her arms.

And somehow, suddenly, they were free, the prow shuddering as it shot forward, the canoe catching the current. Behind her, Jack drove the boat with powerful strokes. Lexie risked a glance over her shoulder. Just before they rounded a bend in the stream, she saw the ranger standing chest high in the dark, cold water, blood running from his face.

"Steer," Jack grunted.

Obediently, she turned around and drove her paddle into the water in time to miss the rocks on their right. Adrenaline bubbled in her system like champagne. "We did it!"

Slick with moss and curtained with spring, the bank glided by on either side. The canoe rode a current down to another eddy, wallowed, and picked up again.

"We fucked up," Jack said.

Her strokes faltered. "What are you talking about? We got away."

"We assaulted a state officer. We stole a canoe from a church group. The Disciples are after us, and if my sister and her kid show up now, they're screwed." His voice was grim. "Other than that, yeah, we're doing great."

Lexie's mood deflated like a balloon on a convention floor. The canoe wobbled as it grabbed another ribbon of current, spooling, spiraling away. The water was high and fast. Her shoulders started to burn from the unaccustomed exercise. She drove the blade of her paddle deeper into the water, trying to negotiate a tree that had fallen from the opposite bank.

At least things couldn't get any worse.

"Watch it!" Jack ordered sharply behind her.

The canoe hit the sunken tree and tilted. The paddle ripped from her hands. The canoe whirled. Jack swore. A branch loomed in the corner of her vision and cracked against the side of the boat.

The canoe tipped, dumping them both in the freezing water.

TEN

WATER, stinging with particles and cold, filled her eyes, her ears, her nose. Cold seized her chest and gripped her lungs.

Which way was up?

She couldn't see. Couldn't breathe.

The current shoved her. The branches of the tree snatched her hair, scraped her arm, pushed her down, down. *Down.* So up must be . . . Lexie grabbed a branch, orienting herself, straining her eyes in the cold, murky water. A patch of light, a burst of bubbles. *There.*

She twisted to get her legs under her and kicked. Her head broke the surface in a rush. She gasped in shock. Gulped in air. Looked for Jack.

He wasn't there.

Clinging to the fallen tree, she took another breath and choked. *Don't panic.* Panicked swimmers drowned.

"Jack?" She coughed.

The canoe, trapped between the current and the tree, bumped her shoulder. The bowed red hull was dented. Intact.

Upside down.

Jack.

She sucked in a breath and jack-knifed into the cold, silty water, groping, searching, diving for the bottom. Her fingers brushed something soft as weed. His hair? No. Fabric, floating. Flesh, cold and heavy as stone. She grabbed, hauled, tugged.

She pulled him with her to the surface and anchored him to the log, using her weight and the water to hold him.

His head lolled. Blood crawled from a gash on his forehead and melted away in the water. His eyes were closed. His mouth open, like a fish's. She couldn't tell if he was breathing.

"Jack?" Her voice was thin and frantic.

Not breathing.

Don't panic.

"Shit!" she yelled.

Rolling him to his back, she grabbed his chin and pushed off from the log toward the nearest bank. She was a decent swimmer. To her father's disappointment, she'd never gone out for the team, but her mother had made sure she passed the lifesaving class at the Y.

She kicked, pulled, and struggled to the side. The tree's root ball had ripped an enormous hole in the bank, clay-slick and impossible to climb. Lexie clutched a root, testing her weight against it. Maybe.

Out of deep water, Jack weighed a ton. She tried crawling out, keeping one hand fisted in his shirt, but his weight dragged against her hold on the root. Her palm slithered and burned. She kept praying for that adrenaline thing to kick in, the one that helped mothers lift cars off their careless toddlers, but it never happened for her.

Panting, she scrambled to her knees on the muddy bank, grabbed Jack under his armpits, and pulled.

Her back muscles screeched in protest. She scraped, dragged, and hauled him onto the bank, leaving him lying with his feet still dangling in the water.

His face was pale. His chest hadn't moved. Blood

streamed along his hairline. If he had a concussion . . .

Don't think about concussion. Get air into his lungs.

With one hand against his bloody forehead and the other supporting his stubbled jaw, she tilted his head back to open his airway. Pinching his nose shut, she inhaled, sealed her mouth to his open mouth, and exhaled into his lungs.

Breathe. Check. Nothing.

Don't panic.

She did it again, feeling her own breath return to her uselessly against her cheek. Maybe she was doing it wrong.

Don't think about that. Breathe. Check. Again.

She listened for the return flow of air, feeling her own heart pound against her ribs, watching Jack's big chest. Nothing.

And again.

His chest rose. Fell.

Maybe . . .? Dizzy with hope, she raised her head. Jack coughed. Convulsed. Grabbing his thigh and shoulder, she pushed and rolled him onto his side. He choked and spewed. Water dribbled and gushed.

Thank you, thank you, God.

"It's okay," she murmured, though she was pretty sure it wasn't yet. "You're okay."

Turning his head, he gave her a glassy stare. His pupils were big and dark. That was good, wasn't it? Anyway, they were the same size.

"Swa . . . Wha . . . ?" He coughed.

"The canoe tipped over. You hit your head." It still bled, streaking his pale face. An interesting lump was forming under his hairline. "You're going to be fine now."

Unless the Disciples found them. Or the ranger. Or a pissed-off church youth group. The canoe was still trapped against the log, a bright red beacon to anyone searching: *Here we are. Come and get us.*

Lexie shivered. She was cold. Jack must be freezing. He needed blankets. Dry clothes. Stitches.

Jack swayed to his hands and knees. Blood dripped onto the back of his hand.

"Where are you going?" she asked sharply.

"Got to . . . hide . . . the canoe."

Was he crazy?

"Jack." She hugged her legs to her chest. "Maybe it would be better if it was found. If we were found."

"*No*. Sally—" Coughing shook him.

"Okay," she said soothingly, although she wasn't sure exactly what she was agreeing to. Anything that would get him to lie down.

He crawled to the bank. He was actually serious about hiding the canoe. Damn it.

"Stop," she said. "I'll do it."

"Can't," he grunted.

Oh, yeah? Who just saved whose life? "I can do anything," she said.

"You're amazing."

He met her gaze, and the look in his bleary, heavy-lidded eyes warmed her to her bones. "Wrong," he added, "but amazing."

She gritted her teeth and jumped into the stream.

The sound of him calling her name was drowned by her splash. The shock stopped her breath. Dear Lord, it was cold. Her arms felt heavy, useless. She couldn't feel her legs at all.

She was dimly aware of Jack cursing as she floundered through the water. At least this time she wasn't dragging his deadweight behind her. And there was the tree to cling to, although that was a mixed blessing, because she kept banging into the trunk. Branches scraped her legs and tangled in her hair.

Her fingers were raw, red, and white. Hanging in the current, trying not to swallow the water that surged around her face, she studied the canoe.

If only she wasn't so *cold* . . .

She yanked on the canoe, but she couldn't budge it

along the trunk. No way could she haul it to shore. It was too heavy. She was too tired. Too weak.

I can do anything.

She closed her eyes in despair.

Ranger Long had seen them steal the canoe. He had a truck. He could follow their path downstream. And if he found the boat here, he would search for them on the banks nearby.

But if he found it farther downstream . . .

"I'm coming in," Jack rasped. White-faced and grim, he lowered himself into the water.

"Wait!" she called.

She couldn't hide the canoe. She couldn't move it. But if she could flip it over and angle it just a bit, the current might move it for her.

Grasping a branch with one hand, she braced her other palm against the rim of the canoe and shoved. The canoe lifted, clearing the log. But instead of flipping safely over to the other side, it slipped her grip and rolled—crashed— down on her.

Bounce on her arm. *Oops.*

Thump on her head. *Ouch.*

Splash in the water. *No!*

She went down gasping and surfaced sputtering and shivering with cold. The canoe bumped and scraped against the tree, its bow sliding out into the stream. The rear end swung back at her head. She threw up her arm, and it smashed her elbow. Pain radiated up her arm. Splintered behind her eyes. She opened her mouth to cry out and swallowed icy water.

Don't panic.

Frantically, she pushed and shoved at the side of the canoe. It glided by like a shark brushing a swimmer at the beach. An eddy snatched the prow.

Breathless, she watched as the slim craft wobbled, wavered, and finally flowed around the fallen log. Downstream. Away.

Lexie sagged, still clinging to the log for support. The current dragged at her clothes and bubbled under her chin. God, she was cold.

Her hands clamped like claws to the tree branch. She had to get back to the bank, that's all. One more little effort, and then . . . and then . . .

Her thoughts wavered and spun away like the departing canoe. Okay, so she'd worry about *then* when she got there.

Jack staggered waist deep in the churning water, his head moving from side to side like a wounded bull's.

"What are you doing?" she yelled.

His jaw set. "Help," he said stubbornly.

Her heart melted. He was coming in after her. The dumbass. And then she'd have to drag both their butts back out.

"I don't need help," she lied.

She hoped. Reluctantly, she uncurled her stiffened fingers from the wet branch. Her legs were leaden. Her muscles cramped with cold. She eyed the yards between her and the bank, and her skin shrank and her heart quailed.

Lexie took a deep breath. A little swim would warm her up. Do her good.

Or kill her.

HE hadn't killed her.

Sally Blaine lay on her stomach on the double bed she'd shared with Ray every night for the past fourteen years, a towel folded under her head so her blood wouldn't stain the pillowcase. She ran her tongue around her swollen mouth, taking inventory of her teeth. Two chipped, one missing. The sharp pain when she inhaled meant a cracked rib. The hot lump on her forearm was only a bruise. She hoped. She wasn't very good at setting bones herself. She'd arranged the covers below her waist, unable to bear their weight on her back. She would have preferred no covers, no nightgown at all, but she was cold. And anyway, Ray didn't like her to be naked in bed.

Once he had. When they were young, when they were dating, he used to touch her with reverent hands and look at her as if she was holy, murmuring love words mixed with Scripture. *Thou art all fair, my love; there is no spot in thee.*

Sally turned her head on the pillow. A long time ago.

After fourteen years, she knew what to do. Knew how to curl to protect her head and stomach, how to use cold water to avoid setting stains in the rug, how to tape and bandage and splint, how to brush her teeth with her finger so she wouldn't gag on the taste of her own blood.

She knew how to do everything except make her husband stop hitting her.

She'd tried. Tried to find inside this cold-voiced husband who beat her the lover she'd run away with, the young man who promised her a family, who watched her with hot, possessive eyes, who touched her and made her shiver. In the early years, she'd tried to reach that man, the good Ray, with arguments, tears, and pleading. Mostly now she simply tried to avoid triggering his temper. His displeasure. His fists.

When that didn't work, she'd tried writing to Jack.

Not for her sake. She wouldn't have put aside her pride and her vows for herself. The brother she adored had abandoned her, gone off to war and left her locked in lonely battle with their father in a fight she couldn't win. *You made your bed, you little slut,* her father had screamed at her when she left their house for the last time. *You lie in it.*

Her fingers plucked the sheet. Well, she was lying in it now. Ray had made sure of that.

He was furious she might have betrayed him by turning to another man, even a brother. Maybe especially her brother, Sally thought as she lay chained by pain in the dark, taking shallow, careful breaths, waiting to heal. Ray had always been jealous of her attachment to Jack.

Or maybe he was just jealous of Jack, because her brother was tall and liked to laugh and had served in a real army.

"You sent for him," Ray had accused her coldly before his fist came down like the wrath of God and knocked her into a table.

But no matter what he did to her, she wouldn't admit it. Alone in their room, she hugged that small defiance to her like another pillow. He didn't know. He couldn't know for sure, and his uncertainty had saved her.

His uncertainty, or maybe his pride. How could a man whose rank depended on his ability to command others admit publicly he couldn't control his own wife?

And so Ray hadn't ordered her disciplined. She hadn't been stoned, the way poor, silly Tracy had been after her husband discovered she was sneaking out at night.

Sally would live. She would heal. She'd missed her rendezvous with Jack, but that didn't mean there would never be another chance for her.

She lay dry-eyed in the dark, her heart numb and her bruises throbbing. But would there be another chance for Isaac? Her beautiful boy. Her only child. Ray's son.

What were Isaac's chances when Ray took him away from her and put him in the Men's House?

JACK was weaving like a drunk walking a line beside the highway. Lexie didn't know how the man stayed upright.

Heck, she wasn't sure how she stayed upright, and she wasn't sporting a two-inch gash in her forehead. He was shaking with shock. She was shuddering with reaction. Both of them were exhausted, wet, and cold. As the hours passed and the sun dropped, they might get dryer. But without some kind of shelter, they were definitely going to get colder.

They didn't even have a blanket. Jack's backpack had been lost when the canoe tipped over. He still wore his compass and his gun, but they'd lost their map and Lexie had a lousy sense of direction. She had no idea where they were going. Away from the stream and pursuit, obviously.

But how did Jack know they weren't walking into a road-block? Or around in circles?

He stumbled, and she reached for his arm.

He shook off her touch. "I'm fine."

Well, excuse me, Captain Invincible.

"Really? Because you look like an extra who's wandered off the set of a zombie movie."

A smile lightened the grim set of his face. He looked terrible, haggard and pale. The blood had started to crust around the oozing gash on his forehead. But something inside her still softened and loosened in response to that smile.

She was pathetic.

"Really," he assured her. "We'll find something soon."

"A Holiday Inn would be good. Or . . ." Lexie blinked. Pathetic, and hallucinating.

"What is it?" Jack asked, instantly alert.

Speechless, she pointed up the hillside. A pink plastic flamingo leaned against a massive oak tree.

Jack grinned. "Well, it's not a Holiday Inn sign, but it's still good."

Clearly, the bump on his head was affecting his brain. "A tacky lawn decoration in the middle of the forest is a good sign?"

"It's a private property line marker," he explained. "We must be close to a house."

"And that's good?" She desperately wanted to believe it could be. But after Clyde and Mrs. Clyde, she needed to be sure.

He changed angle, shambling uphill toward the flamingo. "It is if nobody's home."

"And if they are?"

Jack shrugged. "Then we'll sleep in the shed or the boat house or the garage."

Lexie didn't want to sleep in a shed. But it was better than a cave with bats.

Her wet sandals squelched and slid on the decaying

leaves. The straps had rubbed blisters through her socks. If she ever made it out of here—*when* she made it out of here—she was going to burn them. Or have them bronzed, a monument to her trusting stupidity and eagerness to please a man she never even cared about.

They struggled up the rise. The ground fell away, revealing a landscape textured with trees and shadows and a sky brushed with gray and gold clouds. Through the dark leaves of the surrounding rhododendrons, Lexie could see the pitched roof of a house and a broken ribbon of road spooling into the distance.

They staggered down the hill toward the cabin, a sturdy shingled box with bright curtains at the windows and a stone fireplace rising from the roof.

"How do we know if anyone's home?" Lexie whispered when they reached the yard.

Jack gave her a you're-new-at-this-aren't-you look as he approached the back of the house. "We knock."

He did, right below the "Home, Sweet Country Home" wreath on the kitchen door.

Lexie huddled in the shadows, hugging her elbows to protect the wisp of hope in her chest.

No answer. No lights. No car in the driveway. Maybe there really wasn't anyone home.

"Can you open the door?" she asked.

"I can if they don't have a security system."

She watched as he paced around the house, looking at all the windows. On his return, he picked up the cement squirrel perched on the back stoop.

One of those faux garden sculptures, she thought, with a spare key hidden inside.

Jack smashed the squirrel into a door pane, breaking the glass. Her heart jumped. Reaching through smoothly, he unlocked the door.

Lexie gaped. "What did you do?"

His eyes gleamed. "Opened the door."

"But—"

"Don't stand around waiting. I don't think we need to worry about the neighbors, but you can never tell."

She scooted inside. The narrow kitchen was decorated in blue-and-white checks and black-and-white cows. Lots of cows. The air was stale and cold.

Jack lifted and listened to the handset on the kitchen phone. Shook his head. "They must have cut off service," he said. "At least that answers the question of whether they'll be back tonight."

He was shuddering in his wet clothes.

"We should build a fire," Lexie said.

"We can't risk having somebody report smoke from the chimney if this place is supposed to be empty. It's okay," he assured her gently. "There's a refrigerator, so they must have a generator wired into the house circuit. I'll turn on the heat while you take a shower."

"You first," she said. "You're hurt."

"And you're cold."

She was freezing. She was also really worried about him. But standing here arguing about his stupid women-into-the-lifeboats-first attitude wouldn't help either of them.

The tiny bathroom was down the hall. Mindful of Jack's warnings about the "neighbors," Lexie closed the blinds before flicking on the lights. A riot of red hearts and country stencils jumped out at her from every available surface. But there were towels and an unopened bottle of shampoo in the linen closet and a forgotten sliver of soap in the shower. Blessing her unknown, unknowing hosts, Lexie cranked on the hot water and attacked her hair.

JACK squinted at the white paper filter, trying to focus his blurred vision. His head throbbed. His hands shook with cold, spilling coffee grounds from the plastic scoop onto the white kitchen counter.

Too bad Lexie wasn't a tea drinker. He thought he could

handle filling the kettle with water and setting it on the gas stove.

But he knew she liked coffee better than tea. Just like he knew she was afraid of bats and didn't get on too well with her parents. He knew that those baby-doll looks disguised a stubborn determination and a sharp sense of humor, that even without makeup her skin and eyes shone, and that her nipples were rosy brown.

He sucked in his breath. Okay, there was a piece of knowledge he didn't need. Not with her wet and naked down the hall.

What he didn't know—what he needed to know—was why the Disciples were so desperate to get her back.

He could understand a husband, boyfriend, coming after her. He'd seen that before. The most dangerous time in an abusive relationship was when the victim decided to leave her abuser. He gripped the edge of the counter. *Don't think about Dora, don't go there, don't, let it go . . .*

But this was about more than some asshole who wouldn't accept it was over. What had Lexie said? *I was kidnapped. Because of who I know.*

Who did she know—*what* did she know—that would account for the old guy with the gun stationed at the forest access yesterday? And the forest ranger today?

Jack's head ached. Unless the ranger's presence at the rendezvous site had nothing to do with Lexie at all.

Unless he was there to stop Sally.

Jack dumped out the filter and counted scoops again, concentrating so he wouldn't think about Lexie and her nipples down the hall. *Wet, round, rosy, soap sliding down the slope of her belly, the curve of her ass . . .*

Yeah, he really wasn't going to think about that.

Jaw clenched, he filled the well of the coffeemaker with water and turned on the machine. He needed to think about Sally. He needed to plan.

Something had happened to keep his sister away from the waterfall today. Had she changed her mind? Or had that son of a bitch she married somehow stopped her from leaving?

Jack needed to find out.

He couldn't storm the Disciples camp with Lexie in tow. They still wanted her back. And taking on fifty armed militia men without backup was a really stupid idea.

Not to mention Blaine hated his guts. If Jack showed up demanding to see his sister, Blaine was likely to get pissed off and take it out on Sally and the kid.

The rich aroma of brewing coffee filled the kitchen, but it didn't do a damn thing for Jack's shakes. Or his sluggish thoughts.

His sister's letter was postmarked from town. If he could find whoever helped her mail that letter, he might be able to contact her. His best bet was to go to Benson, the way Lexie wanted him to all along.

And hope he was basing his decision on what was right for Sally, not the slim possibility Lexie would be so grateful for his escort that she'd agree to have sex with him.

He closed his eyes in self-disgust. He'd always looked with scorn on the guys who used the protection of their badge, who abused the public trust or their own authority. Cops who traded in favors, sexual or otherwise.

But the truth was, he was so hot for Lexie Whatever-her-name-was, he didn't give a damn about her motives anymore. If she wanted to sleep with him as a payoff for falling in with her plans, that was fine with him.

And maybe, you know, she felt something more than gratitude. She'd been willing last night. Eager, even, once he'd figured out her hang-up about taking responsibility. He was the one who'd called a halt. Because he didn't know enough about her and whatever game she was running against the Disciples to trust her.

He still didn't know what she was up to.

But he knew *her* in almost every way that mattered. She'd saved his life today. Hell, she'd waded back into the water to save the damn canoe and throw off their pursuit.

She was resourceful, uncomplaining, and a lot stronger than he expected.

Strong enough to enter into a relationship without making him jump through a bunch of hoops first? Without promises? Without expectations?

Yeah, right. And maybe he'd hit his head harder than he thought.

"I left you some hot water."

He opened his eyes, and she was there, wrapped in a towel, her short hair in damp curls. He couldn't see her nipples, but the tops of her breasts plumped above her crossed arms. Her feet were bare.

"I made you some coffee," he said gruffly.

"Mm. Good." She smiled her pleasure as she moved to take a cup. A drop of water trembled at the hollow of her throat. A hot, heavy pounding started in his head. And lower. He caught a whiff of unfamiliar shampoo as she reached around him, and he wanted to sniff her hair. Strip her towel. Lick her neck.

She shivered a little. "It's cold in here."

He almost laughed.

"Baseboard heat," he explained. "It'll warm up soon."

She nodded and sipped her coffee, watching him over the rim. "This is great. Thanks."

His wet jeans strained at his crotch. He felt like he was going to burst out of his pants. Out of his skin.

Her earlier words haunted him. *You were hoping for naked and grateful?*

Oh, yeah, babe.

"I'm hitting the shower," he said abruptly, pretending not to notice the question in her eyes. "Rustle us up some dinner, okay?"

LEXIE watched him walk away from her, stiffly, like a man hiding pain. He was battered, bruised, and bleeding, the gash on his forehead barely crusted over, his pupils wide and dark. Her big, wounded warrior. Her breath caught.

"Do you want me to take a look at that cut?" she called after him.

"No." He kept walking.

Big, wounded dummy.

She did not want to repeat her mother's mistakes, attempting to comfort and care for a man who had no time for tenderness and no patience with sympathy. But maybe the Chinese were right. If you saved a man's life, it belonged to you. Maybe this terrible yearning she felt, this clutch of attachment, was no more than a sense of responsibility.

Served him right if he fell in the tub.

But alone in the kitchen, she worried, her attention drifting down the hall, unable to do more than pull a few cans from the cupboard and set them on the counter.

She heard the gurgle of water into the sink and then the rush of the shower. He was fine. A grown man. He was used to taking care of himself. Showering by himself.

Clunk.

Her heart stopped. Had he fallen?

She hurried down the hall and stopped outside the bathroom, her heart beating faster.

She tapped on the door. "Jack?"

No response.

He could have slipped and hit his head. He could be lying in the bottom of the tub, unconscious. Drowning.

She opened the door cautiously. Steam billowed to greet her. Sweat formed on her upper lip, but her arms prickled with goose bumps. "Jack?"

The water hissed.

She tugged back the curtain.

Jack lowered his head from the water and stared at her, surprised. Conscious. Naked.

He was a big man. He crowded the white-tiled tub, broad shoulders, muscled chest, powerful legs. Dark hair clung to his chest. His thighs. Between.

She gulped. "Are you, um . . ." She was staring at his penis. His very naked, splendidly grown up, fully aroused penis. "Is everything okay?"

He didn't answer. Lexie dragged her gaze up to find him watching her, heat in his eyes.

Slowly, he smiled. A shiver rocked her.

"You tell me," he said.

ELEVEN

HEAT bloomed in Lexie's cheeks. Warmth flooded her stomach. "I came to, uh . . ." Her gaze flickered down again.

"Scrub my back?" Jack suggested wryly.

He hadn't made any attempt to cover himself. Clearly, the man was comfortable with his nudity. And his arousal.

All right, not comfortable, exactly, but he obviously didn't have issues with it. She snuck another look. Well, he wouldn't. Anyway, she wasn't going to react like some trembling virgin who'd never seen a penis—a very nice, erect penis—before.

She lifted her chin. "I just wanted to make sure you were all right. I thought you'd fallen."

"Not me." He bent to pick up a plastic bottle from the bottom of the tub—nice ass, too—and set it on the side. His mouth quirked again. "Although I appreciate the way you charged in here to rescue the shampoo."

Okay, now she felt really stupid. "Right. Well. Since you don't need me—"

"I didn't say that," he interrupted softly.

The air left her lungs.

She crossed her arms more tightly over her towel. "Is this the part where you go, 'Ooh, baby, I want you, I need you, I'm gonna hold you in my arms forever'?"

His eyes were watchful. "Is that what you want to hear?"

"I want the truth," she said crossly.

Jack leaned one shoulder against the tiled wall, water running down his back. "And what will the truth get me?"

Her heart beat faster. He was calling her bluff.

Because if she were honest with herself, this wasn't about what he wanted or needed.

It wasn't even about what she was willing to accept.

It was about what she wanted and how far she was willing to go to get it.

She stared at Jack, tall and dark and attainable in the shower, a sign of all the risks she'd never taken and all the feelings she'd ever denied. The steam of the bathroom lay on her skin like desire. Her throat felt thick with possibility.

She'd gotten into this mess by denying her own instincts, by trying to please Ray, a man she didn't even want. Maybe it was time to break the pattern and make a play for a man she did.

Because she did want him. Jack. Wanted him with an intensity and certainty that surprised her.

He was waiting for her answer. *What will the truth get me?*

She took a deep breath. "Me."

From his sudden stillness, she guessed she'd surprised him, too. He said, slowly, "The truth is, I want you. But I've never been good at forever."

Her brain shut down with *I want you.*

"That'll do," she said. "For now."

Now was all she could deal with anyway. She didn't want to think about tomorrow, about her lies or their danger, about his sister or her father. Now was enough. Now was more than she'd ever let herself have before.

She dropped her towel and stepped into the shower.

Oops. The ceramic was slippery, and her ankle still wasn't steady. She grabbed Jack to save her balance.

And Jack, thank goodness, grabbed her back, steadying her against his hot, male, reassuringly solid body. He smelled great. He felt even better. He adjusted her against him so she could feel him everywhere, the hard, smooth length of his erection against her stomach, the intriguing texture of hair against her breasts and her thighs.

She opened her mouth to breathe and he kissed her, his tongue in her mouth, his hands sliding around and behind her to pull her flush against his wet, aroused body.

Good, she thought muzzily. Squashed together like this, Jack wouldn't notice she could stand to lose a few pounds. Like, ten. If she'd planned this, she would have chosen someplace less brightly lit for seduction. She wasn't having second thoughts. She just didn't share Jack's hi-I'm-nude confidence. Three days of hiking and starving didn't make up for a few too many chevre quiches at wedding receptions and far too many Saturday nights spent with the B.J.s—Bridget Jones and Ben & Jerry's.

But then he eased her away from him, holding her hands out from her sides, his dark gaze raking her, taking her with his eyes. She flushed with heat and embarrassment, her nipples beading, her thighs pressing together.

"You're staring," she said.

"Damn straight. You're beautiful."

The heat and embarrassment grew. "Oh, please."

"You are," he said huskily. "Here." His finger traced the upper slope of her breast. "And here." His broad-palmed hand spanned the curve of her hip. "Here." The backs of his fingers barely brushed the insides of her thighs.

She sucked in her breath, grateful she'd found and used the disposable pink razor in the back of the linen closet. And that's when she noticed.

"You shaved," she said with a fleeting touch to his smooth jaw.

He turned his head and caught her fingers in his teeth. Her bones melted.

"Disappointed?" he asked.

"No, I . . ." With the stubble scraped off, he didn't look younger or less dangerous. His face was too edgy, too angled, for comfort. And there was that gash at his hairline to remind her he was a hard man in a dangerous job.

But without the beard, he looked more like someone she could have known before. Someone she could have dated. Someone she might actually have a relationship with.

Her heart wobbled. She wasn't looking for a relationship. She was trying to break a pattern.

"Why did you?" she asked.

"I figured it was better for what I had in mind."

She nodded sagely. "So you won't be recognized."

His slow smile made her toes curl against the bathtub tile. "No, so I can do this."

He lowered his head and nuzzled her neck, nipping, licking, making her knees go weak and her nerves jump and celebrate. She arched her throat, giving herself up to the pleasure of his mouth and the friction of his wet, hard body.

"And this," he growled in her ear, and knelt in the tub and buried his face between her legs.

Lexie gasped. She moaned. She was wracked, blinded, assaulted by the hot water pounding her breasts and the hot, wet slither of his tongue. She squeezed her eyes shut against the sensory overload, against the warm spray and the shocking image of his dark head against her pale thighs. He was kneeling in front of her like a suppliant warrior seeking a lady's favor. Only he wasn't begging for anything. He took and gave without asking, his mouth urgent and knowledgeable, his lips and tongue busy, busy, his teeth scraping with exquisite skill.

Her hands curled, sliding vainly for a hold in his short, sleek hair, against his broad, slick shoulders. He held her up, held her in place with his powerful arms and strong hands while he stimulated and devoured her.

She was drenched. Dying. Buffeted by pleasure, drowning in sensation. She couldn't hold it. It filled her, flooded her, swept through her, a liquid current that rippled and swirled and crested. Everything inside her contracted to a hard, bright point. She screamed, the sound bouncing around the steamy tiles, and convulsed. On and on, quaking and shaking, while Jack supported her in his arms. Water ran down her face. Suns exploded behind her closed eyelids.

He stood and pulled her boneless body against his.

"Wow," she mumbled into his bare shoulder.

She hadn't simply broken a pattern here. They must have set some kind of record.

Or she had.

She felt too good for guilt. But she couldn't help noticing Jack wasn't as limp as she was. On the contrary. His heavy erection pressed her hip.

She licked her lips, trying to get her mouth to work. "Do you, um . . ."

He kissed her ear, his big hand gliding up to capture her breast. Okay, he did. She was done—satisfied, sated, *sunk*—but it seemed only fair to let him finish.

He toyed with her nipple, and a nerve twinged low in her stomach.

And really, she didn't mind, she thought muzzily as his blunt, hot penis bobbed against her. Some time after college, she'd quit having sex because it was easier than saying no, because it was fair or expected, or because she was afraid of hurting her date's ego. But any guy who worked as hard as Jack to bring his partner to screaming ecstasy deserved at least compliance in return.

As long as the hot water didn't run out.

He shut off the shower and reached for a towel. She blinked at him as he dried her gently, thoroughly, brushing and patting her with the towel, making her oversensitized skin prickle. Warmth pooled in her belly.

A little thrill of excitement and alarm ran through her. She was *done*.

"What are you doing?" she asked.

His eyes gleamed. "Drying you."

"I can see that." She sucked in her breath as he rubbed tenderly between her legs. "But what about you?"

He swiped the towel over his broad chest and arms and tossed it into a corner. "Now I'm dry, too."

"That wasn't what I—" He scooped her up and stepped with her out of the tub. She clutched at his neck. "Careful, tough guy. You're recovering from a head injury, remember?"

"How else am I going to carry you to bed?" he asked reasonably.

She settled in his arms as he strode with her down the short hall. Struggling would only put him off balance. Besides, while it was kind of primitive and probably un-PC, there was something deeply satisfying about being carried in his arms. And he smelled delicious, clean, and male. Without meaning to, she put her mouth to his skin, delicately tasting him. His grip tightened.

Lexie's soft mouth on his neck almost brought Jack to his knees. He needed a bed. Fast. Or he was going to dump her on her feet and nail her against the wall.

Control, he ordered himself. He'd nearly exploded in the shower, seeing her all rosy wet, tasting the soft and the sweet and the pink of her, feeling her tremble and come. But he'd held out. Held back. It was important, this first time, to do her right. And that meant showing finesse. Keeping control, to bring her pleasure and to prove to himself that he could.

He kicked open a door. Not so controlled, but effective. And it was a bedroom, which was good.

He laid her down, pink and white against the dark blue spread, delectably naked. Blood pulsed in his loins, throbbed in his head.

Lexie shivered, her hands moving instinctively to cover herself from his hot gaze.

"Cold?"

She smiled politely. "I'm fine."

He shook his head. Fine wasn't good enough. Not for her, and not for what he had in mind. Deliberately, he set himself to warm her, to tempt her, to tease her back to a state of wild responsiveness.

She shifted and sighed under him, neither evading nor encouraging his touch. "Really, Jack, I'm . . . You don't need to . . . *Oh, God, there.*"

She arched into him. Ruthlessly, he exploited what he'd learned from her before, keeping himself on a short, tight leash as he made her flush and quiver, made her stretch and open, made her writhe and moan.

"Now," she gasped, reaching for him.

Oh, yeah. He kneed her thighs apart and settled himself between her legs, pulsing, rubbing himself against her, ready to bury himself to the hilt in her creamy wet sex. She was beautiful, warm and beautiful, vulnerable. Open. Unprotected.

Really unprotected.

The realization hit him like a bat across the base of his skull.

Shit.

"Now," Lexie said again, twisting under him. "Jack!"

He was dying.

"I can't," he said tightly.

She opened her eyes and glanced down at his eager dick, which apparently hadn't gotten the message from mission control that this launch was aborted. "You certainly can."

If he'd been less miserable, less grimly determined, he would have laughed. "Can't. No condom," he explained.

Her eyes rounded. Her mouth opened. "Oh. You don't . . . Don't you carry protection?"

"Not usually." Although after this, he was going to reconsider the habits of a lifetime and start keeping a rubber in his wallet.

She rolled over, away from him, without another word.

Disappointment speared his gut. Well, what did he expect? That she'd be so impressed with his technique, so overcome with lust, that she'd beg to have unprotected sex with him? He knew better.

But he'd hoped . . .

She flipped on the light beside the bed, her rosy, round buttocks turned toward him. He resisted the urge to shape them with his hands.

"What are you doing?" he asked.

"Looking for condoms. I thought maybe in the nightstand . . ." She rustled around.

His blood pounded. She was beautiful. She was resourceful. And she still wanted to have sex. "Find anything?"

"*Field and Stream,* a flashlight, and three cough drops," she said, disgust plain in her voice.

He forced a light tone. "Something for every emergency."

"Except this one." She flopped onto her back. Her breasts quivered. The curve of her belly, her light brown bush, attracted his gaze like a flag.

So he was frustrated. She was frustrated. That was no reason to break another lifetime habit.

He opened his mouth and said, "Look, I don't expect you to believe this, but I'm clean. I could pull out."

She bit her lip, like she was actually considering it. Anticipation dried his mouth and surged in his groin.

"My mother would kill me," she said.

He raised an eyebrow. "You're not in high school, babe. I don't think your mother is going to get upset if you have sex."

Lexie smiled wryly. "My mother bought me my first box of condoms when I was fourteen and demonstrated how to use them. On a banana."

"Jesus," Jack said, startled.

"Religion didn't have anything to do with it. She's a doctor," Lexie explained. "She doesn't care if I have sex. But she'd be horrified to know I was contemplating unprotected sex with a man I've known less than a week."

Jack was still trying to wrap his mind around the image of Lexie's mother—any mother—wrestling a banana in front of her teenage child.

"It's not that I don't trust you," Lexie said, her smoky blue eyes sincere. "I do. I trust you with my life. Just not . . . not another life."

Something inside Jack cracked and bled tenderness like another wound. She wasn't afraid he'd give her HIV. She was worried he'd get her pregnant.

And she trusted him.

He studied her earnest eyes and tousled blond hair in the yellow light of the lamp. "You're a nice girl, you know that?"

"Don't say that," she begged. "Nice girls get screwed."

His mouth twisted. "Not tonight, they don't."

Unless she didn't cover up that come-and-fuck-me body sometime soon. Jack stood and flipped back the spread. No sheets, but the cover was thick and the mattress pad looked clean.

"Come on. Into bed."

She hesitated. "Don't you want to . . ."

Yeah, he did.

". . . eat first?"

He almost laughed. "Food would be good," he agreed.

"I found soup and chili in the pantry." Lexie climbed eagerly off the bed, making everything shift and jiggle in interesting ways. "And I noticed a washer and dryer off the kitchen. I can get our clothes clean while we eat."

Jack watched, bemused, as Lexie wrapped herself in a towel and headed purposefully down the hall. Hot food, clean clothes, and no messy conversational postmortem about what had just happened, or hadn't happened, in bed. It was like a fantasy come true.

His ex-wife had never been what you might call domestic. They'd met in a bar, and neither of their habits had changed much after marriage. Patty had liked sex, but even in the beginning he couldn't take her to bed without a lengthy re-hash and replay of their relationship.

Lexie had spared him that.

So why was he so dissatisfied?

SHE couldn't put off talking to him forever.

Lexie hunched her shoulders as they trudged down the road, the chill seeping through Jack's fatigue shirt. The morning lay gray and cool as a cloud between the hills, obscuring her view of the highway.

But how did you tell a man you'd almost had sex with you were carrying evidence that might convict his sister of murder?

"Why are we going to Benson now?" she asked, breaking the silence.

"You want to go to Benson," Jack said. "And I owe you."

He looked worse this morning, his dark eyes bleary, his skin pasty white, the gash on his forehead raw and purple. But even in the cold light of morning, with his face all the colors of a meat counter, he made her bones melt.

She moistened her lips. "Because I was willing to sleep with you?"

"Because you saved my life."

His matter-of-fact acknowledgment added to her burden of guilt.

"Besides," Jack continued, his boots striking the gravel at the side of the road. "Sally's letter was postmarked from town. Somebody must have helped her mail it. If I can find out who, maybe I can get a message to her."

"Sounds like a long shot to me," Lexie said without thinking.

"It is. You have a better plan?"

Oh, dear. Now she'd offended him. That was bad. But much worse was her deepening realization that her feelings last night weren't solely the product of a hot shower and hot sex. She hadn't simply been swept away by the illusion of safety and the allure of danger. In the cold light of morning, she was still attracted to this hard-eyed stranger making irritated conversation with her as they tromped through a ditch on the side of the road.

"I'm not so big on planning," she said in excuse. "I'm more of an improviser."

"You've got to have a plan," Jack said positively, sounding so much like her father that it set off an alarm bell, pushed a button hardwired in childhood.

"No, *you* have to have a plan," she said. "That's the way it goes. You have one person who plans and one person who sucks it up and goes along. Or doesn't go along, in which case you don't have a relationship. Not for very long, anyway."

Jack raised his eyebrows. "Are we still talking about Benson?"

Oh, God. Heat swept her face. Her whole body burned. "No. Sorry. Yes, I do want to go to Benson. I'm sorry, I—"

"It's okay."

"It's *not* okay." Distress shook her voice. She wasn't being fair. She wasn't being nice. It was completely unlike her.

A muscle bunched in his jaw. "Look, if you're upset because I stopped last night—"

"You think this is about sex?"

He looked confused. "Isn't it?"

He was such a guy. Lexie shook her head, amused and relieved. "No! That was a totally mutual decision. I was talking about my parents."

"These would be the strong-minded parents who fought a lot."

Not just a guy, she realized with a tiny jolt. He was a cop, with a cop's attention to detail. "You have a good memory."

"A doctor and a cop. Both planners, right?"

She had to tell him. Her stomach hollowed. Sooner or later, she had to talk about her father. She no longer believed Jack would trade her to the Disciples for his sister's safety. *I trust you with my life.*

On the other hand, he had no real reason to trust her. Or

her father. Despite the development of the Critical Incident Response Group, for many people "FBI" and "militant group" still raised the specters of Waco and Ruby Ridge. Jack's sister was still inside the compound. Why worry the guy?

"That's right." She cleared her throat. "Unfortunately, their plans didn't leave a lot of room for each other."

"Or for you, either?"

She flinched. "That's not true," she said automatically.

He didn't say anything.

"They had important work to do."

"Babe, you don't have to convince me. I'm the one who screwed up my marriage, remember?"

She didn't want to think about it. Didn't want to remember that last night she'd nearly given herself, body and soul, to a man trained to depersonalize and compartmentalize his feelings, who put his job above his family.

She had a sudden image of him, heavy-eyed above her, as she clutched him and begged. *Now, Jack. Now.*

She flushed. "It wasn't like they didn't care about me."

"Uh huh."

"My father used to run background checks on my friends in high school." Now, why had she told him that?

"Control." Jack nodded. "It's a cop thing."

She glared at him and changed the subject. "Should we be walking this close to the road?"

"We should if we want to hitch a ride."

A different kind of discomfort moved into Lexie's bones.

"You know," she said, proud there wasn't so much as a quiver in her voice, "the last time I got into a car with strangers, I was nearly abducted."

She didn't hear Jack's reply.

Because grinding down the road behind them, she could hear the unmistakable, threatening throb of an engine.

TWELVE

✦

Ray Blaine hated to sweat. He resented the reminder he wasn't in complete control of his body. He loathed the whiff of possible failure, the sour smell of weakness. Standing in front of Locke, he felt the spreading wetness at his armpits and damned his wife for lying in bed instead of attending to his laundry.

"We'll get her back," he insisted. "We have watchers on all the roads. It's only a matter of time."

"So you said." Daniel's vague blue eyes rested on him a moment. Judging him. Finding him wanting. "Two days ago."

"The canoe was found this morning by the Tsula Bend. She can't get far."

"Not by herself, perhaps. But she has help now. This man, John Miller?"

Ray ignored the question in Daniel's tone. He had to hide his connection to Miller. It wasn't right, it wasn't fair, that he should have to deal with his brother-in-law now. He didn't understand how things could go so wrong, how the man he hated and the woman he wanted could conspire together to ruin everything. Had Miller found Alexandra and seized on her as a likely weapon? Or had she seduced him, lured him, corrupted him with the promise of her warm smile and soft flesh?

Ray forced himself to breathe evenly. It didn't matter. He wouldn't let it matter. He would get her back. Once he had Alexandra, Daniel would have to acknowledge the rightness of his plan.

"I'll take care of Miller," he said.

"That won't be necessary." Daniel shifted a paper on his desk. "Brother Long has already spoken with the sheriff's department about Miller's assault."

Ray stared at him in consternation. The forest ranger was a tool. A useful tool. But to turn to the agents of Satan in the fight against the godless, instead of to Ray himself . . . What was Daniel thinking?

"Do you think that's wise? Wouldn't it be better to depend on"—*me,* he thought—"God's own people for deliverance?"

"We are all God's people, Brother Ray. And we need the goodwill of this community to survive."

Impatience pricked him. Survival wasn't enough. They were engaged in a holy struggle, a revolutionary war to establish a new, moral order in America.

"We can't rely on the existing order to further our goals."

"We can't ignore it, either," Daniel answered. " 'Even zeal is not good without knowledge, and the one who acts hastily sins.' "

The implied rebuke robbed Ray of breath like an elbow to the ribs. "If this is about Martin's wife, you pronounced her guilt."

"But not her punishment."

"You were there when the sentence was carried out."

Daniel's lips folded. "She shouldn't have died," he said stubbornly. "You went too far. Some of our members are speaking out against it."

Speaking out against *him.* Ray's blood beat in his head.

"Our members carried out the judgment," he pointed out. He'd made sure of it. "They can't go to the authorities without implicating themselves."

"And if they do?"

"There's no evidence. No body." He'd made sure of that, too.

"There's a witness," Daniel said.

Ray stiffened. "We don't know what she saw."

"She had a camera."

"I took the camera. Besides, it won't matter once I get her back."

"I don't want you to do anything. We can't afford to attract the sheriff's attention."

They couldn't afford to stand idly by, either. The final struggle was at hand. They needed bold, symbolic action to rally the faithful. Was Daniel blind?

"All the more reason to focus our efforts on finding Alexandra," Ray said with an effort. "And Miller. If the sheriff finds him before we do . . ."

"That's why Brother Long's testimony is so useful," Daniel said. "Miller is a fugitive accused of assaulting a government official. Why should the sheriff listen to him?"

Reluctantly, Ray acknowledged Daniel had a point. "He'll still listen to the woman. That could be a problem for us."

"That will be a problem for you," Daniel said. "If she tells him how you brought her here."

Ray burned with the injustice of it all. How *he* brought her? If his plan succeeded, Daniel would reap the credit and the benefits. But if it failed, Ray would get the blame.

He tried to make it clear they were in this together. "I'm just saying, if Tucker comes here, to the compound—"

"You'd better have some story that will satisfy him," Daniel finished for him, his voice as cool and smooth as marble. "I appreciate your faith, Brother Ray. But I will not allow your zeal to endanger this community."

* * *

AIR brakes squealed as the truck barreled down the hill toward them. Lexie flinched and waded deeper into the weed-clogged ditch. Too late to avoid being spotted. *Please, let the driver not be one of Locke's men. Please, let him drive on by.*

Jack turned to face the road, thumb out for a ride.

Her heart crowded her throat. "What are you doing?"

"Relax," he said, infuriatingly calm. "It's a truck."

Hadn't he ever seen the psychotic trucker in *Joy Ride*? "So?"

"So the driver's not from around here," Jack explained. "Out of state plates. Smile."

"What state?" Lexie demanded.

"What?"

"What state are we in?"

"North Carolina," Jack said. "Now, for God's sake, would you smile?"

Obediently, Lexie bared her teeth in a rictus grin. Of all her father's strictures and prohibitions, the one against hitchhiking actually made sense. You never knew what weirdo loser maniac would cruise by.

Of course, she was safe with Jack. She glanced at him, battered and solid, the gash on his forehead still oozing and angry, and suffered another qualm. What driver in his right mind would stop for a man who looked like he'd been hit with a bottle in a bar fight?

Not to mention she looked like roadkill.

The big rig, dirty white, with Dawson's Trucking painted on the side in blue and Georgia plates, gusted and groaned to a stop on the shoulder of the road.

"Where you folks headed?" A woman's voice. A woman trucker.

Well. To a woman, Jack might not look so bad. Didn't look so bad.

And it didn't matter how Lexie looked at all.

Jack stepped up and smiled through the window. "Going to Benson?"

"Can't avoid it on this road. What happened to your head?"

Jack's smile turned rueful. Charming. "I had a little accident on the trail."

"City boy, huh?"

"From now on. Can you give us a lift into town?"

Bright blue eyes studied Lexie from the shadow of the cab. "That your girlfriend?"

Lexie held her breath.

"From now on," Jack deadpanned.

The woman's chuckle rolled from the cab. "Okay. Hop in."

Jack swung open the door and jerked his head for Lexie to get in.

She started forward, her thoughts whirling. *From now on.* It didn't mean anything. He didn't mean anything. He was simply protecting himself and her with a plausible cover story.

She put a foot on the step.

"Him first," the trucker said. "No offense, honey, but I like a handsome man next to me when I drive."

Jack laughed. "Thanks," he said, and Lexie wasn't sure if he was talking about the ride or the compliment.

She clambered into the cab after him and sat in bemused silence as the truck driver—"Call me Dotty"—shifted into gear. Dotty had a ginger ponytail, a strong, weathered face, and a decal on the inside of her windshield that read "Mother Truckers Handle Big Rigs."

She had a host of stories, too, and joked and shared them with Jack as the truck barreled down the hills. Lexie sat on his other side, small and undaring and unnoticed.

She told herself she didn't mind. It wasn't as if she had any real claim on him. Except for the lifesaving thing yesterday and the naked wrestling last night.

But that didn't mean anything, either. At least, nothing

permanent. Jack had warned her he was no good at forever. Last night wasn't about the future. It was about lust and risk and going after what she wanted.

And kindness, she thought, remembering Jack's concern when she'd confessed her fears about getting pregnant.

And control.

Depressed and confused, she stared down at Jack's large, square knee as he made easy conversation with the lady trucker. The problem with getting what you wanted was it made you dissatisfied with what you could have.

"APPRECIATE the ride," Jack told Dotty sincerely as Lexie jumped from the cab to the gravel drive of the Bo-Lo Biker Motel. "And the recommendation."

"Anytime, honey," Dotty said. "Bobby and me, we go way back. You tell him I said to take good care of you."

"Will do," Jack said, and climbed down. Carefully, because sudden movement still hurt his head.

The morning mist had burned away, revealing long, low buildings set like spokes around a central cabin. Picnic tables huddled under the dripping trees on one side. Extended porches stretched along each building. Motorcycles—a couple wide glide hogs, a custom chopper chromed to the max—parked in front. The metal doors were scratched, the paint shabby, but the ground-level rooms promised privacy and a quick escape.

They needed a base of operations, a place to stay while he tracked down and tried to contact his sister. Someplace close to the center of town, where two rough-looking strangers without luggage or I.D. would be welcomed without question.

The Bo-Lo was perfect.

Jack raised his hand in salute as the truck roared off. Turning, he trudged toward the cabin's wooden steps. Lexie followed him without a word.

She sure was quiet this morning. Her face was pale and

heavy-eyed in the cool light. But even the overcast sky couldn't dim her bright, messy curls or rob the warmth from those eyes.

She must be tired, Jack decided. It had been a rough couple days, and despite the warm bed and their fatigue, he suspected she hadn't gotten much sleep last night. He sure as hell hadn't.

He was hoping—planning—they wouldn't sleep much tonight, either.

But first he had to find a drugstore.

Behind the motel counter, a large woman in faded overalls played *Free Cell* on her computer. A sullen kid with spiked hair and an iron bar through his lower lip slumped behind her. *Green Acres* goes Goth.

"Bobby?" Jack asked, with his best I-just-want-to-take-a-look-around smile.

"Lois," the woman said, but she smiled back, revealing uneven teeth. "Bobby's unclogging the drain in 5-C. And you are . . . ?"

"Jack. Friend of Dotty's. I was hoping you had a room."

The teenager snorted. "We got a bunch of rooms."

Lois gave him a look. He buried his head under the desk and came up with a wastebasket. Her gaze flicked to Lexie. "How many do you need?"

"Just one," Jack said, before Lexie got any ideas. He didn't know how long they'd have to stay. He couldn't afford two rooms. And he didn't want Lexie too far out of reach, for security and . . . other reasons.

"Is there a phone in the room?" Lexie asked.

"Phone, coffeepot, microwave, minifridge, and 150-channel TV," Lois said, pushing the register across the counter. "But if you want to call long-distance, I'll need a credit card."

"That'll be—"

"—unnecessary, thanks," Jack interrupted. Credit cards could be traced. Until he knew why that ranger was looking for John Miller and how he'd found them, Jack was operating on a strictly cash basis. "Cash okay?"

Lois studied his nearly illegible scrawl in the register and the extra two twenties laid on top. Her brows raised. "Friend of Dotty's, you said?"

He held her gaze. "Yes, ma'am."

The kid hoisted his trash bag.

Lois looked again at Lexie and apparently drew her own conclusions. "Guess cash is fine." She tucked the bills away in the bib covering her massive breasts. "You can park your bikes on the porch."

"We don't have a bike," Jack said.

"You looking to rent while you're here?"

"I'll let you know," Jack said. "Keys?"

She handed them over. "Anything else I can get you folks?"

"Directions to a drugstore?" Jack suggested.

"Dillard's Pharmacy is about a mile down at the light with the Piggly Wiggly. And if you don't mind going farther, there's a Kerr Drug at—"

"We need a Wal-Mart," Lexie said.

Jack narrowed his eyes at her. "What?"

"Well, it doesn't have to be a Wal-Mart," she said. "But somewhere with a photo center. For printing digital pictures?"

"There's a Wal-Mart out toward Asheville," Lois said doubtfully. "'Bout an hour away. They maybe could do it."

"Too far," said Lexie. "Is there a camera shop in town?"

"In Benson?" Lois shook her head, hugely amused.

But Lexie didn't give up. "What about an electronics store? Someplace that sells or services computers. I have an xD picture card I—"

Judas Priest. Didn't she get that couples checking into a roadside motel under assumed names didn't spend their time developing pictures? Unless they were into dirty Polaroids or porn sites or something.

"Babe, it can wait."

"But I—"

He hardened his voice. "I said, it can wait."

She stared at him, her eyes troubled, her mouth mutinous. Jack felt a warning tick, like the click of a latch in a quiet house. These photos must be really important to her. What had she called them? Identifying pictures for her family. In case her body was found and her parents needed a place to start searching.

But she was safe now. Why was she so hot to get them printed?

"Let's get our keys," he said, more gently, "and you can make that phone call."

LEXIE stood between the two double beds with her arms at her sides, feeling as if, once again, events were moving too fast for her.

Jack did a swift check of the closet and windows before disappearing into the bathroom.

When he came out, she said, "I've never checked into a motel with a man before."

His mouth quirked. "You picked the wrong one to start with."

Her heart thudded in her chest. The wrong motel? Or the wrong man?

Their room wasn't all that bad, decorated in early American knock-off with a hunter green carpet and slick veneer furniture. The TV was bolted to the dresser. The headboards were bolted to the wall.

Lexie lifted her chin. "I didn't have much choice."

"No, you didn't." Jack's face sobered. His dark eyes studied her. "You okay?"

His concern made her feel strangely weepy. Which was ridiculous. She was fine. She was safe. She was well on her way back to her old life, her own apartment, her things, and her routines. No more running. No more danger. No more lies.

No more Jack.

All it would take was a phone call.

She nodded.

"Make your phone call," he said gently.

She should. She would. But . . .

"I thought I needed a credit card."

"That's what the second twenty was for," Jack said.

"Oh." She sat on the edge of the mattress. "What's today?"

"Thursday."

Her mother would be at the hospital today. Taking a deep breath, Lexie picked up the receiver. Jack moved to the other bed and sat down, watching her.

The switchboard operator put her call back to the OR. The OR nurse couldn't say if Dr. Scott was still in surgery.

"Can you check, please?" Lexie asked, her stomach tightening. "This is her daughter. It's kind of important."

Jack raised his eyebrows. Lexie looked away.

"Lexie? Are you all right?"

At the sound of her mother's voice, Lexie's throat closed with sudden tears.

"Lexie?" Still concerned. A little impatient.

Lexie cleared her throat. "I'm fine, Mom. I'm, um, in North Carolina. In the mountains."

"Sounds beautiful."

"Yeah, it is. But—"

"Can we talk about it later?"

"Okay, but—"

"Lexie, I just got out of surgery, I've barely scrubbed, and I still have to talk to the patient's family. You can tell me about your vacation when you call on Sunday."

Lexie clutched the receiver tighter, as if she could keep a grasp on the conversation, hold on somehow to her mother's interest. "Mom, have you talked to Dad recently?"

"Your father? Why?"

"Well, if he . . . Has he said anything about me?"

"Alexandra, this is not a good time to talk about your father's judgments. He is what he is, and it's not your fault. Or, thank God, my responsibility any longer. Call me this weekend, and we'll talk."

Lexie's chest ached. "All right, Mom."

"I've got to go now, darling. Bye."

"Bye." Very carefully, Lexie cradled the phone.

"You didn't tell her." Jack sounded disbelieving.

"She just got out of surgery," Lexie explained.

"So?"

"So her patient needed her."

"Her daughter needs her. You were kidnapped."

Driven on the defensive, Lexie pointed out, "She doesn't know that."

"Because you didn't say anything."

"Because nobody noticed I was missing."

Saying it made Lexie slightly sick. It was surreal. For four days she'd lived in fear, pushed herself harder, stretched herself further than she'd ever thought she could go. She'd been determined not to be used for her connections, desperate to forestall a massive manhunt and a fatal siege of the compound.

And her parents had never even realized she was missing.

She smothered hysterical laughter. Obviously, Ray had kidnapped the wrong girl.

Jack kept his dark gaze on her face. "Then you tell her."

Lexie had never demanded her parents' attention. Or enjoyed it when she'd gotten it. And now was a terrible time to start. Appealing to her mother—stirring up her father— would only complicate things at this point.

"She wouldn't have heard me. She wasn't in mother mode."

"There's a mode?"

"Sometimes," Lexie said.

Jack shook his head. "You've got to call somebody."

Realities and consequences pressed on her lungs, making it hard to breathe. Her ordeal wasn't over at all. A new phase was just beginning.

"I should call Barbara. A planner I work with," Lexie explained in response to Jack's questioning look. "I'm supposed to shoot two weddings this weekend. If I can't get back in time, she'll have to find someone to cover for me."

"I'm not talking about your workload, babe. You've got no money. No credit cards. No I.D. You need help."

No money, no credit cards, no I.D. . . . just evidence of a murder in the lining of her bra. Evidence that could implicate the sister of the one man Lexie trusted to help her.

"I'll talk to the sheriff," she said.

"You going to press charges?" Jack asked.

"Against . . . ?"

"Against the guy who kidnapped you."

He wasn't talking about Sally. He didn't know about the stoning and his sister's possible participation. He was talking about Ray.

Lexie swallowed. Jack didn't know about Ray yet, either. At least, he didn't know about Ray-and-Lexie.

She didn't want him to know. She was ashamed she'd ever let herself be flattered and fooled into going out with the short, dark, charismatic Ray Blaine. She wasn't the first woman to be duped into dating a liar and a married man. But a violently abusive religious zealot, the leader of a survivalist hate group? She bit her lip. That definitely put her in the running for Needy Sucker of the Year.

If she pressed charges, her lousy judgment would be on trial, too. She didn't want to be the Disciples' bold, symbolic gesture that would spark the new revolution. Or the poster child for Women Who Trust Too Much. If her case against Ray went to court, the media would have a field day. Her stupidity would be a matter of public record, for all the world to read about and speculate over.

Her father would be embarrassed. Furious.

Jack scowled at her. "This is a no-brainer, Blondie."

His tone jabbed her insecurities like a finger poking a

bruise, so that instead of agreeing with him, which she did, really, she said, "What do you know about it?"

A muscle jumped in his jaw. "I was a cop, remember? If you don't press charges, he's free to come after you again."

That was the least of it. If she didn't press charges, Ray was free to kidnap, bomb, and murder in pursuit of his twisted interpretation of God's will and biblical law. And if she did press charges, if her father learned she'd been targeted by religious terrorists, it could bring a federal task force down on these mountains that would make the hunt for abortion bomber Eric Rudolph look like a children's game of hide-and-seek.

Not to mention Jack's sister and nephew could be caught in the fiery fallout and die, and Jack would never forgive himself.

Or her, either.

She had to tell him, Lexie realized with a sick feeling in her stomach. Jack had to know what helping her could cost him.

"It's more complicated than that," she said. "The circumstances—"

"It's always complicated," Jack said, sounding certain and disgusted. "There are always reasons not to press charges. You don't have money or you do have kids or maybe you fucking love him, I don't know."

"I don't love him. But—"

"But you can't protect the guy. You have to protect yourself."

"I'm trying to do that," Lexie said, shaky and nervous and misunderstood. "But there are other people to consider, too."

"Yeah? Like who?"

"Like your sister," Lexie snapped.

Jack's eyes narrowed. "What are you talking about?"

She had to tell him now. She felt terrible.

She took a deep breath. "The man who kidnapped me— the man you want me to press charges against—is your sister's husband. Ray Blaine."

THIRTEEN

JACK felt like he'd been shot. He registered the shock of impact, but everything else around him slowed and blurred. He heard Lexie talking, but he couldn't make sense of the words.

"Son of a bitch," he said.

Lexie winced. "Well, yes, he is." Her blue eyes sought his. Earnest. Worried. "But I didn't know that when I met him."

Feeling returned slowly, tingling in his extremities, rushing in his head.

Him. Blaine. Son of a *bitch*.

"How?" he demanded. The pain, he knew from experience, would come later. Now he was numb. Disbelieving.

"How did I meet him?" Lexie asked carefully.

Jack nodded.

"He came into the store on a day I had portraits scheduled. Renae was out grabbing a cigarette, so I was behind the counter." She waved her hand, but whether she was imitating her smoker friend or trying to brush off the seriousness of the encounter, Jack couldn't say. "He dropped off some film. We chatted."

"And based on that conversation, he decided to kidnap you," Jack said with heavy sarcasm.

"Um, no." She cleared her throat. "Actually . . . Well, he came back later to pick up the developed pictures and . . ."

"What aren't you telling me?" Jack asked.

"I'm trying to tell you," Lexie said, sounding annoyed.

"Something about the pictures?"

"No. Well, yes. That is, not those pictures, but—"

Pictures.

The image of that damn photo card, black against her pink and white skin, flashed through his mind.

We need a Wal-Mart. Somewhere with a photo center. I have an xD picture card . . .

My God. "You stole his pictures," Jack said, his mind racing. What kind of pictures? Something bad, something Blaine wouldn't want made public. Evidence of a crime, maybe, or pornography, something that could discredit him or his organization. "That's what's on the photo card."

"Oh, no," Lexie said, looking so startled he would have believed her if she hadn't been lying to him since the minute they met.

Later he would think about that, later that would hurt, but right now he had to figure out what else she was hiding.

"What's on the card, Lexie?"

"Pictures I took."

"What kind of pictures?"

Her eyelashes fluttered. Was she anxious? Or preparing to lie again?

Memories of her soft voice taunted him. *I'm not going with anyone else. I don't trust anyone else. I'm staying with you.*

It's not that I don't trust you. I do. I trust you with my life.

He was such a fool. She'd been playing him all along. He was torn between outrage and admiration.

She didn't answer him directly. "I told you I had my camera with me when—when I went with Ray. In my jeans pocket, remember?"

He remembered. That didn't mean she wasn't lying. But at least she had the wits to keep her story straight.

"That was on Sunday," she said. "On Monday—"

"What happened to Sunday night?" he interrupted.

"I don't know." Her throat moved as she swallowed. "Ray had a cooler in the car. We were supposed to be going on a picnic. I drank some lemonade, and after that I don't remember much of anything."

"He drugged you?" Bastard.

"I think he must have. I was sick when I woke up. And groggy."

"Woke up where?"

"Some kind of storage room. But there was a window. I remember thinking some fresh air might help." Her eyes were huge in her face, as big as if she was still drugged instead of remembering. "Anyway, the rope reached that far. To the window."

His gaze flicked to the fading marks on her wrists, and despite his skepticism, rage coiled inside him. Fuck.

"There were a lot of people outside. In the yard?" she said, making it a question, making sure he was with her. And suddenly he *was* with her, in that musty storage room, tied—my God—to a strange bed.

"At first I was glad," Lexie said, "because I thought, okay, maybe if I call for help, somebody would hear me. Only then I saw them. Ray and the other man, Daniel Locke. He was saying something to the crowd, but I couldn't really make out the words. There was sort of a circle, with the women inside. And the women started throwing things. Stones. Throwing stones."

Jack knew in his gut what was coming. But he didn't want to believe it. Nine years on the job, and he still couldn't believe what human beings were capable of.

"I heard screaming," Lexie said. "They were stoning her, this woman, and she was running and screaming, and I couldn't do anything, I couldn't stop them. I think I screamed, too, but of course it didn't do any good."

He couldn't imagine how it must have felt to stand there, helpless, fucking useless, knowing a woman was being murdered and powerless to prevent her death.

Oh, wait, yeah, he could.

"Did they hear you?" Jack asked. If Blaine knew she'd witnessed a cult killing, no wonder he wanted her back.

Lexie shook her head. "I don't think so. The window was nailed shut. And there was . . . other noise."

Jack could imagine that, too. Thuds. Sobbing. Screams. He swore, long and quietly.

"That's pretty much what I thought." Lexie tried to smile, but her eyes told the truth. She hadn't just been helpless and angry and frustrated.

She'd been terrified.

And she'd still had the guts, the brains, the sheer will to get away.

"Good thinking," Jack told her, and he wasn't talking about his burst of expletives.

"Well, it beat some of my other thoughts." She bent her mouth into another smile, no more successful than the first. "Like, how long could I make it without a trip to the bathroom, and were they going to kill me next."

Jack closed his eyes briefly. *Ah, Jesus, don't tell me that.*

He liked it better when she was holding out on him. Maybe that made him a fool, but at least then he didn't have to imagine her terror. He didn't have to think about what she might have suffered at their hands.

He didn't have to worry about Sally, still stuck inside the compound with her freaking nut-case husband and his band of throw-the-first-stone religious psychos.

Jack's blood ran cold. Forget the lies and his wounded ego. He had to get his sister out of there. Now.

"We'll go to the sheriff," he said. "You can tell him what you saw. Is the woman—Did you see the woman fall?"

Lexie nodded.

Shit. "Then there will be a body. He may not believe you, but he'll have to investigate. If—"

"Oh, he'll believe me," Lexie said.

Her trust, her sunny confidence, were almost too much for Jack to bear. Even though he knew now that her baby-doll innocence was only an act, even though she'd fooled and misled him, he couldn't stand the thought of letting her down. The way he'd let down Dora Boyle and her little girl. The way he'd let down his sister.

"I hate to be the one to break it to you, babe, but the real world doesn't always work that way. Even when you do everything by the book, cops still fail. Women still die."

Her smoky blue eyes were soft and troubled, but Lexie's voice was clear and sure.

"He'll believe me," she said, "because I took pictures. They're on the photo card."

LEXIE fretted by the wire rack jammed with dated brochures of local attractions—Tail of the Dragon thrill road, the Stecoah Valley cultural center—while Jack loomed over the hotel counter.

"Where the hell is everybody?" Jack muttered. "We need transportation."

"You can't rent a car without a credit card," Lexie said.

"I have a credit card."

She frowned. "But before you—"

"It doesn't matter now."

Now that he knew the Disciples were capable of murder, he didn't care about keeping his identity secret.

Everything had changed, Lexie thought, and not for the better.

Jack had changed. He'd closed down, closed off, gone into cop mode. She knew the signs. She recognized the posture. She'd seen it often enough in her father. Interview stance—head up, feet planted, gun side back, ready to take on the room. Or the world.

Her heart sank into her sandals. It wasn't that she objected to Jack's focus on getting her and her precious evidence into the hands of local law enforcement as quickly as possible. But honestly, the man had developed tunnel vision. He'd stopped really seeing her, Lexie.

He definitely wasn't listening to her.

And as long as he was doing his master-of-the-universe routine, she wasn't sure anymore how much she wanted to tell him.

He drummed his fingers on the counter. "Wait here. I'm going to find us a ride into town."

She should stop him. She could make him listen.

Maybe.

But it was much easier to go with the flow, as she'd always done.

"Okay," she said.

Anyway, Lexie rationalized as Jack banged through the screen door, now probably wasn't a good time to tell him everything. He was already freaked out about his sister. He hadn't even wanted to listen to Lexie's other fear, that Sally could have been among the women throwing stones.

They had argued about it as Lexie washed her face in their room's dinky sink, trying to make herself look like a reliable witness.

"I wouldn't recognize Sally if I saw her. I don't know if she's in those pictures."

"Babe, at this point you don't even know if you have pictures. They could have been damaged when we got dunked."

"No. A memory card isn't like film. As long as it dries out completely, you can retrieve the images."

"So what's the problem?"

"The *problem* is your *sister* could be an accessory to *murder*. I don't want to get her into trouble."

"She's already in trouble," Jack had replied grimly. "At least if she's locked up, that bastard she married can't kill her."

He was right. Of course he was right. But . . . "I still think you should look at them before we take them to the sheriff."

"Look at them where? Look at them how?"

"There's a Wal-Mart . . ." Lexie had suggested tentatively.

"That specializes in snuff shots?" Jack gave her a jeez-you-are-so-dumb look that silenced her more effectively than a slap. "I don't think so."

He was determined not to hear her. Which meant further confessions had to wait.

Lexie stood in front of the display rack, hugging her elbows and waiting for Jack to come back.

Maybe if she'd come clean with him from the very beginning . . . Yeah, like that would have worked.

Even if she had been able to trust him, once Jack knew who her father was, he would have realized Lexie's very identity posed a threat to his sister. If Trent Scott learned Lexie had been kidnapped, he'd come after the Disciples with everything he had.

And if Ray found out Jack had helped his prize hostage to escape . . . Lexie shuddered. Ray would go after Sally.

The door behind the counter opened. Lexie's heart moved into her throat. But it was only the sullen teenager with the spiked hair.

Adolescence was hell. Lexie remembered being trapped in a house that no longer felt like home with parents who seemed like strangers and a body that didn't feel like it belonged to her anymore. Poor kid. She smiled at him.

He didn't smile back, but he shuffled forward. "You want something?"

She shook her head. "I was just . . ." She gestured at the rack of once-glossy brochures, not sure what she was doing.

"Yeah, okay." He stood there, watching her.

Lexie tried not to fidget. She didn't feel threatened, for heaven's sake. He was just a boy, sixteen or seventeen, tops. But he was big, big and soft, and he was staring at her, breathing through his mouth.

"I could help you," he said.

She jumped. "What?"

His gaze met hers with unnerving intensity. "Those digital pictures you were talking about?"

Oh, dear. "What about them?"

"This computer has imaging software."

"Does it?"

His head bobbed. "I wanted to design a website for the Bo-Lo. So, you know, bikers from all over could find us. I can download pictures, adjust them, crop them. Lots of stuff."

"That was very—" Lexie caught herself. *Don't patronize him, he'll hate that.* "Wow," she said instead. "I bet that took a lot of time."

He shrugged. "You live around here, you got time. Unless you do fucking 4-H club or start a meth lab in your kitchen or something."

She laughed.

He smiled, shifting the bar in his lower lip. "So I've got, like, this universal memory card reader. You want, I could download your pictures for you."

Lexie was breathless with hope and doubt. "You would do that?"

His shoulders rounded even more. He ducked his chin to his chest. "Sure."

"That would be great." Lexie beamed at him. And then she realized the impossibility of enlisting a seventeen-year-old boy to develop the graphic photos of a woman's ritual murder. "Oh, but I couldn't let you."

"Well, the quality would be shit," he acknowledged. "I don't have the right kind of paper to print on. But I could do it."

"I'm sure you can," Lexie said gently. "It's just these are, um . . ."

Snuff shots, Jack mocked in her head.

"Private pictures," she said.

The kid's face flushed the color of an overripe tomato. "Yeah. Well. Whatever."

She had embarrassed him. He thought she and Jack had been snapping dirty pictures of each other. Lexie blushed, too. But his reaction gave her an idea.

"I want to give copies to my boyfriend," she said. "But I don't want him to see them unless they turned out. I mean, what if I look awful or something?"

The boy's Adam's apple moved as he swallowed. "I bet you look good."

"You're sweet." She smiled and stepped closer to the counter. She couldn't believe she was doing this, trying to take advantage of a sexually frustrated teenager. She couldn't believe it would work. "But I can't be sure, you know? Not unless I see them."

His gaze darted over her and away. "I could set it up for you. Like, the program? The office is pretty quiet right now. Private. You could look at your pictures, and nobody would see."

"Oh, that would be perfect," Lexie said.

As long as Jack didn't come back anytime soon.

The kid practically stumbled in his eagerness to get to the computer and show her how everything worked. Lexie sat in the chair as he reached around her, turning on the printer, fiddling with the mouse.

"All set," he announced. "You got the card?"

"Oh." Oh, dear. "I, um . . ."

He watched her expectantly, like a dog waiting for its walk. Lexie took a deep breath and dug inside the neckline of her T-shirt. His eyes widened.

Face hot, she handed him the picture card, still warm from her body.

He inserted it into the reader and cleared his throat. "So, uh, you click here—"

"Just a minute." She put her hand over his on the mouse. "Do you think I could . . . Would you mind if I looked at them alone?"

His mouth fell open. "Uh . . . No. I mean, yeah, sure, whatever you want."

"This is so great of you," Lexie said in her most encouraging smile-for-the-camera voice. "I really, really appreciate it."

"Sure." He straightened and stuck his hands in his jeans pockets. "No problem. I'll just, uh . . ."

"Maybe you could let me know if anyone comes in. While I'm printing the pictures."

And erasing them from the computer's hard drive, she thought but did not say.

"Yeah. Yeah, I can do that." He moved away to the other side of the counter.

Swiftly, Lexie clicked on the download button and got to work.

MAYBE he'd been a little hard on Lexie, Jack thought, his good humor partially restored by the keys in his hand.

After all, she'd been abducted and abused by Blaine, a man she thought she knew. No wonder she hadn't immediately put her trust in a total stranger.

He crunched across the drive to the motel office. Actually, she was pretty shrewd, playing him like that. It had pissed him off, but she'd had her reasons. Good reasons.

She'd come clean with him now, that was the important thing. And maybe tonight she'd decide to make it up to him.

Images of Lexie, naked and grateful, naked and contrite—naked and anything—improved his mood even more. Definitely, he'd been too hard on her. Jack grinned. So maybe *he* could make it up to *her.*

After he found a drugstore. He'd show her some guys could be trusted. Some men could be relied on.

The thought stopped him cold at the bottom of the office steps. He was not somebody any woman should rely on.

He'd told her that. He'd been straight with her, too. *What will the truth get me?*

And she'd answered him. *Me.*

He took the porch steps two at a time. "Okay, babe, we're good to—"

A shadow loomed behind the screen. A kid, a punk,

blown up with importance and testosterone. "You can't come in here."

The hell he couldn't. Lexie was in there. Alone.

Shit. He should never have left her here alone.

Jack yanked on the door, jerking it from the kid's grasp.

But the punk was brave or dumb enough to stand his ground. "I said—"

Jack moved, fast, throwing the kid back and against a wall, holding him still with the weight of his body, a forearm hard against his throat. "Lexie?"

"I'm here," she said shakily behind him. "I'm fine. It's all right. Let him go."

He glanced over his shoulder. She was standing behind the counter, clutching some sheets of paper to her chest. Her face was red. Her eyes were bright.

Safe. His head swam with relief. His arm loosened.

"What the fuck is going on?" he growled.

"He was helping me." Lexie came around the counter, eyes still bright and narrowed.

Not scared, Jack realized with a thump. Angry.

"I said, let him go."

Jack eased his weight from the punk kid, steadying him until he found his balance and his breath. "Helping you how?"

"He let me use the motel computer."

"To do what? Check your e-mail?"

Her round chin came up. "Download my pictures. So you could look at them before . . . So you could look at them."

Shit. When he thought Lexie was threatened, when he imagined her hurt, his brain shut down and he lost it. He'd lost control. Again.

Now the kid was goggle-eyed and scared and Lexie was looking at him like he was gum on the bathroom floor, something disgusting stuck to her shoe. A hole opened in his chest.

"Did he see them?" Jack asked, which wasn't what he meant to say, but he'd lost control of his mouth, too.

Lexie tightened her lips, in perfect control of her own mouth. "No."

Great. He'd assaulted a kid for no reason. He made sure the boy could stand on his own feet and then asked gruffly, "You okay?"

"We didn't *do* anything," the kid insisted.

Jack winced. "Yeah, I—"

"I never touched her."

Hello. Jack looked at Lexie for guidance, but she wouldn't meet his eyes. The color in her face deepened.

He was still missing something here. She was keeping something from him. Jack felt the muscles in his jaws and shoulders bunch with tension. But he wasn't going to over-react this time.

"Well, that's good," he said lamely. He jerked his head toward the door. "You ready to go?" he asked Lexie.

"Yes." She gathered up her papers and slipped the thin black picture card from a device hooked up to the computer. She wasn't leaving that evidence behind.

She approached the doorway. Jack held on to his curiosity and his temper as she stepped close to the kid and gazed up into his eyes.

"I don't even know your name," she said softly.

The kid swallowed, which had to hurt. Jack was pretty sure he'd bruised his windpipe. "Travis," he croaked.

Lexie smiled at him. "Thank you, Travis."

Shit. Why didn't she just offer to kiss him and make it better?

But Travis clearly was feeling better already. His chest puffed. "No problem." He shot Jack a hostile look, which Jack returned impassively. "You let me know if I can take care of anything else for you."

"I will," Lexie promised. "Thanks."

Jack waited until they were outside and down the steps

before he said, "Does that 'Rescue me, I'm blonde' routine work with everybody?"

Lexie's spine straightened. "I think so," she said. "It did with you, didn't it?"

Jack wanted to laugh. But it was true, wasn't it? Was it? How much did Lexie really trust him, and how much was she manipulating him?

"So, what's in these pictures?" he asked.

She sat on one of the picnic benches, holding the papers folded on her lap. The wind blew her bright hair around. She pushed it behind her ears, looking so fresh and pretty and earnest his chest hurt.

"They're not as clear as I hoped," she said. "I was too far away, and when I tried to enlarge the images, the pixels just broke down. But they're still pretty bad."

He stood over her, willing her to turn over the photos to him, wanting her to give him . . . Something. Everything.

"I've cleaned up an accident scene on a Saturday night involving six teenagers and a semi," he said. "Nothing can be worse than that."

Wordlessly, she handed over the pictures.

Jack looked at the first one and sucked in his breath. He was right. The images were no worse than some of the scenes he'd been called to. But she was right, too. They were bad.

Not graphic. Not gory. The picture quality was poor, and Jack had seen more blood in video games. What chilled him was the sheer ordinariness of the scene. The women clustered in the sunny yard could have been gathered on the church steps after Sunday service or watching their children play in a park. A few bent double, like old pictures of field workers picking cotton or planting potatoes. Most of them wore long, full skirts and triangular kerchiefs, like the Jewish women he sometimes saw walking their kids to school.

He tried to study faces. *The problem is your sister could*

be an accessory to murder. But the small, blurred images defeated him.

He thumbed through the printed half sheets, like a child's flip book, watching the composition of the crowd bunch and shift. Women stooped. Arms raised. *And the women started throwing things. Stones. Throwing stones. They were stoning her, this woman, and she was running and screaming . . .*

There. Almost hidden in the crowd, a white, frightened face, a blur of motion. Another shot, a crouching form, her arms braced over her head. More pictures of the circle tightening like a noose, cutting off, closing in.

Nine pictures in all.

The last showed an almost empty yard, a few desultory figures . . . and a woman sprawled in a puddle of blue skirt and red blood, her palm turned in silent appeal to the sky.

Jack stared at her long dark braid dragging in the dust of the yard and wanted to puke.

FOURTEEN

JACK looked like death.

Lexie's chest hollowed. "Do you recognize her? Your sister?"

"I haven't seen my sister in eight years," he said harshly. "What makes you think I would recognize her?"

He was answering a question with a question again. That couldn't be good.

"Well, what did she look like the last time you saw her?"

"Like an extra from *Oklahoma*. Like every other woman in these shots."

Oh, dear. "I know it must be hard to imagine your sister—"

"You don't know anything. And I'm not imagining anything."

"Jack?"

"My sister is a young white female with dark hair. The last time I saw her, she wore it in a long braid down the middle of her back. Just like the victim in your photograph."

Sympathy welled inside her. She risked a touch on his tensed forearm. "I'm so sorry."

He shook her off. "Don't be. This woman isn't Sally."

Confusion swamped her resentment. "But you said—"

"I thought she might be. But she's not. If you look at these two photos, you can see that even when the victim is crouching, she's tall. See how big she looks next to this woman, here? And how long her legs are, here? Sally was short. Shorter than you are. So I'm fine. I'm happy. Save your pity for somebody who needs it. Like the real victim and her family."

Lexie closed her mouth. She wasn't going to argue with him. Not now. Not after giving him those pictures.

That didn't mean she believed him.

But she believed he didn't want to accept his sister could be dead. Not on the basis of her hairstyle.

And he was right about one thing. All those women did look the same, especially through the not-particularly-powerful lens of her camera.

She looked at him, at his hard, impassive face; his tight, angry jaw; and his miserable eyes, and her heart turned over.

"What do you want to do?" she asked quietly.

His expression eased, just a little, around his mouth and the corners of his eyes. Refolding the printed sheets, he tucked them away inside his jacket. "Same as before. Go to the sheriff."

"All right, then," she said, accepting. "Did you get a car?"

"Something better."

He tugged her from the bench and started across the gravel, forgetting, apparently, he still held her hand.

She quickened her steps to keep pace with his long stride. "What's better than a . . ."

Oh, no. He couldn't be serious.

Lexie stared at the vehicle parked by the yellowed strip of grass. "It's a motorcycle."

"Yep," Jack said with satisfaction.

"Did you know a motorcyclist is sixteen times more likely to die in a crash than a person in a car?"

His mouth twitched. "Who told you that? Your mother?"

"My mother the doctor, yes. And three times more likely to—"

"You know, those statistics improve if you wear a helmet. Put this on." He fit a bright blue helmet over her hair.

"I feel like a bobble-head doll," she muttered. But she stood still while he fit the strap beneath her chin, his touch warm and light.

While he adjusted his own helmet, she faced the bike. The blue metal frame hovered above the wheels like a beetle's carapace.

"Why are the tires so narrow?"

"Because it's a dual-purpose bike. Touring and off-road," he explained when she looked at him blankly. "Vacation rental, babe. Get on."

It looked awfully unstable. "Will it even carry two people?"

Jack grinned and slung his leg over the vinyl seat, grabbing the upright handle bars. "It will if you hold on tight."

Straddling the engine, his helmet shadowing his eyes, he looked like every swaggering, macho hunk she'd ever turned down for a date, every bad-boy fantasy she'd never allowed herself to have, every risk she'd never allowed herself to take.

She'd wanted to break her pattern. She just hoped she didn't break anything else—an arm, her head, her heart— while she was at it.

Taking a deep breath, she got on the bike.

She had to clutch Jack's shoulders for balance while she found the pegs for her feet. He kicked the starter. The engine chugged and rumbled. Nervously, she shifted her grip to Jack's broad waist, and they lurched off in a roar and a stream of gas fumes.

He shouted something. She couldn't make out a word. The bike snarled and attacked the pavement. Her teeth chattered. Her seat vibrated. The wind drummed her helmet, chilled her arms, cut through her jeans. She hugged him tighter, for safety and for warmth, and closed her eyes as they took the first curve. The bike bucked, and she opened them hastily again.

The two-lane road swooped and twisted down, down, and occasionally up the mountain. Jack leaned into the turns. Gradually, Lexie got used to the feeling she was going to leave her stomach and assorted other body parts by the side of the road and started to enjoy the ride.

The hills cut down to the road on one side and fell away on the other in a tumble of weeds and rock. A battered silver guardrail clung to the edge, following the kinks and curls of the road.

And really, she thought, squinting through half-shut eyes at the rushing landscape, the scenery was beautiful. After hiking through the dark gorges of Nantahala, she welcomed the wide views of pale blue sky. The bare branches of the trees shrouded the peaks like smoke. Mist lay in the valleys. The green pines and slender white trunks stood against the winter brown woods like sentinels. Their stark beauty brought a lump to her throat.

A car approached them, well over the double yellow line in the middle of the road, and the lump in her throat choked off her scream.

Jack eased the bike over, hugging the white line, and the car flashed by with a flash of glass and a blare of its horn. Lexie buried her head against Jack's shoulder, grateful for his solid warmth to cling to.

Was that how she saw him? Was that all this was? An attraction sparked by danger and adrenaline on his side and instinct and fear on hers?

Oh, no. Really. No.

But the thought rattled in her brain like a stone thrown up by the bike's wheels.

All her life, she had struggled to stand on her own two feet. She'd resisted her mother's half-hearted efforts to protect her and rejected her father's more obvious attempts to control her. Even her job, Lexie realized, allowed her to choose her own projects and set her own schedule. And as for the men she dated . . . Nice guys, every one of them. Supportive. Evolved. Nonthreatening.

The bike thundered around another bend and whizzed down a straightaway. She was independent, Lexie told herself. Self-sufficient.

Sure she was.

As long as she was safe in her own environment.

But thrown—literally—into the wilderness, stripped of her usual comforts and defenses, maybe she'd reverted to some more primitive type.

Maybe she didn't want Jack at all. Maybe what she really craved was the security he represented. She could be responding to him out of some primordial instinct for survival, like a wolf bitch attaching herself to the nearest alpha male.

Lexie grimaced. Not a good image.

Sure, that hard-bodied, tough-minded confidence was attractive now. But once she reached safety and civilization, she might come to her senses and realize a divorced ex-cop with control issues didn't suit her temperament or her lifestyle. What then? Jack would go back to rescuing the rest of womankind and salvaging what was left of his career, and she could go back to . . .

Taking pictures of other people's weddings.

She squirmed on the narrow vinyl seat, cramped with the effort of keeping her balance on the bouncing, rattling bike. Somehow, the prospect of going back to her former life wasn't quite as appealing as it had been a few days ago. Like slipping on a favorite pair of shoes, shoes that looked great and matched everything in your wardrobe, and finding they didn't fit as well as they used to.

Okay, so maybe she was ready for a change.

Maybe she was, heaven help her, contemplating a no-frills relationship with man's man Jack Miller.

Leaving aside for a minute the thorny question of whether he was interested in pursuing a relationship with her (*from now on*—what did that mean?), there were still a bunch of things she didn't know about him.

And one very significant thing he didn't know about her.

She still hadn't told Jack who she was. Or rather, who her father was.

The engine throbbed as the bike topped another rise— blue sky, massed trees, and another life-threatening drop over nowhere—and started another twisty descent. She couldn't see the road ahead. All she could do was cling to Jack and hope he knew where they were going.

They passed a side road and then a couple houses snuggled against the side of a hill and finally a gas station. Telephone poles began appearing at regular intervals.

Jack reduced speed as the traffic increased around them. They must be close to town. Vacant lots and convenience stores gave way to clapboard houses and brick storefronts. White steepled churches sprang up at every intersection. At the biggest one, a three-story brick structure with a large white cross on top, Jack pulled to the curb and cut the engine.

"I thought we were going to the sheriff's department," Lexie said.

Jack took off his helmet. "This is the sheriff's department," he said dryly. "Also the county courthouse, the office of deeds, and the Bureau of Veterans Affairs."

"Oh." Gingerly, Lexie crawled off the bike. Her cheeks stung with wind and cold. Her legs wobbled. Her butt and her brain were both mercifully numb. She fumbled with her chin strap.

"Here." Jack pushed her fingers aside and dealt competently with her helmet.

And then he tipped up her chin and kissed her.

His mouth was hungry and hard. He kissed with heat and tongue and teeth, warming her from the inside out, making her want more. Want him. He fisted his hand in her short hair, holding her still for his kisses, and she forgot where they were and why he didn't belong in her life and kissed him back eagerly, straining on tiptoe to meet the demands of his urgent mouth.

When he let her go, his cheekbones were flushed, and she was shaking.

Lexie pressed the back of her hand to her swollen mouth. "What was that for?"

He hesitated briefly. "For luck."

Her gaze sought his. "How much luck do we need?"

"Let's find out," Jack said, and strode toward the courthouse doors.

ACTING Sheriff Will Tucker was having a bad day.

He was shorthanded. More shorthanded than usual. Billy Lewis was at the hospital with his wife having their first baby, and Dickerson was down with the flu, though Will suspected that was Dickerson's way of excusing his hangover.

An increase in traffic accidents along 129 had forced Will to step up patrols there, taking Bobby Greene out of the office just as a report came in of a busted window on a hunting cabin in Nantahala. Cal Carson radioed in about bleached soil and strong fumes from around a trailer in Scrub Hollow, which likely meant another member of the extended Tucker clan was manufacturing methamphetamines. Will wasn't looking forward to bringing in some second cousin once removed for questioning.

The last straw was a request from state patrol to remove a dead deer in the road by Carter Farm, as if the Triple A-with-a-badge boys had never shoveled road kill themselves.

No, Will thought, wishing he'd never quit smoking, the very last straw was the blonde and her bodyguard.

Since no one else was in to take her statement, he'd escorted them back to an interview room himself. He'd gotten her name—Alexandra Scott—which for some reason made the big guy stiffen. And then his, Jack Miller. Something familiar about that.

Will thanked them for coming in and offered them something to drink. "Water? Coffee?"

"No. Thank you," the little blonde added politely.

Her accent was soft, her voice refined as any officer's wife. Not a local, Will decided.

Miller, the big guy with a cop's eyes and a brawler's hands, shook his head.

"Sure?"

The blonde, the one who said she was carrying evidence of a crime, looked bewildered by his persistence.

Miller raised an eyebrow. "Not for me."

"Well, I could use a cup myself," Will said. "Would you folks excuse me a second?"

He closed the door to the interview room quietly behind him and walked down the hall to Debby Jenkins's station.

"Debby, look up a Jack Miller for me."

While the department assistant searched, Will poured himself a cup of sludge and added a slug of milk from the battered refrigerator. He eyed the resulting mud-colored beverage with distaste. The way his day was going, he might actually have to drink it.

He checked in with Debby and then walked back to the interview room, wishing he could dump his cup in the men's room as he passed.

"Thanks for your patience, folks."

They didn't look patient, Will thought. The blonde looked nervous. The brawler was tense. Well, that figured.

"So, what have you got for me?" he asked the blonde.

She started by handing him the pictures, which was a point in her favor. Of course, anybody could do anything with a computer these days, but she turned over a memory card, too, that she said contained the original digital images.

Frankly, without the photographs in front of him, Will wouldn't have known what to make of her story.

Even with the pictures, he didn't want to believe what he was seeing.

Right-wing extremist groups were nothing new in this part of North Carolina. The Klan and the White Racialists had held cookouts and cross-burnings in Polkville and Lenoir. A few years back, when the feds came hunting abortion bomber Eric Rudolph, some drunk with a shotgun and a grievance had fired on the FBI task force over in Andrews.

The Disciples, however, were neighbors. While the most militant lived and trained at the old Locke farm, they had plenty of sympathizers in the community. Locke's hate radio broadcasts had a local following. Occasionally the group's flyers found their way onto windshields in some church parking lot. But to Will's knowledge, in the seven years he'd been with the sheriff's department, the group hadn't actually killed anybody.

He looked again at the blurred print-out of the woman lying on the ground, her dark braid draggled with dust and blood, and felt his gut tighten like a fist.

Until, apparently, now.

If these photos weren't staged, if this witness was for real, he had a hell of a situation on his hands.

Too bad the picture quality sucked. No way could he identify individuals from these print-outs. Will sighed. Which meant the loss of another man and another day while one of his deputies hand carried the picture card to the state lab in Asheville.

"What were you doing at the compound when these pictures were taken, Ms. Scott?"

Her eyes slid to Miller. Seeking his guidance? Worried about his reaction? What kind of relationship did these two have, anyway?

Miller never moved. His gaze remained fixed on Will, flat. Unnerving.

The blonde's chin came up. "I was kidnapped."

Fuck, Will thought, startled.

"And that would be by . . . ?" he asked cautiously.

"By Ray Blaine."

Will didn't like Blaine. It was hard to warm to a man who believed you were one of the mud people. But he knew him—and the respect most folks around here had for him.

He didn't know Alexandra Scott at all.

"And how did you get away?" he asked.

"I escaped."

Will looked her over carefully. She didn't look like the kind of woman who busted out of a compound of mostly armed men. But he kept his face neutral and his questions to the point, taking her through her story again, this time with questions. As much as he wanted to dismiss her complaint, he couldn't ignore those photographs.

"That's very helpful," he said when they were through. "Thank you for coming forward."

Alexandra Scott moistened her lips. "Are you going to arrest him? Ray?"

"We're going to talk to him. Then we'll see what we have to do."

She sat up straight on the molded plastic chair that was all the county could provide. "But—"

"Mr. Miller, we have some papers for you," Will said. "You'll need to go with me before the magistrate."

Miller nodded.

"What papers?" The blonde asked anxiously. "What is he talking about?"

"Arrest papers," Miller said. "That's why he left the room before." His gaze met Will's. "What is it, an outstanding warrant for assault on a government official?"

"And misdemeanor larceny," Will said, grateful that at least he wasn't going to have to wade through a bunch of protests and explanations. The canoe had been found downstream and returned to the rental company, but those church kids had been pretty unhappy at having to hike to their pickup point.

He read the charges out loud. "I need to ask you to—"

Miller placed his big hands palms down in plain sight

on the table. "I'm a law enforcement officer. I have my duty weapon in a belt holster on the right side."

Well, that explained the eyes. And the ease with which Miller had accepted the charges against him.

The blonde, however, wasn't feeling nearly as understanding. "You can't arrest him. He hasn't done anything wrong. He was helping me."

"Yes, ma'am," Will said politely.

LEXIE watched in horror as the Jim Chee–looking officer patted Jack down and secured his wrists behind him.

"Aren't you going to do something?" she appealed.

Jack raised his eyebrows. "Yeah. I'm going to stand here very quietly so I don't upset the sheriff while he removes my property."

Which the sheriff proceeded to do: wallet, keys, cell phone, belt, change. He opened the wallet and started to count the money out on the table. "That's twenty, forty, sixty—"

"Don't bother," Jack interrupted. "Give it to her."

"I have to document—"

"I know what you have to do. I'll sign whatever you want. But give her the money."

A look passed between the two men.

The sheriff shrugged and opened the door to the interview room. "Debby, can you come back here, please?"

"I can't take your money," Lexie said to Jack.

"You have to, babe. I need you to hire a bondsman."

Oh, God.

"Okay." Don't panic, she could do this, she could take care of whatever she had to. "Um, how will I do that?"

"This is the court house. There's bound to be a bail agent within a block or two. After the magistrate sets bail, you pay the bondsman's fee out of what I give you, and he'll put up the cash to get me out."

She nodded to show she understood.

The sheriff smiled at her reassuringly. "I'll tell the magistrate your friend came in on his own. He'll set bail low. Bondsman'll cost you under a hundred."

"See? Easy," Jack said.

"Easy," Lexie echoed, trying to ignore the hollow feeling in the pit of her stomach.

But an hour later, she stood in front of the greasy counter of Gus's Guns, Bonds, Bait, and Tackle, arguing with Gus himself.

He smacked his hand down on the bond guarantee and tugged it away from her. "Listen, honey, he's from out of state, you've got no I.D., and I'm not losing three thousand dollars on a bad flight risk."

She hated confrontation. She did. But she was not letting Jack rot in jail because she was incapable of doing something as simple as co-signing a stupid piece of paper. "There must be something you can do."

Gus rubbed his whiskered face with the back of his hand. "My cousin's got a pawn shop down the street. You got any collateral you can put up?"

Lexie thought. Everything she owned was back in her apartment in Lovingston or had been stripped from her in the Disciples' compound. For one wild moment, she considered offering Gus the rented motorbike. But he'd probably demand I.D. for that, too.

She tried again. "If you can just loan me the money until tomorrow, I can have my mother fax a copy of my birth certificate."

Gus grinned, exposing yellow teeth. "That's real nice. Maybe she could send me some oatmeal cookies, too."

"You don't understand," Lexie said despairingly. "Jack has to get out tonight."

Gus's grin faded. His eyes hardened. "No, you don't understand, honeybunch. Your boyfriend's staying in jail."

FIFTEEN

JAIL was a new low in a year that already scraped bottom.

Jack rested his head against the cinderblock wall and closed his eyes, shutting out the stainless-steel toilet in the corner and the bars. Real bars. No wired glass and reinforced metal door in the sheriff's holding cells. The county never had any money to upgrade their small facilities, the deputy had explained when he escorted Jack back and locked him up.

Like Jack gave a shit what his prison looked like.

He'd known the risk in accompanying Lexie to the sheriff's office. Known, and done it anyway because there was a chance that the only way he could protect Sally now was by building the best possible case against the Disciples.

Unless, of course, the cult had the sheriff in their pocket. In which case, delivering Lexie to the sheriff would be sending her alone into a trap. Jack *had* to go with her.

But now . . . Shit. What the hell had he been thinking?

He hadn't been thinking. That was his problem. Had always been his problem.

Jack stood and paced the length of his cell. Eight feet, end to end. He might as well be six feet under. He wasn't doing a damn thing for Sally locked behind these bars.

And Lexie was alone in this godforsaken town, dealing with bail bondsmen, criminals, and rednecks with guns.

Where was she?

It didn't take that much time or money to secure a three-thousand-dollar bond. An hour, tops, to fill out the paperwork, and three hundred cash. He'd given her more than that.

Maybe she'd taken the money and skipped with it.

His jaw bunched. If she did, she wouldn't just be screwing him, but Sally, too.

But no. No, Lexie wouldn't do that. He might not know everything about her—Alexandra *Scott?*—but she had too much heart and grit to leave him.

Even if she should.

Jack paced to the bench and sat, hitting the back of his skull against the wall with enough force to snap his teeth together.

He'd screwed up. Again. First, by going after that kid who was only trying to help, and then by getting himself arrested when Lexie was in town and vulnerable.

Talk about a fuckup.

She didn't need him. She deserved better than him. Even that Sheriff Andy wannabe, Tucker, was more use to her now than he was. Hell, even the computer geek teenager had been more help.

Jack thumped his head against the cinderblock. The best thing he could do for all of them was to separate, physically and emotionally. Let Lexie get on with her regular life while he tried to sort out this mess with his sister. Yeah. That's exactly what he had to do.

As soon as he got out of here, he was sending her home.

As soon as he got out.

He stood and stalked to the bars. Where the hell was she?

"YOU'RE free to go." Sheriff Tucker unlocked the door to Jack's cell, looking him over critically. "Your girlfriend paid your bail."

Jack set his jaw. Call him macho, call him stupid, but he refused to let the other man see how much he hated not being in charge. Being locked up in someone else's house, dependent on a five-foot-four blonde for his freedom.

"Took her long enough," he growled.

Tucker stepped back from the cell and gestured for Jack to proceed him down the hall. "It's not easy to come up with three thousand cash."

Jack pivoted. "What are you talking about? A surety bond should only have cost three hundred."

"She couldn't get a surety bond," Tucker said, opening the door to his office. "So she paid the full amount. Cash."

"How did she—"

"Why don't you ask her?" The sheriff pushed a fat manila envelope across his desk. "*After* you thank her."

Jack picked up the envelope, his mind whirling, and did a quick check of the contents. Wallet, keys, cell phone . . .

"Gun?" he asked.

Tucker shook his head. "Not until your case is disposed of."

"How about a professional courtesy?" Jack suggested.

"I can smile when I say no," Tucker said. He slid more papers across the desk. "Your agreement to appear in court. Sign."

Jack read, signed, threaded his belt through the loops in his jeans, and pocketed his change. Tucker escorted him past the dispatch desk.

"Y'all come back now, hear?" one of the deputies called, and somebody laughed.

The tension flowed from Jack's jaw across his shoulders, along his arms, down his spine. His fists clenched. He wanted to hit something.

But he didn't. He walked. He walked all the way to the lobby, and when he got there, Lexie was waiting.

She jumped up when she saw him, glad and anxious. "Jack!"

Relief knifed his chest. She was here. She was safe. She was happy to see him.

She was amazing, and she looked great with her soft, bright curls and soft, bright smile.

He had to get rid of her.

He walked by her as if they'd never met, across the lobby, through the doors, and up the stairs to the street. He stood on the curb with his hands clenched in his pockets and his face lifted to the sky, taking great gulps of clean air. The cold bit through his jacket.

"Jack?" she asked behind him.

The knife twisted. He was being a dick, and he knew it. He didn't look at her. He couldn't.

"You got money?" he asked.

"You know I have money," Lexie said, her voice still bewildered but stronger. Less hesitant.

"Good." He stepped off the curb and strode toward the motorbike. "Let me know where I can drop you. It's time for you to get home and me to get to work."

"You are *such* a jerk," Lexie said, not hesitantly at all, and her unexpected spirit nearly made him grin. "I just got you out of jail. The least you can do is buy me dinner."

"I'm broke, remember?"

"Well, I'm not. So I guess I'll buy you dinner."

He glared down at her. "Yeah, how did you get—"

"Over dinner," she insisted. She smiled at him, and something tore open in his chest. "My treat."

He could still say no, he thought desperately, gazing down at her hopeful, determined face. He should say no and send her on her way.

Yeah, and then he could find and kick a litter of puppies.

"Dinner would be great." He cleared his throat. "Thanks."

BROTHERS' Bar-B-Cue was half a block down and across the street from the courthouse. A red-lettered sign and a handful of trucks decorated the outside. The inside featured a long, smoky bar, a couple pool tables, and a stage behind chicken wire. This early on a Thursday night, the band wasn't playing. Judging from the chicken wire, Jack figured that was a good thing. His control was tenuous enough. And there wasn't a judge alive who would look sympathetically on a man fresh out of jail who took on a bunch of locals in a bar fight.

Lexie's voice, bright as a candle in the darkness, burned in his memory. *So, what do you do to blow off steam?*

Oh, baby.

Their young waitress had a tattoo of a butterfly on her arm and a rose twining up from her low-rise jeans. She settled them in a booth at the back and took their drink orders.

"Whatever's on tap is fine," Jack said.

"A glass of Chablis, please," Lexie said with a smile.

He considered warning her about the house wine in places like this and then shrugged. If she was determined to live dangerously, there wasn't a hell of a lot he could do to stop her.

Except send her home.

And he would. After dinner.

The waitress handed them long, laminated menus and went to fetch their drinks. Jack watched the rose tattoo riding her waistband and felt nothing more than basic male appreciation, which would have worried him if he wasn't getting rid of Lexie. Soon.

She shifted along the bench, and for the first time, he noticed she had bags with her, white plastic shopping bags.

He raised his eyebrows. "You do some shopping this afternoon?"

"Just a little. Do you want the onion rings or the hush-puppies to start with?"

"Rings," Jack said. "You went shopping while I was in jail?"

"Before. While I was waiting for the magistrate to set bail." She continued to study the menu, the tip of her tongue caught between her teeth. "What's Brunswick stew?"

"How the hell should I know? Get the ribs."

"Okay."

"Where'd you get the money?"

She blinked at him. "You gave it to me."

The waitress came back and set their drinks on the table with a smile just for Jack. "Y'all ready to order?"

"Onion rings, ribs, a side salad with blue cheese dressing and . . ." Lexie looked expectantly at Jack.

She was taking charge. That, or making her claim on him clear to Miss Rose. Either way, Jack wasn't sure if he was amused or offended.

"Two orders of ribs," he said. "And fries."

"You got it." The waitress collected their menus and sashayed away.

Jack waited until she was out of earshot before he said, "Not that money. The money to get me out."

"Oh. Well, I couldn't co-sign the bail agreement. All the bail agents wanted someone with a regular job who either rents or owns a home in the area, and I can't even prove who I am." Lexie sipped her wine and made a face. "But when I was walking, you know, trying different places, I saw my bank—a branch of my bank—down the street. So I went in there and said, 'Rescue me, I'm blonde.'"

Jack narrowed his eyes, ignoring her sly appropriation of his earlier gibe. "And they just let you have the money."

"Not exactly. But I explained this was an emergency, and the branch manager here called the account manager at my bank, and she got on the phone with me so she could be sure I was who I said I was, and then she authorized a withdrawal of funds."

"The bank will do that? It's legal?"

"Well, they won't do it unless they have a personal relationship with you. If they make a mistake, then the funds are debited against the account manager's own account. But she's authorized to do it, yes."

Jack took a long pull of his beer. "A personal relationship," he repeated slowly. "What does that mean?"

"Just that I'm in there a lot." Lexie's face brightened. "Oh, look, here comes our food."

The sharp aroma of the ribs and the rich, greasy smell of the fries reminded Jack he was starving. But he couldn't let it go.

"So, if I'm Joe Construction Worker, and I go in every Friday to cash my paycheck, your bank would hand over three thousand dollars, sight unseen, because of our 'personal relationship.'"

Lexie nibbled on a rib bone. "Maybe."

Jack waited.

"Okay, probably not," she admitted. "You need to have an account with them."

"I bet you do."

He couldn't believe it took him this long to fit the pieces together: her educated accent, her careful manners, her dissembling of her name.

Her kidnapping.

He must have been blind. Or thinking with his dick.

Of course, "Scott" wasn't as recognizable as "Vanderbilt" or "Kennedy," but maybe Daddy was sitting on a fortune in toilet paper.

"How much?" Jack asked grimly.

"Excuse me?"

"How much in the account?"

He couldn't be sure in the dim light of the booth, but he thought she blushed. "Not a lot. Contract photography doesn't pay as well as whatever you're thinking."

So she was independent, or trying to be. He respected that. But maybe Blaine hadn't.

"What about your parents?" Jack asked. "Do they have a personal relationship with the bank, too?"

Lexie jabbed her fork into a piece of lettuce, her eyes on her salad. "I don't know what you mean. They bank at a different branch than I do."

"But the same bank, right?"

"Yes. So what?"

"So I think you should go home." Home to safety and comfort and her parents and her parents' money. Home to be taken care of the way he could never take care of her.

Jack ripped the meat off a bone. Good thing he'd never wanted to be her white knight. Princess here wouldn't need him to rescue her for much longer. Not if "home" was a freaking castle.

"Why?" Lexie asked.

"Because you belong there. Away from Blaine."

"Away from you?"

"Hell, yes." But saying so made him feel odd inside. Empty. He picked up his beer.

She met his eyes squarely across the table. "I'm not going anywhere. I have an investment here."

"No, you don't." He held her gaze deliberately. "We've known each other less than a week."

"Excuse me, I just paid three thousand dollars to get you out of jail. I call that an investment."

She was making it damn hard for him to do the right thing. He wanted to kiss her. Or strangle her. He took a long swig of beer instead and set it on the table. "I'll send you a check."

"Do that. In the meantime, I'm staying."

His jaw set. "Not with me."

"You're right," she said, a snap to her voice. "Because of course I'll be so much safer staying alone in a strange place in a strange town where anyone I meet could have ties with the man who kidnapped me in the first place."

Shit. She'd tripped him up as neatly as a DA in cross-examination.

He eyed her with frustrated admiration. "You're a real pain in the ass, you know that?"

She relaxed a little, smiling at him as she sipped her wine. "You've said that before."

"Did I thank you before?"

She cocked her pretty head to one side. "For dinner? I believe you did."

"How about for bailing me out?"

She set down her glass. "I don't want you to thank me. I want you to tell me this is about more than you're under stress and I'm convenient."

It was more. At least on his side, it was a lot more. But he had no reason—he had no *right*—to tie her up by telling her so.

"Babe . . ."

Her chin firmed. "You're no good at forever? Fine. But I want to know that when all this is over you'll look me up and ask me out. I deserve that much," she said.

He was shaken to the heart. "You deserve more than that."

"Who are you to decide what I deserve?" God, she was on a tear now. "Who are you to tell me what I need? I'm telling you what I want. Are you going to give it to me?"

The blood rush from his head to his groin was enough to make him dizzy. He had to think. He had to stay in control. He had to . . .

She watched him, heat in her eyes and challenge in the tilt of her chin. She was everything he'd ever wanted.

He was toast.

"I'll give you anything you ask for," he promised hoarsely.

"Good." Lexie beamed and wiped her fingers on her napkin. "Let's go back to the motel."

Jack wrestled his lust, which had grown teeth and was gnawing holes in his self-control. He was not going to let his desire to get her naked and horizontal—*Lexie naked, another rush*—blind him to his need to keep her safe.

"There are a couple things we should get straight first."

Like, first thing in the morning, he was putting her on the next available train or bus out of here. Out of danger, away from temptation, and back to her regularly scheduled life.

Lexie's smile broadened as she held up the shopping bag from the seat beside her. "I know. I bought condoms."

Totally toast. Seared. Scorched. Burnt to a cinder.

Before Lexie could pay, he slapped his credit card on the table—the sheriff already knew where to find him— and signaled the waitress. As soon as he'd signed for the meal, he hustled Lexie from the restaurant.

W HAT was she thinking?

Lexie stood just inside the motel room door, shaking with cold and nerves. Roaring through the darkness with a freezing wind buffeting the motorbike on every scary curve had provided her with plenty of time for second thoughts. Even third thoughts.

What was she doing?

She'd practically demanded that Jack bring her back here and make love to her. As if that could close the gulf between them, a gap created on his side by the things she had told him and on hers by her one big, fat, glaring . . .

Lie was too harsh a word, she decided.

. . . omission.

The latch clicked behind her, and the chasm widened at her feet.

Jack came up behind her and turned her in his arms. The cold clung to his jacket and his hair, but his mouth was hot. His hands were urgent. He smelled male, like engine grease and mountain air, and despite her second—and third—thoughts, she felt a clutch of desire in her stomach. And his erection, hard against the curve of her belly.

She returned his kisses, letting her hands re-learn the shape of his shoulders, letting her mouth be warmed and persuaded by his. But when his thigh nudged between hers, when his palm skimmed her ribs to close over her breast, she felt the situation spinning away from her and took a step back, literally, from the edge.

"Obviously, the ride didn't chill your mood," she said.

"Nope." He grinned down at her. "It's the man/motor connection. Comes with the Y chromosome."

She arched her eyebrows. "So, it's not the vibration?"

"Not really." Jack slid his hands to her hips, pulling her back against his body.

She cleared her throat. "Or me?"

He frowned. "What is this, a quiz?"

"It's a question," she said coolly, while her heart hammered in her chest. "Is this because of me, or under these circumstances, would any woman do?"

"It's you. Christ." His hands left her butt. "You think I *want* a woman right now?"

She glanced at the evidence pressing against his zipper. "It's pretty obvious what you want."

He gave a short laugh. "Not to me. I don't want—I don't need—this kind of aggravation. This kind of distraction. You're complicating things, babe, and I like them simple."

She winced. That was the problem with asking questions. You were stuck with the answers.

Jack swore. "See, that's what I mean. Half the time I don't know what you're thinking or how you're feeling or what the hell you want. And if you were anybody else, if you were any other woman, I wouldn't fucking care."

Her breath stopped. So he . . . did care?

He paced a few steps and turned to glare at her. Her nerves jittered at the look in his eyes, hot and amused, exasperated and . . . something else.

"I'm dying to get inside you," he said tightly. "All the way inside, as hard, as deep, as often as I can. But it's your call, babe. Your choice."

A shiver ran through her at his words. Her mouth went dry with desire and a dizzying sense of her own power.

Her call. Her choice. *She* was in control.

She tested the idea, intimidated and intrigued. With the power of choice came the possibility of mistakes. Could she live with the consequences if she took Jack as her lover?

Could she live with the regret if she didn't?

Lexie licked her lips. Jack watched the tiny movement, his big body rigid as stone. He had accused her once of being afraid to take responsibility. Was she still waiting for him to make his move?

Or was she ready at last to make hers?

"What do you want from me, Lexie?" he asked harshly.

She wanted him. Wanted him inside her, as hard, as deep, as often as possible. Tonight. Next week.

Forever.

The thought caused another hitch of doubt and excitement.

No thinking, Lexie ordered herself. Thinking was for wusses. From now on—well, at least for tonight—she was a woman of action.

"I want this," she said, and stood on tiptoe to kiss him.

His mouth was hot. Hungry. Welcoming. When she finished, Jack was breathing as hard as if he'd carried her a mile, but he didn't grab her. Didn't touch her. His arms stayed down by his sides.

Encouraged, emboldened, Lexie reached for the top button of his shirt. "And this."

She slipped the button from its hole, and then the next one, and the next, gradually exposing his broad, muscled chest. He was hairy, which should have been a turnoff. She'd never gone for hairy men, but she kept thinking—*No thinking*—she kept remembering how he had looked last night in the shower, how he had felt against her, full and hot, the slide of his skin, the tickle of body hair.

"I want everything," she whispered, and her hand slithered down his belly and cupped him through his jeans.

THE rush of pleasure blew Jack's mind.

It wasn't just the pressure of Lexie's hand, rubbing him through his jeans.

The idea that she wanted him enough to get aggressive, to make a grab for him, was a big turn-on. So was the way she looked, soft lips parted, smoky eyes dark with concentration.

Not that he needed to be any more turned on. He'd been a walking hard-on for days.

He bent to kiss her, but she was already rising on tiptoe to taste him, one arm around his neck and her hand busy between his legs. He took her mouth hard, and she hummed with pleasure, fumbling with his zipper.

Heat collected in his balls. Too much. Too fast.

He was thirty-five, for God's sake, not nineteen. After days of frustration, of delayed gratification, he had enough control left to slow things down. To draw things out. To make this good for her.

Yeah, before he sent her away, he could fuck her blind and make sure she really missed him.

He started to caress her breast, but she had already yanked down his zipper. Her cool fingers burrowed beneath the waistband of his briefs and seized her prize.

His vision blurred. His control slipped. His blood pressure threatened to blow off the top of his head.

"Lexie, babe, what are you trying to do?"

She looked up, her face flushed, her teeth worrying her soft lower lip. "I'm trying to get naked with you."

Right. He forced his brain to function. That would work. Naked first; slow, deep, full-penetration sex afterward.

Jack helped, shucking his boots and pants, losing his shirt and socks, reaching for her.

Lexie drew back and smiled into his eyes. "You can watch."

He sucked in his breath. It was like some fantasy come true. She was his fantasy, round and pink, shy and smiling, bold and irresistible.

And she wanted him.

Wanted this.

So he stood, every muscle rigid and aching with the effort of control, and watched her wriggle free of her jeans in front of him. It was amazingly awkward. And arousing. He needed her naked. He needed her now. Did she know? Could she tell what looking at her did to him?

Maybe so, because she was still smiling, reckless and a little smug, as she hooked her thumbs in her panties and shimmied them down her legs.

It was that smile that did it, that freed him from the bounds of patience and control. He lunged for her, swept her up and onto the bed, landing heavily on top of her, between her legs, feeling her along the length of him, beating in his blood, engulfing his senses. Her taste. Her smell. Her skin, smooth, sliding against his.

"Condom," he choked out.

"In the bag."

He dived and dug for it while her breasts rubbed his back. Her hands streaked over him, sneaky and irresistible. His brain screamed at him, *Hurry, hurry, hurry.* His hands trembled.

He covered himself, rolled over, and shoved her back. Her eyes were glazed, her lips curved. He wanted to savor, wanted to linger, wanted to . . . *Hurry.* His hands sought and gripped hers. Lacing their fingers together, he thrust home and groaned.

Her body bowed, braced, under his, and she made a sound deep in her throat. Of pleasure? Or pain? Their eyes locked. Jack froze, his breathing labored, his muscles straining, his heart pounding out of his chest.

Too much? Too fast?

"Too rough?" he asked.

Her small hands pushed hard at his shoulders. Cursing himself, Jack rolled to his back.

But she followed him, straddled him, her thighs on either side of his, her wet sex brushing his.

Too much, he thought, drawing desperately on the tattered edges of his control. *Too fast.* They had to slow down. He had to—

She bent and nipped his lower lip, and he exploded, surging off the mattress and into her, all the way into her, as deep, as hard, as close as he could get. She surrounded him in smooth, wet heat and rode him. Milked him. Destroyed him.

Violent with need, he squeezed her breasts and heard her gasp, gripped her hips and felt her come, felt her cling and convulse, felt her shake apart and shatter in his arms as he thrust into her, slammed into her, pounded into her, again and again. He was relentless as he drove to his satisfaction. Brutal as he demanded hers. Her head dropped forward onto his chest. Turning his face into her hair, he felt the shock that rocked her explode his world and bury him.

SIXTEEN

DEPUTY Bobby Greene leaned back in his chair, his boots propped on his desk. "You're going to the compound yourself?"

Will Tucker retrieved his service pistol from the gun locker and strapped it on. "Why not?" he asked, although he knew why. They both did. The Disciples didn't take kindly to any official presence on their land. A nonwhite acting sheriff would be even less welcome.

"We're shorthanded until Lewis gets back," he continued. "And I'm sheriff, whether they like it or not."

"You go in there alone, you won't be sheriff much longer," Bobby said. "Send Dickerson."

Will selected a shotgun. "Dickerson's in Asheville. I told him I wanted enhancements of those photographs today."

Photographs that still haunted him.

"You have a better chance of getting a warrant if you wait till he gets back."

"I don't need a warrant to drop by. What if the victim's not dead? She could need help. Medical care."

"She sure looked dead in those photos. And there's not

a soul in that compound who's going to own up to murder."

Will tamped down his anger and secured the locker. "You saying I shouldn't ask questions?"

"I'm saying you're not going to like the answers you get today."

"At least I could find out who she is. It's a start."

"It's a risk."

Will shrugged. He wasn't sheriff for the glory of it or the lousy thirty-five thousand a year. He took his charge to preserve the peace and protect the county seriously. However risky it was—physically, politically—he wasn't sitting idle while a woman was murdered on his watch.

Bobby swung his feet down from his desk. "I'll go with you."

Will considered. Dorset County wasn't New York City, or even Charlotte. His department handled fewer homicides all last year than most big-city police departments saw in a day. But there were enough guns at the compound that things could get out of hand fast. He needed somebody to ride shotgun today. But Bobby? The deputy was ambitious enough to be a pain in the ass and young enough to think he would live forever.

"Be awkward for you," Will said. "You've got friends in there."

Bobby's grin flashed. "So, I'll keep things friendly. Don't worry, Chief, I've got your back."

Will looked at him sharply. "That's what I'm worried about. Remember whose team you're playing on."

Bobby flushed, but his smile stayed in place. "I know what color uniform I'm wearing."

Will nodded. "Good enough."

LEXIE hummed in the shower. Well, why not? Didn't she have everything a woman needed to be happy? Clean underwear, the right brand of moisturizer, and a man in the next room who made her feel . . . Her lips curved as she recognized the tune she was humming. Like a natural woman.

She felt powerful. Sexy. Strong enough to seduce Jack from his awesome control and survive—no, revel—in the consequences.

She stretched to soap her hair and winced. Okay, so this morning she was a little sore. She had a few kinks to work out. Not only in her muscles, but in her approach. She needed to tell Jack who she was. And then they had to figure out what they were going to do to help his sister.

But Lexie was confident now they could tackle their problems like equal, rational, cooperative adults. Together.

She tipped her chin, letting the hot water pulse against her scalp. And really, after Jack got over his initial irritation at her lack of candor, he'd see how much she could help. She'd bailed him out, hadn't she? That proved she could contribute. She had money now. She had connections.

Connections that could provoke a deadly standoff between federal forces and the militia inside the compound. Lexie shut off the water, some of her optimism dissipating with the steam.

Sound rumbled from the other room. Jack's voice. He must be awake, then. On the phone?

The thought of him, the memory of the night just past, made her insides soften and contract. She felt him in every twinging, aching muscle, along every plucked and shattered nerve. It was as if he had imprinted himself on her, pressed himself inside her so deep and hard and often she carried his mark in her womb and her bones. *One flesh,* she thought, and shivered.

She wrapped a towel tightly around her, under her bare arms, over her peaked breasts. She was hardly dressed for a serious discussion. On the other hand . . . Lexie's gaze stole to the mirror. Her reflection peered back at her from the foggy glass, bright-eyed. Smug.

Last night, she'd held her own naked.

Her heart quickening, she padded into the bedroom.

Jack sat on the edge of the bed, fully dressed, his weight depressing the mattress, the phone cradled in his big hand. Just the sight of him, solid and strong, the rough shadow of his jaw contrasting with the tender line of bare skin at the back of his neck, made that surge go through her again like electricity, flooding her with power, making her glow from the inside.

He saw her and hung up the phone. "There's a Greyhound station in Asheville with buses to Charlotte. You can transfer almost anywhere from there."

She felt as if a light had been cut off. A hollow opened in her chest. "What are you talking about?"

"The bus schedules," he explained. "So you can go home."

Her toes curled into the cold carpet. She crossed her arms over her breasts, holding in her hurt and panic, holding on to her light tone. "You know, even Britney Spears had a longer honeymoon than this."

His mouth quirked, but his eyes were watchful. Wary. "I'll call you," he said, which was what guys always said the morning after on their way out the door.

And even though she had told him that would be enough—*I want to know that when all this is over you'll look me up and ask me out*—the words formed a hard little lump under her breastbone.

"When?" she demanded.

"What?"

"When are you going to call me? So I can be waiting by the phone. Knitting," she added, in case he didn't get the point. "Or maybe I should bake cookies."

"Baking cookies would be good." Jack left the bed and prowled toward her. "Especially if you were wearing one of those frilly apron things and nothing else."

She refused to smile. Taking a step back, she lifted her chin. "I'm serious."

He raised a hand to the edge of the towel, tracing the

swell of her breasts with the backs of his fingers. Her breath came short.

"So am I," he said, his voice deep. "I don't want anything to happen to you."

Her knees wobbled. Her resolution faltered. It would be so easy to lean her head on his broad chest, to bask in his concern, to go along with whatever he wanted. But she was not going to let Jack banish her to the margins of his life. He was too important.

"Too late," she said. "If we're going to be involved—"

He tugged on the ends of the towel. "We are involved."

She swayed toward him. Oh, my. Oh, yes.

Oh, no. She was not letting him placate her with sex.

"Don't change the subject."

He grinned, and the glow started again, in the soles of her feet, in the pit of her stomach. Jack Miller in a playful mood was even harder to resist than Jack Miller, Macho Warrior.

"I'm not changing the subject." He kissed her shoulder as his hands loosened the towel. "I'm proving how involved—"

His breath hissed in. His face changed, hardened, as he stared at her body. "Did I do that?"

Lexie blinked. "Do what?"

"Did I hurt—" He bit the words between his teeth. "Did I *mark* you?"

"Oh." She looked down. A faint shadow the length of his thumb smudged the curve of her breast. A string of red marks—his fingerprints—lay along her hip like an exotic belt. She'd noticed them in the shower. "I guess."

She glanced again at his face and tried to close the towel. "It's fine."

"It is not fine. I was rough with you." His voice was viciously controlled, his eyes blank. "I apologize."

Uh-oh.

She sighed. "We're going to have to talk about this, aren't we?"

"There's nothing to talk about. I lost control. I shouldn't have. End of story."

She'd heard this before. He'd said this before. *You should know the job is all about control. Being in control. Staying in control of yourself and the situation. And I lost it. I lost control.*

"Obviously not," Lexie said. "Since it's still bothering you. Do you want to tell me why?"

He shot her an incredulous look.

She swallowed. "Okay, you don't want to. Does this have anything to do with"—*the suspect you beat up in custody? Can't say that, do not say that*—"your suspension?"

"We are not discussing this," Jack said, his face like stone. "We don't have time. You have a bus to catch."

She didn't do confrontation, Lexie reminded herself. She didn't like to argue.

Uh huh. And look where that had gotten her.

"I am not running away," she said. "Why are you?"

WHEN the summons came, Sally wanted to run. Which was stupid, because she couldn't manage much more than a hobble, she didn't have anyplace to go, and she would never leave Isaac behind anyway.

She'd been expecting—dreading—the call to Daniel's office since the black-and-tan sheriff's car first pulled to the gates of the compound. Daniel was always unhappy when outsiders took an interest in the affairs of the community. And if Daniel was unhappy, Ray would be furious.

Fuck Ray, cried the rebellious girl inside her, the teenager who used to fight with her father and sneak out at night.

We did, Sally said wearily, to shut her up. *And look where that got us.*

Sally adjusted her kerchief and ran her hands down her skirts, but there was nothing she could do to put her face in order. Her bruises were fading, purple to yellow and green, but her right eye and jaw were still swollen, and the split on her lip should have had stitches. When Isaac had seen her face, his own face had crumpled, just for an instant, before he re-formed it the way his father had taught him, into a carved saint's face, a wooden replica of a boy.

She hadn't cried when Ray hit her, but the change in her son's face made her want to weep.

When Sally reached Daniel's office, she was surprised to see two sheriff's uniforms waiting with the Disciple leader and her husband. Why would Ray admonish her with deputies present? She shrank in the doorway, ashamed to show her face. What did they want?

She recognized the sheriff from her visits to town, a big, quiet man with black eyes like a Labrador. Kind, black eyes. The smaller man, with the easy smile and the bristling brown mustache, she'd never seen before.

But he knew Ray. That was clear from the way they talked together, shoulders almost touching, heads thrust forward in obvious communion.

Years ago, when Ray first hit her, she used to threaten she would go to the police. He'd shaken his head over her stupidity. *"The head of the woman is the man,"* Sarah. *Even the godless know that. The police won't interfere between a man and his wife.*

She guessed he was right.

Swallowing nausea, she waited in the doorway, her hands twisting in her skirt.

The sheriff stood apart from the others the way she remembered her brother standing sometimes, feet planted, one side back. Her legs trembled. Was he here because of Jack? Had her brother gone to the sheriff when she had failed to meet him?

She felt briefly less alone. She just hoped his concern wouldn't get her killed.

Daniel sat in the big leather chair, his long, pale fingers steepled over his desk. Sally didn't think he saw her, but all of a sudden he interrupted them, Ray and the deputy, saying, "Here she is now."

They all turned to look at her.

Sally cringed inside.

"Mrs. Blaine?" The sheriff's dark eyes were unreadable.

Her heart thumped. He'd bought her an ice-cream cone once, did he remember that? Isaac had begged for one from the stand on the corner, and she didn't have any money. None of the Disciples' women carried money when they went into town. All their purchases had to be approved by the brother who accompanied them. But it was so hot that day, and it seemed like such a small transgression, an ice cream for a child, that she had given in to Isaac's longing eyes and the sheriff's persuasion. She had been embarrassed when he'd brought her one, too. Embarrassed and guilty and joyful, eating an ice cream in the sunshine with her son.

Of course he wouldn't remember.

Or if he did, he wouldn't connect that happy woman with the way she looked now, her face bruised and swollen.

Sally ducked her head, hoping he wouldn't recognize her. Her husband would approve of her modesty. He wouldn't understand her shame. "Yes?"

"Could I speak to you alone a minute?" The sheriff's voice was quiet. Polite. She remembered that about him, too.

Panic clogged her throat. Was he going to ask her about Jack, about meeting Jack? Or about the blond woman, the one who ran away? What should she say? What could she say?

"Not alone," Ray said.

"It's against our teachings for a married woman to go apart with a man not her husband," Daniel explained smoothly.

"Mrs. Blaine?" the sheriff asked again, still quiet, still respectful.

But she had her answer from her husband.

"It's against our teachings," she mumbled, her gaze on the floor.

"There's not a problem if we talk to her, though, right?" the younger deputy asked. "With Ray here? Is that okay, Ray?"

"I don't see why it's necessary," Ray said stiffly.

Sally knew that tone of voice and quailed.

But either the deputy didn't know, or he was less intimidated. "But it's okay, right?"

Sally watched from the corner of her eye as Ray threw up his hands, like a reasonable man forced to deal with fools. She could have told them, the black-eyed sheriff and the smiling young deputy, that you didn't want to mess with Ray when he got this way, you better not argue.

But they didn't know, and she was afraid to say anything that might make things worse.

The sheriff—what was his name? Fear was making her stupid, she couldn't remember—came toward her. "I have some photos here, Mrs. Blaine. I'd like you to look at them for me, please, and identify the woman in the picture if you can."

Bewildered, obedient, Sarah glanced at the first fuzzy image and gaped. These were pictures of the stoning. Of Tracy.

Her stomach cramped. Whatever she was expecting, it wasn't this. She looked to Ray for guidance.

But it was Daniel who spoke. "Is this really necessary? You asked to see the woman in the photographs. Here she is. You can see for yourself she's fine."

Sarah blinked.

"Actually, she doesn't look so good," the deputy said.

"But her injuries are consistent with the ones in the photographs," Daniel said. "That's Sarah Blaine."

But it isn't, Sally thought, looking at the pictures. It was Tracy, with her harmless, foolish giggle and her pretty, silly face . . . Her face, Sally realized numbly. In the photographs, Tracy's face was battered. Blurred.

"We still need to speak with her," the sheriff said.

"You're wasting your time," Ray said. Her husband's face was white. His eyes shone with suppressed emotion. "We don't need or want your interference."

"Hey, Ray, sheriff's just doing his job," the deputy said. "We get a complaint, we have to investigate."

"Who complained? Where did you get those pictures?"

The deputy shrugged. "All I'm saying is, he's got to ask some questions."

"Mrs. Blaine." The sheriff quietly reclaimed her attention. "Is this you?"

Poor Tracy. It wasn't fair.

Sally nodded, not meeting the sheriff's eyes, his black eyes that saw too much.

"Can you tell me what happened?" he asked, his voice gentle.

"It was an accident," she said, which was what she always told Isaac when the bruises bloomed on her face and arms, when a bedtime hug produced a wince. *I tripped, I fell, I bumped into a door . . . I scorched his shirt, I raised my voice, I talked too little or too much.* All accidents.

The answer had stopped satisfying Isaac a long time ago.

Apparently it didn't satisfy the sheriff, either, because he frowned.

"Don't be stupid, Sarah," Ray said. "Tell them what happened."

"We have no secrets here," Daniel intoned.

Sally felt giddy, as if she'd been released blinking into the sunlight after days locked in the closet. But she wasn't really free. She knew that.

"Well." She twisted her fingers together. How did she explain what had been done to poor Tracy? She'd barely processed the horror herself. How could she justify it to an outsider? "It was supposed to be, like, penance." She looked up quickly at the sheriff and down quicker still. "Public penance?"

"A purification rite," Ray amended smoothly. "To restore the health of the community."

The sheriff's dark brows drew together. "Are you telling me *this*"—he tapped the photos in his hand—"was a religious ceremony?"

"The apostle Paul commands us to mortify those members who are guilty of fornication and uncleanness," Ray declared.

" 'For which things' sake the wrath of God cometh on the children of disobedience,' " added Daniel.

"This wasn't the wrath of God," the sheriff said. "This was people—this was *women*—throwing stones."

Sally cringed.

"God's instruments," Ray said.

"Tell me who did this," the sheriff said. "You can get help. We want to help you."

He was talking to her, Sally realized.

He thought he was dealing with a case of domestic violence. Maybe that was what Daniel wanted him to think. Better for Ray to be accused of spousal assault than for the community to be implicated in ritual murder.

But was it better for Sally? For Isaac?

The police won't interfere between a man and his wife.

Sally hesitated, paralyzed by her lie and her fears. What should she say? What could she do?

"This might be easier for Mrs. Blaine if we could talk at my office. With a female deputy present," the sheriff added before Ray could object. "If you'll come with us, ma'am, I'm sure we can get this whole thing straightened out."

Ray's eyes glittered in his pale face. "My wife does not wish to go and leave our son. Isn't that right, Sarah?"

She recognized the threat. If she left, Ray might not hurt Isaac, but she would never see her son again.

She licked her broken lip. "I want to stay here."

"We could take him with us," the sheriff pressed.

"Plenty of room in the patrol car," said the other deputy.

"My wife has said she does not want to go," Ray said.

"Your wife needs medical care," the sheriff argued. "Let us take her to the hospital."

"God will heal her," Daniel said serenely.

The sheriff looked at him with dislike. "A doctor would help."

"You can't make her go with you," Ray said.

"I can commit her involuntarily," the sheriff snapped.

"Not without a warrant," Ray said.

Daniel Locke folded his hands. "There's already concern in the community about you holding an office you weren't elected to, Sheriff. How will it look, you dragging a woman against her will away from her family and her church?"

The sheriff tossed the pictures on the desk, spilling horror across the leather blotter. "What kind of church does this to its members?"

Daniel's face lengthened. "Those photographs are deceptive, I assure you. The gesture was purely symbolic."

"And the bruises on her face?" demanded the sheriff. "Are those symbolic, too?"

"Sarah sought discipline and repentance," Ray said. "She accepts the judgment of the community. Don't you, Sarah?"

She stared at him, stricken.

"Sarah," Daniel prompted gently. "Tell the sheriff who's responsible for what happened."

Despair clogged Sally's throat as she realized what he was saying. What he was asking. It wasn't fair. Daniel had denounced Tracy in the assembly. Ray had called for her execution. But they hadn't dirtied their hands with the job. They hadn't cast a single stone.

The women bore the guilt for the death of one of their own. And even though Sarah had hung back, even though she'd flung her stones wide, taking care to miss, who would believe her?

She shared in their guilt.

She bore responsibility.

Certainly the sheriff would see it that way.

Her knees shook. Telling the truth wouldn't help poor,

dead Tracy. All it would do was get her arrested as an accessory to murder, leaving Isaac motherless. Defenseless. To protect her son, she had to protect herself.

Or put herself in even greater danger. She didn't even know anymore. Her head hurt. Her jaw ached. She wanted to sit down.

Defeated, she ducked her head. "I am," she whispered. "It was my fault."

Daniel smiled serenely. "You see? No complaint. No charges. No case."

"Yeah. Too bad there's a witness," said the deputy with the mustache.

Ray stiffened to attention like a dog spotting a deer. "What witness?"

The sheriff stifled a quick movement of . . . Annoyance? Sally wondered dully. But his voice, when he spoke, was mild. "Alexandra Scott," he said. "Do you know her?"

The name didn't mean anything to Sally. But Ray and Daniel exchanged glances.

"Could my wife be excused?" Ray asked. "This discussion is bound to be painful for her."

"Your wife's pain doesn't seem to be an issue for you," the sheriff said. "She stays."

Tense seconds ticked by. Ray glared.

"Whatever you require," Daniel said.

Sally released her breath.

"Alexandra Scott?" the sheriff prompted.

"I met her," Ray said. "On one of my trips. My ministry occasionally requires me to travel."

That much was true, Sally knew. She never questioned her husband's infrequent absences from the compound. She only accepted them with guilty relief.

"I was actually quite pleased when she expressed an interest in our discipline and an enthusiasm for our way of life. I invited her to the compound to hear Father Daniel and to experience our community for herself."

"All this after one meeting?" the sheriff asked.

"We actually met several times," Ray admitted.

"Where?"

"At the camera shop where she worked. Later, as our discussions became more detailed, we had to meet elsewhere—a coffee shop, a park."

"Her apartment?"

Ray hesitated. "Once or twice."

Her husband had been meeting another woman. Out of town. At her apartment. And Sally hadn't known.

Had he been faithful to her?

She didn't know that, either.

"So after these—discussions—you invited her here. Did she come?" the sheriff asked.

Ray looked surprised by the question. Well, he was a persuasive man. Very few women would resist him.

She hadn't, Sally thought, a clutch at her heart.

"She came last weekend," Ray said. "But the visit wasn't what either one of us apparently hoped for. She was—how do I say this?—disillusioned."

"With the community?"

"No." Ray grimaced slightly. "With me. Unfortunately, Alexandra mistook my interest in her spiritual development for something more personal."

"How personal?" the sheriff asked.

"She imagined herself in love with me." Ray's eyes were dark and sincere. His voice was deep and regretful. "It was quite a shock to her when she learned I was married. I'm afraid she made some, well, rather wild accusations."

"What kind of accusations?"

Ray's lips pressed together in annoyance. "I don't know, do I? Obviously, she came to you with some kind of story. Nothing would surprise me. She could have told you anything. Breach of promise. Seduction. Even kidnapping."

" 'A false witness that speaks lies and sows discord among the brethren.' " Daniel supplied. "We have our laws against that, Sheriff, just as you do."

"Such a shame," Ray said. "Clearly, she's a young

woman with deep problems. I'm only sorry I was unable to bring her to a fuller understanding of God's plan. But I trust in time she may come to experience all that is in store for her."

"How is she going to do that?"

Ray raised his eyebrows. "Why, through prayer. I will pray for her."

Sally fought a shudder. She didn't know if this Alexandra was guilty of lying or not. But she knew her husband was.

She glanced at the sheriff to gauge his reaction. But he wasn't watching her husband. He was looking at her, a gleam of awareness in his dark, dark eyes. Recognition? Or accusation?

SEVENTEEN

JACK glared at Lexie. Gutsy, fine, but right now he really didn't need the hassle. "I told you, we are not having this discussion. You're getting on a bus."

She stood there, with bare shoulders and stormy eyes, and stuck out her chin like a target. "Really? Well, unless we have this discussion, I'm not going anywhere near a bus."

Jack felt his back molars grinding together and deliberately relaxed his jaw. "Listen, I don't want anything to happen to you. I'm trained to deal with this. You're not. I have a personal stake in this. You don't."

She crossed her arms over her towel, barefoot and indignant. "Excuse me. I got screwed by Ray, and I fucked you. How much more of a personal stake do I need?"

Jack smothered a grin.

"What?" Lexie demanded suspiciously.

Affection moved in him, unexpected and painful as a cramp. *This* was the girl who had trouble turning down a date, who couldn't confide in her own mother?

He tweaked her soft curls, tapped a finger on the point of her chin. "You're really something, you know that?"

·

Her eyes snapped at him. "Don't you patronize me," she said. "I know all the words you know. I—"

He tightened his hold on her chin and kissed her. Her lips were cool and tasted like mint. He only meant to calm her down, or maybe to shut her up. But then she twined her arms around his neck, her mouth warming, opening under his, her bare feet climbing his shoes, and the heat rose from her body and fogged his brain. He was having trouble focusing. Her hair was damp and cool. Her skin was smooth and warm. She was soft and curvy and—*oh, yeah*—naked under her towel, and he forgot about bus schedules and his reasons for not getting involved and kissed her again, harder, his tongue in her mouth, his knee pushing between her thighs.

"I'm not done talking to you," she said between kisses.

"We'll talk," he promised rashly, his hands on the towel. "Later."

Much later. After-sex later. After he'd touched her, tasted her, taken her, all over again. His heart was racing, pounding . . .

Pounding.

On the door.

Jack raised his head. Somebody was at the door. He should have been relieved. *Saved from the edge of more mind-blowing, control-shattering, life-altering sex, thank you, Jesus.*

He was frustrated as hell.

"HOPE I'm not interrupting," Will said politely, though it was obvious from the big guy's scowl and the hastily closed bathroom door that he couldn't have come at a worse time.

Tough. He didn't have time to accommodate their nookie schedule.

"Come on in," Miller said. "What have you got?"

Will stepped over the threshold. He understood Miller's desire to be kept in the loop, but he wasn't here to talk shop with another cop. "Is Miss Scott available?"

Miller rocked back on his heels, easy on his feet as a fighter. "She'll be out in a minute. You get an I.D. on the victim?"

"Yep."

Miller narrowed his eyes. "You going to share, or are you just here to yank my chain?"

Will smiled without answering.

"Right." Miller jerked his head toward one of the room's two chairs. "Might as well sit while you're waiting."

Will angled the chair so he had a view of both doors and sat. Miller slouched against the wall, his hard face giving the lie to his relaxed pose.

The bathroom door opened and Alexandra Scott came out wearing a T-shirt clearly purchased in the motel lobby and a hesitant smile. She cleaned up pretty, Will thought. Despite the biker babe shirt and complete lack of jewelry, there was something classy about her. The tilt of her head, maybe, or the shape of her haircut or her straight, white teeth.

Will stood. "Miss Scott."

"Sheriff." She swallowed. "Have you—did you find out the woman's name? The one in the photographs?"

Same question as Miller's. Eager, weren't they? No, anxious. What were they afraid of? What did this victim's identity mean to them?

"Sarah Blaine," Will said. *The wife of the man you were involved with.*

The blonde went white and then red.

Miller didn't move, but his very stillness made the hairs stand up on the back of Will's neck. "I don't believe it. Did you see the body?"

Alexandra Scott touched Miller's arm. In comfort? Or in warning?

"I saw her," Will said, watching them both. "She's not dead."

The blonde blinked. "But I saw—"

"How bad?" Miller interrupted.

A vision of Sarah Blaine eating ice cream flashed across his brain. And then the memory of how she'd looked in Locke's office, her smiling mouth split, her pretty face transformed into a horror mask.

"Bad," Will said flatly. "But she could walk, and she could talk."

Miller pushed off the wall. "Where is she?"

"At the compound."

"You *left* her there?" Miller's voice cracked like a rifle shot.

Will stiffened. He wasn't any happier about the way things had gone down than Miller. Which was why he was here. "I didn't have much choice."

"You could have taken her to the hospital."

"She wouldn't go."

Miller scowled. "So did you arrest the bastard who did it?"

"Couldn't," Will said tersely.

"Why not?" Miller started to pace. "You had the pictures. That should have been enough for a warrant."

"On what charge?"

"Any charge."

Will didn't need some Yankee cop out on bail telling him how to do his job. "I don't have probable cause. You want me to arrest every woman in the compound? Because that's all those pictures show."

"I want you to arrest Blaine. Her bastard husband."

"He didn't do it."

"Bullshit," Miller said.

"How would you know?" Will demanded. "And why would you care?"

Miller pivoted, brought up short by the question. Or

maybe he'd run out of room to pace. "Because Sally Blaine," he said tightly, "is my sister."

Well, hell. Will hadn't seen that one coming. In God's name, why hadn't Miller done something to help her before this?

"You might have mentioned it yesterday," he said mildly.

Miller's gaze challenged him. "I didn't see the need. Yesterday."

Will turned this new development over in his mind, trying to see how this piece fit the pattern of his investigation.

"Maybe that makes what I came for easier. I need your help."

Miller bared his teeth in a smile. "Give me back my gun."

Will shook his head. "Not your help. Hers."

The blonde's eyes got even bigger, and Will stifled a pinch of guilt. That innocent, helpless look was perfect for what he had in mind.

"What kind of help?" she asked.

"Something hinky is going on there. Locke and Blaine are covering for each other now, but this afternoon Locke was ready to give Blaine up for domestic violence if it would make us go away. I want to keep pressing, see if I can get either one of them to flip on tape."

"You don't need her for that," Miller said. "Send in a deputy. Undercover."

"There is no undercover in a community this size," Will said wryly. "We have nine male deputies on uniform patrol, and Locke knows every one of them."

"So send in somebody he trusts. Somebody he can talk to."

"He won't do that. It takes too long to establish the kind of trust you're talking about. Unless . . ." Will let his voice trail off.

Miller was too cagey to bite.

But the blonde leaned forward, hooked. "Unless what?"

"Unless the deputy I'm thinking of went in with something Locke wanted," Will said.

"Like what?" Jack demanded.

THE sheriff looked at Lexie.

And she knew. Her heart beat in her throat.

"Me," she said in a small voice. "He wants to give him *me*."

"You're out of your mind," Jack snapped. "She's not doing it." He glared at her. "You're not doing it. It's too dangerous."

"I don't have a lot of options left," Tucker said. "You really want to risk your sister's life while we wait for a lucky break in the investigation?"

"You can't send her in there alone," Jack insisted.

He was right, Lexie thought, relieved. Of course he was right. Returning to the compound was not only dangerous for her, but for Sally and every innocent inside. If her father found out . . .

"She wouldn't be alone," the sheriff said. "I told you, she'd only be there to accompany my deputy."

"Wearing a wire, though, right?"

"For her own safety," Tucker said.

Jack snorted. "Yeah, right."

"Come on. You can't tell me you've never wired an informant before."

"For drug deals, yeah. Gang busts. Not infiltrating some backwoods hate group."

"Same principle," the sheriff said.

"The hell it is," Jack growled. "She's a civilian. She shouldn't be mixed up in this."

The sheriff's dark eyes hardened. "She's been inside. She's already mixed up in it."

"Because Blaine fucking kidnapped her," Jack said.

But not for the reasons he believed. Lexie bit her lip.

Sheriff Tucker shrugged. "That's not what he says."

Lexie felt a warning drop in the pit of her stomach, as if she'd reached her foot for a step that wasn't there. "What does he say?"

"It doesn't matter," Jack said. "Who the hell are you going to believe?"

But Sheriff Tucker continued as if Jack hadn't spoken. "He said you agreed to meet with him several times. You entertained him in your apartment. You assumed his interest in you was personal, and you were upset to learn he was married."

Lexie listened with growing indignation. "That's not true!"

"What's not true?"

"Well, that I . . ." Lexie stopped, feeling the ground give way under her. Forget the stairs. She felt like Wyle E. Coyote, poised over a void the size of the Grand Canyon. Because in some horrible, twisted fashion, it was true. All of it.

"We ran a check on you," the sheriff said, not unkindly. "Alexandra Scott, 215 Magnolia Court, Apartment 8H, Lovingston, Virginia. Self-employed contract photographer, single, organ donor. No wants, warrants, or prior convictions."

Her heartbeat quickened. He knew where she lived. He knew what she did. Did he know who her father was?

"Is that all?"

The sheriff pursed his lips. "Well, we talked to a Renae Somebody at Your Image photography. Do a lot of work with them?"

Lexie nodded dumbly.

"She confirms seeing you with Blaine. So . . ."

"Bullshit," Jack said with bracing conviction. "Blaine drugged her, he forced her to go with him, and he tied her up. Even if they did have a personal relationship, you can make him on felonious restraint."

"You got any witnesses to the abduction?" Tucker asked Lexie.

"No," she admitted reluctantly.

"Evidence of drugging?"

"I don't think . . . No."

"Signs of force or coercion?"

"Show him your wrists," Jack commanded.

Mutely, Lexie extended her hands. The bruises left by the rope circled her wrists like a bracelet.

The sheriff studied the faded marks and shook his head. "I can take pictures," he offered. "But you know these aren't conclusive."

"Why not?" Lexie asked.

"A defense attorney would argue any injuries you sustained could be the result of consensual activity."

"Why would I agree to be tied up, for heaven's sake?"

A stain spread under the sheriff's dark skin.

"He means you might like it rough," Jack said, his voice impassive, his face like flint. "Or your partner might."

Lexie remembered what they had been to each other, what they had done to each other in the night, and blushed.

The sheriff coughed. "Why would Ray Blaine kidnap you?"

Lexie looked into his plain, no-nonsense face and thought about saying, *Because Ray Blaine is a religious terrorist who wants to use me to discredit my father and the United States government and further his own ideological agenda.*

The sheriff might believe her.

Or he might not.

But even if he dismissed her as a complete lunatic, he wouldn't risk sending her into the compound until he had verified her father's identity. At which point, any chance she had of helping Jack save his sister would be lost. ·

On the other hand, what if she went in there and things somehow went horribly wrong? Adolescent screw-ups could be forgiven. But did she really want to be known as the girl who diverted the war on terror to the hills of North Carolina?

While she hesitated, Jack said, "Money."

"You have money?" the sheriff asked Lexie.

She should tell him the truth. She should tell both of them the truth.

I don't have a lot of options left. You really want to risk your sister's life while we wait for a lucky break in the investigation?

"Her family does," Jack said.

"Maybe we can use that," the sheriff said. "Did Blaine make a call? Send a ransom note?"

Lexie swallowed. "No."

"Her parents didn't even realize she was missing," Jack said, disgust plain in his voice.

"I live alone," Lexie said in excuse. "And they're very busy."

Thank God. If Trent Scott had any idea she was even contemplating the sheriff's proposal, he'd lock her up for the rest of her life.

Sheriff Tucker frowned. "But if Blaine expected to collect a ransom—"

"She got away before he could contact anybody," Jack said. "Fooled her guard and got over the wall, all by herself."

The approval in his eyes warmed her to her bones. If she could do that, she could do this. Couldn't she?

"That was real resourceful," the sheriff said. "But without a phone record, without a note, we're still dealing with a he-said, she-said scenario."

"You want to take the word of that psycho bastard over hers?" Jack asked.

"Doesn't matter what I want," Tucker replied evenly. "Ray Blaine is one of us. You all are strangers. Folks around here are going to believe in Ray. Which is why I need Miss Scott to go in wearing a wire."

Lexie felt sick. Jack's face was tight. Frustrated. She knew it was killing him to think of his sister, battered and at Blaine's mercy, while he was powerless to help her. Obviously, he didn't think much of the sheriff's plan. He didn't want Lexie's help. But she knew if there was a way she could remove that look from his face, she would take it.

"If I agree to this," she began carefully, "what would I have to say?"

Jack shot her a flat, dangerous look, intended, she supposed, to shut her up.

"You won't have to say anything," Tucker promised her. "My deputy will do all the talking."

"And he'll protect me, right?"

"Some protection," Jack said. "One man against a militia."

"*Jack.*" She took another breath to control her voice. She was touched he was concerned for her safety. She really was. But she had to work through this, weigh the options, and consider the dangers for herself.

"What if Ray won't let me leave?" she asked the sheriff.

"Blaine isn't in command at the compound," Tucker said. "Locke is. Deputy Greene won't leave your side. And Locke isn't going to turn the community against him by taking out a local patrol officer."

"What about backup?" Jack asked.

"We have a six-member special response team. And I'm calling in units from the neighboring counties to provide additional support. If they're needed," Tucker added. "Which they won't be. You're not going in to provoke a gun battle."

She hoped he was right. She hoped she wasn't letting her adolescent rebellion against her gung-ho enforcer father color her perception of the whole situation.

"Would it be better to get another agency involved? Not that I don't trust your department's ability to do your job," she added hastily. "But—"

The sheriff shook his head. "Locke's got a lot of people around here fired up against the federal government. But we've never had any trouble with him. Better to keep it that way."

Okay. No calling Daddy to bail her out of this one.

Lexie worked moisture into her mouth. "How far away will they be? The backup, I mean."

"Quarter mile. That's about the range of the transmitter in these hills."

"You're still outmanned," Jack said.

"My team is trained and prepared. The Disciples call themselves an army, but most of them are inexperienced. And they won't be expecting us."

"And outgunned," Jack added.

"According to my sources, the majority of their weapons stores are underground. There's no reason to believe Blaine's going to break out the grenades and rocket launchers for Miss Scott's visit."

Big problem. Because there was a reason the Disciples might break out the big guns to keep her. But it wasn't anything Lexie could discuss in front of Jack. He had too much at stake already. She knew he was torn between concern for her danger and worry about his sister's well-being. She couldn't force him to choose between her and what little family he had left.

"This is a bad idea," Jack said flatly.

"Right now it's the best idea I've got. She gets the evidence, I get a warrant, Blaine gets arrested, and your sister has a chance to get out of there."

They were talking about her as if she wasn't there, Lexie thought. As if this weren't her decision. And she was letting them. Because a part of her, this meek little girl part, this part that used to disappear into her room for hours on end and let her parents talk over her at the dining room table, was secretly hoping Jack was going to win this argument and she wouldn't have to face Ray Blaine ever again.

She was such a wuss.

How could she know if she was acting out of appropriate caution? Or sheer funk?

The problem was, she didn't know enough to decide. She would have to tell the sheriff and trust his judgment.

She opened her mouth. But what came out was, "I could do it."

"No," Jack said.

Lexie's spine stiffened. Because whatever Jack said, she had a personal stake in this, too. She was not going to let Ray get away with deceiving her and drugging her and terrorizing her. She was not going to let him get away with murder. This once, she was not going to take the easy way out.

"I didn't say I would," she said. "But you heard the sheriff. If it helped his investigation—"

"It could be your sister's best chance," Tucker said. "If we can get Locke to turn on Blaine, we can put the bastard away."

"Then I'll go with you," Jack said.

Despite her big brave act—yeah, right, like she wasn't ready to throw up at the thought of wearing a body mike and delivering herself into Ray's hands—hope flared inside her. It wouldn't be so bad, if Jack was with her. She wouldn't be so scared.

But Tucker shook his head. "The point is to gain Locke's trust. Miss Scott's presence is a bargaining chip. A gesture of good faith. You, on the other hand, are a threat. If she goes in, she goes in with my deputy."

Lexie wasn't going anywhere until the sheriff knew exactly who she was and what he was up against. She had to talk to him. Soon. She glanced at Jack. Privately. Maybe tomorrow?

She licked her dry lips. "I'm supposed to call my mother."

"When?"

"Sunday."

"That's fine," the sheriff said.

"Should I tell her . . ." What? What could she say that wouldn't precipitate exactly the kind of crisis she hoped to avoid?

"You can tell her everything went fine," Tucker said.

She blinked at him.

"You're going in tomorrow," the sheriff explained. "By Sunday you'll be back, safe and sound."

TUCKER tugged the motel door quietly closed behind him. But the scrape of the door in its metal frame echoed in Jack's soul with the hopeless finality of a prison lockdown.

"You know he doesn't give a shit about you," he said harshly.

Lexie blinked at him, her beautiful face hurt and bewildered. "Excuse me?"

Jack felt like a puppy murderer. But she had to see, had to understand, her danger. It was the only thing he had left to give her.

"Tucker doesn't care what happens to you. You're a tool to get what he needs."

"I know," she said.

"Then why would you let him use you?"

"Because then I get what I need, too."

Frustration surged in Jack's throat. He clamped his teeth on it. "What do you need that's worth risking your life for?"

"Self-respect?"

The way she said it, with that little questioning lift in her voice, with that small, self-deprecating smile, invited him to take her comment as a joke. Not to take it too seriously. Not to take her too seriously.

But Jack knew better.

"Babe . . ." He cleared his throat. "You are one of the gutsiest, most resourceful people I've ever met. You don't need to play the sheriff's game to respect yourself."

"But I'm not really," she said. "I'm scared all the time."

"Not being scared makes you stupid. Being scared and doing something anyway makes you brave."

"Right." Her smile twisted ruefully. "The bravest thing I've ever done was run away."

Ah, babe. "Under the circumstances, running away was the best thing you could do. The only thing you could do. You couldn't take on Blaine and his whole damn army."

"I couldn't then. But I can now." She looked up at him, her big eyes pleading for his understanding. For his acceptance. "Don't you see? This is my chance to do something. For myself, and for Sally."

Jack felt his resolution slipping and scowled. "You don't even know Sally."

"I know you," Lexie said softly. Unanswerably. "I know what she means to you. I want to do this, Jack. For both our sakes."

She was so brave. So amazing.

And he felt like shit.

"If you do, you know the sheriff's right," he said hoarsely. "I can't be any part of this operation. I can't help you."

She nodded solemnly. "Because of Ray."

She didn't have a clue.

He had to spell it out for her.

It was the hardest thing he'd ever done. But her courage deserved his honesty, at least.

"Because of me," Jack said. "Because I can't trust myself to maintain control when I'm emotionally involved."

He waited for her to look shocked. To condemn him, or worse, to pity him.

But she still didn't get it.

"That's okay." She bit her lip. "Actually, I wouldn't want anyone in my family involved for the same reason."

He closed his eyes. God, let her think that. Let her think he was taking himself off the case because Sally was his sister. But this wasn't about Sally, either. This was all on him.

Say it, asshole. Get it over with.

"I fucked up on the job. I lost control. I went after a suspect with my bare hands like an animal. Like a criminal."

"You must have had a reason," Lexie said.

A picture of Dora Boyle flashed in his memory, her sightless eyes in her ruined face, her mouth open in a silent scream. Her daughter's body sprawled like a broken doll against the wall on the opposite side of the room, her skull crushed. The stench of fear and failure, of urine and blood, rose and choked him.

"There is no good reason," Jack said. He had to accept that. Otherwise, how could he accept what had happened to him? "No excuse."

"I don't believe that." Certainty shone in Lexie's eyes. "The man I know wouldn't strike a suspect for no reason."

Her faith in him was unexpectedly sweet . . . and totally undeserved.

"Let me tell you something about the man you don't know," Jack said. "I was working on a repeat domestic this year. Nothing special about that. You got a domestic disturbance, it's almost always a repeat. But this one, nice woman with a little girl, I let it get personal. I told her to call me, not just the 911 business, but my number, my cell phone. Call anytime. Just to talk. Christ, her life sucked, and mine was . . ."

How could he explain how it had been, how he had felt, with Patty gone and Dora calling and her little girl looking up at him like he was Superman and Mr. Rogers rolled into one?

"Lonely?" Lexie suggested softly.

He glared at her. Jesus.

Yes.

He looked away. "Anyway, we're talking a couple times a week, nothing romantic, just how are you, how's the kid, did she have a good soccer practice, did that bastard you married bust your jaw yet?" He had to move. He started to pace, his hands jammed into his pockets. "I'm leaning on her, you know? To take pictures, to press charges, to keep money and shit in a safe place so she could get away if she had to. And all the time I'm doing this, I'm getting called back to that house, I have to hear that son of a bitch ragging on her, I have to listen to her defending him.

"So I tell her—I talk her into getting a restraining order. Finally." His hands curled to fists inside his pockets. "And that afternoon, while I'm giving a deposition at the courthouse, he shows up at the house and kills them both."

Lexie drew a short, shocked breath.

But he wasn't finished. He plugged on, determined now that he had started not to spare her or himself the whole ugly story.

"He was already under arrest when I pulled up. And I get out of the car and he says, 'Fucking cop. You fucked my wife. You can't fuck with me.'" Jack's jaw set. "So I went for him. It took four officers to pull me off."

"I bet they didn't try very hard," Lexie said.

He looked at her sharply. Her gaze was soft and clear. Uncompromising. Uncondemning.

Why didn't she get it? Why didn't she blame him?

"Not until I broke Rooney's nose," he said.

Lexie smiled, a wry and tender curve to her mouth. "I bet he forgave you."

Maybe. Eventually.

"He shouldn't," Jack said. "I shouldn't have lost control."

Her eyes were bright with tears. Shit. Now he'd made her cry. One more sin to add to his growing list.

But maybe she didn't see it that way, because she got off the bed and walked toward him, not stopping until she was close enough that he could feel the warmth of her body. He could smell the shampoo scent of her hair and look into her incredible, tear-filled eyes.

Jack stood, rigid as stone, as Lexie touched the tips of her fingers to the lines of tension in his forehead, to the tightly bunched muscles in his jaw. He shivered under her touch, each light brush of her fingers a torture and an absolution.

"That's not what you can't forgive," she told him. "You haven't forgiven yourself for not saving them."

It was true.

And so he gave her the rest of it, bared the last of his soul and with it, his heart. "I won't forgive myself if anything happens to you, either."

She moistened her lips, her eyes searching his. "Because we're personally involved."

Personally involved didn't cut it. Personally involved wouldn't stop her tomorrow from marching into the Disciples' compound and delivering herself to Blaine like a package from UPS.

He had to come up with something better than personally involved.

"No," he said harshly, and watched her eyes widen. "Because I love you."

EIGHTEEN

"I told you before your zeal would cause us problems," Daniel said coldly. "I won't tolerate outside interference in our affairs."

Resentment burned in Ray's veins. Daniel was talking as if this was Ray's fault. As if Ray had invited the sheriff here. "You can't stop it, Daniel. Isn't that what you preach? The federal government is out of control, pushing Satan's agenda on good Christians. That's why we need a revolution in this country."

"A revolution in men's thinking," Daniel said. "A revolution in their souls. Not armed conflict."

Wrong. Ray's head throbbed. He had worked his entire adult life to raise and train an army. An army of God. Was Daniel so jealous of his accomplishment he would deny their cause?

"We are at war," Ray said, making an effort to speak calmly. "Conflict is inevitable."

"Not inevitable. This is your fault."

Ray's heart thumped in his chest. Unfair. Unjust. Untrue. "It wasn't my guilt that brought the sheriff down on us. It was the woman. We can't allow fornication and adultery to stain this community. America needs our leadership. Our example."

"Those pictures are hardly the example America is looking for," Daniel said, unexpectedly dry. "How did the sheriff get pictures?"

The blood pounded in Ray's head. He didn't know. He couldn't think. He'd taken her camera.

It was a test, he told himself. Daniel was testing him.

Or God was.

"It doesn't matter," he told Daniel. "The sheriff believed us. And when we get the woman back—"

Daniel's face lengthened in displeasure. "We're not getting her back. I don't want her back. She's trouble. You must see that."

Ray's stomach clenched like a fist. Daniel was the one who didn't see. The old man was too blinded by safety and self-interest to have the vision necessary to lead the Disciples anymore.

But Ray still tried. No one could blame him for Daniel's short-sightedness.

"She's a sign," he said. "A symbol of corrupt society, subdued and redeemed by the power of God." The thought of Alexandra subdued, of Alexandra subject to his will— that is, to God's will—caused a hot flare of satisfaction.

Daniel looked at him with opaque blue eyes. "Maybe her escape was a sign as well. Examine your heart, Brother Ray. Examine your motives."

Nonsense. His heart didn't need examining.

Alexandra's escape wasn't a sign of anything, except the incompetence of the people around him and Daniel's own willingness to excuse failure.

Ray would not excuse it.

Ray would not accept it.

He had to get her back.

* * *

LEXIE'S breath abandoned her. Little spots danced before her eyes.

Jack had actually used the L-word. *Because I love you,* he'd said. He hadn't sounded too happy about it, either, which meant he was probably sincere. Or he thought he was sincere.

Or he was manipulating her. Maybe he'd say anything to prevent her from going back to the Disciples' compound.

And now he was glaring at her, expecting her to say something back.

Oh, God, oh, God, she was in such deep trouble here.

She opened her mouth. Closed it. Swallowed and said, "I think I might be falling in love with you, too."

"You think," Jack repeated expressionlessly.

She felt light-headed. "Well, we haven't known each other very long. Less than a week. Five days? That's hardly enough time to develop a lasting relationship. You don't even know who I am, really."

And wasn't that the truth, she thought miserably.

"You might be," Jack said, still quoting her, which was kind of annoying, especially since all her little qualifiers sounded even stupider the second time around.

"Yes. We've been thrown together in a highly emotional and intense situation." Lexie faltered. Oh, God, was that really her mother's lecturer voice coming out of her throat? "Under the circumstances, it would be natural to mistake gratitude or excitement or simple adrenaline for, well, for falling in love."

Jack's deep-set eyes glinted with ironic amusement. He was enjoying this. The bastard. "Only 'falling'?"

Lexie stuck out her chin. "What would you call it?"

He smiled, a slow, toe-curling smile. "I already told you. But if you don't believe me, I could show you instead."

Her heart thumped. "Show me what?"

The grin broadened. "*This* is gratitude."

He kissed her forehead. The warm pressure of his lips and the nearness of his big, solid body made her eyelids droop. Her head sagged, too heavy for her neck's support. She had to fight the urge to lay her head against his chest.

He caught her chin between his finger and thumb and lifted her face for his kiss.

"This is excitement," he whispered against her lips before his mouth covered hers.

He kissed her, hard and deep. Their mouths dueled. Fed. Mated. He kissed her until she was shaking with need and breathless with desire.

His hand came up to cup her breast, to cover her racing heart. The nipple tightened under his palm.

"Adrenaline," he said, his voice rough and warm, satisfied, and tumbled her back on the bed.

Okay, this was the kind of superior, macho, man-on-top routine she objected to. Or she used to object to. Or she ought to object to.

Only this was Jack, his weight welcome and already familiar, his scent male and musky and somehow right. He was still smiling as he nudged his way between her thighs, but there was a darkness in his eyes, an uncertainty, that told her this had stopped being a game for both of them. She could feel his erection, thick and hard against her belly.

Supporting himself on one elbow, he reached his other hand between their bodies, tugging, unzipping, adjusting. She wriggled, trying to help, but his weight defeated her.

"*Jack.*" Not a protest. A plea.

"Just a minute." A promise, as he found and used a condom.

She was panting as he slid the first inch inside her. She cried out and contracted around him. He stopped, linking their hands, holding her gaze.

"This," he told her solemnly, pushing inside her, thrusting all the way inside her, "this is love."

And maybe it was, because in that instant she felt closer to him than she had ever felt to any other human being. She tightened around him, holding him with her hands and her eyes, gripping him with her inner muscles. He pulled out, almost all the way out, and her body wept in protest. She wrapped her legs around his waist. He rocked into her, harder, higher, the sudden fullness making her gasp and clutch at him.

Time collapsed. The air thickened. The shabby motel room ceased to exist. The headboard bolted to the wall, the faded green spread didn't matter. The world wheeled and spiraled, narrowing down to this. To them. To touch and taste, to giving and receiving. The wonder of him moving inside her swelled her heart and swamped her senses. Each aching withdrawal and deliberate thrust, each slow, thick slide and full, deep possession built the heat and quickened the rhythm until they moved together, melted together, pounded together like metal in a forge, and the world erupted in a shower of sparks and an explosion of feeling.

Jack buried his face in Lexie's neck and exhaled into her hair.

She stroked his damp back, holding him as their bodies cooled, as his breathing slowed and her heart shattered.

They were joined now. Tied. Connected.

If this wasn't love and he left her, it would tear something inside her, and she would have to cope with the internal bleeding the rest of her life.

But if this was love, oh, if it was, and he found out she was lying to him, he might never forgive her.

"WE need to talk," Lexie said the next morning when Jack came out of the bathroom.

Those four words guaranteed to kill the mood. Even after the best sex of his life.

We need to talk, Patty had said right before she asked for a divorce.

We need to talk, his captain had said when he called Jack into his office to relieve him from duty.

But Lexie was right. They did need to talk. And because Tucker was picking up Lexie in less than half an hour, they didn't have much time.

Lexie tilted her head. "What's wrong?"

She was sitting on the edge of the bed, pale and pretty and so determined it hurt his chest to look at her.

"Nothing."

"Then why are you doing that thing with your jaw?"

Jack scowled. "What thing?"

"That thing you do when you're upset. Like you're grinding your teeth together."

His jaw relaxed. He even smiled. She could do that, make him smile even when his world was teetering like a drunk on the side of a highway. "Busted. Listen, I—"

"I know what you're going to say," she interrupted. "I know you don't want me to do this. But there's something I need to tell you. I—"

He held up his palm to stop her. "Me first."

He'd given this a lot of thought since last night. He'd rehearsed what he had to say in the shower. He wanted to get it right.

Hell, mostly he wanted to get it over with.

He hated not being in control. Of the situation. Of her. Of himself.

But then he had figured out that wasn't exactly true. Okay, he didn't have the power to stop Lexie from going back to the compound. But he had the ability to make her feel like shit about it.

He could go on fighting her decision. But all that would accomplish was to send her away scared and doubting herself.

Or—Jack inhaled—he could give her his support.

At least he could try.

"Listen," he said, "I want to thank you for what you're doing for Sally. And for me."

Lexie bit her lip. "Jack, you don't have to—"

"Yeah, I do. Tucker was right. Even if he could get a

warrant, he'd never get the charges to stick without more evidence. He needs you."

Jack shook his head. He could do better than that.

"Hell, I need you," he said. "Nobody else could do what you're doing." He brushed his fingers down her cheek, touched his thumb to the corner of her mouth. "You're amazing. I just wanted to tell you so."

Lexie stared at him, her face white with emotion, her eyes wide. Dark. Stunned.

He cleared his throat, uncertain what more he could say. "Your turn."

"What?" She sounded dazed.

He felt an unfamiliar satisfaction. Maybe he'd said enough.

"You had something you wanted to tell me?" he prompted.

"Oh." She swallowed. "No."

"Sure?"

A faint flush crept into her pale cheeks. "Yes. It's not important now."

THE clearing looked like a parking lot at the state fair, with four wheelers in haphazard rows, pickups, trailers, even a shiny red firetruck. It would have made a great photo.

"Where's the fire?" Lexie joked weakly, but Sheriff Tucker took her question seriously.

He seemed to take everything seriously, which didn't reassure her at all. At least he wasn't underestimating the Disciples.

Oh, God, she had to find a way to talk to him without Jack overhearing. She was afraid once Tucker knew the truth, he would never risk sending her into the compound. The investigation into the Disciples could drag on and on, and who knew what could happen to Sally in the meantime?

But the sheriff had to know what they were up against. What he was dealing with.

Who she was.

"Forest service wanted a tanker," Tucker explained. "You always need to be prepared for fire in the mountains."

Fire was bad enough. But . . .

"Forest service?" Lexie asked.

She had a sudden image of the ranger standing hip high in cold water, blood streaming down his face.

"How many people are in on this operation?" Jack growled beside her.

Tucker returned his look blandly. "Probably more than we need. Everybody and his cousin wants to try out their new antiterrorist gear. This is more excitement than we've seen in years."

He had no idea.

"What about Long?" Jack asked.

Tucker shook his head. "District Ranger sent Long on an errand to Raleigh today. He's going to be real sorry when he gets back tomorrow and finds out he's missed all the fun."

"And you don't think Blaine's patrols are going to see all this?" Jack challenged.

"Only if they know where to look," Tucker said.

Lexie watched four men with headsets and binoculars milling around a pickup truck. They looked more like storm troopers than sheriff's deputies, dressed all in black from boots to gloves, bulging with pouches and pockets, and bristling with guns.

"You said there wasn't going to be a gun battle," she said to Tucker.

He shrugged. "In this job, you hope for the best and plan for the worst."

Which was exactly what she was trying to do.

She licked dry lips. "What's the worst?"

"The worst is, Greene hollers for help. We threaten to use tear gas," Tucker said. "Locke fusses about his Second

Amendment rights and how the federal government is ruining America, and then we all go home."

Jack started to say something else, stopped, and
jammed his hands into his pockets.

Lexie looked at his hard, bleak profile and felt her heart
push into her throat.

Nobody else could do what you're doing.

"Ms. Scott?" The female deputy, her trim figure distorted by the Kevlar vest she wore, touched Lexie's arm.
"They're ready for you now."

Her heart expanded with panic.

"All right." Lexie swallowed hard. "Sheriff Tucker?
Could I speak to you a minute?"

Jack's eyes narrowed. "What is it? What's wrong?"

"Nothing."

Everything.

"Sure," the sheriff said easily. "We can talk while you're
getting wired up."

"This won't take long," Lexie told Jack with a weak
smile.

His gaze burned like a brand between her shoulder
blades as they walked away.

Inside the trailer, Lexie faced Will Tucker with the same
mix of dread, embarrassment, and resolution she'd felt at
her first GYN exam. "There's something you need to
know."

"Okay," he said calmly. "Give us a minute, will you,
Ginny?"

Lexie waited until the trailer door closed behind the female deputy. Taking a deep breath, she said, "My father is
Trent Scott."

The sheriff's expression didn't change.

She tried again. "That's why I was kidnapped. Because
he's Trent Scott. The FBI director."

Tucker stared at her, his black eyes like coals.

Lexie's heart beat in her throat. She cleared it. "I thought
you, um, should know. In case it makes a difference."

Tucker exploded. "You're damn right it makes a difference."

Lexie flinched.

"Why the hell didn't you say something before this?"

The door opened. "Chief?" The female deputy stuck her head into the trailer. "Everything all right in there?"

"Fine. Close the door."

The latch clicked shut.

"Fuck," Tucker said with great feeling. "You know this puts you in a lot more danger."

Lexie raised her chin. "I'm still willing—I still *want* to help."

"Not just you. Greene, too. The deputy going in with you."

"I know," Lexie said humbly. "If you need more time . . ."

"I don't have more time." Tucker patted his pocket in the gesture of a habitual smoker and then sighed. "Every law enforcement officer, firefighter and paramedic in three counties is here this morning. How fast do you think the news will spread if I send them all home now? Locke will circle the wagons so fast I'll never get a man inside. It has to be now or not at all."

Lexie winced.

Tucker stood with his head bent and his gaze fixed on the high-tech console, but she got the impression he didn't really see it.

Well, no wonder.

If he went ahead with this operation, he was risking her life, his deputy's life, and his own career.

If he called it off, he looked like a fool to his professional peers in three counties, and any chance he had of mounting an investigation while the Disciples were relatively unaware and unprepared was lost.

And every day he delayed, innocents like Sally were at risk.

"Whose idea was the kidnapping?" Tucker asked abruptly.

"Ray's." Lexie swallowed. "I mean, he did it."

"Okay." Tucker thrust out his lower lip in thought. "Okay, we can use that. We want Locke to think he has something to gain by talking to Bobby. If he goes in with you, lets Locke believe we're talking with you, Locke may decide his best bet is to cooperate."

Lexie felt light-headed. "So . . . we're going to do it?"

The sheriff nodded grimly. "Unless you have a better idea."

She didn't. She couldn't think at all.

She stood as stiff as a post while the female deputy taped a small, flat microphone to her right breast, away from the rapid, distracting beat of her heart. On the other side of the trailer, behind a bank of equipment, the sheriff briefed the deputy who was going to accompany her.

"Of course I can do this." Greene's light, impatient voice broke through the sheriff's murmur. "I've got the contacts, and you've taken more precautions than a new mommy taking baby on his first car trip. We'll be fine."

Lexie looked down as the female deputy ran a wire from the mike to the transmitter on her hip. "Isn't this the first thing they're going to look for?"

The woman looked up with a reassuring smile. "Locke and his men know Bobby. They didn't pat him down yesterday. There's no reason to think they'll be more suspicious today. But we've got to take precautions," she said, echoing Greene. "We can't let anything happen to you."

Jack's words, his face, rose to haunt Lexie. *I won't forgive myself if anything happens to you.*

Lexie's heart clutched. She should have told him. She should have said . . . something, so he wouldn't blame himself if things went wrong.

"Time to go," Tucker announced.

And then it was too late.

Bobby Greene—dimly Lexie registered his cheerful

young face, his cocky brown mustache—escorted her to a waiting patrol car.

Too late for more admissions. Too late for regrets.

She looked around for Jack. Her lover stood motionless and isolated against a backdrop of bare trees, wearing his cop mask.

I want to thank you for what you're doing for Sally. And for me.

Lexie sighed. It had been too late from the moment she realized she was in love with him.

And she hadn't told him that, either.

JACK watched the grinning young deputy open Lexie's door and put his hand automatically on the top of her head, as if she was a handcuffed criminal who had to be guided into her seat.

Asshole.

Lexie didn't appear to mind, though. She smiled and thanked the deputy, smiled and thanked the female officer who had accompanied them, smiled and said something to Tucker, leaning against the frame of the car. He answered—Jack couldn't hear what—and closed her door.

Just for a second, her gaze sought Jack's over the sheriff's broad shoulder. Their eyes met and clung. Her smile flickered.

Jack nodded once in acknowledgment, fisting his hands inside his pockets so he wouldn't do anything stupid like drag her from the car. With her bright curls and pale face, she looked small and pretty and vulnerable against the black upholstery.

Which was the whole point. Tucker had chosen his tool carefully. Her vulnerability, her desirability, was the wedge that could split the Disciples' leadership apart. Jack respected the sheriff's strategy and the extent of his operation.

That didn't mean he had to like it.

He watched the back of Lexie's blond head as the patrol car bumped over the ruts to the road, helpless to do a damn thing to stop her. Powerless to protect her.

DEPUTY Greene flashed Lexie a quick, reassuring grin as he parked before the stockade gates. "You let me do the talking, now," he said.

Lexie nodded. She didn't trust herself to speak anyway.

An acne-scarred young man, his hair shaved close to his head, opened the gate and approached the car. He had a gun, a big gun, a black rifle with a heavy stock, cradled in one arm.

Compensating for something, Lexie told herself, but her stomach quivered anyway.

"What are you doing here?" he called.

Deputy Greene kept his hands on the steering wheel, where they were plainly visible. "Hey, Hawley. I wanted to talk to Daniel Locke. He around?"

Hawley shifted his gun so it pointed at the ground by the driver's side door. With one jerk, one squeeze, he could fire through the window. "You got a warrant?"

"I've got something better," Greene said. He leaned back in his seat to give Hawley a clear view of the car's interior.

Lexie squeezed her hands together in her lap as the gunman leaned forward. His eyes widened.

"Want to let him know we're here?" Greene asked, all friendly.

"Yeah." The kid straightened and backed away from the car. "Yeah, he'll want . . . Get out of the car. I'll take you to him."

"Great," Greene said. He winked at Lexie before he swung out of the car, still keeping his hands in plain sight. "That's great."

Lexie swallowed, trying to summon the nerve to follow him.

They were in.

Just great.

GOD had delivered her into his hands.

It was the sign Ray had been waiting for.

Satisfaction filled him as he stood at the common room window, watching Alexandra cross the yard, small and womanly between Hawley and the deputy. Excitement throbbed in his chest. In his loins.

Now Daniel would see Ray was right. Now the world would see.

She was like a vessel, sullied by her association with her father and by the world's possession. But Ray had saved her, taken her from her Satanic father's protection. He would scour her of corruption. He would restore her to her heavenly father and fill her with the power of God.

He would fill her. Possess her. Ray breathed faster, thinking about it, Alexandra filled.

Of course, the deputy shouldn't be with her.

But it didn't matter. Everything was going to be all right now. God's will would be done. The deputy was only a tool, Ray told himself. An instrument of God's will, a part of Ray's plan.

He heard the knock on the door and composed himself.

Show me the way, Lord, Ray prayed.

LEXIE blinked, blinded by the light flooding through the common room windows. A man stood silhouetted against the glass like Lucifer framed by heaven's gates, his arms folded behind him like wings.

"Ray?" Deputy Greene squinted against the light. "What are you doing here?"

Lexie's lungs emptied. Ray Blaine? It couldn't be. But even with his face in shadow, Lexie recognized his short, compact figure, the careful incline of his head.

She drew a shaky breath. She wasn't going to panic. Exactly. Yet.

"I could ask you the same thing." Ray's deep, remembered voice raised the hair on the backs of her arms.

Greene scratched his jaw and flashed his aw-shucks grin. "Well, I was hoping to speak with Daniel Locke. Is he here?"

"I told Hawley to bring you to me." Ray's dark gaze settled on Lexie. She shivered. "Why is she with you?"

"Maybe it would be better if I talk to Father Daniel," Greene said.

Ray shrugged. "If that's what you want. Hawley will escort you. You can leave the woman with me."

Lexie froze.

She did not want to be alone with him. She wanted to beg Greene—*Don't let him touch me, don't let him take me, don't leave me, don't*—but she'd promised to let him do the talking, so she pressed her lips together and waited for him to say something.

Greene stroked the ends of his mustache. "I'm not sure I can do that, Ray. I brought her here, I kind of feel responsible for her."

"Why did you bring her?" Ray asked.

Greene shifted his weight. "You know I've always been a friend to you folks out here. Well, I got to thinking about what you said the other day. How this was all, like, one big misunderstanding? So, I figured if I brought her out here, kind of talked the situation through, we might be able to clear this whole thing up."

"I don't believe you," Ray said.

Greene shook his head. And then he chuckled. "Guess I can't pull one over on you. Truth is, I found her at the bus station, trying to leave town. She's obviously valuable to you. For all I know, she's valuable to somebody else, too. I thought it might be worth my while to find out just how much you want her back."

"Are you trying to make a deal with me, Bobby?"

"Actually, I was trying to deal with Daniel," Greene confessed, with another of those wide grins. "But if you want to make me an offer, Ray, I'm listening."

"Who else?" Ray asked, and Lexie stiffened.

The deputy looked confused. "What?"

"Who else is listening?" Ray asked softly.

Greene hesitated.

No, don't, Lexie thought. Answer him. Answer him now.

But Greene didn't.

He didn't say anything.

Come on. Come on. Before it's too . . .

Ray pulled one arm from behind his back and pointed a gun at the deputy's head and shot him—*blam*—in the head.

Dead.

NINETEEN

LEXIE screamed.

The doors burst open and men, armed men, five or six of them, muscled into the room. She ignored them, scrambling across the floor to Deputy Greene.

One second he was standing there, smiling and rubbing his mustache, and the next instant he lay with a small dark hole in his forehead and blood and brains sprayed over the floor and the wall behind him.

She wanted that second back.

She threw herself toward him as if she could still push him out of danger. As if she could shove back time. As if, even now, she could stop the bleeding and give him back his life.

"You shot him!" she cried, in case the listening sheriff had any doubt. "You *killed* him. You bastard."

Ray caught her around the waist and hauled her against his hard, wiry body, his breath hot against the side of her face. She twisted, kicking his legs, clawing at his restraining arm, her throat raw with shock and tears. The gun clattered to the floor. Ray thrust his hand up under her shirt, and she screamed again.

His hand groped. Probed. With a grunt of satisfaction, he dug his fingers into her flesh and ripped the microphone from her breast.

Lexie struggled as he raised it to his lips.

"I'll shoot her, too," he threatened, his voice thick. Unrecognizable. "Tell that to the FBI. If you attack, if you approach at all, I'll shoot her and blow the compound."

Horror gripped her, strong as nausea, sharp as bile. It wasn't supposed to be like this. This wasn't supposed to happen.

"What are you doing?" Daniel Locke raged from the doorway with the anguish of an Old Testament prophet. "My God, what have you done?"

What had she done?

Oh, Jack.

INSIDE the trailer that served as temporary command center, confusion flared as the leaders of three special response teams, jolted from Saturday training mode, jockeyed to Do Something. To Fix Things.

"Make entry. Make entry, now."

"What did he mean, tell that to the FBI?"

"Who the fuck does he think she is?"

But Will knew. This was his command.

His mistake.

The responsibility burned a hole in his gut.

"Negative," he snapped. "Wait for my order. Do we still have contact?"

The tech guy, Johnson, from over in Franklin County, fiddled and flipped his dials. "Motherfucker killed the mike."

The motherfucker had killed Bobby, too, along with Will's career, but he didn't have time to think about that now. Not with Scott still inside and all hell about to break loose.

"Which mike? They're both wired."

"Copy. Girl's mike is down. I've got nothing but static on Greene's."

Will could hear it now, buzzing through the receiver. "Fix it. And I want contact with Locke. Phone, radio, I don't care. Just get him. Now."

Johnson got on it.

"Alert the medical team," Will ordered. Sweat soaked his armpits and the back of his shirt, but his voice was steady. Cool. "We may need a doctor." Probably too late for Bobby, but Will wasn't taking any more chances. "And expand the second perimeter. Carl, take a look at the map."

Carl bent obediently over the laminated map, marking the new boundary that would keep the Disciples in and the public out. "At least we don't have to worry about the neighbors."

Right. No frustrated homeowners barging through police lines trying to get home. No neighborhood kids getting struck by stray bullets. That wouldn't stop the news crews from crowding the barricades as soon as word leaked out. That didn't mean the airwaves and telephone lines weren't going to burn with calls from outraged citizens. Will's miscalculation was going to cost him the election.

It had cost Bobby his life.

HE'D killed Deputy Greene.

Held tight by Ray's constraining arm, Lexie swallowed bile, fighting down terror and nausea.

Would he kill her, too?

Or would he only make her wish she was dead?

She had known Ray was capable of violence. But she'd never imagined this. Deep down, she really believed he would follow the same rules of logic and law as everybody else. She really thought Greene's role as an officer of the law and her own value as a hostage would protect her.

The young deputy's eyes stared sightlessly at the ceiling. Dark blood pooled under his head.

Lexie shuddered. She didn't believe that anymore.

Jack.

She wanted Jack. Wanted him fiercely, instinctively, desperately. *Rescue me.*

SOMETHING was wrong.

Jack could feel it in the ripple that went through the makeshift camp, hear it in the other men's sharpened voices.

He knew it in his bones. Call it cop's instinct or concern over Lexie or . . . Shit, call it love. Something was wrong.

He was halfway to the command trailer, worry wrenching his gut, when he heard that Greene was dead.

Jack started to run.

"I had no choice," Ray told Daniel and the other men. His voice was flat and assured, but Lexie was close enough to feel his sweat against her back through his shirt. He stank of fear and aggression. "It was self-defense."

Liar, Lexie wanted to say.

But she didn't. Better a live wimp than a dead smartass.

Anyway, she didn't need to say anything, because Daniel wasn't buying Ray's explanation, either. "He attacked you?"

"He threatened me. Threatened all of us." Ray nodded to the disabled transmitters on the floor. Lexie had watched in horror as the men with Daniel had ripped the wire from Greene's fallen body. "You saw. He was a spy."

"They are both spies," Daniel said coldly, and Lexie's blood chilled. "I told you the woman was trouble. You've mismanaged this business and endangered the entire community. Give her to me."

"God delivered her into my hands," Ray insisted.

God hadn't delivered her. She'd delivered herself. Dumb, dumb girl. She should have listened to Jack. She should have told him . . . lots of things.

"God had nothing to do with it. Your obsession with this woman could ruin us all. We must turn her out."

Lexie's stomach lurched again, this time in hope.

Out, like in out of here?

Out, like free?

"Too late," Ray said spitefully. Triumphantly. "If we release her now, the Beast at our gate will destroy us all."

Oh, God.

Lexie cleared her throat. "Not all."

The gunmen stared at her. Hostile. Uncomprehending. As if one of the planks in the floor had suddenly dared to address them. Well, she was only a woman. *The woman.* Nobody had once referred to her by name.

"You had nothing to do with this," she said to Daniel. She broadened her appeal to include the other men, hoping to strike a spark in one of them. Not compassion. But maybe . . . self-preservation? "None of you had anything to do with this. They're after Ray. If you let me go—"

A vise—Ray's arm—closed on her waist, constricting her lungs, cutting off her air. His hand clamped over her face. She tried to bite him, and his fingers dug into her jaw. She struggled to breathe.

"Lies," Ray said viciously. "Satan's lies. He wants you to believe her. Give up your souls for a chance at a plea bargain. Let her go, and his forces will lay waste our fenced city to a ruinous heap."

He might sound like something out of a biblical B movie, but he was really serious. His spittle flecked her cheek. She clawed at his hand, desperate for air.

"Keep her, and we sacrifice our homes to your lust and ambition," Daniel intoned.

"Better to die in glory than live as cowards."

"It's not cowardice to live in peace with our neighbors."

"Defeat is not peace," Ray shot back, loosening his lock on Lexie's jaw. "Surrender is not peace. We are at war. And you gave up your command a long time ago."

Lexie dragged in her breath. And noticed she was the only one in the room breathing.

Tension pulsed in the air like warring weather systems over a divided map. Hot and cold. Ray and Daniel. The pressure was suffocating.

Daniel drew himself up. Despite his bulk, he seemed suddenly hollow, his menace about as real as the Stay Puft Marshmallow Man's in *Ghostbusters*.

"Bring her to my office," he snapped.

Ray's arm tightened. Lexie's heart pounded against her ribs.

Nobody moved.

The old man didn't repeat his order. He must have understood—he must have feared it wouldn't be obeyed.

He strode across the room, ponderous and alone, and stopped in front of Ray and Lexie. He grasped her wrist. His fingers were cool and trembled slightly. His grip was strong.

"I'm taking her with me," he announced.

Lexie froze, afraid to speak, afraid to blink, afraid to do anything to tip the balance of power.

"Where?" Ray demanded.

"To my office."

Another pause, while the air crackled and hummed and Lexie's stomach quivered.

Slowly, Ray's hand trailed from her mouth down her throat—a warning squeeze—and across her breasts. Indolent. Possessive.

She shuddered. *Jack. Rescue me, rescue me.*

Ray's other hand kneaded her waist.

If his touch roamed any lower, she was going to throw up. It had worked before.

He released her.

She stumbled in her haste to get away from him, Daniel's grip on her arm a fetter and a support. They crossed the room, Ray's gaze jabbing between her shoulders like the muzzle of a gun.

She held her breath, fear warring with relief. She heard, as the door closed behind them, Ray order, "Follow them."

JACK stared across the crowded trailer at Tucker, fear and rage making him temporarily stupid. Or deaf.

"Her father is who?"

His voice was dangerous enough to make the trailer's other occupant, a skinny guy wearing headphones, glance over and frown.

But Tucker never flinched. "Trent Scott. Director of the FBI."

"I know who Trent Scott is," Jack said savagely. She'd told him her father was in law enforcement. Fuck. "Why didn't you tell me before?"

Tucker returned his gaze levelly. "Why didn't she?"

Jack didn't know. He didn't know anything.

You don't even know who I am, really, she'd said to him last night when he tried to tell her he loved her. And he'd brushed aside her uncertainty, confident his heart and his dick couldn't be that wrong.

Surprise, surprise.

Wounded, he went on the attack. "What the hell were you thinking, sending her in there?"

"I was hoping to further an investigation."

"Further your career, you mean," Jack growled.

Shit. He was going to get his ass kicked out of here. But Tucker, surprisingly, didn't lose his temper.

"My career is shot," the sheriff said. "I knew that when she went in. But I hoped I could save some lives. Including your sister's."

Hell.

"So what are you going to do?" Jack asked.

"Right now I'm trying to talk to Locke."

"You don't want to do that," Jack said automatically.

Tucker gave him a hard look.

He should have kept his mouth shut. But that was Lexie in there, and Sally and his nephew. Terror surged inside him. He throttled it.

"In a hostage situation, you need to give the negotiator a way to stall," Jack said. Do the job. One step at a time. " 'I got to check with my boss.' 'He'll never go for that.' 'Let me help you here.' That kind of thing. You never want the guy in charge talking directly with the hostage takers."

Tucker nodded.

The terror beat against Jack's barriers, looking for a way out. He set his jaw. "So, have you had any contact with inside? Is she—"

His throat closed. Shit.

Tucker pretended not to notice. "The line into the compound is working, but so far nobody's picking up."

Jack got enough control of his voice to ask, "What about a two-way radio?"

"If we can get one to the gate without getting shot at, sure. But then everybody in Scannerland will be listening in on the negotiations." He dug in his breast pocket. "M&M?"

Jack shook his head at the offered candy. "Maybe that's what Locke wants."

The sheriff shrugged and popped a handful of candies. "Maybe."

It had to be asked. "You call in the FBI?"

Tucker swallowed. "Didn't have a choice, did I?"

No. But it couldn't have been an easy call. Tucker's decision, Tucker's operation, had delivered the daughter of the FBI director into the hands of religious extremists in the wilds of North Carolina.

The sheriff was in deep shit.

Jack fought a tug of fellow feeling. "How long?"

"Before they're here?" Tucker glanced at his watch. "Special agent in charge of the Charlotte field office will arrive within two hours with a crisis negotiator and a couple field agents. They're calling in the Critical Incident

Response Group—Hostage Rescue Team, SWAT personnel, profilers, more negotiators. I have until maybe midnight tonight before the director sets up shop in my office."

The director. Trent Scott. Lexie's father.

And she hadn't told him, hadn't trusted him with the truth. Hadn't trusted him to help. That hurt, damn it.

Jack raised his eyebrows. "I bet they get you a phone line."

"Yeah." Tucker looked over his command trailer. "They just won't let me talk on it."

Jack understood the sheriff's resentment. It wasn't just a turf fight over jurisdiction. Any good cop had to believe he had the right stuff to get the job done. Like Gene Hackman in that stupid movie saying, *Winners always want the ball when the game is on the line.*

Tucker was about to lose the whole damn stadium.

On the other hand, at least he was in the game. Jack wasn't even going to get to play. Tucker's career was at stake. But it was Jack's life, his sister, his nephew in there. His woman.

The frustration was killing him.

The frustration was better than the fear. As long as they got out safely, Jack didn't give a fuck who was responsible. "At least the feds know their job."

"But they don't know these people," Tucker said. "Locke hates the feds even more than he hates us."

Jack struggled to keep his voice flat. Expressionless. "You think Blaine will make good on his threat to blow up the compound?"

Tucker stiffened like a wooden Indian. "Where'd you hear that?"

Jack jerked his head toward the open door of the trailer. "People talk."

Tucker closed his eyes wearily. "Shit. Already?" He didn't wait for a response. "You get Locke on the phone?" he asked the guy with the headphones.

"Not yet, Chief. Line's working, though."

"Great. Fucking great."

"Blaine?" Jack asked again, trying to focus on the investigation so he wouldn't have to think about what might be happening inside the compound. One step at a time. "Would he blow up the compound instead of surrendering to the feds?"

Tucker shrugged. "He has the capability. Weapons and explosives. But there are women in there. Children."

Sally. Isaac.

Lexie.

"I don't think Blaine gives a damn about the women and children," Jack said harshly.

"Let's hope Scott does, then."

Jack jammed his hands in his pockets. He felt cramped, hemmed in by the crowded trailer and his own inability to do anything. "He should. Lexie is his daughter."

"Oh, Scott will negotiate," Tucker said. "But it's going to be bad either way."

"How can negotiating be bad?"

"Because the people of these hills don't trust the federal government. They'll hole up. They'll hold out. You know how long the Freemen standoff lasted in Montana?"

Jack didn't.

"Eighty-one days," Tucker said. "This community can't stand being torn apart for eighty-one days. Those people inside are our neighbors, cousins, brothers. We have to live with them—and with whatever happens—long after Scott and his daughter are gone."

Jack would be gone, too. And while he sympathized with Tucker's frustration, it was the "whatever happens" part that really bothered him.

Blaine was sitting on a powder keg. He'd murdered one deputy already. He had a damn short fuse and nothing left to lose. No way would he tolerate a protracted siege. And when he blew, everybody Jack cared about could be caught in the fallout.

Yeah, that bothered him a lot.

TWENTY

L EXIE huddled in stiff, blank terror. Things had gone wrong, all wrong. Terribly wrong. She was pretty sure she was going to die, and Jack's sister and a bunch of other people could die, and it would all be her fault. The horror of Deputy Greene's death and the responsibility of all the other deaths paralyzed her. It was easier not to feel, not to think, not to move at all.

The phone shrilled in the silence, startling in its normalcy. Somebody out there was trying to reach her. To help her. The sheriff? Or Jack?

I won't forgive myself if anything happens to you.

Lexie shivered. She wouldn't forgive herself, either. But since she'd be dead, maybe her feelings didn't matter.

She raised her head from her knees.

Daniel Locke slumped at his desk, ignoring the ringing phone, his face slack and his eyes dull. He looked a lot like she felt, and that annoyed her.

Ray Blaine had just threatened to blow up the compound and everybody in it.

Daniel should do something.

She should say something.

"You can fix this," Lexie said.

Daniel didn't glance at her. He hadn't bothered to tie her up. Obviously, he didn't consider her either a threat or a flight risk.

And she wasn't.

Even if she could overpower him, she would never get past the guard at the door. And beyond the guard was Ray. She really didn't want to mess with Ray.

No, she had to take her chances with Daniel.

If Daniel would just take a chance.

"There is no fixing this," the Disciples' leader said heavily. "There is no going back."

The phone fell silent.

Lexie felt another welcome spurt of adrenaline. Impatience. "But you can look forward," she said. "You can still save yourself."

"My fate is in the hands of the Lord."

"Well, the fate of everybody else is in your hands," Lexie snapped. She lowered her voice in case the pimple-faced guard was listening through the door. "So maybe you should *do* something."

IT was up to him to do everything.

Ray looked from Gary's sweaty face to Eric's blank one. Good men, loyal men, but not leaders. They were simply tools, suitable for the task at hand but not particularly sharp.

He was the one with the intelligence to plan this operation. The only one with the will to carry it out. It was right he had been chosen by God to lead them.

He had tolerated Daniel's flimsy show of authority in the common room. As leader of the militia, Ray had taken care to model discipline for his men. Restraint. Respect. He wasn't going to undercut their training by wrestling an old man for possession of a woman.

Not in front of witnesses.

Besides, Daniel was only taking Alexandra to his office. Ray could put his hands on her anytime he wanted her.

His hands. On her. He opened his mouth to breathe.

"Anything else, sir?" Gary asked.

Ray shook his head, shutting away the thought of Alexandra—*warm, soft flesh yielding*—the same way he shut out the sound of the phone ringing on the guard room wall. "Post a guard at the tunnel entrance."

Eric frowned. "Shouldn't we bring the weapons up? To, you know, prepare for an attack?"

Ray suppressed his irritation at having his orders questioned. "Aren't you armed already?"

"Yeah, I mean, yes, sir, but—"

"We can't spare the manpower to move weapons around. I want every man over the age of ten on the wall with his rifle. Our extra stores can stay where they are. For now."

To bring the cause power through victory, Ray thought. He flushed with excitement.

Or glory in defeat.

DANIEL regarded Lexie with open dislike.

Not the reaction she was hoping for.

Or accustomed to. Most people liked her. She was good at making people like her, damn it.

She moistened her lips and tried again, as if Daniel were a recalcitrant toddler she was coaxing to smile for the camera. "I know you want to see this end as peacefully as possible. It would be a shame if people were hurt because things got out of hand."

Still no response.

Maybe she should be more direct. "Can Ray really blow up the compound?"

Daniel's mouth tightened. He stared stonily over her head.

Okay, not that direct. "Come on, I'm not wearing a wire now. If there's a way for you to stop him . . . If you talked to the sheriff . . ."

"Negotiations cannot change what will be," Daniel pronounced.

Lexie sighed. Maybe he was right. She tried to remember anything her father had ever said about hostage negotiations, but all she knew was what she'd learned from movies and TV. The United States did not negotiate with terrorists.

But admitting that meant admitting defeat.

"It might be more useful—for you," she said carefully, "if you told the sheriff where the bomb is."

"There is no bomb," Daniel said.

No bomb was good. "So Ray is"—*don't say lying, don't make him mad*—"bluffing?"

Daniel looked at her bleakly.

Her heart quailed.

"Okay, not bluffing." *Give me something,* she thought. *Something to work with. Something to hope for.* "So . . . What? He has explosives? Weapons?"

"You want me to betray my cause."

She fought to keep her voice steady. "I think we want the same thing. You want to save your people, and I want . . ."

She wanted to live.

She wanted to see Jack again.

She wanted to tell him she loved him, without waffling or holding back.

The phone rang again, jangling. Insistent.

Lexie started.

Daniel froze.

"Pick it up," she whispered. "Please."

SALLY usually didn't mind cleaning detail. She wasn't afraid of hard work. She enjoyed the chatter of the other women as their young children played nearby, and if her soul sometimes shrank from the cheerless order of the public rooms, well, at least her husband couldn't find fault with her scrubbing.

But today her back ached, her hip hurt, and her bruises protested. She'd been excused from heavy duty all week. So what was so urgent it required her attention in the middle of a Saturday afternoon, a time when most women were baking for the Sabbath?

The women in her detail, sturdy Joan and plain Elizabeth, waited silently by the common room door, looking put upon and sulky. Ray had banned the children from coming with them today.

Despite her cracked lip, Sally did her best to smile. "Let's see what kind of mess they've made for us this time," she said cheerfully, and pushed open the door.

Joan gasped.

Blood.

Blood everywhere.

Red spots danced before Sally's eyes. Her heart drummed. She blinked and heard Elizabeth being sick into her bucket.

Blood sprayed the wall and the long window at the front of the room. Blood puddled in the planks of the floor. So much blood, it was hard to believe it could all come from one source, one man lying in—Sally's breath froze—the stained brown uniform of the sheriff's department.

She swayed and gripped her mop handle tightly for support. Forcing her legs forward, she stared down into the dead man's face.

It wasn't him. The sheriff. Sally was ashamed of the rush of relief she felt. This was the face of the younger man, the man with the mustache.

The one who had been friendly with Ray.

"We're going to need more water," she said, amazed her voice only shook slightly. "And a tarp. Elizabeth, will you get them, please?"

Elizabeth covered her face and moaned.

"I should go with her," Joan said.

Don't leave me here alone, Sally thought.

But she nodded and said, "Close the door behind you. We don't want the children to see this."

She listened to their footsteps escape down the hall. Her breath rasped in the silent room. The air stank of blood and urine. She could see the dark stain on the front of the young man's uniform trousers. He lay as he must have fallen, with his legs crumpled under him and his brains fanned out on the wall behind him.

Poor man. Poor boy.

She set down her bucket and reached with trembling fingers to close his pale blue eyes. That was better. Encouraged, she tugged at his body, arranging his arms, straightening his legs, trying to restore some dignity to his death.

His body was heavy. Panting, she wrapped both hands around his ankle to pull his leg straight and fumbled. Some kind of lump made it hard to get a grip. She pushed up his pants leg to see.

Her heart leaped into her throat. Strapped above his boot was a small black revolver in an ankle holster.

She stared at it a long time.

DANIEL glared and picked up the phone.

Lexie sagged with relief, so giddy she almost missed his first words.

"This is Locke. Who is this?" A pause and then, "I want to talk to the sheriff."

A longer pause, while Lexie's heart threatened to beat out of her chest and Daniel's face lengthened in displeasure. "She's here. I can't . . . I suppose." He scowled at her. "This man needs to verify you're all right."

Lexie snatched the receiver. "Yes?"

"Miz Scott?" She didn't recognize the tenor twang, up-beat as a morning DJ on a country music station. "Hold a minute, please."

Her fingers cramped on the receiver.

"Lexie? That you, babe?"

Tears sprang to her eyes and burned in her throat. She swallowed. "I . . . Yes, it's me, Jack, I'm—"

"That's affirm," she heard him say, his voice slightly muffled, before it flowed, warm and strong, over the line. "Lexie, we need to know if everybody there is all right."

"No," she choked out. "Deputy Greene . . . Oh, God, Jack, Ray—"

"Give me the phone," Daniel demanded.

"He shot him," Lexie said, as rapidly as she could. "He took his gun and both the wires. Locke got me away to his office, but there's a guard outside with—"

"The phone," Daniel said, and wrested it from her, shoving her to the floor.

Pain shot through her wrist as she landed. She grunted. "Lexie?"

" 'For how can I endure to see the evil that shall come unto my people?' " Daniel declaimed in a terrible voice. " 'Or how can I endure to see the destruction of my kindred?' "

"What the hell . . . ?"

Lexie curled in a ball on the floor, cradling her wrist.

"Emmanuel 3:50," Daniel said.

"Yeah. Yeah, okay." She could hear Jack's voice, faint and distorted but still calm. Controlled. "I can hear you're . . . I hear that you're concerned. I'm going to give you to Larry here, and he'll talk to you about that destruction stuff. But can I speak to Miss Scott again? Just for a second. Just to make sure everybody's okay."

To Lexie's astonishment, Daniel meekly handed her the phone.

"Babe, you all right?"

"Yes, I'm . . ." Hurt. Scared. *Rescue me.* "I'm fine. Don't worry. Jack, I'm so sorry."

"It's okay," he said, strong and reassuring. "You did what you had to do. Listen, babe, I've got to put the negotiator on the line now. He's going to get you out of there."

She clutched the phone, blinking with pain, desperate to hold on to him. "No, I . . . I should have told you. I meant to tell you—"

"It's okay," he said again quickly. "I know. Tucker told me."

He was talking about her father.

She shook her head, forgetting in her frustration that he couldn't see. "Not that. Remember when I said I thought I might be . . . I should have . . . Jack, I might not get another—"

"Don't say it."

"Excuse me?" She wasn't offended. Just hurt and confused. She wanted to tell him she loved him, the dumbass.

"I want to hear it in person," Jack said gently. "Let the negotiator do his job, and whatever it is, you can tell me when you see me, okay?"

THE phone jangled again.

Gary jerked. "Should you get that?"

"It's only the sheriff," Ray said. *Big, stupid Indian.* "Let him wait. Let him wonder."

Ray was in control. It felt wonderful. Right.

"Maybe he wants to talk to Father Daniel," Eric suggested.

Ray twitched with annoyance. "Father Daniel is indisposed," he explained patiently. "Until he recovers, I am in charge here."

The ringing stopped.

Was it Ray's imagination, or had the last ring been cut short?

Had the sheriff given up? Or . . . Uncertainty gnawed at Ray. Had Daniel actually answered the phone?

"Get the women and children to the church, and the boys under ten." It was a shame his own son had to be in the group, but as tall as he was at seven, the boy could barely handle a rifle. "I'll speak to them there."

It was important for Ray to be seen calming the flock. And if the sheriff ignored his warnings and decided to attack, the old barn made an easy target. Even the liberal Jew media could not ignore the spectacle of women and children burning.

As soon as his lieutenants departed, Ray strode to the wall phone and silently lifted the receiver.

THE negotiator—they'd been introduced, but Jack only remembered his first name, Larry—huddled over the communication console, the tension in his neck and shoulders giving the lie to his relaxed, good-old-boy twang. Daniel Locke's voice came through his headset and droned over the speakers, a rambling accompaniment to the terse dialogue inside the van.

" 'The wicked shall be a ransom for the righteous,' " Daniel announced, " 'and the transgressor for the upright.' "

"What does he mean, 'ransom'?" asked the female deputy. "Is he offering to give up Blaine?"

"Or he's talking about Scott." Cal Carlson, who was coordinating with the entry team, spoke up. "She could be the transgressor."

"Either way, he's willing to deal," the woman observed. "I don't think he wants a showdown."

Tucker rubbed his face with his hand. He looked tired, Jack thought. Hell, they all were tired. And it had barely been an hour since Greene was shot and Lexie was taken.

Taken. Rage and panic pulsed inside him, shortening his breath.

Jack exhaled and folded his arms, trying to concentrate on the conversation.

"If Locke really wanted to save his people from destruction," Tucker was saying, "he'd get down to talking and knock off the Bible quotes."

The fine hair rose on the back of Jack's neck. He'd been quiet until now, afraid to draw the sheriff's attention and get kicked out. But something had been bothering him, a tickle at the back of his brain, a prickle between his shoulder blades. And now he knew what it was.

"That wasn't a quote from the Bible," he said.

Daniel's voice continued to buzz through the speakers like an angry fly throwing itself against a window.

Tucker barely glanced at him. "Sure it was. Emmanuel something."

Jack shook his head, feeling the prickle grow to an itch. "There is no book of Emmanuel in the Bible."

"Oh, and you would know this because . . . ?"

"Sister Theresa," Jack answered promptly. "Second-grade catechism. I had to memorize all the books of the Bible as punishment for setting off a firecracker under her desk."

Tucker turned to the woman deputy. "Find it on the tape."

The recorder whirred. The tape stuttered. Jack winced to hear Lexie's voice, shaking, eager. *Yes, it's me . . . There's a guard outside . . .*

For how can I endure . . .

"Here it is," the deputy said with satisfaction and re-started the tape.

The negotiator hunched forward, turning down the volume of Daniel's real-time diatribe, listening through his headset as the recorded message rolled tinnily from the speakers. *"For how can I endure to see the evil that shall come unto my people? Or how can I endure to see the destruction of my kindred?"* And then, an instant later, *"Emmanuel 3:50."*

The deputy leaned back in her chair. "Miller's right. I don't know what that's from—Esther, maybe?—but there's no book of Emmanuel."

Carlson shrugged. "So Locke made a mistake. It's not important."

"Important enough that he grabbed the phone," Jack argued. "It was practically the first thing he told us. And the only time he gave a, what do you call it, a citation. He's trying to tell us something."

"Then why not come right out and say it?" Tucker demanded.

Jack met the sheriff's eyes and felt the tension in his gut twist a little tighter. "Maybe he's afraid somebody else is listening."

RAY'S head throbbed. His heart pounded with a terrible and righteous anger.

Daniel was going to ruin everything.

"Give me the phone," he said thickly from the doorway of Daniel's study.

He caught a flash of Alexandra's white, frightened face as he closed the door behind him, as he advanced on Daniel, sitting slack-jawed at his desk.

That was good. She should be afraid. Temptress. Unclean vessel.

Daniel should be afraid. Betrayer.

Ray strode forward, his anger burning within him, swelling within him, filling him with power, like Moses when he saw the calf and the dancing, like Jesus when he chased the money changers from the temple.

Daniel stood, shaking. His chair scraped and fell over. "This is your fault," he said, and resentment crashed through Ray.

This was not his fault, it was Daniel's. He was to blame for betraying their cause, for undermining Ray's plan.

"What did you tell them?" he demanded.

He saw the phone still dangling from Daniel's hand and reached for it, but Daniel clutched the receiver to his chest with both hands.

Rage boiled in Ray. That was wrong. Daniel should give the phone to him. He never, never gave Ray what he deserved. Ray was the one who had finally brought the light

of publicity to their cause. And if they went out in a blaze
of glory, his action would shine as a beacon to freedom-
loving men. He should be the one to talk to the sheriff. To
the sheriff and the media and the FBI.

"Give it to me," he repeated.

"This can't go on," Daniel said into the phone. "I can't
let this go on."

Traitor. Ray had to stop him.

He had to fix this.

He had to fix everything.

He lunged across the desk.

INSIDE the trailer, the air-conditioning labored, but air
and tempers kept getting hotter. The space stank of old car-
peting and bad coffee and frustration. A line of sweat
crawled down Jack's spine.

Tucker shook a cigarette from the pack sitting on the
console. "So, if it's not a book in the Bible, what is it?"

The female deputy stirred on her chair. "Emmanuel? It's
another name for God, isn't it? The Messiah."

Jack frowned. "Some cult thing?" That didn't feel right.

"Or the old copper mine," Carlson offered.

Jack's instincts sprang to attention.

Tucker stiffened. "What?"

"The old Emmanuel works aren't far from here."

"How far?" Jack asked, while everything inside him
jumped and screamed, *This is it!*

Tucker gave him a sharp look but didn't interfere as
Carlson bent over his maps.

"Yeah, here it is," Carlson said. "The main shaft is
about a mile away."

"Any numbers?" Jack asked.

"You want a street address?" Tucker asked dryly. He
looked at the unlit cigarette in his hand as if he'd never
seen one before and put it in his pocket.

"I want to know what '350' means. Locke didn't pull those numbers out of his ass. Does your map show elevations?"

"Three hundred fifty feet is barely above sea level," Tucker said.

"There are three entries into the mine," Carlson said. "Abandoned now, of course."

"Emmanuel 3?" Jack looked at Tucker, trying to keep his excitement in check. "You could check it out."

The sheriff met his gaze, stunned speculation in his eyes, and then shook his head. "I don't have time or manpower to spare on a wild goose chase. Not with your Miss Scott's daddy and the Critical Incident Response Group coming in."

Jack's jaw tensed. "What if it's not a wild goose chase? You said the Disciples stored their munitions underground. What if Locke was trying to give you directions? Coordinates?"

"To a mine a mile away?"

"Maybe there are caves. Tunnels."

"You want me to pull men off my containment team to go crawling around the mountain looking for a crosscut that might not exist to an arms store we've only heard rumors about?"

Jack grinned suddenly. "Yeah."

"Shit," Tucker said in disgust.

"I could go."

"I'm not deputizing somebody who'd be sitting in my jail if he hadn't made bond."

"It's public forest," Jack pointed out. "I'm a member of the public. I could hike up there and check it out."

"You get lost underground, I'll have to send a search and rescue team after you."

"I won't get lost."

"And what would you do if you found something?"

"Report in," Jack said so promptly Tucker laughed.

"Sure you would. After you helped yourself to the nearest M-16 and rushed the compound to rescue your girlfriend."

If there was a way in, there was a way out. If he could get to Lexie and his sister before all hell broke loose, he could bring them out with him.

Jack held the sheriff's gaze, careful to keep his thoughts out of his face. "Just give me a radio. And a gun. You can trust me."

Tucker sighed. "I might say yes just to get you out of my hair."

"Something's happening," Larry reported suddenly.

Jack's heart rate spiked.

Tucker pivoted. "Put it on."

A thump.

A wheeze.

"Mr. Locke?" the negotiator said. "Daniel? Sir, can you—"

Lexie screamed, and Jack's heart died in his chest. "Help! Stop it! Stop!"

Agonizing images—Lexie fighting, Lexie struggling, Lexie raped and beaten—flayed his brain and scraped him raw. His head damn near exploded.

Larry was talking, spouting questions, a continuous spate of words that flowed unchecked across the line and broke against the muffled sounds of struggle.

Another thud. A clatter as something—the receiver?—slid and fell.

And then, amazingly, Lexie's voice, staccato. Clear. "He's choking him. Ray. Ray is strangling Locke. I have to—"

A grunt and then a crash. "Bitch! Whore!"

A cry.

Jack's whole body jerked.

"Do something," he said through his teeth, but Tucker was already huddled with Carlson, ordering the entry team forward, and there was nothing, nothing he could do but stand there, clenching his fists and listening, fear and rage pumping through him.

"Miz Scott? Ray? This is Larry. Somebody talk to me. What's going on? Nobody has to get hurt, I just need you to talk to me . . ."

Jack heard sounds of breathing, a man's rasp, a woman's soft gasps. His body clenched like a fist. *Oh, God, Lexie.*

A soft click, and the line went dead.

TWENTY-ONE

SQUATTING, Ray thrust his face in Lexie's face. His usually pale, clean-shaven skin was flushed. Sweat beaded his forehead and gleamed on his upper lip. She shrank back, nursing her wrist.

"If you do anything, if you say anything, I'll kill you, too," he said thickly.

She believed him.

Her neck and jaw throbbed where he'd hit her. He had never hit her before. No one had ever hit her, really hit her, before. She was surprised how much it hurt.

Daniel Locke's body sprawled across the desk. From her angle on the floor, she could no longer see his blood-congested face, his contorted mouth, his bulging eyes. But she knew he was dead. She'd heard him die, heard the drumming of his feet slow and stop as the flow of oxygen to his brain gradually failed and he slipped into unconsciousness. Cowering on the floor, woozy from Ray's blow, she hadn't been able to save him.

Deputy Greene, dead.

Daniel Locke, dead.

Both men had tried, in their own ways, to protect her. She had never felt so scared in her life.

Or so alone.

Or so angry.

"Killing me won't get you what you want," she said.

Ray looked down his nose at her, which was easy, since she was on the floor. "What do you know about what I want?"

Lexie swallowed. She didn't know. She didn't know him at all. Everything he had said to her before her abduction was a lie. Most of what he'd said afterward was blurred, lost in a haze of drugs and fear.

Maybe he wanted her dead.

She shuddered.

Not a productive thought.

She moistened her lips, trying not to notice how he watched her mouth, and said, "Why don't you tell me?"

"There's no time."

Time. She seized gratefully on the idea. Time was on her side. The longer she delayed Ray, the longer the sheriff had to coordinate a response outside the compound.

"I'm not going anywhere," she said.

Especially not with the guard at the door.

"No, you're not." Ray sat back on his heels, regarding her with satisfaction. "I have plans for you."

Ick. She released her breath. Okay, he was crazy, but he was a religious crazy. A *married* religious crazy. He couldn't mean . . .

She remembered his touch on her breasts and felt cold.

"You said I was a symbol," she reminded him.

Ray nodded. "A child of the darkness. When you are transformed, when you are made holy, then others will see our power and believe."

Another spurt of anger warmed her. Steadied her. She wanted to shout at him that you didn't make people holy by kidnapping them, beating them, or fondling their breasts. But she didn't.

You are one of the gutsiest, most resourceful people I've

ever met, Jack had told her. *You don't need to play the sheriff's game to respect yourself.*

She didn't need to play Ray's game, either. She wasn't going to feed his inflated delusions, his sense of his own importance, with her anger.

She swallowed blood and said, "So, I'm like your celebrity spokesmodel."

Something shifted in Ray's face. Behind his eyes. She thought he was going to hit her again and flinched.

But somebody was pounding on the door, calling. "Sir? Blaine? Father Daniel?"

Ray stood. "Just a minute!"

Seizing Daniel's body under the arms, he dragged it off the desk. Thump. Lexie turned her face away. When she looked back, Ray had somehow folded and stuffed the bigger man's body into the cubby under the desk. The black toe of one shoe peeked out. Her stomach lurched.

Ray tugged his shirt and ran a hand over his neat, dark hair. "Not one word," he warned her and went to open the door.

"They're moving up!" the young guard's excited voice reported. "What should we do?"

"Stay here," Ray ordered. "Stand guard. The sheriff needs to be reminded of the consequences for defying the will of the Lord."

"*FUCK.*" The voice of Jimmy Purdue, point man for the entry team, came clearly through Will's headset. "That's Bobby."

Sick at heart, Will raised his binoculars. The command unit had moved up to within a few hundred yards of the stockade. From his new position he could make out the roofs of the compound buildings, the furtive movement along the top of the wall . . . and the body that had just been dumped outside the gates. A body in the tan uniform of the Dorset County sheriff's department.

"Make entry on my word," Cal said.

Will lowered his binoculars. "Negative," he snapped.

"But, sir." Cal turned off his mike so every word of his protest wouldn't be broadcast to the team. "He's fucking with us. We need to respond."

"He wants us to respond," Will said grimly. *The prick.* "Which is exactly why we can't."

He couldn't afford another mistake. There was more than his career on the line. The lives of the sixty-seven law enforcement personnel and emergency responders circled outside the compound, plus the lives of the fifty-odd armed militia men and their families inside, rested on what he decided now.

If you attack, if you approach at all, I'll shoot her and blow the compound.

Will fished the unlit cigarette out of his breast pocket and stuck it between his lips. "Try phone contact again. And if that doesn't work, get out there on the bullhorn."

While Larry tried vainly to raise the compound, Miller came up beside them.

"Let me help," he said tightly. "Let me do something."

His jaw was tense. His eyes were haunted.

Will took the first slow, blessed drag of nicotine deep into his lungs. He understood the other cop's frustration. Hell, he shared it. They all did.

In an hour, the feds would be here. For Will, whatever the official line was about crisis assistance and support, an "integrated task force" meant he was losing command. He wasn't looking forward to explaining to Trent Scott how he'd prompted, pressured, and persuaded his daughter to go inside the compound in the first place.

But for Miller . . . that could have been his girlfriend's body dumped outside the gate.

And from that look in his eyes, he knew it.

Will blew out a stream of smoke. The last thing he needed complicating a potentially bloody standoff was a vigilante cop from out of town playing Rambo. The last thing he wanted at his first meeting with Scott was Scott's daughter's boyfriend explaining how this was all Will's fault.

If he could get Miller off the scene . . .

Will crushed his cigarette underfoot and turned to Miller. "You want to go on a wild goose chase?"

"YOU can't go in there." Tod Hawley's voice didn't crack, he was too old for that, but it had the same note of bravado Sally sometimes heard in Isaac's voice, defiant and uncertain.

I don't want a bath. I won't go to bed. You can't make me.

Of course, Tod was only five years younger than Sally.

And Isaac had never pulled a gun on her.

Sally tightened her grip on the tray, praying Tod wouldn't notice how badly her hands were shaking. "Ray told me to bring her something to eat."

And the magic phrase—*Daddy says*—worked as well on Tod as it did on Isaac.

Sally held her breath as he glanced at the soup and flipped back the napkin covering the bread basket. "Okay. Be quick."

She didn't move.

"What are you waiting for?"

"I need you to open the door."

Scowling, he complied.

A woman scrambled from the floor by the desk. Blonde. Pretty. Ray's "important guest." She looked up anxiously as the door opened, and Sally got a good look at her face. She winced in sympathy.

"Hey." The blonde smiled tentatively. "I remember you."

"No talking," Tod ordered.

Sally set the tray on the desk. Something in the room smelled bad. "I brought you some lunch."

"Thanks." The blonde's smile twisted ruefully in her swollen face. "Got any ice? Or aspirin?"

"No talking," Tod repeated.

Sally shook her head. "Just soup and bread."

"I'm not sure I can chew. But soup sounds good."

Sally's heart beat faster. She met the other woman's eyes, desperate for her to see. To understand. "You should try the bread."

"And you should shut the fuck up," Tod said.

Sally ducked her head. There was nothing else she could say. Nothing else she could do. Shame and hate and hope wriggled inside her like snakes.

Tell the sheriff who's responsible for what happened.

I am.

She just hoped she'd done enough.

THE tunnel was breathing. Odd currents fretted and sighed along the dark passage.

Up ahead, Jack could see his guide's light dance on the broken floor and rough arched walls of Emmanuel entry 3. The light from Jack's borrowed helmet chased after him.

Ron Bailey, a firefighter for Dorset County, had groused about being pulled from the Disciples' stakeout to baby-sit Jack on his way over, and then under, the mountain.

"What if there's a fire?" he had demanded.

"Think of this as fire prevention," Tucker suggested, and since then, Bailey hadn't talked much or slowed down at all.

But Jack was grateful for his company. Despite the map and compass in his pocket, the lantern and battery pack, the rope and even—thanks to God and Tucker—the service pistol Jack now carried, he felt disoriented and ill-equipped underground.

They were barely inside the tunnel's entrance, making their way along an uneven surface under curved, irregular walls, and already it was black as hell.

Jack's heartbeat pounded in his ears. The cold breath of the tunnel touched the back of his neck. He concentrated on counting his steps, struggling to take even strides over the sloping, uneven floor. Forty-two, forty-three . . .

"Well, shit," Bailey said softly.

Jack stopped. "What is it?"

"Fifty yards, you said?"

"Fifty feet, fifty yards, yeah, whatever."

"Fifty yards," Bailey confirmed. "And we got ourselves a tunnel opening on the right."

His flashlight beam swept over it. *Emmanuel 3. Fifty.* A rough-cut hole banded by rotting timber.

Jack's pulse quickened. "Not such a wild goose chase after all," he murmured.

"What do you want to do?" Bailey asked.

The hole yawned, black and cold.

"Follow it," Jack said, which was a lie.

Bailey shrugged. "Your call."

They radioed first, reporting their findings. Reception was already breaking up. When they went in, they would be without contact. Without backup.

Bailey patted his gear: ropes and friction devices butter-flied over his chest, a battery pack looped to the webbing belt on his waist. "All set."

Jack stooped and followed him into the tunnel.

It was quiet and dark. Really quiet. Really dark. Only the scuff of their boots and the rasp of their breathing broke the silence. The ceiling was lower and the air was closer here. Dank. Still. Choking.

Something moved high on the wall, just out of reach of the light. Bailey's beam shifted and froze on two tiny, furry forms, clinging to a cleft in the rock.

Bats.

Jack thought of Lexie and smiled in the darkness.

Name one thing you're afraid of.

Being buried alive.

His smile faded. He took a deep breath and moved on.

LEXIE stared at the disabled phone and wished, now that it was too late, she'd called her father. *Hi, Dad, you were right, the world is a dangerous place full of terrible men, and I don't have the sense God gave a goat.*

It would have made him so happy.

It might have kept her alive.

Of course, there was a good chance the sheriff had called Trent Scott by now. In which case, her father was definitely unhappy and making life for everyone around and under him absolutely miserable.

I'm sorry, Daddy.

She hugged her knees, trying to summon the energy to think. To fight. But the throbbing of her jaw distracted her. Exploring the inside of her mouth with her tongue, she tasted blood.

Damn it, she wasn't like her brilliant, disciplined mother or her ambitious, aggressive father. All that fabulous genetic material, and she was still only Lexie, whose best efforts were never quite good enough.

She had already checked the window—no exit—and the desk—no gun. She'd pocketed the long letter opener in the top drawer, although her father had told her once that a knife was a man's weapon and any woman who armed herself with a blade could expect it to be used against her.

She remembered the almost casual way Ray had knocked her to the floor and shivered, frightened. Angry.

She'd told Jack she couldn't let Ray win. But he was racking up points, and she hadn't even scored. He'd shot Deputy Greene. He'd strangled Daniel Locke. He'd hit Lexie, and she was pretty sure he must have beaten the dark-haired, defeated woman with the tray, too. She had the split lip. The swollen jaw. Hey, they probably looked enough alike to be sisters . . .

Lexie's breath caught.

Not her sister.

Jack's.

*   *   *

Prayer For All Souls

Beloved Mother hear my prayer.
I ask you to remember my loved ones
who have passed.

I pray that you will hold them
in your loving embrace,
just as you held your Son
and wept by His side.

Comfort us who have lost a loved one
and quiet our pain with the knowledge
that they are at peace in heaven.

You, who are our compassionate Mother
and understand our suffering,
bring our sorrow and petitions
for our beloved deceased before your Son.

Fill us with new hope and joy
that you will keep each of us
close to your heart now and forever.

Amen.

Franciscan Friars • 143 E. Pulaski St. • Pulaski, WI 54162-0100

THE ceiling gradually lowered on Jack's head. Or maybe the floor rose, built up over years of drifting dirt and falling debris. Either way, it made progress a bitch. Jack went from standing to stooping, from stooping to crouching, from crouching to . . .

He eyed the hole in front of Ron Bailey with disbelief. "Who mined this place? Dwarfs?"

Bailey shrugged. "Roof's down," he answered, as if Jack couldn't see that for himself. "We crawl, or we go back."

They crawled.

Unlike Bailey, Jack didn't have kneepads. Rocks struck through the soil at his unprotected knees and scraped his hands. His helmet bumped the ceiling. The darkness pressed his lungs. Despite the cold, sweat collected at the waistband of his pants and ran down his face. He concentrated on breathing in and out, in rhythm to the same four notes playing over and over in his head. It was several minutes before he recognized them. *Heigh ho, heigh ho . . .*

Yeah, off to work.

If you were a cop, you knew not every lead would pan out. For every minute of action, there were hours of boredom. For every moment of triumph, long days of frustration. For every kid saved from the street, every bad guy put behind bars, there were a dozen others gunned down, gone bad, let loose.

That was your job. The only thing you could count on was the lousy odds.

But Jack had never crawled through stifling blackness, cut off from all communication, with no clue what was going on over his head and the life of everybody he cared about on the line.

He'd failed them before. The knowledge pressed on him, colder and more implacable than the dark.

What made him think he had a shot at saving them now?

Lexie's face, Lexie's eyes, glowed like a candle in his memory. *You haven't forgiven yourself for not saving them.*

Fucking A, babe.

But he kept crawling, pushing his weight forward with

his toes to save his abused knees. Because whatever he thought, whatever he believed, whatever he feared, he had to try.

The light from his helmet bobbed ahead of him. He could just make out the bottoms of Bailey's boots.

And then they stopped.

Jack wriggled forward, wedging in beside Bailey. Ahead, the passage angled and broadened, opening into a man-made cave. Jack played his light over massive posts like tree trunks, pounded into a slope supporting the roof. And piled between the supports, in wooden crates and plastic tarps, were weapons. Explosives. An arsenal of destruction.

Holy shit.

They'd found the guns.

A few minutes later, Jack raised a corner of tarp covering a pile of assault rifles—Soviet AK-47s and Israeli Galils, mostly—and pursed his lips in a silent whistle. The Disciples had more weapons than Iraq. Hell, if Jack kept looking, he might even find those weapons of mass destruction.

But he didn't have time for a thorough search or even a complete count. Bailey had to go back. Tucker was waiting to hear from them. And Jack needed to go forward. Lexie was waiting, too.

At least he hoped to God she was.

LEXIE inhaled carefully, as if the extra oxygen would help her think.

Jack's sister Sally had been stoned. The sheriff said so. She was the victim in the photographs.

Soup-and-Bread Lady could not be the victim in the photographs, because it was after the stoning when she escorted Lexie to the bathroom, and she hadn't had a mark on her then.

Therefore, Jack's sister could not be Soup-and-Bread Lady.

Or . . . Lexie pressed her fingers to her temples. She

couldn't think. Maybe watching people die killed your brain cells. Her head hurt. Her jaw radiated pain, and the inside of her cheek bled.

Or the sheriff was wrong, and Jack was right, and Sally had never been stoned. Beaten, maybe, after Lexie's escape, but not stoned.

Okay. Lexie drew another shaky breath, trying to ignore the pain in her head and the stench of death that thickened the air. That made sense. Who better to serve Ray's prisoner than Ray's wife?

So Ray had tricked the sheriff into believing Sally was the victim, and Ray had gotten away with murder. Score another point for Ray.

For a minute, Lexie felt pretty good. She'd figured it out. But then a lifetime of doubt reasserted itself. What did it matter if she knew what Ray was up to? Pretty soon the whole world would know, courtesy of CNN and half a dozen network special reports. Ray wanted them to know. That's why he'd kidnapped her in the first place.

She had to do better.

She had to do more.

She struggled back to her feet. She could start by eating. Keep up her strength, as her mother would say. She drank a little water, rinsing the taste of blood from her mouth, and then a spoonful of soup, but the smell turned her stomach.

You should try the bread.

Right. Blessing Sally, Lexie picked the soft center from a piece of bread and chewed cautiously. Not bad. Swallowing, she reached for another slice. Her fingers brushed something beneath the bread. Something hard. Something hidden under the napkin.

Her heartbeat quickened. With shaking hands, Lexie pulled back the cloth lining of the basket.

And uncovered the snub black shape of a Smith and Wesson .38.

TWENTY-TWO

A noise floated out of the darkness.

Echoes. Voices. Fuck.

Jack dropped the tarp and grabbed Bailey's arm.

Yep. Voices and boots, coming from the other side.

They both shut off their lights. Jack melted behind a pile of crates. He heard Bailey scuffle back toward the passage, the sound masked, thank you, Jesus, by the approaching boots.

Voices, boots, and lights, all coming toward them.

His heart pounded.

Flashlights darted and circled on the floor beyond the crates. A snap, a hum, and shop lights flickered feebly from the supports overhead.

The sudden light made Jack squint. He turned his head, hardly daring to breathe. No Bailey. That was good. Maybe the firefighter was already on his way to report to Tucker.

"Grab the other end, will you?"

They were moving the munitions. Shit.

"Not that box," another voice ordered.

"Why not?"

"We're supposed to leave the rifles. Just bring up the explosives."

"Why?"

"Blaine's orders. C-4, blasting caps, and detonator cord."

"You can't throw C-4 at an enemy," the first speaker objected.

No, Jack thought, his blood running cold. But you could use it to blow up a compound and every living thing inside.

The second man—from the sound, there were only three of them—ignored the protest. "Heavy boxes first."

A grunt. "Where are we taking this?"

"The barn."

Jack closed his eyes. He couldn't take on three armed men without backup.

Three armed men with their hands full who weren't expecting an attack. That evened the odds.

Three armed men with their hands full of plastic explosives on their way to blow up everybody Jack cared about and a bunch of people he didn't. That changed the equation altogether.

He waited until he heard them shuffle across the dimly lit cavern and re-enter the dark tunnel to the compound.

Silently, he rose—stopping once to fill his pockets—and followed them.

TRENT Scott was possibly the biggest blowhard Will had ever met.

In a career that spanned eight years in the Army and seven dealing with backcountry politicians, that was saying a lot.

The suits accompanying the FBI director were professionals—buttoned-down, uptight career bureaucrats. But Scott had the hard-line ideology and fervor of a political appointee. He even looked like a politician, with his starched white shirt and his thick, graying hair and a smile that never reached his eyes.

Not that the poor bastard had any reason to smile, Will admitted as he stood sweating on the carpet inside the crowded trailer.

That was his daughter inside the compound.

And Will's operation that had put her there.

But Will knew men on his own team who had loved ones inside the compound, too. Not daughters, but neighbors, friends, cousins, brothers. And to Will's mind, Scott was making a big mistake taking the operation away from them and turning it over to a task force with no ties and no personal stake in the outcome.

He'd said so, first politely, and then, as time wore on and the Disciples continued to ignore the FBI negotiator talking to them through the newly rigged loudspeaker system outside their walls, less politely.

At least one of the blue suits with Scott—a behavioral scientist named Roberts—agreed.

"Most of these militia don't want to fire on their neighbors," Blue Suit argued earnestly. "You send in federal agents wearing SWAT gear, and they're going to fight like you sent in the devil himself."

Scott's face was red. "I'm sending in a fully equipped, professional force. Those insurgents are not going to get away with threatening our national security and defying our system of government."

"They won't," Roberts assured him. "An ongoing investigation—"

"An ongoing investigation will not free my daughter. I want her out of there. If they don't give her up—give her up now—they're going to pay."

"Or she will," contributed another suit quietly. Special Agent Laura Haggerty, middle-aged, poker-faced, with the reserved calm of a psychiatrist. "Sir, we need to negotiate."

Scott fumed. "We can't negotiate if this Blaine character won't talk to us."

"Blaine is a wild card," Haggerty conceded. "I'd expect him to use our presence as an opportunity to get his message out. It's unusual that he hasn't made any contact. Any demands. We have very little to work with."

"Maybe he's waiting for CNN to show up," Roberts said.

"Maybe he won't wait," Trent Scott said. "We need to create a diversion—tear gas, something—and go in."

"Those are exactly the strategies that didn't work at Waco," Haggerty said tightly. "We need to resolve the situation peacefully."

"We need to resolve it," Scott said. "I'm not having my bureau or this administration depicted in the media as being soft on terrorism just because a bunch of Bible-thumping backwoodsmen have got their hands on my daughter. I'll make them sorry they messed with me."

Silence in the trailer.

And even though his own career was now officially in the crapper, Will caught himself feeling sorry—not for Blaine, that bastard didn't deserve his pity—but for poor Alexandra Scott.

JACK tugged on the belt securing the third guard's arms and then slumped against the wall, breathing hard and clinging to the cold stone for balance. Sweat ran down his back. Blood ran down his face. He swiped at it absently and hissed in pain. The gash on his forehead must have reopened.

But he was three down and nobody dead yet, although he was pretty sure the second guy he took down was going to need medical attention soon.

He'd stopped them. He'd stopped Blaine from blowing himself and everybody around him to kingdom come.

At least until Blaine noticed his thugs weren't back yet with his C-4 and sent somebody else to investigate.

Jack sagged. He was so close to Lexie, so close to playing the hero she needed and he wanted to be. But he couldn't leave the weapons cache unprotected while he searched for her. He couldn't stay and defeat the Disciples one at a time as they came down the passage.

He had to seal the tunnel.

If he did, he'd be blocking his planned escape route.

But if he didn't, and Blaine wired the compound with C-4, there would be no escape. Not for Lexie, not for Sally and her son, not for anybody.

Jack fingered the grenade in his pocket. He didn't have to be a member of the bomb squad to know he couldn't pull the pin here without detonating the kind of explosion he was trying to prevent. He would have to set it off from the other end.

Staggering to his feet, Jack grabbed the first guard under the shoulders and began to drag him up the tunnel toward the compound.

"CHRIS got a rifle," Isaac said, dragging his feet as Sally tried to hurry him along. "And Danny got a rifle. And Ben and Gideon both got rifles *and* they got to go with their dads. Why do I have to go to the barn with the babies?"

"Because it's safer, ba—" Sally bit the word back a moment too late.

Isaac scowled at her, looking so much like a miniature Ray that her heart quailed.

She looked back at him helplessly. Her son. Her baby. She might already have lost him even though he hadn't gone to the Men's House yet, even though he wasn't with the other boys on the wall.

He hung his head. "It isn't fair."

It wasn't safe, either, Sally realized. What was Ray thinking, crowding the women and children into the largest, most flammable building in the compound? Painted red, for heaven's sake, like the bull's-eye in the center of a target.

"Then let's find someplace else," she said. "Just the two of us."

Isaac looked at her through his lashes, a gleam of interest in his eyes. "Like where?"

Sally felt a flutter of panic. Where? Not on the walls where the shooting would start, not in some outbuilding that could be shelled and forgotten . . .

"The big house?"

Father Daniel was in the main building. And Ray's "important guest." Surely they would be safe there?

"The kitchen?" Isaac suggested with another upward gleam.

Of course. She had missed the Sabbath baking. So had he.

She smiled at him, her insides dissolving in relief. "Why not?"

JACK grunted as he rolled his last burden under the protective tarp. The son of a bitch weighed a ton, and he wasn't even grateful. Of course, Jack hadn't exactly been gentle, either.

Every second he spent saving these losers took time from his search for Lexie. Every minute gave Blaine another opportunity to notice his men were missing. Each time Jack headed down the tunnel, he expected to hear a rifle ratchet at his back.

Lurching, sweating, bleeding, and cursing silently, he made the trip three times, lugging each bound, gagged, and mostly unconscious bundle twenty yards to the passage mouth.

He was done now. Finished.

Bracing himself against the wall, he dug for the grenade in his pocket.

His hands shook. Exhaustion, he told himself. He depressed the clip. Inserted his finger through the safety ring.

Name one thing you're afraid of.

Ah, Lexie. I should have let you say the words when we both had the chance.

He pulled the pin and lobbed the grenade back down the tunnel. *Clink. Clinkity clink.*

Boom.

And everything went black.

Boom.

The trailer rattled. Will jerked his gaze to the compound. Smoke rolled over the wall. Debris rained down.

"What the hell is that?" Trent Scott demanded.

"It's your diversion," Roberts exclaimed. "Go now, go now."

"Our people aren't in position," Special Agent Haggerty protested.

Will smiled for the first time all afternoon. "Mine are," he said.

Boom.

The floor trembled. The windows shook in their frames.

Lexie squeaked and shivered, reaching out blindly for balance.

Shouting. Gunfire. Confusion. Was the compound under attack?

Uncertainty rooted her feet. She glanced anxiously out the window. Beyond the broken glass, smoke drifted over the ground. Her heart hammered. Was the house on fire? Was the guard still at the door? She tightened her grip on the gun.

Footsteps running in the hall outside.

Hope pushed the air from her lungs. *Rescue me.*

The door burst open, and Ray strode in, his mouth implacable as a marble saint's, the gun he'd murdered Deputy Greene with at his side. His gaze swept the room and caught her. His eyes glittered.

" 'I will render vengeance to mine enemies, and reward

them that hate me.' I warned them. I warned you." He raised his gun.

And she shot him.

"WE'VE secured the gate," Carson reported. "But we're still taking sniper fire."

"Return it," Scott ordered.

"Some of the snipers are kids," Will protested. "Twelve, thirteen years old."

"Kids with semiautomatics," Scott said.

"It would be better if we could negotiate a surrender," Special Agent Haggerty intervened. Thank God for bureaucrats. "Where's the main resistance?"

"The Disciples are still in command of the guardhouse. And there appears to be a large contingent in the barn."

"So smoke them out."

Scott's daughter was inside, Will reminded himself. Fear must be clouding his thinking.

Special Agent Haggerty, on the other hand, was clear and cool as ice. "We don't know how many of those inside are women and children. We can't be sure how the gas will affect them. We don't want to create a scenario where even if we win, we lose."

"Then they have to surrender." Scott stared over the smoking compound. "Why won't they goddamn surrender?"

LEXIE sighted down her pistol barrel and watched Ray die. She didn't want him to die—she had aimed for his shoulder—but her bullet had plugged him high in the right quadrant of his chest. His gun lay where he had dropped it, two yards from his feet. At least he wasn't coughing up blood.

Yet.

Outside, the yard crackled with intermittent gunfire.

Lexie almost wept with tension and fatigue. Her arms ached from the recoil of the shot. Her head throbbed. Her knees trembled. Her palms slipped on the butt of the gun.

Someone had to come soon.

Why didn't someone come?

Ray stirred, as if he could escape the pain.

"Stay where you are," she ordered. Great. Her voice trembled, too.

Ray cocked his head, his dark gaze fixed on her face. "Or what, Alexandra? Or you'll shoot me again?"

She gripped the gun, pointing her shoulder at the target the way her father taught her. "If I have to."

"No, you won't." He sounded almost kind. He was harder to resist when he was kind. Now he sounded like the man who came into the camera shop. Interested. Sympathetic.

Manipulative.

She shuddered.

"I'm dying, you know," he said conversationally. "Do you really want to live with my death on your hands?"

Her gun wavered. She jerked it up. "You were prepared to live with mine."

"But we're different," Ray said gently. Unarguably. "I always knew I was called to do my Father's business. And you . . . Well, you've never really cared for your father's business, have you?"

"So what?"

"So why are you doing what he would want you to do?" Ray raised himself slightly, his breathing fast and shallow.

Oh, God, was he going for his gun?

Something moved in the hallway behind him, but she didn't dare turn her eyes or her gun away from Ray. What should she do? What could she do?

"You're not like him," Ray continued. He was very pale. The blood seeped from his shoulder as he pushed himself to a sitting position. "Isn't that what you told me? He's violent. Controlling. Overbearing."

"You move another inch, and you'll see how violent I can be," Lexie said through her teeth.

"No." Ray smiled at her. "You don't have that kind of confidence. You won't shoot me. You can't."

Her arms shook.

"I can, asshole," Jack said from the doorway, and Lexie sobbed once in relief.

He had a rifle in his hands. He was covered in dirt, his face streaked with blood and sweat and grime like a pinup poster from *Soldier of Fortune* magazine. She'd never seen anyone so beautiful in her life.

"You okay, babe?"

She nodded, but Jack didn't look at her. His face was hard and cold. All his attention was fixed on Ray, bleeding on the floor.

"Do it then," Ray hissed.

"Nope. I'm not making any fucking martyrs today." Jack's voice sharpened. "Get away from that gun."

But Ray lunged forward, his hand reaching desperately. Jack exploded out of the doorway. His foot shot out. The handgun went skittering across the floor. Lexie scrambled for it, aware of the two men struggling behind her.

As soon as she had the gun, she whirled, but the fight was already over. Jack, breathing hard and plenty mad, was on top, his forearm across Ray's throat.

"Where's my sister?"

"Dead," Ray spat.

Jack's face set like flint. "No."

"All the women. All the children. In the barn. You couldn't save them."

Lexie choked off a small sound of distress.

Jack's forearm trembled. *"No,"* he said hoarsely.

"Do it," Ray spat in Jack's face. "You know you want to."

"Yeah. And that's why I'm not going to, you son of a bitch."

"Didn't you hear me?" Ray raised his voice as Lexie

listened in horror. "They *died.* I killed them. I packed the barn with C-4 and I—"

"No, you didn't. Your men never brought the explosives out of the tunnel, you little prick, because I stopped them." Jack eased cautiously off the smaller man's chest, one hand reaching for his own waist. "*Damn* it."

Lexie blinked away tears, her heart so full she could hardly speak. "Jack, I know you're upset. But you made the right choice."

He looked at her as if she were speaking another language.

She tried again. "I'm proud of you. I know it's not easy."

"It's not easy because I used my belt on another guy," Jack explained patiently. "I don't have anything to tie him up with."

"Oh." Disoriented, she glanced around the room for inspiration. "Um . . . how about an extension cord?"

"That would be good."

She yanked one out of the wall and then stood back as Jack secured Ray's arms behind him with cool efficiency. Ray groaned.

"He needs a doctor." Jack glanced at the desk. "Phone working?"

Lexie struggled to function, to focus on what needed to be done. In the yard, another burst of gunfire punctuated the confusion. "No, Ray ripped it out of the wall after he . . ." Why couldn't she stop shaking? She hugged her elbows.

"Murdered Locke?" Jack supplied, with a lift of one eyebrow.

She nodded, afraid if she opened her mouth he would hear her teeth chatter.

"Okay." Jack dug a radio from his pocket, in perfect command of himself and the situation.

Cop mode, she thought, and fought another shiver.

"This is Miller. I'm on scene. Get me Tucker." Jack scowled. "I guarantee he'll want to talk to me. Tucker? Go ahead." His face cleared. "Yeah. Yeah, she's with me. In Locke's office. He's dead. We have Blaine in custody. Tell the gunmen outside unless they want him to die, too, they better give it up." Jack paced. The radio crackled and squawked. "Hell, no, but he needs a doctor. He's been shot."

More squawking. "Copy that. No, it's not a problem. Go ahead. Because they can't access them, that's why. I'll tell you when you get us out of here."

He ended the call.

Lexie tried to control her trembling. "It's over."

"Everything but the parade." Jack grinned at her crookedly and opened his arms.

Thank God.

She ran to him and laid her head on his chest as he held her tight.

TWENTY-THREE

LEXIE waited at the bottom of the trailer steps, shivering despite the heat and the navy FBI windbreaker draped over her shoulders.

Jack, looking solid and competent and tired, comforted his sister in the shadow of the fire truck. Sally was crying and clinging to his arm. Her husband had been taken away in an ambulance accompanied by federal agents. Lexie wondered when Sally would see him again. Or if she would want to.

Their little boy, Isaac, pressed against his mother's skirt. Jack reached over to ruffle his hair. Lexie saw the boy duck his head, flinching from his uncle's big hand. Jack pretended not to notice, hunkering down to pat the boy's shoulder instead. He said something, and Isaac responded with a quick, fugitive smile.

Watching them together, the tough, muscled cop talking so gently to the anxious, awkward boy, made Lexie's heart wobble. She didn't think she might be falling in love with Jack anymore. She knew. And as soon as she got the chance, she would tell him so.

The trailer door opened, and her father exited, flanked by Special Agents Haggerty and Roberts. Haggerty offered Lexie a slight smile on her way to confer with the jacket-and-tie crowd a few yards away.

"There you are," Trent Scott said.

Here she was. Right where she'd been for the past fifteen minutes. But who was counting?

Scott cleared his throat. "They said you were all right."

Lexie clutched the lapels of her borrowed jacket a little tighter. "I'm fine, Dad."

He squinted down at her. She could only guess what he saw. Her face felt tight and swollen, and she tasted blood at the corner of her mouth.

"He didn't rape you or anything, did he?" her father asked abruptly.

Lexie flushed, conscious of the hovering agents. "No."

"Good." He frowned. "You should still have your mother check you out when you get home."

It was the closest to an expression of concern he would allow himself. Lexie smiled.

"I will," she promised.

Even if she had to make an appointment.

Her father shoved his hands into his pockets, apparently relieved to have the mushy stuff out of the way. "This is a fine mess you've gotten us all into."

Lexie stuck out her chin. "I know. I'm sorry."

"How could you let yourself be used by a screwball like that?"

"I didn't know he was a screwball when I met him. He didn't come with a sign."

Special Agent Roberts covered his mouth with his hand.

"Haven't I taught you anything?" Scott said. "It doesn't look good when someone personally connected to this president's administration gets mixed up with some right-wing extremist group. You're lucky things turned out as well as they did."

She was aware of movement around them, furtive

glances, halted conversations, as everyone hushed to listen. It was like the silence in the school lunch room when the class big shot took on the unpopular kid.

Her throat burned. She laughed. "Yeah, I feel really lucky."

Her father glared at her. "Do you think this is funny? Do you know how much of our budget we wasted today on this Hatfields-and-McCoys operation?"

Lexie drew breath to defend herself when Jack stepped up beside her. She hadn't even known he was there.

"For the record," Jack said, "your daughter didn't get mixed up with the Disciples. She was kidnapped. She wasn't lucky. She apprehended Blaine before I showed up, before your hostage rescue team was even on the ground."

Every point he made sharpened the edge in his voice. "Your daughter participated in a multi-jurisdictional investigation with no regard for her own safety because she had reason to believe a crime had been committed and was determined to see the perpetrators brought to justice.

"And if the federal government makes a successful case against this group of well-armed, antigovernment extremists," Jack concluded, very firmly, "it will be in large part because your daughter is going to make a hell of a witness for the prosecution."

Lexie wanted to cheer. She wanted to cry. She wanted to throw her arms around him and never let go.

Scott's face was red. "Who is this dickhead?"

"I'm the dickhead who's in love with your daughter." Jack put his arm around Lexie's shoulders, where it felt heavy and warm and wonderful. "Now you can thank her, you can question her, but I'll be damned if I'll listen to you bully her anymore."

"THE dickhead comment was pushing the envelope," Will Tucker said to Jack. The two men were back in his office after hours of interviews and debriefings. "The rest of it was good, though."

Jack grimaced and rubbed the back of his neck. He was tired, deep in the bone tired, and sore, but adrenaline still buzzed in his blood. Even with arrests made and investigations launched, there were things left unsettled.

And unsaid.

He thought of Lexie. He wanted to see her. He wanted to be with her. He wasn't in any doubt about his feelings or hers. But he'd never been any good at forever. He had no control over their future, and that worried him.

"You heard about that, huh?"

Will smiled. "Everybody heard. I think some of the feebies were taking a collection to buy you a nice gift certificate."

"I thought they'd started a pool on how many hours were left of my law enforcement career."

"Get real. The feds may take all the credit, but everybody knows you saved the day. Along with my ass. If you hadn't stopped Blaine from blowing up the compound, we'd be shoveling body parts tonight instead of processing arrests. You kept a lot of people alive and made a lot more grateful."

"I pissed off the director of the FBI."

"Nobody's perfect." Will pushed a manila envelope across the desk. "But that was one of your finer moments today."

Jack picked up the envelope, hefted it in his hand, and raised his eyebrows. "You're giving me back my Glock?"

"That gun you're carrying is the property of Dorset County. I need it back. Besides, the DA's dropping your case. Ranger Long is no longer considered a reliable complainant."

Jack fought the sudden constriction of his throat. One black mark, at least, was removed from his name. "Good to know."

"Something else you'll be glad to know," Will offered.

Jack paused in the act of holstering his gun.

"Somebody's waiting for you." Will jerked his head toward the door of his office. "Out in the lobby."

Jack's heart began to pound. Trent Scott had made it clear he was bundling his daughter back to Washington despite Jack's claim on her. Or maybe because of it. If Lexie had decided to stay over her father's objections . . .

Jack cleared his throat. "Sally?"

"Your sister and her boy got a room at the Bo-Lo. Courtesy of Miss Scott. I had one of the deputies drive them there. The kid was pretty beat."

Jack told himself not to overreact. Lexie's actions didn't prove she was ready to take him on for good, baggage and all. It was like her to do what needed to be done without making any fuss. Without taking any credit.

But he thought of her voice on the phone that afternoon and the look in her eyes when he took her into his arms, and hope lodged in his chest, bright and sharp as shards of glass.

"In the lobby?" he repeated.

Will nodded.

Jack strode out.

IT was stupid to feel nervous.

Lexie gripped her hands together in her lap, avoiding the curious, sympathetic gaze of Debby Jenkins, the department assistant.

Jack loved her, she reminded herself. He'd said so. Not only in the heat of lovemaking and the privacy of their motel room—her body contracted at the memory—but in the light of day and in front of her father.

I'm the dickhead who's in love with your daughter.

The recollection curved her lips and stiffened her spine. Bolstered, she waited.

But when Jack blew through the door a few minutes

later, her breath and her confidence deserted her. Despite a hasty cleanup in the sheriff's locker room, he looked big and bloodied and dangerous. He was a lot of man. It would take a lot of woman to love him. To live with him.

He stopped in front of her chair, his hands jammed in his pockets and his eyes unreadable. "Tucker said you got my sister a motel room."

She searched his face. Was he offended? But she'd come too far to apologize for trying to help, for doing what she thought was right.

She raised her chin a notch. "You can pay me back."

"I will. Along with the bail money. They're dropping the assault charge," he explained.

She beamed at him, her nervousness forgotten in genuine pleasure. "Jack, that's wonderful!"

"Yeah."

Their eyes met. Her stomach jittered. Jack was a proud man. It couldn't be easy for him, admitting the marks on his record or acknowledging his debts. But he'd done it.

Surely she could do the same?

"I owe you something, too," she said, her heart beating wildly.

"What's that?"

I want to hear it in person . . . Whatever it is, you can tell me when you see me, okay?

She moistened her dry lips. "I . . ." But she wasn't as brave as he was. She was too aware of their surroundings, phones ringing, footsteps echoing, Debby Jenkins watching from behind her desk.

"I wanted to thank you," she said.

His dark, intense gaze never left her face. "For what?"

"For rescuing me." It wasn't what she'd intended to say, but at least it was true.

His mouth quirked. "Babe, you rescued yourself. I just helped with the cleanup operation."

She smiled back, her heart suddenly lighter. "I meant from my father."

Jack shrugged. "You were handling it."

"Yes, but it was nice not to have to," she admitted.

"He loves you, you know," Jack offered unexpectedly. "He's just too big a jackass to figure out how to say it."

She blinked. Well. Maybe she should try to learn from her father's mistakes.

"Ready to go?" Jack asked, a gleam in his eyes.

"Not yet." She stood. "I have something to say to you first."

"You can tell me in private."

He was teasing now. She should have been intimidated. Or annoyed. But everything inside her lifted and lightened at the challenge in his voice.

At the promise in his eyes.

"I want to tell you now."

He rocked back on his heels, grinning at her. "So go ahead. I'm ready."

"Are you?" She put her hands on his hard chest. His heart thudded under her palms.

"Yeah," he said, suddenly serious. "I'm not saying it will be easy, you being in D.C., me in Pennsylvania. The timing could be better. I've got a commitment to my sister, and I still have my suspension hanging over my head. I don't know what's in our future, babe. But I'm ready. I'm ready for you."

"I don't need easy anymore," Lexie said. "I don't want easy."

"What do you want?" he asked, his eyes heavy-lidded.

"You." She touched her lips to his, giving him her kiss. Her trust. The words. "I want you, Jack. I love you."

EPILOGUE

"I can't believe you brought me camping," Lexie said three months later.

Summer lay like a quilt on the North Carolina hills, spread out below in rippling folds of green and gold and smoky blue, beautiful enough to make your breath catch or your heart sing.

"Hey." Jack sounded injured. "I bought you your own sleeping bag."

She glanced over her shoulder where he had finished setting up their tent. With the sun on his face and forearms, he looked fit, tanned, and more relaxed than she'd seen him in weeks. She didn't know how much of his playful mood was because his hearing was behind him and he was back on active duty, and how much of it was because they were together again. For three long, glorious days this time.

She smiled back at him. "What if I don't want my own sleeping bag?"

Jack came up behind her and nuzzled her throat, jolting every nerve in her body to life. "Then maybe you'll share mine."

She turned and looped her arms around his neck. "Sounds good to me."

Later, much later, she lay with her head on his chest, savoring the feel of the crisp whorls against her palm, relishing the strong, steady beat of his heart. Content, replete, and satisfied after too many days and nights apart.

She sighed. "This may sound really selfish, but now I'm glad Sally and Isaac decided not to come on this trip."

Jack patted her bare bottom. "Isaac wanted to. But I think Sally's ready for some space."

Lexie could believe it. Living with Jack in Clarksburg had required a lot of adjustments. A new home, new routines, a new school for Isaac. It had been a much-needed time of togetherness, a time of healing. But now she heard the hesitation in Jack's voice.

"Problems?" she asked.

He played with the ends of her hair. "Not really. Isaac's doing better since school let out. I think Sally's just ready to move out."

"To move on," Lexie suggested gently. She understood Jack's need to support his sister, both financially and emotionally. But Sally's willingness to be independent was a good thing. Maybe this move was just what she needed. What they all needed, Lexie thought, and flushed guiltily.

"You can still see them," she offered. "Every day if you want to."

Jack's chest expanded with his breath. "She wants to move back here."

"Oh, Jack." Lexie raised her head. "How do you feel about that?"

His mouth quirked. "Girlie question."

"Yes, it is," she admitted. "Now answer it."

"Sally thinks Isaac would have an easier time adjusting in a familiar place," Jack said. "I agree with her."

"But you'll miss her," Lexie guessed. They were just learning to be a family again.

"Actually, I was thinking of moving down here with her. Not in the same house. But close by."

"But your job . . . I thought everything was okay. Are there some kind of repercussions or—"

"Nope. Your father put in a good word for me with the chief." Jack grinned. "He probably figured as long as I'm employed, I won't move in with you."

Her heart beat faster. "But you're thinking of moving anyway."

"Will Tucker seems to think he has a shot at winning the next election," Jack explained. "He asked if I'd be interested in a job with the sheriff's department. I'd have to complete the rookie training to be certified in North Carolina, but—"

"He wants you," she said.

Jack grinned. "Actually, I think he wants my sister. But he'd hire me."

"How long would the certification take?"

"I have a year from the time I'm hired to complete the certification and remain on as a sworn officer. But I figured that would give you time."

"Time for what?"

"Time for you to think about marrying me."

Emotion clogged her throat and flooded her eyes.

In every relationship, she had told him, there was one person who plans and one person who sucks it up and goes along. *Or doesn't go along, in which case you don't have a relationship. Not for very long, anyway.*

She was good at going along. At getting along. But was that enough? Was that what she wanted?

Lexie thought of the life she could make here. One of the most beautiful spots in the world. One of the most photographic, for sure. She thought about the fact that there wasn't a camera store closer than Asheville and the business opportunity that might present for someone confident enough to go after it. She thought about living always in the shadow of the mountains, with their beauty and danger, their changing seasons and abiding strength.

Mostly she thought about Jack and how much she loved him and how nice it would be if their time together wasn't limited to snatched visits and stolen weekends.

He had changed. In the past few months, he'd proved his willingness to put his family before his career.

And she had changed, too.

"Well, I don't know," she said slowly and felt him tense under her. "I don't think it will take me that long to make up my mind."

Jack threaded his fingers through her hair and tugged until he could see her face, so much love and hope and heat in his eyes that her insides turned to mush.

"Is that a yes?" he growled.

She smiled and gave him the words so there would be no doubt ever in either of their minds about her answer. "That is definitely a yes," she said. "Now kiss me."

He did.

Her soul soared.

Outside the tent, a lark rose in the blue sky, its song joyous and clear.

Turn the page for a special preview of
Virginia Kantra's next novel

HOME BEFORE MIDNIGHT

Coming soon from Berkley Sensation!

FOR better or worse, there was no place like home. And nothing hotter or lonelier than a Carolina summer night.

Bailey Wells lifted her heavy brown hair off her neck. Outside her window, a willow drooped, pale in the moonlight, listless in the heat.

Even with the windows locked and the thermostat lowered to sixty-five degrees, the air gripped the house like a warm, damp fist. The grinding whine of the cicadas swelled the night and buzzed in her blood. She had to be crazy to leave New York—the lights, the life, the energy—for this.

Not crazy. The thought slipped in like a breeze under the windowsill, stirring her mood. *In love.*

Bailey flushed and dropped her hair. No, that wasn't right, either.

She had perfectly good reasons, professional reasons, for returning to her hometown of Stokesville, North Carolina, starting with the fact that Helen Stokes Ellis—her boss's wife—had a lot kinder memories of the place than Bailey did. No wonder. Twenty years ago, when Bailey had been the official geek of the fourth grade, Helen Stokes had ruled the high school. With her children grown and her handsome new husband receiving the lion's share of attention in New York, Helen wanted to go home.

And Helen usually got what she wanted.

Paul had broken the news.

"I would never insist that you come with us," he had said, with one of his special looks. "But you know I want you."

Bailey's heart beat a little faster.

"We both want you," he had added. "You must be my translator. We can band together against the natives."

She was one of them. The natives. He knew that. Four years at Bryn Mawr and six years in New York hadn't completely eradicated the South from her vowels.

But she was pleased Paul saw her as something more, as something special. And flattered when, after the move, he insisted she make her home with them, with Paul and Helen, in Helen's house. God knew, he had said with a droll look, there was enough room.

The old Stokes place had been built in the 1930s for a large and prosperous family. The sweeping verandas and imposing columns in front were balanced by two thoroughly modern additions in back, the master suite and a kitchen-and-dining wing, flanking an Olympic-size pool.

Bailey had her own room and bathroom in the original part of the house, with high ceilings and heavy wood trim that more than made up for the uneven floors and cramped shower. Maybe she didn't have a view of the pool, but she was welcome to use it whenever Helen wasn't entertaining or sunbathing or, well, there.

She wouldn't be there now, Bailey thought, glancing at the clock. It was almost midnight. On her "at home" nights, Helen liked to nurse her nightcap through an hour of television and then pass out in bed. No one would notice, no one would care, if Bailey snuck down to the kitchen and fixed a snack to eat by the pool.

Unless Paul was up, working.

Bailey pushed the thought away.

She made her way downstairs in the dark, refusing even to look in the direction of his study to see if his lights were on. All she wanted was to sit by the pool and watch the cool gleam of the water and the bugs committing suicide in the patio lights while she smothered her restlessness in ice cream. *Stress eating,* Dr. Phil called it. *Ask yourself what you really want.*

She knew what she wanted.

And what she couldn't have.

Ice cream was better. Safer.

In the kitchen, she dug deep into a round carton of Edy's butter pecan. The heaped ice cream looked lonely in the bowl, so she added sliced strawberries and then a squeeze of chocolate syrup and then—on impulse—a second spoon.

Two-fisted eater? her conscience mocked.

She ignored it. Carrying her spoils, she slid open the patio door, flipped on the lights . . . and froze. Apprehension squeezed her chest. Something big drifted below the surface of the water, dark against the submerged lights. Something big and dark, with floating hair.

Bailey took a step forward, dread backing up in her lungs.

Helen was not in her room.

She was in the water. Face down. At the bottom of the pool.

Bailey's bowl slipped from her hands and shattered against the Mexican tile.

LIEUTENANT Steve Burke hadn't worked the graveyard shift since he was a wet-behind-the-ears detective. But in a small department, rank was no protection against a shit assignment. Somebody had to be on call through the midnight hours, and it was usually the new guy. Steve didn't mind. It freed his days for Gabrielle.

Of course, Gabby wouldn't be happy if she woke and found him gone, but he'd left a note for her and another for the housekeeper. With any luck, he'd be back before breakfast.

He pulled up the long drive and parked his truck behind an ambulance and a pair of black-and-whites. The big house was lit up like the folks inside were giving a party, which, from what he'd heard, wouldn't have been unusual. Not that he'd ever been invited. He grimaced and got out of the truck. Helen Stokes Ellis might have married a man who was Not From Around Here, as folks delicately and pointedly referred to Yankees. But now that she was back home, she didn't socialize with people who were Not Her Kind.

Steve had never met Paul Ellis, the husband, but he'd heard stories about him, too. The briefing room was thicker with gossip than the barbershop or his mother's Wednesday morning Bible group. Ellis was a real pain in the ass, poking into the old Dawler case, implying the police had railroaded the investigation.

It was all before Steve's time, but his sympathies were with the department. He had no patience with self-styled experts. No reason to believe Ellis wouldn't be equally critical of the police's handling of his wife's death.

No wonder the patrol officer on duty tonight had been anxious to pass the buck to Steve.

Steve prowled up the walk, hands in his pockets. Yellow crime-scene tape was strung around the house like bizarre party decorations. *That* would get the neighbors' attention in the morning. How long, he wondered, before the press showed up? Not just the local press, either, the papers from Raleigh and Durham and even Charlotte. Paul Ellis was a bestselling true crime writer. His wife was a wealthy older woman who'd spent years maneuvering on the social pages. This case had the potential to blow up in Steve's face. And the explosion could attract national media attention.

His lucky night. There were guys already grumbling over Steve's hiring, detectives with more seniority who'd be only too happy to accuse him of hogging the limelight . . . or point their fingers if he screwed up.

Raising the yellow tape over his head, he walked in through the open front door.

Uniforms clustered at the other end of the long hallway. Beyond them, an arch opened up on some big room walled with glass. He'd get sketches and photographs of the layout later. For now, he focused on Wayne Lewis, the responding officer. Lewis, a fresh-faced rookie, was young enough not to resent him and hadn't known him long enough to dislike him.

"What happened?" Steve asked quietly.

Lewis cleared his throat. "The homeowner—Helen Stokes?—was found drowned in the pool."

The majority of drownings were accidental. Most involved the use or abuse of alcohol.

"And you called me because . . . ?"

Lewis turned red to the tips of his big ears. "The victim was fully clothed and has a nonpenetrating injury just above her right ear. She could have slipped and hit her head on the side of the pool as she fell. Or . . ."

Or she could have gotten an assist into the water.

Steve nodded. "Okay. Who found the body?"

"Bailey Wells. Mr. Ellis's personal assistant. She lives with the family," Lewis explained.

Steve followed the patrolman's gaze across the room, where a skinny brunette knelt beside a handsome, haggard man in a leather armchair. Her dark hair hung in lank strands around her pale face. Her plain white blouse clung to her narrow rib cage, revealing her bra and the shape of her breasts. Steve felt an unwelcome twinge of compassion. There was something vulnerable and appealing about her, even though she wouldn't win any wet T-shirt contests, for sure.

"Why is she wet?" he asked.

And why the hell hadn't anybody thought to bring her a towel?

"She pulled Mrs. Ellis out of the pool," one of the other cops volunteered.

Steve looked to Lewis for confirmation.

Lewis nodded. "Apparently she was trying to resuscitate her when Mr. Ellis called 911."

Well, that was natural, Steve conceded. Competent. Even heroic. It was just too bad the brunette's intervention had further messed up an already compromised crime scene.

Despite her bedraggled appearance, she was talking soothingly to the man in the chair, patting his arm.

Steve narrowed his eyes. "Who's the guy?"

"That's Paul Ellis." Lewis sounded surprised he hadn't known. "The writer."

Like he was supposed to recognize him from his book jacket or something.

"Get her away from him," Steve ordered.

"She's comforting him," the second cop said. "The man just lost his wife."

Steve should sympathize. He'd lost his own wife fourteen months ago. But however much he had railed against Teresa's cause of death, at least he'd known what killed her. He didn't know what had killed Helen Ellis yet. And he didn't like the fact that the two major witnesses at the scene had had ample opportunity to coordinate their stories.

He glanced again at the bereaved widower and the stringy-haired brunette, assessing their reactions. Ellis looked suitably distraught, like a man confounded by the accidental drowning death of his wife. Or like a man who had committed murder.

Depending on the medical examiner's report, Steve would have to look into Helen Ellis's will. And her life insurance policy.

Beside Ellis's red-eyed display of grief, his assistant, Wells, looked pale but composed. Maybe too composed?

Steve admired self-control. He had no use for hysterics. But Bailey Wells had known the dead woman. Lived in her house. Discovered her body. He expected her to demonstrate some emotion at her death.

He studied Wells's white face, her dilated pupils. The result of shock, maybe. It definitely wasn't grief.

"She lives here, you said?" he asked Lewis.

"Yes, sir."

He watched Wells lean forward to murmur to Ellis and wondered. Just how personal an assistant was she?

"We need to record the scene and get the body out of here," he said. "In the meantime, separate those two until I can take their statements. And somebody bring that woman a towel."

BAILEY was barely holding it together. She huddled on a kitchen chair, listening to the low voices and slow footsteps outside, feeling as if her head had disconnected from her neck and was floating somewhere above her body.

Her body. Floating.

Bailey shuddered.

"You want another towel?" asked the female officer who had been banished with her to the kitchen. Like Bailey needed a baby-sitter.

Or a guard.

She shuddered again. She couldn't seem to stop shaking, bone-deep tremors neither the warm night nor her now damp towel were doing a damn thing to dispel.

"No. Thank you," she said politely, because her mama had raised her children to be respectful to the law. Anyway, it wasn't the officer's fault Bailey was stuck in here while poor Paul wrestled with his grief and guilt alone.

She'd felt better when she could comfort him. She'd felt useful. Valued. *Glad.*

And then she had despised herself because it was wrong to rejoice in being needed when he was hurting so and Helen was . . .

God, she couldn't believe it. Helen was *dead.*

Bailey hugged the towel around her shoulders as if it could shield her from the memory of Helen's flaccid face and vacant eyes. She had put her mouth on Helen's cold, slack mouth. She had blown her breath into Helen's unresponsive lungs. She'd done everything she knew how to do, over and over until she was dizzy, and it hadn't been enough.

Now she couldn't do anything. She couldn't see anything. The police had closed the kitchen blinds, leaving her to worry. And to wait. She sat, stunned. Numb. Her hands twisted in the towel. Her mind tumbled and spun like a double-load dryer at the Laundromat.

Maybe she should call her parents? Or a lawyer. But she felt too guilty to face her mother's eyes, and she wasn't guilty enough to need a lawyer.

There had to be something she could do.

Bailey stirred on the hard wooden chair. "Do you want some tea? Sweet tea?" she added, in case the cop thought in this house of death and Yankees she might not be served the proper syrupy beverage that lubricated the South.

The woman—OFFICER M. CONNER, read the name tag on her uniform—looked surprised, as if the chair had spoken.

Bailey saw the "no" forming in her eyes and offered, "Or I could make coffee."

"Coffee would be good," the other woman conceded.

Relieved, Bailey stood, forcing her knees to support her weight, her hands to uncurl, her mind to focus on the mundane task of spooning grounds into a paper filter. She had just put the pot under the drip when the door slid open and the tall, plainclothes detective came in from the flood-lit patio.

Bailey remembered him because he stuck out—older than the officers who had first appeared on the scene, younger than Paul, and confident in a macho way that raised her hackles. Beneath his loose sport coat and heat-wilted shirt, his body was solid. Muscled. His eyes were black and bold, his features harsh and so aggressively mas-culine he was almost homely.

She thought at first, stupidly, he had been attracted by the smell of the brewing coffee.

He nodded once to Conner before his hard cop's eyes sought Bailey. "Miz Wells? I'm Detective Burke." His deep-timbred twang plucked her nerves. "I'd like to ask you a few questions."

Bailey nodded, her teeth chattering. Now that he was here, she couldn't think. She needed time. She snagged a mug down from the cabinet, unable to control the trem-bling of her hand. "Coffee?"

"No, thank you, ma'am." He didn't smile.

Her head still felt light. Her heart was racing. "Do you mind if I get some for myself and Officer Conner?"

"You all go right ahead," he said, just as polite, but with a rasp in his voice.

She poured two coffees, added milk to her own, and put the cream and sugar within easy reach of the female officer. The whole time, Detective Burke watched her, a glint in the back of those eyes, like he wasn't used to being put off.

Bailey sat back down, leaving her coffee untouched on the table. Burke had taken the chair opposite hers, his bulk cutting her off, hemming her in, creating an island of pri-vacy in the brightly lit kitchen. His knees were large and square. And too close, she thought, but she didn't know how to scoot back her chair without offending him.

She folded her hands to hide their shaking and waited.

"All comfortable now?" Burke asked.

Bailey flushed. "Yes, thank you."

He pulled a notebook from his breast pocket. She braced herself to relive the horrible moments with Helen in the pool. "Where are you from, Miz Wells?"

She gaped at him. Shouldn't he be asking about Helen? About the accident? But she pulled herself together to answer. "My family is from around here. But I'm from New York."

Detective Burke didn't look impressed. She wasn't trying to impress him, she reminded herself.

"And you moved back here . . ."

"About a month ago." Her throat relaxed as she swallowed. Maybe his questions were intended to put her at ease. "Why?"

Why did it matter? "Because Helen wanted to," she answered evenly.

Burke made a sound, a masculine grunt that could have been challenge or acknowledgment. "Helen. That's the deceased."

A statement, not a question. Bailey nodded anyway.

"What was your relationship with her?"

Bailey tightened her hands in her lap. "I work for her husband."

"And what is it you do, Bailey? May I call you Bailey?"

Despite the drawled intimacy, she didn't think he liked her. Her sister would have known how to make him like her. Bailey nodded again. She felt like one of those plastic dogs in the rear window of a car, her head bobbing with every bump in the road. She stiffened her neck. "I'm his research and editorial assistant."

Burke didn't look impressed by that, either. "For how long?"

"Two years."

"So you've known Helen Ellis . . ."

"Two years," Bailey repeated, bewildered. Uneasy.

Those hard, dark eyes met hers. Bailey felt the jolt in her stomach. "Did you like her?"

Bailey's heart pounded. Nobody liked Helen, not even her children. She was like a wasp, shiny and dangerous, with an annoying buzz and a painful sting.

Bailey moistened her lips. "I'm sorry she's dead," she said honestly.

Burke was silent, his gaze still narrowed on her face. She stared back like a possum caught in the oncoming headlights of a car.

"All right." He flipped a page in his notebook. "Tell me what happened here tonight."

Reprieve. And so she did her best to cooperate. Prompted by his questions, she told him about dinner—just the three of them, cold chicken and a salad prepared ahead of time by the housekeeper—everything as usual, everything fine. She wasn't stupid. She knew he was trying to establish whether Helen's death was an accident, just as she knew in sixty percent of cases a murdered woman was killed by her spouse. But even the indignation she felt on Paul's behalf—poor Paul, what must he be feeling?—was muted and blurred, as if she were still struggling underwater. She clung to facts as if they were lifelines tossed to her by the grim-faced, deep-voiced detective.

After dinner, they had followed their regular routines. Paul had gone to his study to work. Helen had gone to bed.

"Did you see her go to her room?"

Bailey forced herself to remember. "No. I took a walk. I usually take a walk."

"Anybody see you on your walk?"

Dazed, it took her a moment to realize he was asking if she had an alibi. "I don't . . . No."

"You don't know?"

She was so tired. "I didn't see anybody."

"How about when you got back?" he asked. Casual. Relentless. "Did you see anybody then?"

"No."

"Mrs. Ellis? Mr. Ellis?"

"No."

"Wasn't that unusual?"

"Not really," she said, adding with weary humor, "it's a big house."

He didn't smile.

She tried another answer to satisfy him. "I don't like to intrude on the Ellises in the evening."

"But they weren't together, you said."

"No." She didn't think so.

"Do you remember what time it was?"

"Late. After nine."

Burke glanced at his notes. "And Mr. Ellis was still working?"

"Yes." She was pretty sure.

"Why didn't you go to his study? To see if he needed you?"

Her mouth went dry. She reached for her coffee, but it was cold. She took one sip and put it down. She never sought out Paul at night. It was one of her rules, painfully arrived at and scrupulously adhered to.

"You're his assistant," Burke said in that deceptively laid-back voice. "It would be only natural for you to check in with him."

"I went to my room," she said firmly. Too firmly. "To read."

Burke sighed. "And where is your room?"

She told him. She was used to organizing facts. Good at remembering details. She told him the layout of the house and the view from her window and the exact time she had left her room to get ice cream.

"Butter pecan," she said before he could ask. "It's my favorite flavor."

His mouth didn't so much as twitch, but there was a gleam in those dark, dark eyes. Humor, maybe, or respect. Or suspicion. Bailey didn't know him well enough to guess. She didn't want to know him.

"Why two spoons?" he asked.

Bailey felt faint. Her pulse pounded in her head. "Excuse me?"

Burke's face was like a rock. His voice grated. "We found two spoons by your broken bowl. Who was the second spoon for?"

**Romantic suspense from
<u>USA Today</u> Bestselling Author**

Patricia Potter

THE PERFECT FAMILY   0-425-17811-0

In this compelling contemporary novel, a woman
confronts past secrets and present dangers when she
travels to Sedona, Arizona, to attend a family reunion.

BROKEN HONOR   0-515-13227-6

In the waning years of WWII, a Nazi train was captured by
the Allies. Its cargo, a fortune in stolen art and gold dust,
vanished. Today, two strangers are about to become
engulfed in its mystery—an unexpected passion, and
inescapable peril.

TWISTED SHADOWS   0-515-13439-2

A riveting story of a man who thought he'd escaped his
criminal past, a woman who didn't know she had one,
and the FBI agent who threatens to blow both their
worlds apart.

COLD TARGET   0-425-19386-1

Holly Matthews and Meredith Rawson have never met
each other, but they are linked by a conspiracy that could
shatter their lives—and their dreams of love.

**"PATRICIA POTTER IS A MASTER STORYTELLER."
—MARY JO PUTNEY**

**Available wherever books are sold or at
penguin.com**

(B501)

Blazing romance from award-winning author
Kathryn Shay

AFTER THE FIRE
0-425-19304-7

*When widowed detective Megan Hale
moves to Hidden Cove, she is sure she will
never love again. But when she meets
fireman Mitch Malvaso, her heart is set
ablaze, despite the risks.*

"KATHRYN SHAY NEVER DISAPPOINTS."
—*NEW YORK TIMES* BESTSELLING AUTHOR
LISA GARDNER

"[A] PERFECT BLEND OF ROMANCE AND DANGER."
—BARBARA BRETTON

"INSPIRING AND EMOTIONALLY INVIGORATING...A
TRUE HERO'S TALE."
—*ROMANTIC TIMES*

**Visit Kathryn Shay on the web at
kathrynshay.com**

**Available wherever books are sold or at
penguin.com**

National bestselling author
LYNN ERICKSON

WITHOUT A TRACE
0-425-19325-X

With a serial rapist and killer on the loose in
Western ski towns, burned-out police sketch
artist Jane Russo joins FBI agent Ray Vanover
on the case. With his help, she must confront
a demon from her own past to catch a madman.

AFTER HOURS
0-425-19708-5

To earn extra cash NYPD Detective Nick
Sinestra moonlights as a bodyguard—and sells
celebrity secrets to tabloids. Until he meets
Portia Carr Wells, a socialite who doesn't want
to trust him. But her desire can't be controlled.

Available wherever books are sold or at
penguin.com